Ain't No Rest for the Wicked – Cage The Elephant

Oh, What a World – Kacey Musgraves

My Own Monster – X Ambassadors

Cloudy Day – Tones And I

Flaws – Bastille

Rare Bird – Caitlyn Smith

Lasso – Phoenix

Bubbly – Colbie Caillat

Believe – Mumford & Sons

Take a Chance On Me – ABBA

From Eden – Hozier

Could Be Good – Kat Cunning

R U Mine? – Arctic Monkeys

34+35 – Ariana Grande

Ho Hey – The Lumineers

Can't Help Falling in Love – Haley Reinhart

Wildfire – Cautious Clay

White Horse (Taylor's Version) – Taylor Swift

Need the Sun to Break – James Bay

Landslide (Remastered) – Fleetwood Mac

Missing Piece – Vance Joy

Dreams – The Cranberries

THE *Fine* PRINT

LAUREN ASHER

Bloom books

Cover design by Books and Moods
Cover image © diversepixel/Adobe Stock,
Danussa/Addobe Stock, romanya/Adobe Stock
Internal image © ONYXprj/Adobe Stock

Published by Bloom Books, an imprint of Sourcebooks
P.O. Box 4410, Naperville, Illinois 60567-4410
(630) 961-3900
sourcebooks.com

Originally self-published in 2021 by Lauren Asher.

Cataloging-in-Publication Data is on file with the Library of Congress.

Printed and bound in the United States of America.
LSC 28

To the girls who dream of meeting a prince
but end up falling for the misunderstood villain.

CHAPTER ONE

Rowan

The last time I attended a funeral, I ended up with a broken arm. The story made headlines after I threw myself into my mother's open grave. It's been over two decades since that day, and while I've completely changed as a person, my aversion to mourning hasn't. But due to my responsibilities as my late grandfather's youngest relative, I'm expected to stand tall and unbothered during his wake. It's nearly impossible, with my skin itching like I'm wearing a cheap polyester suit.

My patience wanes as the hours go on, with hundreds of Kane employees and business partners offering their condolences. If there's anything I hate more than funerals, it's talking to people. There are only a few individuals I tolerate, and my grandfather was one of them.

And now he's gone.

The burning sensation in my chest intensifies. I don't know

why it bothers me as much as it does. I've had time to prepare while he was in *a coma* yet the strange sensation above my rib cage returns with a vengeance whenever I think of him.

I run a hand through my dark hair to give myself something to do.

"I'm sorry for your loss, son." A nameless attendee interrupts my thoughts.

"Son?" The one word leaves my mouth with enough venom to make the man wince.

The gentleman centers his tie across his chest with fumbling hands. "I'm—well—uh."

"Excuse my brother. He's struggling with his grief." Cal places a hand on my shoulder and gives it a squeeze. His vodka-and-mint-coated breath hits my face, making me scowl. My middle brother might look dressed to the nines in a pressed suit and perfectly styled blond hair, but his red-rimmed eyes tell a completely different story.

The man mumbles a few words I don't bother listening to before heading for the nearest exit.

"Struggling with my grief?" Although I don't like the idea of my grandfather's passing, I'm not *struggling* with anything but uncomfortable heartburn today.

"Relax. That's the kind of thing people say at funerals." Two blond brows pull together as Cal stares me down.

"I don't need an excuse for my behavior."

"No, but you need a reason for scaring off our biggest Shanghai hotel investor."

"Fuck." There's a reason I prefer solitude. Small talk requires far too much effort and diplomacy for my taste.

"Can you *try* to be nicer for one more hour? At least until all the important people leave?"

"This *is* me trying." My left eye twitches as I press my lips together.

"Well, do better. For him." Cal tilts his head toward the picture above the fireplace.

I let out a shaky breath. The photograph was taken during a family trip to Dreamland when my brothers and I were kids. Grandpa smiles into the lens despite my tiny arms wrapped around his neck in a choke hold. Declan stands by Grandpa's side, caught in the middle of an eye roll while Cal raises two fingers behind his head. My father shows a rare sober smile as he wraps an arm around Grandpa's shoulder. If I try hard enough, I can imagine Mom's laugh as she snapped the photo. While the memory of her face is fuzzy, I can make out her smile if I think hard enough.

A weird scratchiness in my throat makes it difficult to swallow. *Residual allergies from spring in the city. That's all.*

I clear my irritated throat. "He would have hated this kind of show." Although Grandpa was in *the* entertainment business, he disliked being the center of attention. The idea of all these people driving out to the edge of Chicago for him would have made his eyes roll if he were still here.

Cal shrugs. "He of all people knew what was expected of him."

"A networking event disguised as a funeral?"

The side of Cal's lips lifts into a small smile before falling back into a flat line. "You're right. Grandpa would be horrified because he always said Sunday was a day of rest."

"There's no rest for the wicked."

"And even less for the wealthy." Declan stops by my other

side. He stares at the crowd of people with an unrelenting scowl. My oldest brother has intimidating people down to a science, with everyone avoiding his pitch-black stare. His suit matches his dark hair, which only adds to his cloak-and-dagger look.

I'm somewhat jealous of Declan since people typically talk to me first, mistaking me for the nicest child because I happen to be the youngest. I might have been born last, but I most certainly wasn't born yesterday. The only reason guests take the time to speak to us is because they want to stay in our good graces. That kind of fake treatment is to be expected. Especially when all the people we associate with have a moral compass pointed permanently toward hell.

An unknown couple walks up to the three of us. A woman pulls out a tissue from her purse to dab her dry eyes while her counterpart offers us his hand to shake. I look down at it like he might transfer a disease.

His cheeks flush as he tucks his hand back into his pocket. "I wanted to offer my condolences. I'm very sorry for your loss. Your grandfather—"

I tune him out with a nod. This is going to be one hell of a long night.

This one's for you, Grandpa.

I stare down at the white envelope. My name is written across the front in my grandpa's elegant cursive. I flip it over, finding it untampered with his signature Dreamland's Princess Cara's Castle wax seal intact.

The lawyer finishes passing out the other letters to my two

brothers. "You're required to read his individual letters prior to me reviewing Mr. Kane's final will and testament."

My throat tightens as I break the seal and pull out my letter. It's dated exactly a week before Grandpa's accident three years ago that led to his coma.

To my sweet little Rowan,

I choke back a laugh. *Sweet* and *little* are the last words I'd use to describe myself since I'm as tall as an NBA player with the emotional range of a rock, but Grandpa was blissfully ignorant. It was the best thing about him and the absolute worst depending on the situation.

Although you're a man now, you'll always be the same little lad in my eyes. I still remember the day your mother gave birth to you like it was yesterday. You were the largest of the three, with these fat cheeks and a head full of dark hair that I was sadly jealous of. You sure had a pair of lungs in you and you wouldn't stop crying until they handed you over to your mom. It was like everything was right in the world when you were in her arms.

I reread the paragraph twice. It's strange to hear my grandpa talk about my mother so casually. The subject became taboo in my family until I could barely remember her face or her voice anymore.

I know I've been busy with work and that I didn't spend as much time as I should've with you all. It was easy to blame the company for the physical and emotional distance in my relationships. When your mother died, I wasn't sure what to do or how to help. With your father pushing me away, I devoted myself to my job until I became numb to everything else. It worked when my wife died and it worked when your mother met a similar passing, but I realize that it set your father up for failure. And in doing that, I failed you all as well. Instead of teaching Seth how to live a life after great loss, I showed him how to hold on to despair, and it only hurt you and your brothers in the end. Your father parented in the only way he knew how, and I'm the one to blame.

Of course Grandpa excuses my father's actions. Grandpa was too busy to pay close enough attention to the real monster his son turned out to be.

As I write this, I'm living in Dreamland, trying to reconnect with myself. Something has been bothering me over the last couple of years and it didn't click until I came here to reevaluate my life. I met someone who opened my eyes to my mistakes. As the company grew, I lost touch with why I started this all. I realized that I've been surrounded by so many happy people, yet I have never felt so alone in my life. And although my name is synonymous with the word "happiness," I feel anything but.

An uncomfortable feeling claws at my chest, begging to be released. There was a dark time in my life when I could relate to his comment. But I shut that part of my brain off once I realized no one could save me but myself.

I shake my head and refocus my attention.

Growing old is a peculiar thing because it puts everything into perspective. This updated will is my way of making amends after my death and fixing my wrongs before it's too late. I don't want this life for you three. Hell, I don't want it for your father either. So Grandpa is here to save the day, in true Dreamland prince fashion (or villain, but that's going to depend on your perspective, not mine).

You each have been given a task to complete to receive your percentage of the company after my death. Do you expect anything less from the man who writes fairy tales for a living? I can't just GIVE you the company. So to you, Rowan, the dreamer who stopped dreaming, I ask you one thing…

Become the Director of Dreamland and bring the magic back.

To receive your 18% of the company, you'll be expected to become the Director and spearhead a unique project for me for six months. I want you to identify Dreamland's weaknesses and develop a renovation plan worthy of my legacy. I know you're the right man for this job because there's no one I trust who loves creating more than you, even though you lost touch with that side of yourself over the years.

I *loved* creating. Emphasis on the past tense because there's no way I would draw again, let alone willingly work at Dreamland.

An independent party will be contacted and asked to vote on your changes. If they are not approved, then your percentage of the company will be given to your father permanently. No second tries. No buying him out. That's the way the cookie crumbles, little lad. I had to work to make the Kane name what it is today, and it's up to your brothers and you to make sure it lives on forever.

Love you always,
Grandpa

I stare at the ink until the words blur together. It's difficult to concentrate on the lawyer when he discusses the splitting of assets. None of that matters now. These letters put every plan on standby.

Declan shows the lawyer out before returning to the living room.

"This is utter bullshit." I swipe the whiskey bottle from the coffee table and fill my glass to the top.

"What do you have to do?" Declan takes a seat.

I explain my impending task.

"He can't demand this of us." Cal rises from his chair and starts pacing.

Declan runs a hand across his stubble. "You heard the lawyer. We either go along with it, or my ability to become CEO is null and void."

Cal's eyes grow wilder with every ragged breath. "Fuck! I can't do it."

"What could possibly be worse than losing your percentage of the company?" Declan smooths out his suit jacket.

"Losing my dignity?"

I give him a once-over. "That still exists?"

Cal flips me off.

Declan leans back in his chair as he takes a sip from his tumbler. "If there's anyone who has a right to be pissed, it's me. I'm the one who needs to marry someone and impregnate them to become CEO."

"You know babies are created by having sex, right? Is that something your internal software is capable of learning?" Cal's pushing for a fight he can never win. Declan prides himself on his reputation as America's most untouchable bachelor for a reason other than sleeping around.

Declan plucks Cal's letter from the floor and gives it a bored glance. "Alana? Interesting. Wonder why Grandpa thought it would be a good idea for you to reunite again."

Alana? I haven't heard that name in years. What does Grandpa want Cal to do with her?

I reach out to grab the letter from Declan but Cal rips it out of his hand before I have the chance.

"Fuck off. And don't speak about her again," Cal seethes.

"If you want to play with fire, then prepare to be cremated." Declan tips his glass at Cal. His gaze flickers between the two of us. "Regardless of our personal thoughts on the matter, we don't have a choice but to proceed with Grandpa's terms. There's too much at stake."

I will never allow our father to obtain our shares of the company. I've waited my entire life for the ability to control the Kane Company with my brothers and I don't plan on losing to my father. Not when we're fueled by something far stronger than the need for money. Because if there's one lesson we learned from Seth Kane, it's that love may come and go, but hate lasts forever.

CHAPTER TWO

Rowan

My new assistant, Martha, is a Dreamland veteran who has worked for all the directors of the theme park, including my grandfather. She's handled my transition with ease. The way she knows everything about everyone has been a bonus, making me breathe easier considering my move to Florida.

Because of Martha's key intel, I know how to find most of the Dreamland employees all in one place to formally introduce myself. I'm able to secure my choice of a seat because I made sure to be the first one to arrive for the morning meeting. I pick the perfect spot in the back of the auditorium, where the fluorescent lights don't reach, cloaking me in much-desired darkness. Sitting away from curious eyes will allow me to observe how the crew interacts and how the managers resolve problems.

Ten minutes before the meeting, everyone files inside the space and fills the countless rows of seats. Whatever energy I give off has the employees avoiding the back row for the more preferred seats in the front and middle. There's only one person who braves the seat in front of me. The older gentleman stares at me like I'm inconveniencing him by sitting in his territory, but I ignore him.

Spotlights at the front of the room focus on Joyce, the daytime crew manager and Dreamland house mom. She has a helmet of white hair and blue eyes that scan the entire room like a drill sergeant. I'm not sure how she knows my location, but her eyes land on mine and she nods with pressed lips.

Joyce taps her clipboard. "All right, everyone. Let's get started. We have a lot to cover and little time before the first guests arrive." She sets the meeting agenda and moves through countless questions with confidence. She barely breathes as she discusses the July schedule of parades, festivals, and celebrities visiting the land.

The door behind me creaks open. I turn in my chair and look over my shoulder. A younger brunette woman slides through the small crack before shutting it softly behind her.

I look down at my watch. *Who is she and why is she twenty minutes late?*

She clutches onto a neon pink Penny skateboard with one golden brown arm as she scans the packed room. I take advantage of her distraction to assess her. She's beautiful in a way that makes it difficult to refocus my attention on the conversation at the front of the room.

I hate it yet I can't look away. My eyes trace the curves of her body, drawing a path from her delicate throat to her thick thighs. The speed of my heart picks up.

I clench my hands into two fists, disliking the lack of control I have over my body.

Get ahold of yourself.

I take a few deep breaths to slow my heart rate.

A lock of dark hair falls in front of her eyes. She tucks it behind an ear decked out in gold piercings. As if she senses my gaze, her eyes land on me—or more so the empty seat next to me.

The woman walks out of the lit entrance and toward the aisle shrouded in darkness. She checks out the seating arrangement as if she wants to figure out how to slide into the chair beside me with as little contact as possible.

"Hi. Excuse me." Her voice is soft with a hint of an accent. She takes a deep breath as she moves inch by inch into my personal space.

I don't say a damn thing as I clutch onto the armrests. I'm given an up close and personal view of her backside, barely constrained by her unregulated attire of jeans and a T-shirt.

There's a reason uniforms are mandatory while on company property and I'm staring straight at it. The back of my neck heats, and the armrests creak under the pressure of my hands. Her perfume hits my nose. My eyes drift shut at the intoxicating smell—a mix of flowers, citrus, and something I can't quite place.

She fumbles around my long legs with the gracefulness of a newborn giraffe.

Wanting to end this, I give her some space by sitting up. My sudden movement has her tripping over my feet. One of her hands smacks against my lap for balance, missing my cock by only a few inches. Electricity shoots up my leg, right to my crotch.

Shit. Since when has someone's touch given me that kind of a reaction?

Her wide eyes look into mine, showing off thick lashes and brown, almond-shaped eyes. She blinks a couple times, proving she possesses some form of cognitive functioning. "I'm so sorry." Her lips gape apart as she stares down at her hand on my lap. She gasps and rips her hand away from my thigh, taking her warmth and the weird feeling with her.

Some older crew member looks over his shoulder. "Do you mind taking a seat already? I can barely hear Joyce over your usual racket."

Usual racket? Good to know that this is a pattern.

"Right. Yes," she sputters.

I consider her ability to slide into the chair beside me without another accident a miracle. She drops her loud, jangling backpack on the floor, causing yet another distraction. Metal rattles and pings as she bends over and unzips the bag.

I shut my eyes and breathe through my nose to calm the dull ache pulsing at my temples. Except I take in more of her perfume with each deep breath, making it impossible to forget her.

Her arm brushes up against my leg during her search. A similar spark shoots down my spine at the contact, like a rush of heat begging to go *somewhere.*

Anywhere but *there* for fuck's sake.

"Do you mind?" I grind out.

"Sorry!" She winces as she finally grabs her notebook and snaps back into a sitting position. Her Penny board slides off her lap and smashes into my two-thousand-dollar shoes.

There's a reason those damn things were banned from the

park decades ago. I kick the contraband item away from me and right into the ankles of the same man who reprimanded her earlier.

"Come on, Zahra." The man turns his head and shoots her a withering look.

Zahra. Her name fits the wildness I've only had a tiny taste of.

"Sorry, Ralph," she mutters.

"Stop being sorry and start being early for once."

I fight the urge to smile. There's nothing I enjoy more than people being called out on their bullshit.

She leans over and places a delicate hand on the man's shoulder. "Can I make it up to you with fresh bread that Claire and I made last night?"

Bread? Is she seriously offering this man food after he got annoyed with her?

Ralph shrugs. "Throw in some cookies and I won't complain to Joyce about you being late again."

I blink at the graying grump in front of me.

"I knew you had a soft spot for me. People say you're mean but I don't believe a word of it." She shoves his shoulder in a familiar way.

I see what she's doing here. Somehow, she wrapped old Ralph around her finger with nothing but a smile and a promise of baked goods.

This woman is dangerous—like a landmine someone doesn't see until it's too late. Zahra grabs a package from her backpack and drops it into Ralph's waiting hands.

Ralph cracks a smile, revealing a chipped front tooth. "Don't let anyone in on our secret. I couldn't handle the fallout."

"Of course. I wouldn't dare." She lets out a soft laugh that reverberates through my chest like someone smashed a damn gong with a sledgehammer in there. Warmth spreads through my body, scaring the shit out of me.

Her white teeth stand out in the dark as she shoots Ralph a beaming smile. There's something about the look on her face that has my heart racing faster in my chest. *Beautiful. Carefree. Innocent.*

Like she's actually happy with her life rather than faking it like the rest of us.

My teeth smash together as I let out an agitated breath. "Are you done? Some of us are trying to pay attention."

The whites of Ralph's eyes grow larger before he turns around in his chair, leaving Zahra all by herself.

"I'm sorry," she whispers under her breath.

I ignore her apology and refocus my attention on Joyce.

"Some big changes are happening at corporate that we will be reviewing over the next week. They're going to be keeping a close eye on us this quarter."

"Great. Just what we need," Zahra mumbles under her breath as she scribbles in her notebook.

"Do you have a problem with corporate?" I'm not sure what I expect to hear or why I even care.

She laughs to herself, and I'm hit with another weird feeling in my rib cage. "The real question is who doesn't have a problem with corporate."

"Why?"

"Because the Kane Company board is filled with a bunch of old men who sit around talking about how much money they've made, without actually discussing the important matters at hand."

"And you're an expert on board meetings all of a sudden?"

"It doesn't take a genius to draw conclusions based on how they treat us here."

"And how's that?"

"Like we don't matter as long as we make them billions of dollars a year."

If she notices my glare, she seems unbothered by it. "Aren't employees paid not to complain?"

She directs her smile at me. "Sorry, that'll cost the company extra, and seeing as most of us make minimum wage, silence isn't part of the deal." Her voice is light and airy, which only annoys me more.

"It should be if only to prevent you from spewing more ignorant statements."

She sucks in a breath and returns her focus to her notebook, finally giving me the quiet I wanted.

"This next quarter is going to be different from the last one." Joyce's eyes brighten.

A few crew members grumble under their breath.

"Oh, come on. It's the truth."

Zahra makes a noise in the back of her throat. She scribbles some notes across her notebook, but I can't make out the words in the dark.

"You don't believe her?" *What the hell are you doing, man? She finally shut up and now you're asking her questions?*

Her head snaps in my direction, but I can't make out her expression. "Because nothing good can happen now that Brady's really gone." Her voice cracks.

My molars smash together. Who does she think she is to call

my grandfather *Brady*? It's insulting. "The park has performed better in the last year alone than ever before, so I find your statement baseless."

Her knee bounces in an annoying fashion. "Not everything is about a bottom line. Sure, the park performed better, but at what expense? Small wages? Cheaper health insurance benefits for employees and unpaid vacation days?"

If she's trying to appeal to my humanity, she might die trying. People in my position don't lead with our hearts because we would never be satisfied with something so ridiculous.

We don't seek to make the world better.

We seek to make it *ours*.

I readjust my position in my chair to look at her. "Spoken like someone who knows nothing about running a multibillion-dollar industry. Not that I'm surprised. You do work here, after all."

She reaches out and pinches my arm. Her small fingers lack the strength to do any real damage.

"What the hell was that for?" I snap.

"I was trying to see if this was a nightmare. Turns out this whole train wreck of a conversation is *very* real."

"Touch me again and you'll be fired on the spot."

She freezes. "Which department did you say you were from again?"

"I didn't."

She smacks her forehead with her hand as she switches between English and a foreign language I'm not familiar with.

"What department do *you* work in?" I counter.

She sits up taller with a grin like I didn't threaten to fire her a second ago. *Bizarre*. "I'm a beautician at the Magic Wand Salon."

"Great. So at least you don't do anything important enough to be missed."

Her chair creaks underneath her as she recoils. "God, you're such an asshole."

Joyce couldn't have planned my entrance any better than this. She calls out my name and everyone's heads turn in the direction of our dark corner.

I rise from my seat and look over at Zahra with a raised brow. Her head hangs low, and her chest shakes. *From laughter?*

What the hell? She should be apologizing and begging for her job.

Joyce calls my name, and my head snaps in the direction of the stage.

I turn toward the crowd and walk away from Zahra. There's only one thing I need to focus on, and my goal has nothing to do with a woman who dared to call me an asshole and laugh about it.

CHAPTER THREE

Zahra

I slam the door to my locker shut.

"What's got you all upset?" Claire takes a seat on the bench across from me and puts on her flats. Her dark, shoulder-length hair curtains around her face, and she shoves it out of the way.

"I met the biggest jerk this morning during the meeting. And you won't believe who it was."

"Who?!"

"Rowan Kane."

"Get the fuck out!" My roommate's brown eyes go wide.

A couple heads snap in our direction. Mrs. Jeffries fumbles for her cross necklace as she stares at us.

"*Claire.*" I groan.

"He's Dreamland royalty. Excuse my shock."

"Trust me. Some things are better left to the imagination."

Whatever sweet stories Brady shared about his youngest grandson were nothing but a fantasy. The rumors circulating Dreamland were right. Rowan has earned a reputation as a ruthless businessman known to stir up the same level of happiness as animal euthanasia. He first gained attention after being the tie-breaker vote against increasing the minimum wage for employees. Because of him, the Kane Company has continued to pay their employees pennies for their hard work. His reign of terror was solidified over the years. He has cut back on employees' paid vacation days, swapped our health insurance plan for one that hurts rather than helps, and laid off thousands of employees.

Rowan might have the looks of an angel but the rest of him is pure sin.

Claire tugs on my dress. "Well, tell me! Does he smell as good as he looks?"

"No." *Yes.* But I'm not about to tell Claire that.

Not only did Rowan smell amazing, but his company photo doesn't do him justice. Rowan is beautiful in an unapproachable kind of way. Like a marble statue surrounded by a red velvet rope, tempting me to cross into forbidden territory for one single touch. His cheekbones seem sharp enough to cut while his lips look soft enough to kiss. And based on the part I pinched and the thigh I touched, he is packed with lean muscle. He seems perfect, looking every bit like a pretty boy with his perfectly styled brown hair, pressed suit, and deep caramel-colored eyes.

That is until he opens his mouth.

"Okay, let's ignore the fact that he's a jerk and talk more about if he's single or not." She bats her lashes.

"Last time I checked, he isn't your type." I shove her shoulder, knowing she doesn't give a damn about boys. She declared herself gay during high school and never blinked at men ever again.

"Bitch, I'm asking for you, not me."

I run a hand down my purple renaissance costume. "Seeing as he told me that my job wasn't important enough to be missed, I'm not interested. Not to mention he's our *boss.*" Even though Dreamland doesn't have any rules against fraternization, I've officially labeled Rowan off-limits. Been there, done that, and bought the souvenir. My ex-boyfriend met my lifetime asshole quota.

"Man. What a dick."

"Tell me about it. I can't believe he's our new director. It was so all of a sudd—"

"Roll call!" Regina, the salon manager, shouts from the main floor.

Claire and I step onto the salon floor and line up with the rest of the staff. We're surrounded by a sea of empty, colorful chairs and lit vanities waiting to house children who dream of being dressed up as princesses and princes during their time in Dreamland.

All the employees stand through our assignments before setting up our stations.

"Ready?" Claire looks over at me from her vanity.

I grab my unplugged curling wand and wield it like a sword. "I was born ready."

Henry, today's floor attendant, opens the doors and lets in a crowd of kids and their parents. My heart warms at the bright-smiling, starry-eyed children who assess all the costumes lining the walls.

Henry rolls a little girl in a wheelchair toward my station. "Hi, Zahra. This is Lily. She's excited to have you make her look like Princess Cara today."

I bend over and give Lily my hand. "Are you sure you need a makeover?"

She nods and smiles.

"Are you sure you're not a princess already?"

Lily muffles her giggle with her other hand. Her straight blond hair falls into her face, shielding her green eyes from me.

I tap her scrunched nose. "You're going to make my job so easy that my boss might think I have superpowers."

Lily laughs. The sound is so sweet, I can't help joining her.

"I like your pin." She points at today's enamel pin that rests above my name tag.

"Thank you." I smile at the *Bee Happy* script covering a cartoon bumblebee. My small rebellion against the uniform code is a hit with the little ones.

I get to work, starting with Lily's hair. Her straight hair stubbornly struggles to hold the classic Princess Cara curls, but I don't give up until she looks perfect.

A weird prickling sensation shoots down my spine. I turn toward the vanity without watching my hands and swipe Lily's cheek with purple eyeshadow.

"Hey!" She laughs.

"Oh God."

"What?"

Rowan stands beside the front desk. His weighted stare in the mirror has my skin heating and my eyes threatening to pop out of their sockets. A flush spreads across my cheeks, and I turn away from the makeup station to hide my reaction.

"Oh, you're getting red. Mommy does that with Daddy." Lily's eyes light up.

"Hmm." *What is he doing here? Am I going to be fired?*

Lily catches me staring at Rowan's reflection in the mirror. "Do you like him?"

"Shh! No!" I wipe the makeup off her cheek.

"Is it a secret?" she whispers.

"Yes!" I'll say anything to get her to shut up.

I take another peek over my shoulder. The asshole-in-Armani's eyes remain focused on me, his scowl adding to my anxiety.

Henry walks up to my vanity under the guise of offering Lily a juice box. "So, care to share why Mr. Kane is asking about you?"

"Because I might have made him angry earlier?"

Henry's eyes crinkle with concern. "I wanted to come over and warn you that he's asking Regina all kinds of questions about you."

I hope Regina keeps her personal dislike toward me to herself. While she would love nothing more than to complain about me, my performance speaks for itself. My client tips are nearly double everyone else's, which only fuels her personal vendetta against me. I don't understand her problem. Her daughter is the one who had an affair with my now *very* ex-boyfriend while we were still dating. I'm nothing close to a threat because I wouldn't touch Lance with a hazmat suit, let alone get back with him.

I straighten my spine. Thinking about Lance and Tammy only dampens my mood. It puts me back in that bad mental place, and I refuse to reduce myself to being that girl who thought she would marry her college sweetheart. That future crashed and burned after finding out about Lance's double life with Tammy.

Let it go. Show them that they didn't break you, no matter how close you got.

"Is he your prince?" Lily grins.

I snap back into the conversation.

Henry shimmies his shoulders. "We'll have to wait and see if he carries her off to his kingdom."

The only kingdom that man resides in is hell and I'm not interested in visiting. He's a devil in a designer suit with a personality to match.

"Good luck! You're going to need it." Henry leaves after patting me on the head like a child.

Every time I look in the mirror, Rowan's emotionless, brown eyes meet mine. I shiver under his stare despite the warm lights of the vanity.

During the entire makeover, I somehow keep a straight face despite my heart pounding against my rib cage. I throw all my energy into ignoring my new boss while making Lily the prettiest princess in the whole park.

As I get closer to the reveal, I turn her chair toward the center of the room and away from the mirror. I finish up the final touches before making a show of swiveling her chair back in front of the mirror for the big reveal. Her eyes water as she checks out her reflection.

"You look beautiful." I bend over and give her a small hug.

"Thank you." She frowns at her chair.

My heart squeezes in my chest, making me wish I could do more for kids like Lily. They always seem to be overlooked.

I wrap my arm around Lily's shoulder and smile into the mirror. "You're one pretty lady. I bet someone is going to mistake you for the real Princess Cara the moment you leave here."

"*Really*?" Her entire face brightens again.

I tap her nose. "You bet. And I know kids are going to

be jealous of your cool wheels when their feet are aching and sore."

She laughs. "You're funny."

"If someone asks you for a free ride, make sure to charge them. Promise?"

"Pinky promise." She holds up her tiny finger for me. We lock ours together and shake on it.

I turn to call for Lily's parents. My eyes lock on Rowan's. Heat blooms in my stomach, spreading like wildfire across my skin from one look.

Am I coming down with a fever? I knew that sniffling kid at my station yesterday didn't have allergies.

Lily's parents come over and rave all about her makeover. While her dad kneels to talk to Lily, her mother turns and clutches my hand with her trembling one. "Thank you so much for taking care of my daughter. She was scared she wouldn't fit in here like the other girls but you went out of your way to make her day special." She throws her arms around me.

I return her hug. "It's my pleasure. But Lily made it easy because you both have one beautiful daughter, inside and out."

Lily's dad blushes while her mom grins. With one last look in the mirror, her parents roll Lily away.

I turn toward the area where Rowan and Regina were chatting only to find it empty. My stomach sinks.

I remain permanently nauseous for the rest of the day. No matter how many smiling kids leave my chair, I can't shake this weird feeling in my gut. I'm not sure what Rowan's up to but I need to keep an eye out. There was a time I ignored my intuition and I refuse to make that mistake ever again.

CHAPTER FOUR

Rowan

Dreamland might be in the business of selling fairy tales, but it brings me nothing but nightmares and bitter flashbacks. The energy surrounding this place chokes me as much as the Florida humidity. Despite the raging summer sun, a chill runs down my spine as I stare up at Princess Cara's Castle. The architectural monstrosity that put my grandfather's park on the map nearly five decades ago reminds me of a past life I've long since forgotten.

Get over it, you worthless piece of shit. Focus on what matters.

I'm not sure why my grandfather tasked me with fixing a theme park that has run seamlessly for forty-eight years. Tickets are always sold out, and we meet maximum capacity every single day. With the park outperforming each quarter, I question how I can make improvements.

To put it simply, this place is perfect. Almost *too* perfect. I've dealt with more issues in one day as the chairman of our streaming service subsidiary than this park manages in a whole year. But with my twenty-five-billion-dollar shares on the line, I'll turn over every single rock in this entire place if it means exposing weaknesses and building upon Dreamland's strengths. There is no other option. My brothers are counting on me to do my part in securing our future, and I don't plan on letting them down.

I abandon my spot on the wooden drawbridge. My breathing becomes easier as I add some distance between the castle and myself.

Think of how much better life will be once you get the hell out of this town.

That's the thought that keeps me sane in a world built on nothing but haunted memories and broken dreams.

My patience is thinning with each roadblock I hit. After back-to-back pointless meetings with Dreamland staff, I'm desperate for news about where the park is underperforming. I've learned nothing worth noting since I arrived forty-eight hours ago.

On paper, Dreamland is hitting new goals with every financial quarter. The demand for *more* is the only common theme I've heard from employees. More rides. More lands. More hotels. More *space*.

There's only one team that can help me with this kind of grand-scale expansion. Dreamland's Creators are world-renowned in the theme-park business. If there's an attraction, venue, souvenir, or consumer experience at Dreamland, the Creators helped design it. So they're the people I plan on working side by side with for the next six months. My micromanaging approach will be a significant change from the laid-back attitude they're used to from the previous director, but quite frankly, I don't care. It helped me turn a start-up streaming company into a billion-dollar empire, and it'll help me here.

I enter my office and shut the door behind me. The two head Creators jump in their seats before regaining their composure. Sam, the male who has the common sense to mix a plaid shirt and a polka dot tie, can barely look me in the eyes. The top of his brown curly hair is the only image I get as he scribbles in his notebook. Jenny, the brunette co-manager, sits straighter than a needle beside him as if one kink in her posture will set me off.

I take a seat. "Let's get started."

They nod in unison.

"I am expected to come up with a new plan for the park that identifies our weaknesses. Together we will evaluate the performance of Dreamland's attractions and determine how we can better serve our guests. That includes renovating current rides, creating new lands, updating skits and float parades that will increase Dreamland's ROI by 5 percent, at the very least."

Sam's eyes somehow double in size while Jenny's face remains stoic.

"Based on my preliminary analysis, our competitors have been growing fiercer over the years. And although Dreamland performs above average each quarter, I'm looking to obliterate our competition and steal their profit margins."

Sam's throat bobs while Jenny scribbles in her notebook. I appreciate their silence, given my limited time between meetings with each department.

"Projects like these take years to go from blueprints to live-action rides. That being said, I'm expecting your two teams to develop the initial plans that I will then present in front of a board in six months."

It was Declan's idea to keep my real reason for being here a secret. He thinks that if I revealed my less-than-altruistic intentions for a project of this magnitude, people might sabotage me for the right price. So no one will be the wiser about my temporary position here for the next six months. In their eyes, I will be the director they always dreamed of. In reality, I can't wait to crawl out of this hellhole and go back to Chicago to replace Declan as the CFO.

"Six months?" Jenny croaks. Her cheeks lose all their coloring.

"I assume that won't be a problem."

She shakes her head, but the hand clutching onto her pen trembles.

"I'm looking to package this whole idea as a fiftieth-anniversary celebration and generate a buzz that pulls at people's heartstrings. The project should appeal to the new and old generations who grew up with Dreamland characters. I want it to emulate everything my grandfather loved about this park while also moving us toward a brighter—and more modern—future."

Sam and Jenny are nothing but two bobbing heads, hanging on to every word as they scribble in their notepads.

"So whatever needs to be done, do it. Time is not our friend."

"What is our budget?" Sam's eyes shine.

"Keep it reasonable—so around ten billion for the entire park. If you need more, my accountants will review the numbers."

Sam nearly chokes on his tongue.

"I expect results. If not, then you're better off applying for the traveling carnival."

Jenny stares at me while Sam's eyes drop to the carpet.

"Sir, may I speak freely?" Jenny taps her pen against her notepad in the most irritating fashion.

I check my watch. "If you find it absolutely necessary."

"Based on your rapid timeline, I was wondering if we could open up the annual employee submissions early this year? That way, the Creators could work with fresh ideas, rather than starting from ground zero."

I blink at her. Annual submissions are nothing but a headache meant to boost employee morale. We have plenty of Creators who have worked at Dreamland for decades already. They don't need the useless input from low-paid employees who don't know the first thing about how to design a park.

But what if someone submits something the current Creators haven't considered?

I work through the pros and cons before determining that I don't have much to lose. "Open up the applications for two weeks only. I want you to personally review the submissions and deliver only the best ones to my desk."

Jenny nods. "Of course. I'm sure we have a good idea about what you're looking for."

Doubtful but I don't bother wasting any words correcting her. "Get to work."

Jenny and Sam exit in a rush, leaving me behind to answer emails and prepare for the next meeting of my day.

"Son."

I instantly regret answering my father's unusual personal call. Stupid curiosity got the better of me because he's been too quiet about the whole Dreamland business. Something about his silence makes me wonder what he's planning behind the scenes.

I settle into a leather couch across from my desk. "Father." Our titles are nothing but a front developed over the years for public appearances.

"How's everything in Dreamland? I assume you'll be attending our board meeting on Monday regardless of whatever plans you've got going on." His tone remains light and indicative of the calm facade he's perfected across decades.

My molars grind together. "Why do you care?"

"Because I'm intrigued by your sudden interest in becoming the director after your grandfather's passing."

Does he think so little of my intelligence?

Of course he does. He's done nothing but mock you for the entirety of your existence.

"Is there a purpose to this phone call?" I ask with a faux indifference.

"I was curious about your progress after reviewing the funding request you put in. Ten billion dollars isn't a joking matter."

Every muscle turns rigid in my body. "I don't need your advice."

"Good. I wasn't offering it."

"God forbid you acted like a father for once in your pathetic life."

"Interesting word choice from my weakest son."

My fist tightens around my cell phone. It was stupid for me

to answer my father's call because of some budding curiosity. I should have expected that nothing would change, even after my grandfather's death. The only thing my father is interested in is reminding me how inept he thinks I am.

He's trying to screw with your head. That's all.

"I've got to go. I have a meeting that I can't be late for." I hang up the phone.

I take deep breaths to lower my blood pressure. I'm not that hopeless boy anymore that craved a real relationship with my father. Because of him, I turned my mind into a weapon rather than a weakness. No matter how hard he tries to poke at me, I'll always come out on top because the child he once knew no longer exists. I made sure of that.

CHAPTER FIVE

Zahra

Claire drops onto our couch and shoves her laptop onto my lap. "This is your chance!"

"What is?"

She pauses the TV, interrupting my binge of *The Duke Who Seduced Me*.

I read the email before putting her laptop on the coffee table. "No way. Not happening."

"Hear me out—"

"No."

"Yes! You're going to listen to my argument without interrupting me. You owe me that much as your best friend and personal chef." She wags her finger in the same way my mom does.

"My stomach might love you but my thighs sure don't."

She only glares at me.

I cross my arms. "Fine. I'll give you a chance."

She readjusts her tiny bun. "Okay, so I get why you're hesitant. I'd be too if someone betrayed me like Lance did."

"Do we really need to bring up Lance?" A cold feeling seeps through my chest, chilling my veins. Betrayal like that is hard to come back from.

Claire's smile falters. "The only reason I'm mentioning him is because this is the final step in the process of letting him go." She waves at her laptop like it will solve the world's problems.

"I've moved on already."

"I know you have, but there's still a tiny part of you that is afraid of chasing after the dreams he stole right out of your hands." He stole a lot more than my dreams.

My eyes sting. "I don't dream about inventing anymore."

"The bullshit he said about your skills was only a diversion to keep you from submitting the same idea as him. You know that, right?"

"But—"

"But nothing. Lance lied because he wanted to hold you back long enough for him to steal your idea."

It makes sense in theory, but I'm still not sure.

Claire grabs my hand and holds on to it. "This is your chance to prove to yourself that nothing anyone says defines who you are. Only your actions do."

My chest tightens. "I'm not sure..."

She squeezes my hand. "Come on. Just submit one teensy little project. That's all. What's the worst that can happen?"

"Well, where should I start? I mean—"

Claire covers my mouth with her palm. "It was a rhetorical question!"

I raise a brow. "Why are you pushing me so hard to apply?"

"Because that's what friends are for. We need to push each other out of our comfort zones. Because if you're not afraid—"

"Then you're not growing." I smile back at her.

"So what do you say?"

I pull out my phone from my pocket and open an email I received last week. "Speaking of comfort zones…I wanted to bring this up to you, and now seems like the perfect time. Because if you're not afraid…" I tease.

"Oh no."

My grin widens. "If I'm submitting a proposal, then you're applying for the apprentice position at the Royal Chateau. They have an opening in the kitchen that has your name written all over it."

Claire's smile drops. "This wasn't supposed to be about me."

"We're a duo. If I'm pushing myself to my limit, then you're coming along with me."

This is my chance to help Claire out. She never wanted to permanently stay at the Magic Wand Salon, but she never worked up the nerve to apply for the position she was initially rejected from.

"I can't apply there. They have a Michelin star!"

"All the more reason to apply to the very best."

"But I don't have a culinary degree from some fancy French school!" She jumps up from her spot on the couch.

"No, but you have *a* degree and heaps of experience working at restaurants during high school and college."

She throws her arms in the air. "Last week I burnt a batch of cookies."

"Only because I forgot to set the timer." I laugh.

"The entire building had to evacuate because of the fire alarm. There's no way anyone would trust me in a kitchen after that."

I laugh. "Don't be so dramatic."

She plops onto the couch and lays her head on my lap. "You weren't supposed to blackmail me."

"What are friends for?"

"Oh, I don't know, anything *but* felonies?"

I smile. "Come on. What do you say?"

"I say you're annoyingly chirpy for someone who was against this whole idea only five minutes ago."

"I'm taking advantage of an opportunity."

"Just so you're aware, I'm only agreeing because I'm okay with being rejected if it means seeing you chase after your dreams again."

My smile wobbles. "Sure thing. Just like I will only agree to your plan because I'd rather see you try again. If not, you'll end up like Mrs. Jeffries, working at the salon until you retire at ninety."

Her lips purse. "Now you're just being intentionally cruel."

Together, we laugh up to the ceiling before shaking on our agreement.

Sifting through the weathered pages of my idea notebook hits me with bittersweet memories. I trace over Brady's cursive handwriting covering the pages where we brainstormed what Nebula Land would look like if it became a new land within the park.

He and I spent weeks on it after he rejected my initial

submission and told me I could do better. The catch? He would be the one to guide me. Together, we formulated a proposal while I was under his mentorship.

Nebula Land was supposed to be the project that turned me into a Creator. But after Brady's accident, it felt wrong to submit it, so I held off. I was surprised to read about my idea in the company newsletter after learning Lance stole the main parts I had shared with him in private.

What would Brady think of Lance manipulating our idea? The ride looks nothing like our original plan. My lungs burn with the heavy breath I let out, and my eyes become watery as I run a finger across a sketch Brady did.

Critiquing Lance's idea isn't going to get you anywhere closer to submitting yours.

I turn on my laptop, sign in to my employee account, and open the annual Dreamland submissions portal. The blinking cursor in the empty text box mocks me, but I refuse to give up. Claire believes in me, and maybe it really is time I stop letting Lance get in my way of believing in myself.

This was a very bad idea. After my first failed draft, I decided wine and a broken heart were a good combination for my second attempt.

Update: It was not.

I'm still nowhere close to having a submission ready. Everything I write about seems too underwhelming and lacks my usual passion. I take another swig of wine straight from the bottle in a way that would horrify my mother.

What if working through your negative feelings about the Nebula Land ride helps open up your mind to more creative ideas?

Yes! Maybe that's what I'm missing. I delete everything from the text box and restart. At the top, I write *The real Nebula Land that would make Brady Kane proud.* My fingers fly across the keys as I let out every single thought I have about the project. I'm done staying silent and pretending the ride doesn't bother me.

When I was with Lance, that's the kind of person I became comfortable being. The silent, demure type who didn't want to make any waves because I prioritized his happiness. In the end, it was all for nothing. I gave up the person I was for a man who couldn't handle the woman I was meant to be.

All my fingers cramp up from typing. It feels empowering to tear apart something that broke me first. By the time I'm done, my vision is a bit blurry and my coordination could be better.

Since drinking and typing have no place in my life, I decide to click the *Save Draft* button at the bottom and shut my laptop for the night.

"Oh no!" *Oh no, no, no.* "Fuck! Fuck! Fuuuuck!"

Claire runs into my room. "What is it?"

I stare at the application portal.

This can't be real. I pinch my arm so hard, I wince. The bright green letters mock me in a way that has my stomach threatening to revolt.

Your application has been submitted.

Claire looks over my shoulder at the screen. "You submitted

it without asking me to double-check for typos? Who are you and what have you done with the real Zahra?"

"It was an accident!" I drop onto my bed, cover my face with a pillow, and scream.

Claire rubs my trembling arm. "What if you send an email to Mr. Kane and the Creators explaining the mistake? I'm sure they would understand."

I tug the pillow away from my face. "Are you kidding me?! What am I supposed to say? 'Sorry I got a tiny bit drunk and submitted an application tearing apart your most expensive ride'?"

She brushes my hair out of my face. "Maybe it's not as bad as you think."

"I called Lance's ride a big metal pile of shit that would make Brady Kane roll over in his grave."

She winces. "Oh, okay. Well. Yeah. You have always had a talent with words. At least you're putting that English degree to good use."

I groan. "I can't believe I hit the wrong button. I should have never been drinking and working. What was I thinking?"

The bed dips under her weight as she sits next to me. Her arms wrap around me in the best hug. "Well, this was the first big step in letting go of the past. Maybe it needed to happen like this."

"Yesterday you said fate was a fool's way of avoiding plans."

Her chest shakes from silent laughter. "Only because you love to blow your kismet horn for everyone to hear. So what, you only believe in fate when things go your way? That sounds like some bullshit logic to me."

I purse my lips. "Yeah, but what if I get fired? I've already made some mistakes."

First, I called Rowan an asshole and made fun of his board, and now this? I'll be lucky if I'm allowed to pick up trash at the end of all this.

Claire pats my hand. "It's too late now. You're in deep." She points at the green font on the screen.

I sigh. "Let's hope for the best?"

What's done is done. I can't change the proposal I submitted and there *was* something cathartic about pouring out all my feelings.

Maybe it really is kismet.

CHAPTER SIX

Zahra

The last week has been hell. It's taken all my willpower to make it through my shifts at the salon because I'm tired from worrying. I've been waiting for the other shoe to drop because it's only a matter of time before the Creators call me out on my proposal.

My worst nightmare came at the most unexpected time when I received an ill-fated summons from Rowan Kane. His single-line email didn't give away much.

Your presence is required at my office tomorrow at 8 a.m. sharp. R.G.K.

I'm not sure what's more shocking: the fact that he emailed me demanding my presence on a *Saturday* morning or the way he signed an email so casually with three initials.

I call Regina to explain the circumstances of why I will be

late to work. She lets me know that she's already aware of my meeting before hanging up.

Damn. I'm totally in trouble.

I rush through my morning routine and ride my skateboard through the catacombs so I can make it to the meeting on time.

My sneakers squeak as I run into the lobby of Rowan's private office suite. It's hidden behind one-way mirrors that look out at Story Street and Princess Cara's Castle.

The door to Rowan's office remains shut. His secretary, Martha, points at an empty chair beside her desk. I recognize her from my visits with Brady.

My strawberry print dress puffs around me as I plop into the seat. I decided to go for an *innocent until proven guilty* look today.

Martha offers me a small cup of water. "Do I have you to thank for his good mood this morning?"

I gasp in mock shock. "Don't tell me you're referring to Mr. Kane. He wouldn't know a good mood if he was overdosing on Valium." I take a sip of water to refresh my parched throat.

Her eyes glitter. "You're trouble."

"And *late*," Rowan calls out.

I turn in my seat, making the water in my cup slosh. I'm about to correct him on the fact that *he* is the one who is running late but I somehow forget the entire English language when I get a look at him.

Rowan in a suit is my kind of corporate kryptonite. Today, the custom royal-blue fabric hugs his body like someone sewed the material onto him. The material highlights the dips and curves of every single muscle, like waves of water I want to drown in. His dark-brown hair is styled without a single hair out of line, and his stubble is nonexistent during this early morning hour.

I let out the tiniest sigh that makes his secretary smile at her computer screen.

All the attraction is sucked out of me once his hardened gaze crashes into mine. The shadows in his eyes douse the small flame in my chest.

I grab my phone from my dress pocket. "I was on time. Right?" I look over at Martha for approval.

She remains silent as she focuses all her attention on cleaning out her junk mail inbox. *The betrayal.*

"Follow me." Rowan steps away from the door to give me space to enter.

I rise from the chair and grab my backpack off the floor. His gaze lingers on my puffy tulle sleeves before eying the rest of my dress like he wants to burn the fabric. His scowl only deepens once his eyes land on my cherry-red sneakers.

I click the heels together twice with a smile.

His eyes snap toward mine. My cheeks heat from the look on his face.

Is that yearning in his gaze or intense dislike?

Let's hope for the first while expecting the latter.

Whatever lingers in his eyes disappears as he blinks and removes any trace of emotion. He turns in a huff, giving me a prime view of his firm bubble butt. I pause and look because I am a warm-blooded human after all.

No man in power should possess a body like *that*. It should be considered a corporate crime to look that good while wearing a suit.

I shake my head and follow him into his domain. Rowan's office is a complete contrast to his personality. The vintage space reflects the romantic charm of Dreamland with crown molding and pale-yellow walls. It reminds me of something I'd find in one of my regency novels, with white wainscoting and elaborate wood furniture carved with an artist's touch.

Rowan frowns, sticking out like a thundercloud on a bright summer day. He stands by his desk and presses his clenched fists against the top. "Sit." He takes a seat in his leather wingback chair.

The dominance emanating off him makes it difficult to take deep breaths of air. I settle into the chair across from his desk, crossing and uncrossing my legs as he grabs papers from a file drawer.

"Do you need to use the restroom?" His face remains blank.

"What?"

"Bathroom?" He grunts, pointing toward a door in the corner of the office. "You keep moving around."

"Oh, no!" My cheeks heat. "Just trying to get comfortable."

"Don't set yourself up for failure like that."

A laugh escapes me before I have a chance to stop it. The side of his mouth lifts a whole quarter of a centimeter before dropping again.

Honestly, what does it take for someone like him to smile? Stealing candy from babies? Blood sacrifices? Watching live feeds of families having their homes foreclosed on? I need to know.

He slides the file over to me. "Here's your new contract. It's quite similar to your previous one with the Magic Wand Salon."

My mouth drops open. "I'm sorry. A contract?!"

When people are fired from Dreamland, are they given a

contract to never come back? How exactly does this whole thing work?

He sighs as if *I'm* inconveniencing *him*. "You'll be joining the Creators' team effective immediately."

The room spins around me. I place a hand against his desk for stability. "I'm what?! Joining the Creators' team?"

He blinks at me. "This annoying habit of repeating everything back to me is a waste of time and oxygen."

"Excuse me?" I rear back. "First off, I have every right to be confused. I thought you were about to fire me!"

This time his face shifts from a neutral stare to something that translates into *You're the dumbest person I've had the displeasure of being around.* "You're getting a job promotion."

How did I go from tearing apart the entire Nebula Land ride to getting a job offer with the most elite employees in all of Dreamland? This has to be some kind of payback for wasting everyone's time with my submission.

"How?"

The vein on his forehead makes an appearance. "Do you always feel the need to ask so many questions?"

"Do you always feel the need to be evasive and curt in everything you do?"

He proves my point by remaining silent. I'm tempted to knock his head around like a busted vending machine until I get some answers.

He taps the top of the file. "Your Nebula Land submission was rather bold. Not many people dare to critique a billion-dollar investment."

"I submitted it while I was drunk!" I blurt out.

He blinks at me. The only noise I hear is the rush of blood pounding in my ears.

Oh God. Why did I admit that?! I rub a sweaty palm down my face.

His lip curls. The look on his face makes me want to curl into a fetal position. "Will this be a habit while you're on the clock?"

I shake my head so fast, I'm hit with a wave of dizziness. "Oh, no! I rarely drink. It was a stupid idea to help me unwind—"

He lifts his hand. "Save me the monologue. I don't care."

Now it's my turn to blink. Rowan might be a man of few words but they serve their purpose in making me feel like an idiot without actually calling me an idiot. It must be his superpower.

I smile to ease the tension between us. "But I'm guessing you liked my idea or else you wouldn't be offering me a job."

"My general feelings on the matter are irrelevant. I make decisions based on facts and years of fine-tuned expertise."

The air escapes my lungs like a deflating balloon. Seriously, was this man not held enough as a baby? There's no other explanation for his coldness.

That's not fair. You've heard the stories about his mother...

I choke on the weird feeling squeezing my neck. "You want me to work as a Creator permanently?"

"Nothing here is permanent. Your job is contingent on your performance, so as long as it meets my standards, then you can consider yourself employed."

Oh my God. This was definitely not a part of Claire's plan. Self-doubt trickles in, erasing my happiness. I was supposed to submit a proposal and earn a stripe of courage, not be hired as a full-time Creator. I might be creative but I'm not *that* creative.

Dreamland Creators are legendary. They've made *history* for their inventions and were even invited to the White House a few years back. I haven't earned the right to serve as part of the team. Plus, I don't fit the typical Creator formula. They're people who graduated from expensive universities and attended specialty internships across the globe—a mix of architects, artists, engineers, writers, and more. I'm a woman with a community college degree who works at a kid's salon. I couldn't work on a team filled with the best talent around the world.

There's no way I could do this. "I'm sorry. I can't accept your offer."

His eyes narrow. "I didn't ask a yes or no question."

My jaw drops.

He slides the contract toward my side of the desk. "You can take your time and review the paperwork but you're not leaving this office without signing the contract."

I stare at my hands, wondering if they would fit around Rowan's tree trunk of a neck. "This is the twenty-first century. You might be my boss but I won't let you tell me what to do."

"That in itself is a contradiction."

I fist the fabric of my dress to avoid doing something stupid like punching his pretty face. "Are you always this cold?"

Rowan stares at me in silence. He rubs his sharp jaw in a way that sends my stomach into a flurry of butterflies. It draws my attention to his plump lips.

Hello! Earth to Zahra!

I glare at the contract. Rowan has every right to fire me after my mockery of a proposal. But instead, he offered me the most coveted job in all of Dreamland. I'd be stupid to turn this down.

Not that you have an option anyway.

I swipe the contract off the table in defeat.

He plucks a pen from the glass holder. "Sign on the dotted line."

I reach out for the pen. Our fingers brush, and heat shoots up my arm like flames licking my skin. I pull back and drop the pen.

Rowan looks down at his hand like it offended him. *Great. Glad to know I elicit that kind of facial expression from him.*

It shouldn't matter either way. He's your boss.

I grab the pen off the desk and refocus my attention on the contract. My heart slams against my rib cage as I reread the bold numbers at the top until they blur together.

I turn the page toward him and point at the salary. "Is this a typo?"

"Do I look like a man who makes typos?"

"But there's a ten-thousand-dollar raise."

"At least your eyesight isn't as impaired as your judgment."

I should be angry at his insult but all I can do is laugh. The kinds of things he says with a straight face impress the hell out of me, and I can't help feeling oddly attracted to his blunt nature. I blame my exposure to *Pride and Prejudice* at a young and impressionable age.

He stares at me with wide eyes. His expression has me going into another fit of laughter. There's something about breaking through Rowan's icy exterior that I find entertaining. I'm not sure what the hell is wrong with me, but I find his matter-of-fact comments funny rather than off-putting. They're awkward and stilted, like he isn't comfortable doing anything besides barking out orders.

Yeah. There's *definitely* something wrong with me.

CHAPTER SEVEN

Rowan

I take the opportunity to observe Zahra while she's distracted with reading the contract. This weird feeling in my chest hasn't stopped since she walked into my space, and the way she looks at me makes me feel alert.

Her feet dangle an inch above the carpet, with the edges of her shoes irritatingly grazing the floor. From the offensively cheery strawberry fabric of her dress to the way she laughs, I'm somewhat disarmed by her presence.

I hate it. There's nothing I want more than for her to be gone from my eyesight and olfactory range.

I pull at the tie wrapped around my collar to relieve some of the tension in my neck. My eyes drop to the stupid pin located above the curve of her breast.

Bloom even when the sun doesn't shine.

She's an uncomfortable bright spot in my office, and I'm tempted to shoo her out the door.

She frowns as she turns the page. The gesture brings my attention to the red coloring on her lips. It stands out against her golden-brown skin, and I find myself uncharacteristically focused on the way her tongue darts out to trace her cupid's bow. Heat trickles down my spine as I imagine those lips doing something else.

What the fuck? No. I let out a huff, ignoring the warmth spreading throughout my body.

Her nose scrunches at whatever she reads.

"Problem?" I grind out with clenched teeth.

She doesn't even flinch. "No."

"You've reviewed the same page twice already."

She tilts her head and looks at me in a way that makes the hair on the back of my neck rise. "I'm flattered you've been paying such close attention to me."

I refrain from releasing a groan. Whatever look she registers on my face has her grinning to herself.

She taps the paper with her pen. "Contracts like these require my full and undivided attention. I'm not signing anything before I have a chance to read the fine print."

"You're not special enough for any fine print."

She doesn't look the least bit offended by my comment which only irritates me more. What is it about this woman, and why can't she fall in line like everyone else? It's like she shits sprinkles and consumes rainbows for sustenance. I'm not sure what kind of fairy tale forest she was raised in, but no one can be this optimistic about everything.

"You're nothing like your grandfather described."

The wooden armrests groan under my tight grip. "What did

you say?" The only reason my voice comes out flat and disinterested is because of years of practice.

She stares at my white-knuckled fists. "Forget I said anything. It slipped out."

One simply can't forget something like that. I'm stuck between pushing her for answers and looking unbothered by her comment. "Whatever my grandfather said to a stranger in passing is nothing short of casual conversation."

She laughs to herself but says nothing else. My skin itches for more information, but she remains tight-lipped as she returns her attention back to the contract.

That's it? "How did you catch yourself in a conversation with my grandfather?" I blurt out.

She shrugs at my wide-eyed expression. "Fate. And it was *conversations*. Plural."

Great. I'm betting my entire fortune on someone who believes in fate. "And what happened during these conversations?"

"That's between Brady and me."

Brady? This is the second time I've heard her call him that.

She interrupts my thoughts with a knowing smile. "He had quite a bit to say about you."

The tightness in my chest intensifies. "Part of me doesn't want to know."

Her grin widens. "But part of you can't help being curious."

I roll my eyes, which only makes her whole face light up like a damn Dreamland firework. I've never seen someone look at me like that before. It's strange. Like she's genuinely interested in my company rather than the idea of getting something out of me.

My skin itches under her assessment.

"Don't worry. He didn't say too much about you except that you were the dreamer of the three grandkids. And he was very excited for you to take over as the director one day. Said it was your calling, so I'm sure he would be happy to see you in his office, destroying his favorite chair." She gestures at the armrests I hold on to like a life preserver. I release my grip and crack my knuckles.

"That's all?"

"For the most part. Sorry to disappoint. We were pretty busy working on other things, but I remember how highly he spoke of his grandsons."

The burning in my chest increases tenfold. I take a few deep breaths to ease the tension in my muscles.

Zahra scribbles her signature on the bottom of the page and passes it back to me. I purposefully swipe my fingers across hers as I grab the contract. The same weird feeling from earlier sparks between us, making me pause. Zahra sucks in a breath and pulls away, tucking her hand under the layers of her dress.

Interesting. It seems our connection wasn't a one-off.

"When do I start?" She rises from her seat and runs a hand down the length of her dress.

I drag my eyes away from the curve of her waist toward her face. "Monday. Be here at 9:00 a.m. sharp."

"Thank you for the opportunity. Really. I might have been shocked earlier when I said no, but I do really appreciate it. I don't plan on letting you down." A flush of color surges to the surface of her brown cheeks.

I find her reactions to the simplest things interesting. What else would make her blush? An image of her red-painted lips wrapped around something incredibly inappropriate flickers through my mind.

She's on your payroll. Get a fucking grip on yourself. I frown at the uncontrollable reaction spreading through my body like a row of falling dominos. I've never been the type to be attracted to those who work under me.

What's different about her and how can I stop it?

I release a tense breath. "See yourself out." I grab her contract and add it to the stack of paperwork for Martha to handle.

Zahra grabs her backpack off the floor. She stands and turns on her heel, giving me a view of at least fifty different pins scattered across the pocket.

What's the story with the pins, and why does she carry them with her wherever she goes?

I stop breathing as I zone in on one pin in particular. It catches my attention not because it's bold but rather because it's so different than all the other ones. No normal person would notice that pin out of the countless ones, but I'm all too familiar with the symbol and what it represents.

Maybe there's more to Little Miss Bubbly than meets the eye, and something tells me it has to do with the understated black semicolon pin.

"How's it going?" Declan leans into the camera.

"My schedule has been slammed with meetings from nine to nine but I finally think I have an idea of what I need to do." *All thanks to Zahra.*

"At least I have one brother taking this seriously." Declan takes a shot at Cal.

His jaw locks. "I'm waiting for a particular moment."

"Sounds like an excuse." I shrug.

He rubs his eyebrow with his middle finger.

Declan sighs. "Rowan, let's concentrate on your plan first. I'll get to Cal after."

"I don't need you trying to micromanage me. Have a little trust in my process and let me go about this my way. I've already proven myself."

Declan rubs a hand across his stubble. "There's a lot more banking on this one project. If any of us fails—"

My molars smash together. "Then we all fail. I got it the first five times you mentioned it. Give me space to figure this all out. You don't see me chasing after you, checking in on whether or not you found a wife that meets your unreasonable standards."

"There are no standards in this process because it's a contractual obligation. All I care about is finding someone who's practical, fertile, and has a face considered proportionate enough to be deemed attractive."

Cal grins. "With that kind of charm, I bet you'll be walking down the aisle in no time."

Declan shoots a withering glare into the camera.

"Will I be your best man? Before you decide, think about it. Rowan wouldn't know the first thing about planning a bachelor party. He considers puffing cigars at your house a good time."

"That's because it is a good time."

"Think about it. I'm talking Vegas. Buffets. Strip clubs. Casinos." Cal ticks off each on his fingers.

"If you're trying to sell me on this, you lost me at Vegas."

I laugh. "Declan's happy place happens to be the four walls of his home."

Cal rubs his stubbled chin. "Okay. I'll compromise and bring Vegas to you."

"Neither of you will be my best man because I'm eloping."

Cal scoffs. "You and Rowan are so boring it's no wonder you get along so well. Only you would skip out on a massive party to elope."

Declan shows off the small smile he saves for us. "You sound jealous."

"Mr. Kane. Mr. Johnson is waiting on line one. A fair warning—he's in a foul mood." Declan's mic picks up on Iris's voice.

"Old man Johnson still giving Iris a hard time?" Cal leans forward.

"Did he threaten you again?" He mutes his mic. Whatever Iris says makes the vein in Declan's neck pulse.

Declan shakes his head and unmutes his mic after a minute.

Cal frowns. "One day, you're going to regret making Iris work on weekends. The best years of her life are ticking by taking care of your old, grumpy ass."

Declan's jaw ticks. "Next week. Same time." He ends the meeting call, leaving me with nothing to look at but a black screen.

Instead of going home and making dinner for myself, I pull up Zahra's electronic employee file. Something in the way she spoke about my grandfather has bothered me ever since she left my office. I'd be stupid to trust whatever she said about Grandpa.

Nothing in my preliminary search reveals much besides the

fact that she's been a dedicated salon worker since her college internship days.

Frustrated with my lack of findings, I dive deeper into her file, reviewing everything from her first Dreamland interview to her college transcripts. I somehow find myself clicking on an old employee submission from over three years ago and scrolling to the bottom. There's a virtual sticky note, signed and dated by my grandfather two months before his accident.

> *Schedule a meeting with Ms. Gulian to discuss rejection and improvements.*

I review the paperwork again. *Zahra submitted a proposal about Nebula Land?* That's odd, given the kind of proposal she turned in that ripped the ride apart.

I pull up the Nebula Land submission that was accepted by the Creators two years ago and compare Zahra's to this version. Someone named Lance Baker submitted the idea with a few more bells and whistles compared to Zahra's more basic proposal. How did they both come up with similar ideas? Were they creative partners who had a dispute?

My questions continue to grow without any real answers to appease my curiosity. I search Zahra's file for more submissions but come up empty. She didn't submit any after the one my grandfather reviewed until this year.

What made her stop in the first place? And who the hell is Lance Baker?

CHAPTER EIGHT

Zahra

"Let me get this straight. You're going to be a Creator? How did you keep this from me all day?" Claire's fork drops against her plate.

I've held back from spilling the news because I wanted to share it with my whole family during our weekly Saturday dinner. My parents are the whole reason we all work at Dreamland together, so I wanted to celebrate with them too.

Ani jumps out of her seat, making her brunette curls fly around her head. She throws her arms around me. "Yay! You did it!"

I hug my sister back, cherishing her warmth. It means the world to me to show her that nothing can get in her way, regardless of her Down syndrome diagnosis. And in other ways, she pushes me to be my best self every day with her infectious happiness.

"We need to celebrate!" My mom's hazel eyes brighten as she runs into the kitchen.

The brown skin around Dad's eyes wrinkles as he grins. "I'm so proud of you! I knew once the right person realized how talented you are, they wouldn't be able to resist."

My chest tightens. Dad has always supported me, ever since I was a little kid who said I wanted to be a Creator when I grew up. He never stopped dreaming enough for the two of us, even when I gave up on myself.

Mom steps out of the kitchen with a bottle of champagne and a few plastic champagne glasses.

"Do you have champagne bottles sitting around now?"

"Your mom was planning on opening it for our anniversary next week but today's news calls for it." Dad claps his hands together.

Mom places a hand on my shoulder and gives it a squeeze. "Forget about our anniversary. We have plenty of those."

Twenty-eight, to be exact. They've been solid since Dad swept Mom off her feet with his stories about Armenia.

Mom wraps her arms around me. "Our daughter is going to be a Creator! Did you hear that, Hayk?"

"Hard to miss since I was sitting right here." Dad winks at her.

I sigh. That's my parents. Voted *most likely to make me nauseous with their love* since the day I was born.

Mom takes her seat beside Dad. "I can't believe Mr. Kane offered you a job after you told him how disappointing his ride was. Now that's our daughter." She shoots Dad a knowing look.

I grimace. "Well, I didn't tell him that exactly..."

"She's lying. She told him that it represented everything Brady Kane would hate if he were still alive." Claire tips her glass of water in my direction before taking a sip.

Ani's brown eyebrows rise. "You didn't."

"I might have gone a little overboard but it's true. The design Lance submitted was only a fraction of the idea I created with Brady."

Dad's smile drops. He reaches out and gives my hand a squeeze. "Well, the joke is on Lance. Now you have a new job and you have the chance to fix it until it's exactly what you dreamed of."

"I'm not sure that's what Rowan wants."

I'm already going into a job grossly underprepared and underqualified. The last thing I want to do is make waves with the Creators, especially after my accidental proposal.

"If he hired you, then he has a good idea of what he's doing," Dad says.

I wish I felt as confident as he did in my skills. Ever since I left Rowan's office, the worrying thoughts have multiplied until they have become overwhelming.

What if I only had one good idea that Brady Kane helped take from average to amazing? What if I was a one-hit wonder who will crash and burn in front of the very people I've looked up to my entire life?

I hate that I'm slipping into these old thinking traps. I'm letting Lance win every time I give his criticisms any airtime in my head, and it only annoys me more.

If you don't believe in yourself, no one will.

My family pulls me out of my thoughts. I pop the champagne bottle and raise it toward the ceiling.

Cheers, Brady.

I arrived ten minutes early today to impress Rowan with my newfound punctuality, but my efforts were for nothing. His door remains shut, so I talk Martha's ear off. It doesn't take us long to become gal pals who bond over our favorite romance author and our forever craving of Chick-fil-A on Sundays.

Talking with her helps pass the time.

Even Martha has to work, so I fiddle with the fabric of my polka dot dress and mess around on my phone.

The door to Rowan's office opens with a bang. I jump in my seat and press a hand to my racing heart. Whatever coffee Rowan drinks in the morning clearly isn't working for him. He walks out of his office without giving his secretary and me a second glance.

She all but shoves me out of my chair. "Go!"

I speed walk out of the lobby to catch up with him. It takes me double the amount of steps to keep up with his long strides because the man is *tall*. How does he fit through a doorframe without ducking his head?

As we continue walking, the silence eats away at me until I burst.

"I'm starting to think you're not much of a morning person." I somehow find myself matching his strides.

Rowan grunts under his breath. He leads us toward the Story Street catacombs entrance.

"Wonderful weather, am I right?"

Cue the crickets. "Why yes, Zahra, I was wondering what's the point of showering in the morning if the humidity does the job for me?" I try to imitate his voice with a low pitch but fail when my voice cracks.

The corner of his lip lifts the tiniest bit and I mentally fist pump in the air.

I take another stab at rescuing this conversation. "How do you like Dreamland so far?"

"I don't," he mumbles under his breath.

I trip on the toe of my sneaker. "Oh." *Well, shit. I didn't expect him to say that.* "Do you have a favorite ride?"

"No."

My brain cells all cheer for his response. *We're getting somewhere, people.* "Me neither! There are too many good ones."

That earns me another grunt.

"What's your favorite part about being the director?"

"The silence at the end of the workday."

I flat-out lose it. My lungs burn from laughing so hard at his response. He stops walking and stares at me for a second before recovering.

He leads us through the tunnels like he does this all the time. Together, we walk up a pair of stairs and through a door marked *The Creators' Workspace*. My breath catches as we walk into a massive warehouse, partitioned into four sections with tall dividers. A certain smell wafts through the air, reminding me of an elementary school art class.

Rowan shuffles me through each room, staying quiet as I take in the beauty of it all. The first space is packed with animatronics and robots for rides, parades, and shows. I run a hand across a cold metal arm of an animatronic. It moves and I jump back and straight into Rowan's chest. His hand clutches onto my arm to stabilize me. Every cell fires off in unison within me, sparking to life at the gentleness of his touch.

My body becomes an inferno from the contact. Skin heats where his hand presses, and I find myself leaning into him. He releases me and exits the room like his shoes might catch on fire.

I keep up with his hurried pace, following him into a designer's paradise where the walls are covered with storyboards and the tables are filled with all kinds of art supplies.

The next room features many tables covered in mini 3D models of Dreamland, and I'm blown away by the attention to detail. I lean over one, finding an exact replica of Fairy Tale Land and Princess Cara's Castle. I can't help myself from running my index finger across one of the spires.

My neck prickles and I look over my shoulder to find Rowan staring at my ass.

Oh my God. Is he attracted to me? As if he has the same thought, his lips press into a thin line. My scoff becomes a full-blown belly laugh as I curl over. He blinks a couple of times, erasing the look of darkness from his eyes.

"Are you ready to meet everyone, or are you still interested in wasting company time with your tour?" he snaps before moving toward the door.

I don't bother correcting him about who started this tour. I'm not too sure who he's trying to fool here because I see right through him. But the real question is *why*. Why bother giving me a moment to take in my surroundings like this? Why lead me through the warehouse himself rather than throw the task on someone more willing and available?

I remember Brady mentioning how Rowan loved visiting the warehouse when he was a child. Is he enjoying this walk-through as much as I am? If so, why is he so angry now?

Rowan is like a secret code I want to crack—a human Fort Knox I'm interested in breaking into, if only to uncover a vaulted heart full of gold. Or maybe that's just the hopeful part of me that wonders if Rowan is truly as sweet as Brady described him to be.

I follow him into the final room, packed with Creators, and the main room seems to be a gathering space surrounded by rows of cubicles. The room is paradise, with bean bag chairs, dry erase walls, and 3D simulation stations.

Welcome to your new home. I can't believe I'm finally here. Brady was right. It was only a matter of time before I would find myself officially trading in my old work badge for a Creator one.

What would he think of me now?

He might have told you to lay off the wine and write something while sober, but beggars can't be choosers.

I blink away the mistiness in my eyes.

Rowan introduces me to the Creators, who he refers to as the Alpha and Beta teams. Different members welcome me to the warehouse. My heart squeezes in my chest at their eagerness and the idea of working by their side.

Jenny, a brunette woman who is the head of the Beta team, claims me as a member of her group once Rowan steps away from me. I look back at him to check if this is part of the plan.

Rowan offers me a bored look. "Go on." He looks around the room. "Get back to work, everyone."

Everyone follows his royal decree like the faithful foot soldiers we are for the Kane brand.

Jenny takes the time to show me my new workspace. My jaw drops open as I take a look inside my cubicle. I've never had my own office, and I'm in awe at the L-shaped desk in the corner with dual monitors taking up a chunk of space. There's even a shiny new laptop in one corner, just waiting to be opened up.

I drop into the luxurious rolling chair and run a hand over the ergonomic keyboard.

Look at me, having grown-up things like a desk and my very own stapler. I click it twice to make sure I'm not dreaming.

Jenny readjusts her already pristine ponytail. "We're thrilled to have you as a part of our team, Zahra. I'm glad Sam backed down pretty fast during our fight for you."

"A fight over *me*?" The words seem ridiculous leaving my mouth.

She grins. "Don't worry. I took it easy on him. I laid on the fake tears and he broke down quicker than a McDonald's ice cream machine."

We laugh. Compared to Regina, Jenny is a breath of fresh air.

"I'm the one who thought Mr. Kane needed to read your submission himself. Sam was a bit hesitant given the nature of the content."

I wince. "I'm sorry."

She waves her hand in the air. "Please. No apologies needed. We're in such a time crunch and there's no reason to apologize for stating how you feel. You're the kind of Creator we need on our team."

"Wow. I mean—thank you." *That went so much better than I'd thought it would.*

"Let me give you a quick rundown of how things work around here. On Fridays, each Creator is responsible for presenting a new proposal. There's a multistep six-month process set in place to give Mr. Kane as many options as possible to choose from."

"Options for what?"

Jenny smiles. "He's planning a fiftieth-anniversary update. A lot is riding on a project of this scale, so he expects us all to be at our best."

"You got it! I won't let you down."

"I'll let you get settled in. I hope you like Italian because the Betas planned a welcome lunch for you."

"Only monsters hate Italian food."

She laughs. "I knew you'd fit right in. See you at noon." She walks out of the cubicle, leaving me with all my shiny new toys.

I might collapse from how nice everyone is here. It's a much different vibe than I expected based on the stories I've heard about the Creators. My worries from before seem kind of silly now.

I slide my backpack underneath my desk before giving my rolling chair a spin. After my dizziness goes away, I swipe the stapler and press it together over and over again. Staples rain around me like celebratory confetti.

I feel Rowan before I see him. My neck tingles, and I look over my shoulder to find his eyes piercing my back like he wants to stab it.

"Yes?" I smile wide because I enjoy the way it makes his right eye twitch.

"Do you mind putting away your weapon before I start speaking?" His eyes narrow at the stapler.

"Is the big bad Mr. Kane afraid of a little stapler?" I click it a few times in his direction. The staples fly in the air before landing a few inches from my ballet flats.

"I wouldn't trust you with bubble wrap, let alone a stapler."

"You're right. That choking hazard warning should be taken more seriously."

A strange noise between a scoff and a groan escapes from his throat, and I classify it as a laugh. *Looks like he has a personality after all.*

I place the stapler back on my desk where it belongs.

"Any other weapons I should know about?"

I roll my eyes as I pretend to grab an invisible gun out from under my desk. I'm sure to make a show of removing the fake magazine and placing it on the desk.

If I squint, I could classify the small smirk on Rowan's face as a smile. He lets out an exaggerated breath and steps inside the cubicle.

Wow. Was that his attempt at a joke?

I reward him with a grin that goes unreturned. The space instantly feels smaller, with his size taking up a quarter of the square footage.

I break the silence. "Can I help you with something in particular?"

He opens his mouth, only to close it a second later.

Does he even know why he's here? The thought makes my chest all tingly.

Bad Zahra. "What do you think of my new digs?"

"Leaves something to be desired." His eyes slide from my face to the gray cubicle walls.

I blink at him. *Would it kill him to be nice?*

Probably. I focus my attention back on my desk. I'm committed to ignoring him until he goes away because I don't want him to rain on my parade.

I press every single button twice on the computer but the damn thing won't turn on no matter what I do.

"Move over." He walks up to my desk, bringing his addictive cologne with him.

"Why?" I rasp.

"For some unknown reason, I feel like helping you."

"*Because*?" I keep my smile hidden behind a curtain of my hair.

"Because you shouldn't be trusted around electrical outlets."

I laugh and scoot my chair out to give him some room.

He kneels down on his perfectly pressed trousers. I shouldn't find it as hot as I do, but the cubicle heats up as he looks up at me from his spot on the floor. His gaze darkens as his eyes scan my crossed legs. My heart thuds in my chest at the pace of a jackhammer, and I'm surprised he can't hear the erratic beats himself.

Whatever passes between us disappears as he crawls underneath the desk, giving me the perfect view of him on all fours.

Now who's the one staring?

I ignore the voice in my head and choose to enjoy the show. Rowan's body is nothing like my ex's. Every inch of his lean body is packed with muscle like he runs for fun. His muscular calves stick out from beneath the desk, and his firm ass moves as he readjusts the cables down there. It takes every ounce of self-control in my body not to reach out and touch him. I take a moment to guess his shoe size. The only conclusion I come to is that I'm hopelessly immature and desperately horny.

Of course I'm attracted to my arrogant boss who lacks any sort of people skills. This has to be some cruel joke on me after everything I've been through. Maybe there is some kind of chemical imbalance in my body or gravitational pull toward assholes like Rowan.

What if jerks are my kink?

Well, at least it explains your unhealthy obsession with Mr. Darcy.

I barely get my breathing under control before he rises back on his feet.

Something about the way he looks at me has my blood reaching a new temperature. Goose bumps scatter across my skin despite the raging inferno spreading through my chest. It comforts me to know my body is just as contradictory as my brain.

Why him? Why me? My smile disappears. His hand flexes by his side before he pockets it.

Jane Austen, are you my guardian angel now? I look up at the high ceiling for answers but come up empty.

"What in God's name are you whispering about?"

Oh shit. I said that aloud? "Is the computer all fixed now?" Sounds close enough to what I mumbled before.

"Yes."

"Great. Thanks! You can see yourself out." I throw his words back at him, half hoping for any kind of reaction. He offers me nothing but a frown and a pinched expression on his face.

Well, it's a start.

He walks toward the entrance of the cubicle, taking his allure with him. Maybe I can finally think again once he's out of my eyesight. There's something about him that throws me off-kilter, like I don't know what to say or do anymore.

He strolls out of my cubicle, leaving me behind with all the thoughts bouncing around in my head. I take a deep cleansing breath only to get hit with another inhale of his cologne.

Why does he have to smell so damn good? My head drops into my hands, muffling my frustrated groan.

I recover and hesitantly press the power button on my computer.

Let's get to work.

CHAPTER NINE

Zahra

I give my presentation one last look through. After Jenny's kind words, I thought I beat back the self-doubt, but it decided to come back with a vengeance.

I groan as I reassess the drawing I created of Nebula Land. While the PowerPoint reflects everything that Brady and I designed together, my sketch proves why I'm an English major. If I were meant to be an artist, I'd move to New York with all the other starving talent and eat ramen every day of the week until I got my big break.

Can I really present this to the group? My skills seem on par with a two-year-old child learning how to hold a crayon for the first time. It's not like Rowan expects us to be perfect at everything, but my drawings are far from it. And seeing as I have zero skills in anything Adobe related, I'm stuck relying on my own two hands, which are severely lacking.

I sigh as I add a photo of my drawing to the last slide of my presentation. Maybe if I go over my allotted time slot, I could hold off on showing this tragedy.

Now that's an idea. I wipe my damp forehead before packing up all of my supplies. "Here goes nothing."

I enter the conference room with my head held high. Everyone smiles up at me before resuming their tasks, and I take a seat toward the back. Despite the group lunches and brainstorming sessions, I still feel like an outsider. My addition to the team was anything but traditional, and I'm afraid people think I'm being favored because I fast-tracked my way into a Creator job.

Jenny walks into the room and starts up the projector. "So who wants to go first?"

A bunch of hands shoot into the air. I don't bother lifting my arm because worry weighs mine down like an anvil.

Jenny calls on the Creator closest to her. They stand at the front of the room and crush their presentation on an update to Princess Cara's Castle. While their idea is nice in theory, it's just that. *Nice.* Not riveting or enthralling, and even Jenny can't suppress her yawn halfway through the discussion.

The conference room door slides open and everyone's heads turn toward the sound. The presenter stops midsentence.

No! As if this day can't get any worse. Rowan waltzes into the space without a care in the world. Today he wears a gray suit that has my mouth watering and my thighs pressing together. The charcoal color brings out the severity in his gaze. His muscles shift under the luxurious fabric as he settles into the chair at the front of the room.

"Proceed as usual."

His air of authority shouldn't be considered an attractive trait to me, but there's something about the way he commands a room that has me wanting more.

The rest of the team sits pin straight in their chairs as the presenter finishes their speech. One by one, Creators take the podium. The series of ideas all follow a similar pattern—some updates here, some immersive line experiences there. I begin questioning if my presentation is too bold for this kind of setting, especially with Rowan right there.

With each presentation, Rowan's frown becomes more pronounced. His reactions add to my already-fraying nerves. I've suffered from stage fright since I was a little kid, but I don't remember it being this bad. My hands remain permanently clammy and my breathing grows heavier with each presentation.

"Zahra. You're up," Jenny calls out.

I rise on wobbly legs. If the pressure I placed on myself wasn't enough already, now it's hit a whole new level of distressing with Rowan's gaze glued to mine.

"Move along with it. I have another meeting in twenty minutes." Rowan taps the face of his watch with finality.

I'm tempted to run out the door, but I control the urge and set up my presentation. With a deep breath, I dive into explaining my idea. I feed off the team's nonverbals, letting their nods and smiles boost my confidence. My self-esteem grows, and I nail my entire explanation without passing out. I count the entire thing as a major win.

When I get to the dreaded final slide with the drawing, I click it so fast that the black screen pops up not a second later. Jenny's timer rings simultaneously, and I thank the big man upstairs for saving me. "Looks like I'm out of time."

People clap and Jenny looks over at me with a massive grin and a thumbs-up.

"Go back to the last slide." Rowan's voice hits me like a bucket of ice water.

"Oh, it's nothing important. Just a mock-up. And you have a meeting now anyway."

His nostrils flare. "I wasn't asking."

Of course you weren't. That requires the kind of manners you're severely lacking.

His jaw ticks. "Now, Ms. Gulian."

I mentally curse him in English, Spanish, and Armenian for good measure. "It's really nothing." I hide my shaky hands behind the podium.

"I'll be the one to decide that."

My teeth smash together as I bring up the drawing. I wouldn't have included it if we weren't required to have some kind of visual aid of our proposal. And of course, if I didn't need another reason not to fit in, I'm one of the only Creators who can't draw to save my life.

The self-doubt comes back again, picking away at the newfound confidence I built throughout my presentation.

Rowan runs a hand across his chin. "Your drawings could use some work."

"I'll be sure to get right on that." My voice is doused in sarcasm.

The entire room goes silent. I wish I could slap a hand over my mouth and apologize.

Rowan appears unbothered. "Everyone better come back with better ideas next Friday. I was underwhelmed to say the least."

Shit. The entire team's faces mirror my own shock. No one dares to move, probably too afraid to do anything but stare at Rowan.

He tilts his head toward the projector. "Use Ms. Gulian's presentation as a guide for what I expect from here on out. Minus the last slide."

My cheeks heat.

"Everyone is dismissed except for Ms. Gulian."

Something takes flight in my stomach at the way he says my name. It's quickly doused by the reality of my situation. *He wants me to stay alone with him. Here?*

Team members funnel out of the room like the floor is lava. Rowan doesn't move from his seat until the last member shuts the door behind them. He prowls toward the podium, giving me no room to escape his thousand-pound stare.

My back hits the wooden frame as I turn to face him. I don't want to test my self-control around him because I feel like it's a losing battle. After he embarrassed me in front of everyone, the temptation to wrap my hands around his neck and give it a squeeze is too strong to be ignored.

"If you talk to me like that in front of anyone again—"

"Let me guess. You'll fire me. It's a bit predictable for my taste but I respect it since you're the man in charge."

He stares at me like he can't believe I spoke to him the way I did. Honestly, me neither. And I can't exactly blame a bottle of wine for this level of bravery and stupidity. There's something about him that makes me want to push all his buttons. I'm interested in seeing who the real Rowan is beneath all those layers of ice and indifference.

His brows scrunch. "There are worse things I'm capable of."

A chill shoots down my spine. "Like?"

"I don't think you want to find out."

I pretend I'm unbothered by his threat despite my racing heart. "You better have a massive dick to back up that attitude or else people will be mighty disappointed."

"Care to bring out a ruler and test your theory?"

"I left my magnifying glass at home, so maybe tomorrow." I'm pretty sure the angel on my shoulder has left the building.

Something shifts between us. His eyes darken as they assess me. I'm not sure if he wants to choke me, fire me, or fuck me into submission. "Are you always this impossible?"

"I don't know. Are you always this much of an asshole?"

One second he's scowling at me and the next his lips are slamming into mine.

Wait, what?!

My brain goes haywire and my eyes shut as Rowan devours my mouth. Both of his hands clutch onto the podium behind me, trapping my body between his thick forearms.

He kisses in the same way he does everything else—with practiced precision and restrained power. I'm tempted to drive him wild because all that pent-up anger must go *somewhere*. I'll happily volunteer as tribute.

I'm a lost cause to my inhibitions as I kiss him back. My hands fist the front of his suit and I hold on like I might fall if I let go.

This is so wrong. He's your BOSS!

Rowan kisses away each thought. Our tongues lash out against one another in a silent battle. Kissing Rowan is a completely new experience. Toxic to the point of overdosing and erotic enough to leave me aching for more. A kiss filled with so much passion, it seems like he might die if he stops. Hell, I might drop dead if he keeps going.

But what a way to go.

Rowan presses his body into mine. I'm hit with a rush down my spine as he rocks his erection into me. I don't need any kind of tool to determine he's *big*. I moan and he sucks up the sound. He pushes harder, and I feel him *everywhere*.

The wheels of the podium roll, and the entire thing moves. I lose my footing. Rowan latches onto my arm before my ass has the chance to hit the carpet.

I rip my arm out of his grasp. He looks at me with dilated pupils and swollen lips. My eyes drop to the bulge that I was *very* interested in only a few seconds ago. I nearly stumble from the sheer size of whatever he has hidden beneath his slacks.

I can't believe I did *that* to my *boss*. What was I thinking?!

I wipe my mouth with my hand as if it can erase the memory of his lips, but it's a hopeless cause. He might as well have branded my lips with his initials.

"Shit." The lust disappears from his eyes, gone in the blink of an eye. His chest rises with each ragged breath.

I snap out of his trance. I'm on an escape mission as I rush to grab my purse and bolt from the room, leaving a silent Rowan behind.

I'm not sure what the hell happened, but I lock our kiss away in the *never think about again if I value my life* file, located in the darkest corner of my brain. Right next to the *stupid shit I did while drunk* and *dick pics* categories.

CHAPTER TEN

Rowan

Fuck. That's all I can say to myself as I walk all the way back to my office. Every time I think I have my urges under control, the memory of Zahra's lips against mine has my body reacting all over again.

It was a bad idea to ask Zahra to stay after the meeting. Things escalated when she talked back to me in a way I've never experienced before. It should have been a huge turnoff. I've never been attracted to anyone who disrespects authority, so I'm not sure what about Zahra draws me in. Instead of listening to the rational voice in my head earlier, I ran face-first into the biggest red flag without blinking.

I don't know what it is about her that stops me from thinking. Threats bounce off her and my glares only make her laugh harder. And after the way she treated me in the meeting, I wasn't sure if I wanted to kick her out of Dreamland or fuck her until she apologized for how she spoke to me.

And the noises she made when my tongue glided across hers... *Fuck.* I groan as blood rushes to my cock again.

I shove my hands in my hair and tug. *Fuck. Fuck. Fuck!*

Declan would string me up by the balls on the Castle's flagpole if he found out I kissed an employee. I consider all my options on how I could get ahead of this impending HR shitstorm but there's no way around it. In the end, I deserve whatever lawsuit Zahra wants to hit me with. I'm the one who kissed her. No matter how she reacted to my touch, it's my responsibility to remain professional and hold myself to a higher standard.

Instead of going back to my office, I head toward my house at the back corner of Dreamland. I pull out my phone and call my pilot, wanting to get the hell out of here for a while before I do something else that could jeopardize the best shot I have at succeeding with this project.

The kiss I shared with Zahra revealed just how dangerous our attraction is, and I need to stay as far away from her as humanly possible. She's nothing but dangerous. For my plan. For my future. And for the voice in my head wondering how explosive everything else would be between us if we hadn't stopped.

My first twenty-four hours back in Chicago have been anything but pleasant. From my driver making me late after struggling to change a flat tire to some random employee spilling coffee all over my shirt, everything has gone to shit.

Monday meetings only add to my growing irritation. I feel as if I'm wasting time sitting through procedural meetings when my time could be better spent at Dreamland.

I rotate my cuff link, twisting the cool metal between my fingers. Declan takes the helm after my father's usual run-through. My brother speaks about our numbers while Iris handles the PowerPoint presentation. Declan's assistant is pretty in an understated kind of way. Her dark, wavy hair is held back with a bright-colored headband, bringing out the warm tones of her brown skin.

She and Declan work together seamlessly. Despite her younger age, she's damn good at what she does. He even lets her answer some questions, which is a rarity for him.

I look over at Cal, wondering if he notices how they work together, but he's focused on a sheet of paper in front of him. This isn't anything new. Cal has always struggled with his impulsivity and attention issues despite how intelligent he is. Sitting through hour-long meetings sucks him dry of any restraint he has over himself.

Today he decided to stay awake by playing a game of tic-tac-toe with himself.

I grab my pen and screw up his game for the hell of it.

"Fucker," he mumbles under his breath.

I write *PAY ATTENTION* across the top of his paper. He draws the wonkiest middle finger, and I scribble below it.

That's one small dick. Is it yours?

He lets out a low laugh.

Declan clears his throat, and we both look up at him.

"Any updates on Dreamland's progress, Rowan?" my father asks. His tone is so neutral that it sets me on edge. If he doesn't sneer, scowl, or glare, I'm automatically searching for a trap he wants to lay in front of me.

I flick an invisible piece of dust off my jacket. "The Creator teams have already been assembled and they're making quick progress on developing some ideas."

Father nods. "Good. I think it would be beneficial to have you present during our next meeting on the preliminary findings. Your ten-billion-dollar budget is drastic, and I'm sure the rest of the board is interested in learning more about the allocation of the funds."

Motherfucker. I grind my teeth to the point of pain. "Of course I can present on my budget. Is there anything in particular that you would like to see?"

He shakes his head. "I'm sure everyone is equally interested in learning more about the creative design process behind an operation this large. There hasn't been a renovation on this scale since the twenty-five-year mark."

Bullshit. I assess his eyes, searching for some kind of tell, only to find they lack their usual redness. That's bizarre. To think of it, I'm not sure I've ever seen my father look *this* sober. He's the worst kind of functioning alcoholic, with his only tell being his red eyes the next day.

I brush it off as a weird coincidence. Maybe he ran out of alcohol last night and was too lazy to hit the store. "I'd be more than happy to share everything I've been working on thus far."

My father lit an inferno under my ass today. It's about time I start pushing everyone to their breaking point because their best simply isn't good enough for me. Not with my father breathing down my neck, waiting for me to fail.

I'll do whatever it takes to ensure the Creators have everything they need to be successful, especially Zahra. She's my best chance at achieving my goal and getting the hell out of Dreamland.

CHAPTER ELEVEN

Zahra

"Any word from Rowan since he kissed you?" Claire takes a sip of her wine.

I'm grateful Ani had to skip out on our weekly girls' night because she had a date with her boyfriend. I couldn't bear having this conversation in front of her.

I lean back into the couch cushions. "No. And you promised not to bother me anymore about it." After I spilled the news about kissmageddon, Claire swore not to bring it up.

So much for that.

"I know. I know. But there's a question that's been bothering me."

"What?"

She grins. "Was it better than Lance?"

I scoff. "It's like comparing a hurricane to a drizzle."

Claire whistles. "Damn. What else do you think his mouth is good at?"

Heat crawls up my neck. "Nothing."

She grins. "Ohh, you're turning red! Admit it. You've totally been thinking about him."

"*No.*" The redness spreads from my neck to my hairline.

"We need to work on your ability to lie. The blush is a dead giveaway."

It's been a curse ever since I was a child.

I raise my chin. "I actually haven't thought about him at all. In fact, I'm grateful he left for the week." His trip gave me time to solidify my spot with the other Creators while strengthening my mental barriers against him.

While his absence was welcomed, I'm worried he disappeared because he thinks I might do something crazy like report him to HR. I considered it for all of two seconds before I decided it was unfair. He might have started the kiss but I was a willing participant. *Very* willing to be honest.

"What's your plan on managing your attraction to him?"

I sigh. "There is no plan."

"Just like there was no kiss?" She grins.

I wink. "Exactly."

Claire rolls her eyes. "If you had to guess, how big was his dick again?"

I slowly separate my two hands to gauge the size. A pillow smacks me in the face, stopping me.

"Hate to break it to you, but if you still remember his dick size, you're totally still thinking about him."

All I do is groan.

"You've got to be freaking kidding me."

Rowan is seated on the corner of my desk like he has every right to the space. After a week of him leaving me alone, I grew too comfortable in his absence. I thought I had everything under control. But the moment he looks at me, my legs shake and my body temperature spikes.

The memory of our kiss floods my brain. The way his tongue dominated. The feel of his chest, tight and strong beneath my palms. The rush of warmth blazing its way through my body toward my lower half.

Yup. I'm screwed. "What are you doing here?" I take a seat to hide the way my knees knock together.

"I'm checking in on everyone."

I make a show of pressing a hand to my ear. Not a single noise bounces off the high ceilings since everyone already left the warehouse for lunch. My intention was to catch up on work since I'm already behind compared to the other Creators, but it looks like Rowan wants to ruin that plan.

"And you decided my office is a good place to start?"

"I'm starting with the person who gives me the most amount of trouble and working my way from here."

"I'm flattered to have earned such a reputation."

He unleashes a smile so small, I need to squint to see it. My chest tightens, and I can't help the panic rushing through me at the flood of attraction.

He's the Devil, Zahra.

Well, that explains why Eve fell for his tricks. If the Devil looked half as good as Rowan, I'd eat the damn apple too. Screw the consequences.

His heavy gaze smacks into me, knocking the air from my lungs. Heat shoots through my veins and sends a new kind of warmth straight to my lower abdomen.

"When you blush, it makes your freckles stand out." He traces the bridge of my nose with the tip of a red pen. His eyes move from my face to his hand, as if he can't believe he did that. *Me neither.*

I brush a hand across my nose, still feeling the burn from his phantom touch.

Get ahold of yourself.

He opens his mouth to speak, but I wave him off, desperate to end this conversation. "I've got work to do."

His brows pull together as if he can't believe he's being dismissed. He ignores my comment as he walks over to the far cubicle wall I covered with half-assed drawings of ideas.

My entire face turns red as he runs a hand across my drawing of Princess Nyra.

"And what's this supposed to be?"

"A new float idea I came up with."

He shoots me a withering glare. "I could guess that based on the shape. But what are they supposed to be celebrating?"

"Are you making fun of my drawings again?"

"No. Now answer my question."

"Would it kill you to say *please* sometimes?"

He blinks at me.

I release a tense breath. "It's a classic Hindu wedding."

He rubs his jaw and stares at it. "Interesting. And when are you presenting this to the team?"

"Friday."

"Hmm." He traces the poorly drawn mandap. My terrible

attempt at the floral canopy mocks me as his hands hover over a stick figure meant to be Princess Nyra's prince. At least my presentation makes up for the poor visuals. I even included real photos this time of Indian weddings since the drawing is anything but professional.

Something about Rowan's stare sets me on edge. "What? If it's a bad idea, spit it out already. I'd rather not look like an embarrassment in front of my coworkers again."

He shakes his head, removing whatever look of longing from his face. "The idea is fine."

Fine. The word repeats in my head, ramming into my skull like bullets. Lance always said everything was fine. Our sex life. Our relationship. Our future. *Fine. Fine. Fine.*

Fine isn't good enough for me anymore and it sure as hell isn't good enough for the team. I stand and go to remove the drawing from the wall.

Rowan's massive hand covers mine, stopping me from removing the tack. The current of energy from last week is back in full force. I suck in a breath when his thumb caresses my knuckles.

His hand disappears all too soon, taking my rush of attraction with him. "I'm sorry. That was inappropriate."

I laugh to myself. "I think touching my hand would be considered tame compared to other things."

His entire body freezes. "What's your angle here?"

"Angle? What are you talking about?"

"Are you trying to get money out of me?"

"What?! Money?" God. Is that what he really thinks about me? I might not have the most squared away finances, but I would never do something of the sort. Especially when I encouraged him.

"It wouldn't be the first time something like that happened," he grumbles.

Oh my God. Does he go around having this issue with others? "Is kissing your employees a repeat occurrence for you?" The question leaves my lips in a whisper.

"What? No." He blinks twice, giving away his surprise.

My muscles relax.

Huh. So maybe I'm special after all. The thought makes me smile to myself.

"But I'd rather you name your price to me in private than go to HR with a complaint, but I can't stop you. I *won't* stop you," he amends.

I'm not sure I'm even breathing at the moment. "I'm not going to HR."

The way he stares at me makes me feel like I'm sitting on the stand, with a lawyer assessing me for any kind of weakness.

"Okay." He refocuses his attention on the drawing. "The idea is good. Great even."

Okay, we're segueing into an entirely different conversation. My brain hurts from the emotional whiplash.

He shoots me a bored expression. "Take a breath. I'm not in the mood to call an ambulance when you pass out and crack your head open."

"How dare I consider for a second that you would catch me before that happens."

"That requires caring and I'm fresh out of fucks to give."

I release a heavy laugh, and our usual cycle repeats of him looking at me with the strangest expression. "I better get to work."

He plucks my drawing off the wall and leaves the thumbtack on the corner of my desk. "I'll be taking this."

"*What*? Why?" I take a seat because I'm not sure if my legs can sustain me anymore.

"Because this drawing isn't going to fix itself."

"And *you're* going to fix it?"

Something flashes in his eyes. Anger? Sadness? Fear? I can't place whatever haunting look crosses his face because none of those labels make sense.

He grips the paper with a tight fist. "No. I don't draw but I know someone who does."

"Really? You have friends?!"

He drags out one long blink. "I don't consider those who work for me friends," he spits out.

Okay then. Moving on… "Do you think they'll help me?"

His eyes move from my lips back to my eyes. "If only to spare me from witnessing your secondhand embarrassment again."

My laugh takes over, making my entire chest shake. "I'm all for that." *But…* "Do you trust them to not share the idea with anyone?"

His head tilts. "Why?"

My eyes drop. "I want to make sure it remains a secret until I present on it. That's all."

"I trust them." He looks as if he wants to ask me something else entirely.

I press my feet into the floor to stop myself from jumping up and down. "Thank you!" My grin makes my cheeks ache.

Rowan stares at me, making my skin flush beneath his scrutiny. He turns on his heels, taking my drawing and my sanity with him.

CHAPTER TWELVE

Rowan

I didn't hesitate when I grabbed the half-assed drawing from Zahra's cubicle. Nor did I even flinch when I purchased a pack of a hundred colored pencils and drawing paper from the local craft store. In reality, the hardest part of everything was forcing Martha to take the rest of the day off so I could have some privacy.

My hand clutching onto a number two pencil trembles. With a stiff arm, I press the tip against the paper. The lead point snaps and rolls away from me, leaving me with nothing but a useless piece of wood.

"What are you doing, man?" I grumble as I drop the pencil and throw my hands in my hair.

"Being a stupid fuck for some unknown reason."

Her drawings are shit and you know it. She almost cried during her presentation when you called her out on it, and it was painful to watch how nervous she was about it.

And you care because…

Because a happy Zahra means a creative Zahra and a creative Zahra means I get the fuck out of here as fast as possible.

My brain cells wage war against one another as I swipe Zahra's drawing out from under the blank page and look at it. Her idea is well-thought-out. She chooses to highlight our more diverse characters who often get left behind in favor of our more popular princesses.

It's that thought that helps me reach for the pencil sharpener and try again. It keeps me grounded despite the rapid beat of my heart as I reconstruct the idea Zahra had.

It doesn't take long for my palms to become clammy. My emotions are turbulent and bordering on volatile. I remove my jacket and roll up the sleeves of my button-down shirt, desperate for some reprieve from the rising temperature of my body. It's as if I'm sweating out my demons, one stroke of the pencil at a time.

Drawing is a useless hobby. Real men don't draw, my father's voice whispers. I clench the pencil tighter at the memory of him ripping up one of my art class sketches.

Yellow wood splinters as the pencil cracks in half.

"Shit." I throw the broken pieces in the trash bin and wipe away the remaining dust from the paper.

What the hell was I thinking by pretending I knew someone who could help Zahra? There's no way I can do this.

My chair rolls back as I jump up and swipe my forehead with a shaky hand. I grab the paper and tear it to pieces. White shreds flutter into the waiting trash can like snowflakes of my failure, falling on top of the broken pencil.

I expect to experience some relief, but all I'm left with is a sick feeling in my stomach and a racing heart that has yet to slow.

My eyes slide from my bunched-up fists to the pail filled with the tattered remains of my drawing.

There's no one here to yell at me or make me feel like I'm worthless. I'm a grown man who can handle anything slung my way, including a stupid, harmless drawing.

I can do this. If not for myself, then for the future my brothers have dreamed of. Instead of focusing on the past, I remind myself of the future. One where Declan becomes CEO with me serving as his CFO. Of Cal finally finding his place within the company once we take control.

I take a seat, grab a fresh piece of paper and a pencil, and get to work.

I stop at the entrance to Zahra's cubicle and take a moment to observe her. She bobs her head to whatever plays out of the white earbuds while she taps away at her keyboard. Her pin of the day flashes under the overhead light. Today's choice features a salt and pepper shaker with the phrase *Seasons Greetings* written below it.

Who could hate themselves enough to wear something so atrocious?

My gaze flickers across her body before landing on the curve of her neck. The soft skin is meant to entice. To kiss and mark while she's fucked into oblivion. There are plenty of things I'd want to do to that pretty little neck if given a chance.

Except that's not possible.

My moment of weakness won't happen again. She might claim she won't report me to HR, but I haven't made it this far in life by trusting anyone but myself. Her options are endless, and she has every opportunity to squeeze money out of me like a wet rag. The media alone could pay for her to retire at her whopping age of twenty-three. The thought leaves a sour taste in my mouth, making my tongue dry and my throat tight.

I stomp toward her desk and slap the drawing on the surface.

She jumps up from her seat before dropping back into the cushion. "Hello! Can you announce your presence like a normal person?"

I don't reply because I'm afraid to breathe while this close to her. All it takes is one sniff of her perfume for my blood to reroute its path from my brain to my dick.

Thankfully, I have enough control over my impulses to stand down and take a step back.

She tilts her head at me. "What's wrong with you?"

I readjust my already perfect tie. "Nothing."

"*Right.*" She turns toward the drawing and stares.

Does she like it?

Of course she likes it, you self-conscious fuck. Who wouldn't?

Her eyes pop as she traces the design. "This is amazing."

I let out a breath I didn't realize I was holding in. At least I still have some of my drawing talent, like Grandpa said. I'll give it to the old man. He was right after all when he said talent doesn't disappear—passion does.

My throat constricts. *Focus on the task at hand.*

Although the drawing took multiple attempts and over twenty-four hours to finalize, the process of recreating Zahra's design was easy. *Too easy.* By the time I realized I had finished the final product an hour ago, a weird emptiness had washed over me. My fingers itched to keep going and chase after that all-consuming feeling where the world shut off around me.

I hate that I want more of it. It makes me feel weak and like I'm teetering on the edge of no control.

"I better get going." I step toward the entrance of her cubicle.

"Wait!" She bolts out of her chair.

"What?" Does she know I drew it?

Fuck. How could she?

She waves her hand. "It's missing a signature."

"What is?"

"The drawing."

I freeze and consider my words as carefully as I can during this kind of circumstance. "And?" *Smooth.*

"And whoever designed it deserves credit for their work. It's the right thing to do." Her eyes drop to the floor.

Interesting. This is the second time her trust issues have come to the surface. Is this because of Lance Baker publishing a similar proposal to hers? Or is there something else that affects her ability to put faith in someone else?

Rather than feel pleased with my assessment, an inky feeling slithers through my chest. I might be many things, but I'm not a thief.

I shake it off. "The artist is a contact I have from the Animation Department. It's a half-assed rush job, so don't worry about giving them credit."

"Will you share their number with me so I could tell them thank you?"

I frown. "They want to remain anonymous."

"Okay, how about you give them my number then. If they don't want to text me, then they don't have to. No hard feelings." She blows out a breath.

A dark lock of hair drops in front of her eyes. She tucks it behind her ear that's covered in a row of unique earrings. I take a step forward to get a look at the designs, only to pull back when she takes a deep breath.

My groan thankfully gets stuck in my throat. "And what do you stand to get out of this conversation?"

She looks at me with knitted brows. "Are you always this cynical about people's intentions?"

"Yes."

Her eyes roll. "Expressing gratitude isn't exactly an exchange program."

"I won't take your word for it."

She laughs as she bends over her desk, giving me a prime view of her firm backside while she scribbles something on a sticky note. Heat spreads from my chest to places that have no business being turned on at the moment.

For some godforsaken reason, I'm suffering from some kind of physical ailment in her presence that makes me act like a sex-deprived lunatic. My fingers tap against my thigh to keep my hands to myself.

You should be keeping an eye on her motives, not her body.

There's something not right about her. Maybe her niceness is a front for what really lies beneath the surface. I don't believe for a second that she hasn't thought about exploiting me because of my position after I kissed her. Anyone in her kind of financial position would.

She turns and passes me the hot-pink sticky note. "Here."

Don't grab it. Tell her no and leave before you make a big mistake.

My hand swoops in and plucks the sticky note out of her hand before I give it a second thought.

CHAPTER THIRTEEN

Rowan

I stop at a trash bin near the entrance of the warehouse. Accepting Zahra's stupid note was only meant to appease her and save me the awkwardness of denying her.

Right. Because you care so much about making others happy all of a sudden.

I linger by the bin, staring down at the hot-pink note like it holds my fate. *Look who's believing in destiny now, you broody, hypocritical asshole.*

Zahra's dainty cursive handwriting sticks out to me.

I'd love to say thank you if you are willing to text me (that is if Rowan wasn't annoying enough to throw this out before you got it). -Zahra Gulian

The sticky note crumples in my fist. What's so damn difficult about throwing this away? She would never find out. I covered my bases and made sure she understood that the Animator values his privacy and that he's busy, which *is* the truth.

You could find someone to work with her with a snap of your fingers. As good a solution as any, yet the idea leaves a bitter taste in my mouth for some unknown reason.

I pocket the sticky note and step away from the trash can. The walk through the catacombs is a decent trek. Fewer and fewer employees pass by me as I near the underground gated tunnel entrance to Grandpa's old house. When I was a kid, I thought it was the coolest thing to explore the tunnels with my brothers at night. Our father would make it into a game, with Mom and him making spooky noises. It was their failed attempt to scare us into never doing it again, but it only worked until the next time we visited Dreamland.

I let out a shaky breath, trying to ease the pressing weight against my lungs. Reminiscing only leads to one thing and I'm not interested.

I enter the gate code, walk up the stairs and toward the house. It's an old colonial-style home with a wraparound porch. I divert my eyes away from the porch swing to avoid the pinching sensation in my chest. No matter how many weekends I've told myself I'm going to grab a drill and take down the damn thing, I always find a reason to leave it up. Whether it's a new pile of papers to sift through or a last-minute meeting with a manager, I'm never able to confront the swing.

Out of all the Dreamland memories, I hate that one the most.

You're so fucking weak. My father's slurred voice booms through my head.

I jam my key into the lock and open the door. It smacks against the wall with a bang before I slam it shut. My heavy footsteps echo through the house as I walk up the stairs toward one of the master bedrooms I've taken over as my own. I throw my wallet on my nightstand before dumping the crumpled note next to it. Before I think to stop myself, I grab my phone and add Zahra's number to my contacts just in case I do something idiotic like rip up the note.

My brain battles it out, going through the positives and negatives of reaching out to her.

What's the harm in one text message?

What do you plan on talking about? The weather?

It's not like I haven't had practice speaking to women. I'm warier about the burning desire I feel toward Zahra compared to my lackluster dates over the years. They were simple and easy, with few expectations. But with Zahra, the idea of texting feels like *more*. More what, I'm not sure of yet. But I know it's something I should be cautious of.

Maybe Declan rubbed off on me in more ways than one. My brother holds us to the highest standard, ensuring we never look stupid to the public. He ingrained in us since a young age that our name carries power and with power comes a responsibility not to fuck up.

Yet you kissed your employee because the Florida heat killed all your working brain cells.

If Zahra planned on reporting me, she would have done it already.

Well…unless she's biding her time to extort money from you.

The thought makes me pause. Could that be the case? Or maybe she wants me to make an even bigger mistake so she can get a bigger payout in the end.

Are you always this cynical about people's intentions? Her soft voice enters my thoughts like it belongs there.

Compared to my brothers, I've always been the most reserved and untrusting, ever since I was a young child. Situations in my life amplified the feeling, turning a hopeful kid into a bitter adult.

Poked holes in condoms. Failed attempts at extortion. People wanting to be my friend with the sole purpose of reaping the benefits associated with my last name.

The list is endless with one universal lesson: *Trust no one.*

I throw my phone on the bed. Hoping for a moment to gather my thoughts and solidify my reasoning against reaching out to Zahra, I go on an evening run.

My skin dampens after a few minutes thanks to the humid summer air. I set an even pace and focus on the sound of my sneakers slamming into the pavement. Despite my best efforts to shut off my brain, it doesn't get the memo. By the time I'm done with my run, I've developed a mental pros and cons list about texting Zahra that helps me come to one reasonable conclusion.

I should text her and find out what her true intentions are. There's absolutely no way she's only interested in messaging me to express her gratitude. No one is that pure—not even Little Miss Bubbly. I can use our conversations as an opportunity to probe around and find out how she really feels about me.

I go back home, shower, and drop onto my bed. I open the Google voice app on my phone because I want to use a fake number that she can't trace back to me.

Me: Hey. Rowan gave me your number.

Okay. Not too bad. It's simple and to the point.

My phone beeps a second later. *How the hell does she type so damn fast?*

Zahra: Hi! I'm not going to lie to you. I didn't expect Rowan to actually do it.

I roll my eyes.

Me: Well, he did.

No shit. You're texting her. I run a hand down my face.

Zahra: Well, I'm glad you messaged me!!!

Who in God's name uses that many exclamation points? It should be considered illegal.

Zahra: I just wanted to say... 1. Thank you for helping me because I can't draw to save my life. 2. Is there some way I can repay you?

She wants to repay *me*? That can't be the true reason she was interested in texting me.

Zahra: I'm broke with real money so I'm not sure if you accept Monopoly bills as currency?

I officially need to find out what kind of woodland fairies raised this woman because there's no way she's a product of the real world.

Zahra: Or I could take you out to dinner? My treat?
Me: I'll pass. I'm not interested in acquiring food poisoning at a place that accepts Monopoly bills as currency.

Oh God. I reread the joke and cringe.

She follows up with three laughing emojis because she lacks subtlety.

Zahra: No worries.
Zahra: I could make us dinner instead as a gesture of gratitude.

My response takes two seconds.

Me: No meeting up.
Zahra: Okay then. You're shy. I get that.

I haven't been called shy since I was a kid.

Zahra: That's all right. Maybe one day.
Me: Are you this hopeful about everything?
Zahra: Sure. Why not?
Me: Because life isn't always rainbows and sunshine.
Zahra: Of course not. But how can we appreciate the sun every morning if we don't live through the dark?

What kind of drugs does she take?

My phone buzzes again as if the silence scares her.

Zahra: What's your name? You know, so I can put a name to a face.

I'm experiencing my personal hell. Turns out Zahra is a back-to-back serial texter.

Me: Except you don't have a face.

Good job stating the obvious. My poor attempt at a joke falls flat, and I'm reminded yet again why I don't bother with them to begin with.

Zahra: Duh. But for now, I'll just picture you as a young James Dean.

James fucking Dean? What kind of old-school shit does Zahra watch? James Dean was someone my grandpa used to talk about.

My fingers fly across the screen before I consider the repercussions of having a conversation that has nothing to do with work.

Me: I'm sorry. How old are you?
Zahra: HAHA.

I'm filled with some kind of warmth at the idea of making her laugh. I frown at the sensation.

Zahra: To be fair, my parents are into retro and iconic American things. It was their dream to move here when they were kids, so I'm afraid James Dean is only the tip of the iceberg. Don't get me started on my love for vintage clothing stores and Elvis Presley.

That's something I can relate to. My grandpa was the same way about American pop culture. He was always obsessed since he immigrated here from Ireland with nothing but a single suitcase and a dream to draw.

My chest pinches and I shove the memory out of my mind.

Zahra: I even taught myself to play the ukulele to impress my parents.

Zahra: I'm quite terrible though, much to my dad's disappointment.

I come to the realization I'm entrusting my livelihood to the hands of someone who happens to be the most bizarre person I've ever met. Zahra is a risk as much as she's an investment. Like putting a million dollars into penny stocks and hoping I don't get fucked over in the end.

Zahra: ...so do you plan on telling me your name now or do you want me to guess?

Zahra: I can pull up a baby-naming website and get cracking. We can even make it into a game.

God, no. Who knows what kind of messages I would open myself up to?

Me: You can call me Scott.

Scott? What the fuck are you doing?

I exit the conversation before I have a chance to say anything else. That was enough crazy for me. I'm not the kind of person who does something as spontaneous and asinine as creating an alter ego to speak to someone. Talk about pathetic.

But that's all you've ever been. A disappointment who doesn't deserve the Kane name in the first place.

I roll over and shove a pillow over my ear as if that can erase the voice from my past.

It's been years. You're not that same rejected kid anymore.

But no matter how many times I tell myself that, nothing is good enough in my eyes. Every time I accomplish a difficult task, I'm already searching for the next obstacle to overcome. To show my father and anyone who doubted me that I turned my weaknesses into strengths.

Shy? I choose my words wisely, turning them into a feared weapon.

Weak? I let thousands of useless employees go to improve our bottom line.

Pathetic? I built my own reputation in the corporate world that has nothing to do with my last name. It might not be a pretty one but it's exclusively mine, and nothing my father says or does can take that away from me.

I'm not a disappointment anymore. Not today and certainly not ever again.

There's only one loose end getting in the way of ensuring my time at Dreamland is smooth and scandal-free. And I plan on keeping a close eye on her.

I check my messages in the morning. I expected maybe one or two messages from Zahra but she surprised me again with a total of five.

Zahra: Scott. Okay. A bit basic but I like it.

The next text was sent ten minutes after the previous one.

Zahra: I see I might have scared you off. It's okay. My mom taught me if you put food out for stray cats, they'll keep coming back.

Zahra: Not that I think you're a stray cat!

She includes a facepalm emoji next.

Zahra: Anyway, I pretty much solidified how weird I am and why I fail at online dating apps! So I don't blame you for running away. The only positive of this entire conversation is that I have no idea what you look like. If you happen to meet someone with my name, pretend for my sake that you have no idea who I am. K thanks!

I find her embarrassment strangely entertaining.

Her last message came in fourteen minutes after the other one.

It's like she wanted to end everything on a positive note because she's a damn ray of sunshine ruining my perfectly dreary day.

Zahra: Have a nice life!

I consider my situation. The easy option would be to ignore all her messages and label her as the strangest person I've ever contacted. She's disgustingly friendly and trusting with someone she's never even met before.

Who are you to call her strange? You count ten words or fewer as a successful conversation.

Only because I'm the guy who prefers to stand in the shadows, letting my work speak for itself.

My curiosity about Zahra's hidden side wins over my sensible rationale. I type up a response before I back out and do something worthy of my time.

Me: Do you always talk to yourself?

The bubbles appear and disappear twice before a new message pops up on my phone. Not that I was waiting around and staring at my phone or anything.

Zahra: Well, let's pretend none of THAT happened. Okay? Okay.

For the first time in a long time, a smile spreads across my face before I have an opportunity to kill it.

CHAPTER FOURTEEN

Zahra

My mom always warned me about stranger danger. But she also taught me to be kind to everyone, so I'm dealing with conflicting advice at the moment.

Would Rowan really give my number to someone dangerous? No way.

Okay, well maybe. But I would sure *hope* he wouldn't.

I make a conscious decision to keep texting Scott and see where our conversation goes. It's not like it's much of a chore. And after everything I messaged him last night, I expected him to run for the hills. And that's saying something because Florida is one of the flattest states in the entire United States.

At least he came back.

Even I was surprised at that. According to my mom, I have the subtlety of a lightning bolt and the personality of a firework. She told me it would take an equally strong man to appreciate that kind of force of nature.

Still waiting, Mom. I'm not sure where I'm supposed to find this *strong man* but I've had zero luck on the dating apps Claire signed me up for. It's my fault. I'm too much of a dreamer who still believes in fairy tales and the possibility of a duke swooping in and marrying me.

I drop my head in my hands and sigh.

"Am I working you too hard?"

I choke on my intake of breath. Rowan stands in the entryway of my cubicle. He looks…*well, damn.* Casual Friday looks really fucking good on him. He's got that country-club feel with a designer polo and khaki pants. I wonder what it's like to have so much money that I could have a collared T-shirt dry-cleaned instead of carrying a spot-corrector pen in every purse I own. Is that how the other half lives?

I let out another sigh. "No. I didn't get a lot of sleep last night."

"Something keeping you up?" The side of his mouth lifts.

"Don't start asking me personal questions. I might do something crazy like assume you care about me."

"Save the fairy tales for your proposals."

I grin. "Do you talk about anything besides work?"

"Why would I? Work is my life." He looks at me like a scientist with a microscope.

"That's sad, Rowan. Even for you."

"I don't see how."

"What do you like to do for fun?"

"People still do things for fun?"

Was that…a joke? If so, his tone could use some work.

I laugh to encourage more of them. "You need to find a hobby that doesn't include watching the stock market."

"One does not simply 'watch the stock market.'"

I roll my eyes. "I can't believe you said that with a serious face. With the way you act, you'll end up in a shallow grave before you have your first gray hair because you're addicted to work."

His glare penetrates my faux confidence. "I didn't ask for your opinion."

"No. But it's not like you can fire me for stating an observation."

"At least not while you're my golden ticket."

Golden ticket? I don't think I've ever been referenced as something so…special.

My shoulders sag. How pathetic is that? I set my standards so low after Lance, I'm obsessing over casual compliments from my boss.

A boss who kissed you like you've never been kissed before.

But my boss nonetheless.

I wipe away whatever look is on my face. "Is there a reason you came by my office?"

"Is that what we're calling cubicles the size of my shower nowadays?"

I flip him off underneath my desk.

"Hiding your hand defeats the intended purpose of such a gesture."

Why does he talk like he was born drinking breast milk out of a porcelain teacup? And even weirder, why do I enjoy it?

"My dad taught me that if I don't have anything nice to say, then I shouldn't say anything at all."

"Shouldn't that rule extend to offensive gestures?"

I raise a brow in his direction. "Because you're the kind of person who gets offended now?"

His grimace doesn't match his lit-up eyes. "Your file never mentioned an issue with talking back to authority figures."

I perk up. "You've been reading up on me."

"I tend to research my investments."

I know his intention wasn't to make me feel all warm and fuzzy inside but my heart leaps in my chest anyway.

We aren't an investment, my feminist brain calls out.

But the big, grumpy man spends his time researching me, the hopeless romantic calls out in rebuttal.

I grin to myself. When I look up, I find Rowan staring at me with a pinched expression. "What?"

He shakes his head. "Nothing." He turns and exits my shower-sized cubicle, leaving me with a weird feeling that sticks with me for the rest of the day.

I add the drawing Rowan dropped off yesterday to the last slide of my presentation. He captured everything I dreamed of showing but lacked the talent to execute.

Today I feel way more nervous about presenting. Despite the amazing mandap drawing Scott did, I'm still unsure about showing off my first idea that doesn't have Brady Kane's approval. I could have chosen one of the ideas we brainstormed together but I wanted to test myself.

Now I'm not too sure if it was the best idea. What if people hate it?

But Rowan said it was great.

I roll my shoulders back as I shut my laptop. There's a reason Rowan sees me as an investment, so maybe it's time I start acting like one. The worst thing that can happen is Jenny telling me no or Rowan deciding the idea isn't as good as he originally thought.

So I walk into the conference room with my head held high.

Rowan's chair remains empty despite the room filling up with Creators. I take my usual seat at the back of the table where I write notes away from any prying eyes.

Jenny calls the meeting to a start despite Rowan being absent. I keep checking the time on my phone as the presenters go up one by one to discuss their idea of the week. When Jenny calls my name, I stand and walk up to the podium.

I pull up my PowerPoint and ignore the weird feeling in my chest when my eyes land on Rowan's empty chair. Why isn't he here? It's not like he mentioned anything when he stopped by my cubicle.

I shake my head and turn on my presenter mode. The excited energy in the room balances the nerves inside of me, and my confidence grows into something stronger. I'm winded by the time I finish. My skin is flushed and the erratic rhythm of my heart has yet to lessen.

One person clapping turns into the entire room smiling and congratulating me on a job well done.

All I can do is grin. If this is what believing in myself feels like, I wish I had done it a bit sooner. Before my ideas were stolen and my spirit was crushed.

I'm done being that woman. From now on, I refuse to let self-doubt get in my way. I'm now Zahra 2.0. The woman who doesn't give much thought to the past because I'm only facing my future.

Lance might have stolen my first idea but it's most certainly not my last, and everyone's response tells me that the only one I need to prove something to is myself.

Claire barrels into me the moment I open the door to our apartment. "Zahra!" Her arms wrap around me and she starts bouncing up and down.

"What?!"

"I got a job!"

"Really?! At the Royal Chateau?" Holy shit. I know Claire's talented but wow.

Her black brows pull together. "Well, no."

"I'm so confused."

"Let me explain." Claire leads me to the couch, where she already has a bottle of cheap wine waiting for us. "So I was a complete wreck during my entire interview."

My smile drops. "Oh no."

She waves me off. "Everything that could possibly go wrong did. I overcooked the chicken and undercooked the fish. Then my souffle deflated before I had a chance to even plate it and I burned my hand on a hot pan." She shows off her bandage.

I cringe.

"It was so embarrassing. The sous chef dismissed me in the middle of the interview after yelling at me for wasting her time. She made me feel this tall." Claire shows me an inch of space between her index finger and thumb.

All the muscles in my body tighten. "I'm so sorry, Claire. I feel responsible for pushing you into this before you were ready. I thought—"

"No! Thanks to you, I ended up landing something even better."

"How?"

She pours me a glass of wine before passing it to me. "I ran into the chef outside the restaurant."

"How did you know they were the chef?"

"It's a funny story. You see, I didn't know who he was at the time. He thought I was an injured animal."

"No way." I smack a hand over my mouth to stop my laugh from escaping.

She nods. "Yes. I don't think he was prepared for the Pandora's box he unleashed when he asked if I was okay. All the emotions exploded out of me. I have to give him credit. He stood there quietly while I went off about how I tanked the most important interview of my career."

"*And?*"

"And then he asked me a couple of questions about my favorite things to cook before telling me to make his favorite meal!"

My jaw drops open. "Get out."

"It was like a movie! So I cooked him the best grilled cheese and tomato soup that man has ever tasted. His words, not mine."

"A chef's favorite meal is grilled cheese? Doesn't that seem a bit…basic?"

"There is no room for basic bitches here." Claire grabs my hand and leads me into the kitchen. We might not have a gourmet size anything but Claire makes our small space work in her favor. She grabs all her supplies and starts preparing everything on the mini peninsula.

My stomach grumbles on cue. Today's small lunch barely held me over, especially since I worked later than usual. I was on a roll and didn't want to stop.

Claire points at the barstool and I take a seat.

"Then what happened?" I pull off my vintage headband and give the sides of my head a massage.

"He offered me a second interview after nearly orgasming on the spot from my food."

I giggle. "Shut up."

"Okay, that was dramatic, even for me. But his eyes did roll the tiniest bit." She grins.

"So what is your new job then?"

"The head chef is being transferred to a new restaurant project with Mr. Kane so he won't be working at the Royal Chateau anymore. And I'm going to be part of the chef's team! It doesn't have a name or anything yet, but I'm guaranteed a spot in the kitchen."

"Claire! This is huge!"

Her whole face lights up from the grin she unleashes. "Right?!"

"We need wine!" I go back to the living room and grab our filled glasses. We clink them together and say a quick cheers.

"Without you pushing me to try, I would've never bombed the interview. And without crying by a dumpster, then I wouldn't have run into the best opportunity yet! So I now believe in fate. You were right all these years." She returns her attention back to the frying pan on the stove.

"So us meeting didn't convince you that fate exists?"

Claire rolls her eyes. "No. I thought you were just an annoying person who crashed into me because you wanted to steal the parking spot."

"One man's accident is another man's fate."

"Tell that to my insurance company."

We both laugh to the point of tears before calling my parents and telling them the good news.

Claire serves us the most amazing grilled cheese I've ever had, not because her skills aren't amazing, but because of everything a simple sandwich represents.

CHAPTER FIFTEEN

Rowan

I had always planned on flying back to Chicago on Saturday for my Monday board meeting. But after my moment of weakness around Zahra, I called my pilot and asked him to prepare for takeoff when I left Zahra's cubicle. I should have never stopped by to visit her. It wasn't like I needed anything from her, but I couldn't stop myself after meeting with Jenny and Sam. It was like a siren calling out to me, leading me toward my demise.

She's an anomaly I can't categorize yet which only fuels my interest. Everything about her is strange. From her vintage attire to her pins, she doesn't fit into the usual neat category of business professionals I'm used to.

I hate that she interests me about as much as I dislike how I keep acting like a thoughtless fool around her. Between my alias and Zahra working her way under my skin, I need some distance from whatever the fuck is getting in the way of my objective thinking.

A sense of relief instantly hits me the moment I enter my penthouse apartment overlooking the Chicago River. It's my silent world up here, away from distracting females with enamel pins and employees who don't understand the universal nonverbal signal for *fuck off*. People say home is where the heart is but I couldn't disagree more. Home is wherever I'm unbothered. That's true peace for me.

I shower, eat some takeout, and crack open a beer while tuning into a Friday night football game.

My phone buzzes and I grab it off the coffee table.

Zahra: I know you don't like any kind of gratitude because you're shy and all, but that drawing is INCREDIBLE. I just left my meeting after receiving a standing ovation.

There goes my plan to avoid thinking about Dreamland for a couple of days. I go to place my phone back on the table but another message shows up before I have the chance.

Zahra: Okay, that was an exaggeration. But everyone DID clap.

I bite on my cheek as if it can erase the need to smile.

Me: Does anyone tell you that you're ridiculous?
Zahra: Of course. Ridiculously Amazing happens to be my middle name.
Me: I'm half convinced that you're crazy.

The next message pops up before I have a chance to breathe.

Zahra: Half convinced? I need to step up my game because I don't half-ass anything.

I can't stop the laugh that escapes me. It's a rough sound I'm not used to hearing.

Me: I see why Rowan hired you.

Am I really going to pretend I'm someone else like this?

Zahra: And I see why he hired you.

Yeah, I am.

Zahra: I'm nothing but smooth if I do say so myself.

I smirk. This is what I've been waiting for because I knew she was too good to be true.

Zahra: In case you missed the subtle clue, this is the moment I proposition you.
Me: I don't think you considered how that sounded.

My text earns me a GIF of someone laughing into their coffee mug. I'm so used to people laughing on cue that I forgot what it's like to genuinely entertain someone.

My phone rattles in my hand.

Zahra: So how do you feel about us establishing a partnership of sorts?

My response is instantaneous.

Me: No.

Zahra: Come on. You haven't even heard my proposal yet.

Me: Sorry. My bank doesn't accept Monopoly money.

I pinch the bridge of my nose. How lame is that? Somehow my comment gets me a trio of laughing emojis.

Zahra: You're kind of funny.

Me: I don't think I've been called funny in my life.

I groan as I read the text a second time. I'm making my alter ego into a complete loser, much like my normal self.

Zahra: That's kind of weird, Scott. Maybe you need to find new friends who appreciate your brand of humor.

Friends? What friends? The higher anyone climbs up the ladder of success, the harder it is to relate to anyone below. Maybe that's the reason why I enjoy talking to Zahra. It's not because of her specifically, but rather the idea of letting loose and being myself.

Zahra: So scratch the idea of Monopoly money. I'll do

you one better. I'm willing to pay with food, booze, or whatever it is you like.

Before I have a chance to think up another response, her next text lights up my phone.

Zahra: Are high-quality crayons considered valuable currency in your department? I have a coupon for our local craft store that I borrowed from my mom.

Something in my chest tightens, and although it's not exactly uncomfortable, it raises an alarm. Yet I don't heed the warning as I send another message.

Me: How does one borrow a coupon?
Zahra: Well, when you put it that way...consider it a donation.

Is she even for real? And more importantly, why am I smiling at my phone? I wipe the grin from my face and grind my molars together.

Me: Can't help you. I'm busy with work.

Good. Get out of this before it's too late.

Zahra: Oh. Right. I understand. Rowan mentioned how the Animators are working hard on some new movies. Are you a part of that?

There's a weird feeling in my gut that has nothing to do with whatever I ate. I'm not sure why it happens, but everything tells me to avoid it.

Me: I've got to go. Ask Rowan for someone else's help.

There's a sense of finality to my words that I hope translates through text. I raise the volume on the TV to drown out the thoughts in my head.

My phone vibrates against my thigh a couple of minutes later.

Zahra: I'll be back with a better offer tomorrow once I sort everything out.
Me: Don't go selling your kidney.

Fuck me. It's like I have no control over myself around her.

Zahra: Of course not. That's plan E. I still have three better options up for grabs.

I curse up to the ceiling, wondering how the fuck I ended up here, joking with someone who doesn't even know who the hell I really am.

And worse, why am I starting to like it?

My presentation with the board goes flawlessly. Even my father has nothing to comment on besides basic logistical questions about my timeline. I expected more from him, so his calm facade only has me gearing up for the worst.

He's up to something. I just don't know what.

"Something's off about our father." Declan takes a seat at his desk.

"I've noticed the same thing. Today was different from what I came prepared for." I take a seat diagonally from him. I'm stuck meeting with Declan on my own because Cal skipped out yet again.

"He's too quiet about the will which only tells me he's hiding something from us. I'm not sure what to make of it but I'm keeping an eye on him. It's only a matter of time before he reveals his cards." Declan rubs his bottom lip.

Iris opens the door with one elbow while juggling our two coffees and a takeout bag filled with our breakfast. "Must you eat so much, Mr. Kane? Your doctor said to watch your cholesterol since you're getting older."

Declan might be pushing thirty-six but he's nothing close to old.

His eyes narrow. "What did I tell you about reading my personal file?"

Iris passes me my coffee and my breakfast sandwich. "Well, how else am I supposed to put together an informational packet for all of your potential suitors without any personal information?"

"Easy. You don't," he dryly replies.

"How is the wife search going?" I ask.

Iris grins as she sets up Declan's breakfast in front of him. Despite my brother's best efforts to remain professional, his eyes slide from me to Iris's skirt.

Iris doesn't even notice. "I can tell you that I've been on more dates with women in the last month than your brother has been on for the entirety of me working for him."

Declan's eyes remain focused on his secretary as she places his plastic-wrapped utensils in front of him. *And here I was feeling bad about kissing Zahra.*

I cough, and Declan snaps out of whatever trance he was caught up in. "Iris is vetting the women before I meet with them."

"And people say romance is dead."

"What do you expect me to do? Fall in love the old-fashioned way?" Declan sneers.

The idea is laughable. After everything we've been through with our father after our mother's death, none of us have any intention of falling in love. Because if we have learned anything, it's that the useless emotion makes people weak and powerless. It clouds judgment and has the opportunity to ruin everything.

My father in love was the best kind of man. But my father nursing a broken heart? Disgusting. Pathetic. So lost in his misery that he ruined his own children because he couldn't stand seeing them happier than him.

No thanks. I'll take my chances staying married to my job. The divorce rate is far more forgiving.

Iris drops into the chair next to me. "Mr. Kane doesn't have time to waste, so I'm the next best thing."

"You do know him best after all these years." I shrug.

Declan grabs the paper bag from the middle of the desk and removes Iris's takeout box. He places it in front of her.

Out of all the weird things I've seen today, that has to be the strangest thing yet.

"So cut the shit and tell me what's really going on at Dreamland," Declan snaps.

I turn my focus from Iris back to my brother, finding his shoulders tense beneath his suit. What about Dreamland unsettles him this much?

Probably the same thing as you.

I go off, sharing my actual report from last week, minus my growing attraction toward my employee.

CHAPTER SIXTEEN

Rowan

My phone vibrates at the corner of my desk. I grab it and open the message without checking who it's from. There's only one person who messages me during working hours and it's sure as hell not my brothers.

I'm surprised Zahra's able to get her work done with so many interruptions. I'd question her work ethic but based on some of the timestamps of her messages, she's up past the time when I go to bed.

Zahra: Mayday!!!

Zahra: I have another meeting this Friday and my sketches look like something from a kindergarten showcase.

Me: Give the kindergarteners a little more credit. Their drawings aren't that bad.

I lean back in my chair and wait, fighting a smug smile.

Zahra: Remember when you said you've never been called funny in your life?
Me: Yes.
Zahra: Turns out everyone is right. You're awful.
Me: Is this how you proposition those you want favors from?
Zahra: I'm glad you asked because I'm ready with my next offer.

Of course she is. I'd expect nothing less from her.

Zahra: I'll buy you pizza and a six-pack of your favorite beer if you help me. I'm BEGGING you.

She doesn't ask before sending a photo. She's right. Whatever mock-up she created is absolutely hideous. I can barely make out whatever idea she originally had.

Me: Is that a dying cat? That's a bit morbid for a children's theme park, don't you think?
Zahra: Ha. Ha. Ha. It's supposed to be a menacing dragon for your artistic information.
Me: At least you nailed the scary part.

She follows up my message with one single knife emoji.

Me: Are you threatening my life? That's something HR would frown upon.

Now I'm jokingly threatening her with HR? I'm fucked. So positively fucked.

Zahra: Slip of the finger. I meant to send this.

She follows up with a series of praying hands. I rub a thumb across my smile.

Me: Liar.
Zahra: All right, you're playing hard to get, so here's plan C.
Me: Only two away from selling your kidney.
Zahra: You really pay attention!!
Zahra: But I think you won't be able to resist this one, so my vital organ could be safe and sound if you only agree.
Zahra: How about pizza, beer, and a year of unlimited access to my TV streaming accounts. I won't even change the password in a few months to spite you.

A whisper of a laugh escapes me. Her offer is ridiculous, especially seeing as I'm the one who acquired any streaming service worth paying a subscription for. It's my pride and joy.

Regardless, I'm impressed by her perseverance despite all my rejections.

Zahra: Do you accept the challenge?
Me: Tell me more about your idea and I'll think about it.

Every siren in my head sounds off in unison, warning me away from her. Yet I can't find the will to send a follow-up message revoking my offer.

She sends a flurry of messages explaining her idea for the new roller-coaster ride featuring Princess Cara. Her texts are filled with such intriguing passion, and I find myself getting lost in her world for a little bit.

Zahra has this way of dreaming that I find intoxicating. It makes me want to create along with her and design something that brings her vision to life. And that alone is terrifying.

I should push her away for good, but I like how she thinks I'm only a guy who likes to draw random shit. My alias is becoming an addiction despite the risks of growing closer to her. But I can't find it in me to assign an Animator to work with her, no matter how much I should. There's something about how she talks to me that has me forgetting my last name for a little while.

Because she has no idea you're her boss.

A sour feeling takes up a spot in my stomach, but I can't find it in me to change the circumstance and admit who I am. I don't feel *that* guilty.

Professionalism flies out the window as I drop off *Scott's* drawing. There's only one reason for the loss of control and Zahra's curved ass is to blame for all of it.

I should clear my throat and get her attention. Hell, I should turn around and come back later when she isn't sprawled out on the floor, typing away on her laptop with her ass facing the ceiling like it needs to be blessed by God himself.

Heat spreads from my chest to the area below my belt buckle. I readjust my jacket to ensure nothing alarming is noticeable, but it doesn't solve the weird feeling spreading through my body.

I call out her name but her head continues to bob to whatever plays through those plastic earbuds.

I squat like I'm not wearing trousers worth an entire month's rent. Zahra's eyes remain shut as her lips move silently to whatever song plays. I'm not sure what possesses me to pluck one of the earbuds out and bring it to my ear. ABBA plays through the tiny speaker.

Huh. That's not what I expected.

Her eyes pop open, and my eyes drop to her parted lips. I'm drawn to her like a moth to a flame. It's fitting given how I act like a complete dumbass around her who is willing to risk everything for a moment of her light.

The way she looks at me tempts me to kiss her again. What's the harm of testing out if our first searing kiss was a fluke? Maybe it was some product of built-up adrenaline and a burning desire to test something forbidden.

I lean forward. It's only an inch, but it feels like I'm wading through cement to get close to her.

Since when do you care about something forbidden? My eyes drop to her lips.

I'm staring at my reason right now.

"Rowan?" She shuts her laptop, killing my moment.

I shake off the lust as I stand and offer Zahra my hand. She clutches onto it and the same energy crackles between us. Her inhale of breath fills the small space, and my hand tightens around hers before letting go.

She peeks at the leather portfolio in my hands. "What's that?"

I open it and grab the drawing. "Here. I was told to give this to you."

She tugs it out of my grasp with greedy fingers. Her entire face morphs into something else as she assesses the drawing. The smile she unleashes makes me feel like I'm staring straight at the sun—beautiful yet blinding. A burn spreads across my body, starting at my neck before spreading to my cock.

How does one look from her make me feel all of *this*?

I scowl. The idea of losing control over myself again has me stepping farther away from Zahra.

She swipes her phone off her desk and taps away at the screen.

"All good?" I snap.

Her smile from earlier dims. "Yeah. Are you friends with Scott or something?"

My back goes rigid. "Why?"

"Because you don't seem like the kind of man who has the time to drop off papers that have nothing to do with you. Aren't you supposed to be busy or something?"

"Or something." I sneer.

She rolls her eyes with a smile. "So sensitive."

The insult has my fists balling up at my sides. "You're right. I do have better things to do than serve as your personal mail courier. If Scott doesn't have the courage to face you himself, then that's his problem, not mine." The lie slips past my lips with ease.

"Oh, sure. No problem. I'll text him myself." While her smile is a dimmer version of her previous one, it still makes my chest tighten.

I really need to get the hell out of here. My eyes remain focused on the exit as I leave Zahra behind with nothing but a string of lies to keep me company.

CHAPTER SEVENTEEN

Zahra

Scott hasn't answered my thank-you text yet and it's been a whole hour since Rowan stopped by and nearly kissed me.

And you almost let him. Maybe it's the way his eyes lock on my lips. Or how my entire body inappropriately heats up whenever he gets too close.

I try to distract myself with working on my presentation but I find my mind drifting. It feels weird to not have spoken to Scott for an entire day, and I'm not sure what to make of that. He's quickly becoming the first person I text in the morning and the last person I speak to before falling asleep.

I might have no idea what he looks like but I know he has a good heart. I'm all about trusting my feelings and there's something about Scott that tells me to keep trying, regardless of how shy he might be.

I shoot him a text message with my streaming log-ins and passwords, hoping to get his attention.

Me: If you comment on my Recently Watched shows, I swear I'll murder you in your sleep.

Me: Once I find out your HP address of course.

I count the seconds that tick by based on the beat of my heart.

Nothing.

I shut off the ringer and throw my phone into one of the drawers of my desk, hoping the dark corners swallow it whole.

During my lunch break, I pull out my phone to find a few messages from Scott.

Scott: If you are trying to find out my location, I suggest starting with an IP address.

Scott: And I won't judge too hard.

I grin like a goof at my phone.

Me: You're totally judging.

Scott: Me? Never.

Scott: But do you recommend *The Duke Who Seduced Me?*

Me: Shut up.

Scott: That's not nice.

Me: It's for research purposes.

Amongst other things. I'm not about to reveal my obsession with Juliana De La Rosa and the TV adaptations of her books.

My phone buzzes.

Scott: Of course. You seem like a diligent Dreamland employee.

Something about the text has my cheeks burning.

Scott: Care to share why you have seventeen versions of *Pride and Prejudice* saved to your Recently Watched list?

Me: Consider it a virtual safety blanket.

Scott: But who needs seventeen versions of that movie?

Me: The same person who would be happy with eighteen.

Scott: You're unique.

Me: Unique happens to be my middle name.

Scott: What happened to Ridiculously Amazing?

My heart squeezes in my chest like Scott wrapped his fist around it.

Me: You've been paying attention.

Scott: It's easy when you're an open book.

Me: Maybe I should play harder to get.

After minutes go by with no reply, I lay my head down against my desk. I've scared him away at the first sign of interest.

My phone buzzes.

Scott: Go ahead. I suffer from a nasty competitive streak.

Scott: But rest assured, I win every time.

Tiny little butterflies take flight in my stomach. Scott hasn't openly flirted like this before.

Me: You sound mighty confident in your abilities for someone who hides behind a screen.

The message was supposed to carry a flirtatious tone but it falls flat. Minutes tick by without a reply and I grow more restless.

Did I push him too hard too fast? It was only supposed to be a joke.

The answer becomes evident as time goes by. Scott doesn't answer my text for the rest of the day, and I'm left feeling empty.

Maybe I made him feel shitty about something he's self-conscious about. He might struggle with body image issues or a bad case of social anxiety that I'm only making worse because I'm too curious for my own good. And the truth is, I'm starting to enjoy our friendship. I'd hate to scare him away, especially with how he made me feel giddy from one flirtatious message.

From this point on, I swear to not bother him about his identity. It doesn't matter. Plus, I'm confident he will open up slowly if I give him time to warm up to me. If I could make Ralph, who hates everyone, smile, then I can do anything.

Shit! I'm late! I shove my laptop and phone into my purse before exiting my cubicle.

The warehouse is empty as I run to the conference room. My breaths come out ragged and forced as I pull the door open, interrupting Jenny. Everyone's heads snap in my direction, and my entire body blushes from head to toe.

"Tardiness will not be tolerated. If this happens again, you'll be required to work additional hours to make up for it." Rowan doesn't bother looking up from his phone.

The dismissal makes me feel small.

A quick assessment of the room reveals no available seats except for the one next to Rowan. This is the punishment I deserve for flirting instead of working.

Great. Fabulous. Today couldn't be going any better.

"Take a seat or get out." His authoritative tone rubs me the wrong way.

I keep my head held high as I take the unoccupied chair beside Rowan. The smell of him hits me first, like an ocean breeze I'd expect while vacationing somewhere like Fiji. I scoot my seat as far away from him as possible without disturbing the Creator next to me.

"Now that everyone is finally here, proceed." Rowan motions for Jenny to continue.

My stomach dips.

Jenny shoots me a soft smile before returning her attention to the rest of the room. "Who wants to go first?"

The group remains silent. No one rises from their chair as Jenny looks around the conference room. It's such a stark contrast compared to our last Friday meeting and I think it has everything to do with the frowning man next to me.

"Come on, everyone." She lets out a nervous laugh. "Do I need to draw names out of a hat?"

Crickets. No one moves an inch.

"I'll go." I rise on wobbly legs that could give out at any

second. Rowan looks up at me with his usual empty gaze before nodding. His dark eyes remind me of space—infinite, dangerous, and something I can get lost in.

I set up my PowerPoint with shaky hands. My stage fright has slightly improved since my first presentation, but the jitters still hit me, especially at the beginning. Rowan's gaze sends tiny pricks of something down my spine. I end up clicking the wrong file twice before I'm able to get control of myself. It takes a couple deep breaths to finally steady my heart rate.

The entire time I present, I ignore Rowan. That's what he gets for treating me the way he did in front of everyone.

The Creators clap as I wrap up my last sentence, and I feel slightly better about everything that happened earlier.

"It could be better," Rowan calls out.

"How so?" I clench my fists against my dress.

"What if we changed the entire layout of the ride."

"The *entire* layout?" *Deep breaths, Zahra.*

"Instead of having the roller-coaster carts created to represent the dragon flying, let's have the dragon be a part of the ride. We will keep your mountain idea, but I want the coaster to dive into the dark caves as if riders are escaping the dragon. I want fire, special effects, animatronics, and backward tracks."

I'm not sure what throws me off more: the fact that Rowan's idea makes mine pale in comparison or the burst of passion in his voice that I haven't heard before. It's like someone plugged him in and turned on his consciousness. His previous scowl is gone, replaced by the smallest smirk on his face as he stares up at the projector. The brightness in his eyes brings out a beautiful shade of honey brown I'd yet to see.

"Backward? We've never had a ride like that before."

"Obviously," he states in a flat tone that makes me feel like I have the IQ of a pea. "Your idea is a good starting point, but we need to up the stakes. Next." He dismisses me with nothing but a wave of his hand.

I want to be angry at Rowan for completely hacking away at my idea until it became a completely different concept but I can't find it in me to be anything but excited. I never even considered a backward roller coaster before.

He wants me to raise the stakes? Fine. But he might need a ladder to reach the levels I'm willing to go.

I raise my chin and retake my seat beside Rowan. I'm stuck sitting closer to him than before and I can only blame the Creator next to me for shoving my chair as far from him as possible. It's not as if my presentation failure was contagious.

I clutch onto my pen in a death grip throughout the entire meeting. Every time Rowan readjusts his leg, sparks shoot up my body, straight to my heart. I'm tempted to go snag someone else's seat during our bathroom break but that would be ridiculously immature of me. It's only his leg after all.

Then why do you blush every time his body grazes yours?

My pen stabs through multiple pages of my notebook.

The other presenters go up one by one, discussing a broad range of topics from a couple new rides to a new hotel based on a Dreamland movie. I'm thankful that I went first because with each presentation, Rowan's frown deepens. He furiously writes notes and treats each presenter like they're on the stand with his line of questioning. The feedback he gave me seemed tame to his other severe comments.

There's a collective sigh of relief as the last person finishes their closing statement.

"The presentations were subpar at best." Rowan's voice carries more bite than usual. He stands and buttons the front of his suit. "I want you all to stop wasting my time and come prepared with groundbreaking ideas that leave me wowed. If I continue to find your proposals lacking, then I'll be forced to find people willing to get the job done right the first time. Consider this your first and last warning."

The Creator next to me swallows loudly. I glance over at him to find a sheen of sweat dripping down his forehead. I'm somewhat thankful I'm seated farther away from him based on the smell coming off him.

"Until further notice, employees will be expected to work twelve-hour days to increase productivity and creativity."

"Will we receive a pay raise?" someone in the back pipes up.

Rowan's blank stare sends a chill down my spine. "Am I supposed to reward you all for being average?"

Oh my freaking God. Did he really say that?

Rowan's frustration, although slightly understandable, isn't justified. The Creators aren't used to coming up with ideas at such a fast pace. To present every Friday on a new concept is tough. I'm even struggling, not that I'll admit it to anyone.

"Raises are earned, not given." Rowan leaves the conference room without a goodbye.

We all sink into our chairs.

Jenny clears her throat. "So that was a lot to unwrap. Are there any questions?"

One person groans and I raise a mental fist in solidarity.

CHAPTER EIGHTEEN

Rowan

After ruining Zahra's team meeting, I did the same to Sam's Alpha team. I don't have the luxury of wasting time on subpar ideas and missed opportunities.

Yet you have time to waste on drawing.

Drawing invigorates me in a way I haven't experienced before—like I can shut off the world and the demands placed on me for an hour. I'm not stupid enough to believe this could be a long-term activity for me. It's only a means to an end.

I drop onto my bed and grab my phone off my nightstand. I've been avoiding Zahra since she sent her message about me hiding behind a screen. It pissed me off more than I cared to admit earlier. I don't hide behind anything, least of all a stupid piece of glass. I'm merely observing.

Me: I'm not hiding behind a screen because I'm scared.

She doesn't respond right away like usual. I add Zahra's streaming account to my smart TV. *If only she knew who helped produce her favorite duke show.*

I choose a random show to pass the time. One episode turns into three, and before I know it, Zahra still hasn't texted me back.

Me: Is Rowan keeping you up all night?

I wince when I reread my message, realizing how it sounds.

I expect some awkwardness on her end but my comment earns me a laughing GIF.

Zahra: No. But I was busy working on a new idea!

Great. That's exactly what I need from her. Just maybe not at midnight when she should be sleeping.

Isn't this what you expect? You're the one who added four hours on to an eight-hour workday because you were pissed off.

Zahra: Why? Did you miss me?

My response is instantaneous.

Me: No.

Zahra: Damn.

Zahra: Do you even have a heart?

Me: I don't suffer from that kind of affliction.

Zahra: Who hurt you?

Her question is meant to be a joke, but it sends a rush of bad memories to the surface. I grip my phone in a choke hold. It takes me five whole minutes to recover and think up a response vague enough to suffice.

Me: Who else?

Zahra: A sucky ex-lover?

Me: Speaking from experience?

The question leaves a sour feeling in my stomach. I never considered Zahra having a lover before, but the idea makes me want to chuck my phone across the room.

The idea of her being with someone else…it's unsettling. Like the way someone feels right before a roller coaster drops.

Zahra: There aren't enough words in the human dictionary to explain that story.

Me: That bad?

Why do you care?

Zahra: All I can say is when one door closes, it's usually because someone slams it in your face.

Me: I don't think that's how the saying goes.

Zahra: I like to put my own spin on things.

Me: I've noticed.

Just like I've noticed a lot of things about her that I probably shouldn't.

Does it stop me from continuing our conversation? It should yet it doesn't.

Does it force me to shut off my phone and give in to sleep? Not in the slightest.

Instead, as Zahra works through an idea, I keep her company via text like the stupid fool she's turned me into.

"You've got a package." Martha opens the door to my office with one arm. The other trembles as she holds on to the box. I get up and grab the box from her, afraid her wonky ankle might give out and smash the contents before I have a chance to use them.

Martha sees herself out without paying me much attention. I appreciate her more and more by the day because she gets her job done while ensuring only people with appointments bother me.

I place the box on my desk before slicing it open with a pair of scissors. It takes a few seconds to pull out the smaller box from the ocean of foam peanuts.

I run my hand over the Wacom drawing tablet picture on the front of the box. If my grandfather saw me using one of these, he would criticize me for giving up on the classics. My initial reason for buying the tablet was to send digital copies to Zahra without stopping by her cubicle.

The tablet caught my eye during online shopping. It has all the gadgets and features that graphic designers love to have. I open the box like a child on Christmas morning, ripping at the cardboard in my rush to pull the tablet out.

My heart races in my chest as I press the power button. I

smile to myself as the screen lights up and the company logo flashes.

I pack away the paperwork I was reviewing earlier and pull up the texts Zahra sent me last night.

This is a means to an end.

You keep telling yourself that. Maybe you'll finally believe it.

I wipe a hand across my five o'clock shadow after creating a pseudonym email and sending Zahra a copy of her newest design. My eyes burn from spending hours watching YouTube tutorials on how to use a hunk of plastic. I almost gave up halfway and assigned an Animator to help Zahra but the idea made me feel deflated. I'm not the kind of person who gives up and I wasn't about to let a tablet beat me.

I check for her reply two hours later, after I went through another series of meetings with our foreign Dreamland directors.

Zahra: I see you've stepped up your game!

Zahra: It's incredible. Seriously.

Me: Do you like the alteration to the original design?

I should have asked her first before I tweaked her original plan. She wanted to feature a new castle for one of the original princesses, but I liked the idea of ditching the cookie-cutter one for Princess Marianna. I changed the classic design into something that matches Mexican culture.

Zahra: I love it! It might impress Rowan.

Zahra: Okay, let's be real. Nothing I do will impress him, but it felt good to say.

Usually, I'm happy pushing people to their limits, but the way Zahra speaks about herself has me pausing. *Does she really think that?*

She doesn't give me much time to consider anything else.

Zahra: Wait!!!

Zahra: OMG. I think you gave me the best idea. Stop everything and help me!

I run a hand across the smile that only appears because of Zahra.

Zahra: What do you think about a ride that takes guests through the afterlife on Día de los Muertos?

Zahra: Feel free to lie and tell me it's amazing even if you don't think so.

Of course I think it's a decent idea. It never dawned on me that a castle could lead to an entirely new ride about a princess who can speak to the dead.

I spend the next thirty minutes entertaining her because I'm interested in seeing where her creativity takes her. It has nothing to do with the way her passion sparks something warm in my chest. Just like speaking to her has no correlation with the sudden burst of energy I feel as I pull out the stupid tablet that's given me nothing but issues all afternoon.

Absolutely nothing.

CHAPTER NINETEEN

Rowan

Like the stray cat Zahra described, I pass by her cubicle after my meetings with Jenny and Sam. If Zahra's suspicious of my growing interest, she hasn't let on to it.

I stop at the wall right outside of her cubicle. A white paper with bold lettering stands out against the gray fabric backdrop, with strips of half-cut paper dangling in the air. They're all accounted for except one.

Join our Buddies team and be a mentor today! If you have any questions, feel free to call me. We'd love to have you.

The rest of the paper is vague, only mentioning an opportunity to join an adult mentorship program for Dreamland employees. I think I heard Martha speak of this during our morning agenda but I was only half listening once she mentioned the word *voluntary*. I only have so much time in a day and discussing some random employee meeting about community service isn't on my radar.

Each strip includes an address for the meeting and a contact number I'm quite familiar with. There's something about everyone having access to Zahra's information that makes my skin all hot.

There's one strip missing out of the ten. I could check the surveillance tapes and find out who snagged it but that's a step too far, even for me.

Who could have taken the number? There aren't too many young Creators around here that might be interested in hanging around Zahra. I have noticed one blond Beta team member staring at Zahra's ass once or twice. When he saw that I caught him looking, he actually shot me a smug smile that made my fists clench. I ended up destroying him during his presentation.

My fists ball up by my sides. I look around the hall before ripping the rest of the numbers. I tuck them into the pocket of my trousers before I have a chance to berate myself for something this ridiculous.

I'm acting like a goddamn maniac.

Who cares who texts her?

Me. I care.

But why?

I rub a hand down my face and groan.

Zahra pops her head out of the cubicle. Her smile drops when her eyes land on me. "Oh. It's you."

"Waiting for someone else?" Don't tell me she's waiting for Chad. Or is it Brad? Either one fits the blond tool.

You sound like a jealous idiot.

Her brows pull together. "Huh? No. Just checking if someone

had any questions about—" Her eyes widen at the paper in front of me. "Wow! I didn't think that so many people would be interested!" Her entire face lights up like a solar flare. She shines so brightly that everything else pales in comparison. I feel helplessly trapped in her magnetic field, so close to the sun I might burst into flames.

A fitting way to go based on the lie that pours out of me. "There was only one left when I got here." I should feel guilty about lying but I can't find it in me to care that much.

Zahra's smile reaches her eyes. "Does that mean you took the last one?"

Fuck. Why does she have to be so smart all the time?

"Yes," I mutter under my breath. My stomach churns, and my throat feels like I have an invisible hand wrapped around it.

"Great! Be there tonight at 8:00 p.m. *sharp.*" Her eyes glitter as if she is amused by the idea of mocking my request for punctuality.

I frown. "Aren't you supposed to be working at that time?"

"What if I told you this is a part of an idea I'm working on?"

I rip the paper from the thumbtack and reread the title. "Doubt it. I can't imagine approving of anything that involves cupcakes and charades. I don't know who you're trying to mentor here but we're not interested in hiring toddlers."

Her smile drops. "Forget you ever read about this and lose my number." She snatches the paper from my hand and returns back to her cubicle without sparing me another glance.

I've never seen Zahra this pissed before. What about this meeting specifically set her off?

Who cares? Now you have a reason to avoid going.

But what is she hiding?

I leave the warehouse and stop at the closest trash bin where I throw away all the slips of paper except one.

Zahra's eyes connect with mine as I step through the doorway of the small meeting room. The reserved space Zahra chose is located at the back of the park within the employee apartment complex. I've never visited this area for anything but a quick glance for my checklist.

Her smile falters as I unbutton my suit and take a seat like I belong here. My neck heats from the way she tracks my movements, with her eyes following my hand as I pluck a cupcake from the tray.

Her small hands ball up by her sides. I don't even love sweets but I pretend it's the best cupcake.

Come on. Show me what you're really hiding beneath those fake smiles and innocent pins. Speaking of, today's offensive dose of serotonin is a ridiculous ghost wearing a sombrero with the saying *Ami-Ghost*. Where does she find these things, and why does she wear them?

Zahra's eye twitches. "What are you doing here?"

I look around the nearly empty room as if the answer is obvious. The lack of a turnout fills me with a sense of accomplishment. "I'm here for a meeting. Carry on."

She leans forward on the table, attempting to intimidate but failing. "You don't tell me what to do. You're not my boss after working hours."

"If you're on company property, then you're still considered my employee."

"Everything here is company property."

"Perceptive as ever."

Zahra's eyes narrow while her cheeks turn an interesting shade of red I haven't seen before. I'm somewhat interested in learning more about this version of Zahra. It's quite the contrast from her pin-loving, happy-go-lucky self that she shares with the world.

A younger brunette woman walks into the room carrying a bottle of soda, followed by a blond male. They both have soft facial features, which is a dead giveaway for their Down syndrome diagnoses.

Shit. It doesn't take much effort to draw conclusions about exactly what kind of mentorship program this is.

For the first time in God knows how long, I feel intense regret. No wonder Zahra was so pissed at my comment. It was wholly deserved based on the kind of program she is trying to create here.

Fuck. You're such an asshole sometimes.

Zahra smirks. "Now's your chance to leave before it's too late."

"I think I'd like to see this through." I meant what I said about challenges. The more Zahra wants to push me away, the harder I'll push back.

The shorter brunette elbows Zahra in the ribs. "Be nice. He's cute." Her almond-shaped brown eyes brighten and bring out the softness in her face.

She officially becomes my new favorite person.

Zahra glares at her. "I am nice."

I raise a brow.

"Why are you really here?" Zahra looks around the room that's empty besides us four.

I could comment on the lack of a turnout but it's my damn fault.

"I'm interested in the mentorship program."

She scoffs. "What happened to not being interested in hiring toddlers?"

"I was wrong."

Both her brows rise. "You—well. Wow. Okay. I didn't think you had it in you to admit when you make a mistake."

"Don't hold your breath waiting for the next time." My comment earns me a tiny smile.

"So, are you going to start the meeting or do you plan on staring at me all night?"

The brunette beside Zahra giggles.

Zahra's eyes move from the shorter woman to me. "You know what, Rowan? I have the perfect buddy for you."

Buddy? I never agreed to becoming a buddy. I'm only here to watch from afar, not become some *mentor*. I don't think I've mentored anyone in my life. It requires too much speaking and not enough working, and I end up redoing their job anyway.

The way Zahra smiles at me has my skin itching. "Ani, you're partnered with Rowan."

The brunette beside Zahra cackles. "Yes!"

Well, shit. That laugh should worry me.

"So my sister told me all about you." Ani and I take a seat on a bench near the apartment complex. Zahra split off with the male, giving us time and privacy to schedule our first official mentorship outing.

"Who's your sister?"

She looks at me like I'm the dumbest man on Earth. "Zahra."

My head tilts. "I didn't know she had a sister."

"Surprise!" She grins.

"Well, is it too late to revoke her sister card?"

Ani looks at me with furrowed brows. "Why?"

"Because no sister who loves you would partner us together."

"Oh, please. I doubt you're that bad."

"And you got that in the two seconds you've known me?"

Ani shakes her head. "Because not many guys would come to a meeting like this. Lance never wanted to."

"Who's Lance?"

"Zahra's ex."

"He sounds like a dick."

She elbows me. "No bad words."

I raise my hands in surrender.

She fidgets with her hair tie on her wrist. "I never liked him."

"Because?"

"Because he looked at me funny. And sometimes I heard him say things on the phone when I wasn't supposed to listen." She looks away. The look on her face has me wondering what kinds of awful things she might have overheard.

"Like?"

She shakes her head aggressively. "Nothing."

"Why are you protecting him?"

"I'm not. It's old news, and I don't want to make Zahra sad again." Her bottom lip wobbles.

Wow. Ani really cares about her sister. While my brothers love me, I doubt they would let anything tear themselves up to protect me.

Ani knocks her shoulder into mine. "So why did you come tonight?"

"I was curious."

"About my sister?" Her grin widens.

"About the meeting. I wasn't sure if she was planning a coup d'état against me."

Ani giggles. "Don't worry. Your secret's safe with me."

"What secret?"

"You wanted to see my sister." She says it in a singsong way.

I steal the cupcake from her. "I'll take that as payment." I forgot what it was like to enjoy sugar but whatever Zahra put in these cupcakes has me craving more.

"Hey! Payment for what?!" She tries to swipe the cupcake out of my hand.

"For the emotional turmoil you're bound to put me through by the time we're done here."

"It's only day one. You still have months left."

"Then you better bring a lot of cupcakes."

I solidify myself as Ani's buddy. Not because Zahra told me to but because I kind of like her.

Maybe Ani can give you a better understanding of who Zahra really is.

I grind my teeth together.

Or what if Zahra really is a nice person and you're too goddamn bitter to accept that?

Something about that thought troubles me. Because if Zahra really is a nice person, it would throw my entire mentality off.

I shake my head. I'd be stupid to trust someone based on nothing but a few interactions.

Scott and I have fallen into a comfortable pattern as the weeks go by. He's consistent with sending drawings every week, and I'm equally reliable at texting him first almost every day.

But on the rare occasions Scott messages me first, I'm hit with a wave of giddiness. And today, he breaks my happiness meter with a single message alone.

Scott: I saw this and thought of you.

My heart races in my chest, betraying exactly how I feel about Scott *thinking about me*. I open up the link he sent of a *BuzzFeed* quiz.

A *Which Character from Pride and Prejudice Are You Most Like?* quiz.

I swear I almost fall out of my chair from swooning so hard.

There's no way he happened to come across this on his own. He must have outright been searching for a conversation starter and thought this was a good option.

I grin as I type up a response.

Me: Did you take it?

Scott: Maybe.

Me: WHO DID YOU GET?

Scott: You want the truth or a lie?

Me: Always the truth.

His text takes a whole ten minutes. I'm afraid I scared him off with my response, but he comes back with a message I wasn't expecting.

Scott: Elizabeth Bennet.

I curl over and laugh until my voice turns hoarse.

Me: Honestly, she's the best character.

Scott: She's a woman.

Me: She's more than JUST a woman.

Scott: Obviously or else there wouldn't be seventeen versions of her story.

Scott: Although I'm partial to 2005 Lizzy.

My cheeks ache from smiling so hard.

Me: You've been watching the movies?!

Scott: Yes.
Scott: But tell a single soul and I'll find your HP address.

I grin at his attempt at a joke.

Me: Was that a joke?
Scott: If you need to ask, then I failed.

I release a heavy laugh.

Me: I'm only teasing.

I want to pull more information from him. No normal man watches *Pride and Prejudice* without some ulterior motives, and I have a feeling why.

Me: Why did you watch the movie?

The dots come and go over and over again before his next message appears.

Scott: I was interested in dissecting it from a purely scientific standpoint.
Me: You're such a nerd.

Seriously, based on the few facts Scott has shared, I've come to picture him as a hot one. I mean the man still has a subscription to *National Geographic* magazine and watches *Jeopardy!* religiously before bed. If he didn't drop a few pop culture references and have the same kind of music taste as me, I would've thought I was being catfished by a senior citizen. I'm pretty aware that's still an option on the table, but I'm holding out for the right moment to pressure Scott into meeting me. And today's conversation is the perfect start.

Me: Did you come to any conclusions?

His reply is instantaneous.

Scott: Yes. You're just as crazy as I had thought.
Scott: But it's bordering on slightly endearing.

In other words, that's practically a compliment coming from him. The warmth in my chest spreads through my body like a wildfire.

I spend the rest of my day thinking about my conversation with Scott. It's hard not to jump to conclusions about it all, but why else would he watch my favorite movies? All *seventeen* versions of them?

I think Scott might like me. If only he had enough courage like Lizzy to face me.

Maybe one day.

If there's one thing no one should look good wearing, it's bowling shoes. But of course the man who wears thousand-dollar suits can make clown shoes look designer. When Ani suggested bowling as our first group mentorship activity, I agreed wholeheartedly.

I thought a bowling alley would make Rowan uncomfortable enough to drop out of the program.

My assumptions were proven wrong the moment Rowan showed up an hour ago with a custom ball and shoes. I'm 90 percent sure he probably bought them at the bowling alley's store because he couldn't bear the idea of sharing anything with the general population.

I spent an hour hoping he slipped up so I could have the opportunity to prove my other assumptions correct. There's no way he could be genuinely interested in participating in my pilot program. *Right?*

Wrong. One hundred and ten percent wrong.

Rowan is completely different from what I expected. Although he might still be the Burberry-polo-shirt-wearing prep, he's nice to my sister and her boyfriend. And it makes me feel *all* sorts of things.

Ani drops into the plastic seat next to me. "So, Rowan's cute."

I shoot her a withering glare. "*Stop.*"

A weird feeling sits in the pit of my stomach at the idea of finding Rowan cute. It feels wrong to be interested in him while also feeling a pull toward Scott—like I'm playing around. It adds to the growing nausea every time I find myself zoning in on Rowan tonight.

It's wrong to be attracted to my boss, but it's despicable to be interested in two guys at the same time. I'd never want to intentionally hurt anyone like that after everything I've been through.

"But look at him teaching JP how to bowl." She points at both men standing side by side.

Trust me, Ani. That's all *I've been doing.*

Rowan demonstrates how to properly launch a bowling ball and JP copies the movement. I'm still not bored after watching them for the last hour.

I shake my head. "Not happening, so whatever you're planning, stop it."

"I'm not planning *anything*."

"You bring him up during every conversation we have."

She smiles. "I like him."

"Doesn't mean I have to."

"But you like everyone!"

I wince. "Not this one."

"Yeah right. You blush anytime he looks at you."

"No I don't!"

She pushes my shoulder. "Do too!"

"Why are you staring at me like a creep anyway?"

"Because it's funny. Rowan gets all nervous too."

"Oh really?" I blame my mother for teaching Ani to believe in fairy dust and fairy tales from a young age.

She taught you the same.

"What else do you notice?"

"I thought you didn't like him?" She raises one sassy brow at me.

I end up laughing at the expression on her face. Rowan's eyes connect with mine, sending goose bumps across my skin. He refocuses his attention on JP right before he almost drops the ball on Rowan's foot. Together, with Rowan's help, JP launches the bowling ball down the lane.

Pins crash in front of us. Ani jumps up and claps her hands as JP dances in place. A hint of a smile graces Rowan's lips before disappearing. JP pulls Ani into his arms and gives her a kiss on the cheek. It makes my heart melt all over the sticky linoleum floor.

The back of my neck tingles and I look over to find Rowan staring at me. "What?"

His brows pull together. "Nothing."

"Your turn, Zahra!" Ani calls out. "Hurry up. We only have thirty minutes left before our time runs out."

I grab my pink bowling ball off the rack and throw it. It rolls forward before veering off straight into the gutter, resulting in zero pins.

"Your wrist is twisting right before you throw it." Rowan speaks behind me.

I turn on my heel. "And you're a bowling expert all of a sudden?"

He shrugs. "I played varsity."

The seriousness of his voice has me curling over and laughing. By the time I stop, I find Rowan's face guarded as ever.

"What?" I frown.

"Forget I offered to help." He turns on his heel and takes a seat next to JP.

Oh God. Was he being serious? I didn't even know there were bowling teams. My stomach takes a dive into dangerous territory, and my cheeks turn hot at the idea of embarrassing him.

What if he was really trying to help me?

If so, then you just grabbed his olive branch and snapped it in half right in front of his face.

I try to fix my wrist like Rowan suggested but my ball only ends up in the gutter again. Ani laughs as she gets up for her turn. JP follows her like always, leaving me alone with Rowan.

"So, varsity, huh?" I try to break the ice as I take the seat next to him.

His crossed arms flex. "I can guarantee that your jokes will be nothing new to me."

I playfully shove him with my shoulder but his body doesn't budge. "I'm sorry. It was a shitty thing to laugh at."

"It was."

"I wasn't laughing at you."

He glares and I laugh to myself again. The sound only makes him scowl harder.

I raise both hands in submission. "Okay, I was laughing at the situation, but to be fair, I didn't even know there was such a thing as varsity bowling."

"Don't beat yourself up too much over it. I've dealt with worse."

Like what?! I want to learn all about the grumpy guy who played varsity bowling and joins a mentorship program for people with disabilities despite being incredibly busy. There's more to Rowan than meets the eye, and I'm dying to learn all about this new side of him I never knew existed.

There's this strange, albeit microscopic, part of me that wants to shield him from dealing with worse, whatever that means.

Whoa. Where did that thought come from?

Abort. "It's kind of cool. Women love letterman jackets."

"I valued my reputation far too much to wear that jacket at school."

"Why?"

"Because I only joined the team to spite my father. He never specified which team I should join, so I liked beating him at his own game."

I blink at his personal admission.

He continues on the same breath as if he might stop speaking if he takes a second longer. "He was pissed I never made it past any of the 'real sports' team tryouts like my brothers. While Declan was the school quarterback and Cal was the team captain of his hockey team, I was…lacking." He clears his throat. "According to my father, that is."

My heart clenches in my chest for the boy who struggled to live up to his father's expectations. Rowan might be rich, but he struggles with the same kind of issues the rest of us do. Parental expectations. Personal failures.

I want to ease the tension from his shoulders. "You're telling me you couldn't buy your way onto the bench?" I fake gasp.

"You're catching onto how things work." The corner of his lip lifts. "On the contrary. I paid the coaches to keep me off those teams."

"Why? I've never heard of anyone trying that."

"I had no interest in being labeled a benchwarmer."

"You were that bad?"

"Yes." The lightest shade of pink floods his cheeks and I find it kind of cute.

Cute? Ugh, Zahra. No.

"I'm kind of loving the fact that you're not the best at *everything*."

He shakes his head. "One thing, Zahra. *One*."

"So did you win a bowling championship?" I grin.

Rowan's tense shoulders drop an inch. "I don't lose. Ever."

"Your cockiness knows no bounds."

Rowan says nothing but the smile on his face speaks volumes. It's stiff, like he hasn't practiced the movement in quite some time. I'm tempted to touch it to make sure I'm not hallucinating but I keep my hands to my sides.

I shouldn't find it as endearing as I do. And I most definitely shouldn't crave more of that stupid, timid smile.

During my next turn, I call out Rowan's name. "Will you help me, please? I've been told by an expert that I twist my wrist."

His small smile makes a reappearance. I want to do everything in my power to make him smile like that again. Now that I know a little bit about the kind of guy who hides behind suits made of armor, I'm interested in discovering more about him. Consequences be damned.

He walks with a sense of self-assuredness that screams *I have a big dick and I know how to use it.*

Don't think about his dick.

Rowan grabs his ball off the rack and keeps enough room for Jesus between us. I'm disappointed this isn't like the movies.

"So, this is the way you're swinging your ball." He rears his arm back, making it twist at an odd diagonal angle. "Which makes your follow through curve to the side and head straight toward the gutter." He demonstrates the way my arm swings like a pendulum in the opposite direction. I try my best not to focus on his veins as he shows me the correct positioning, but I'm a lost cause to the way his body moves.

"You try." He pulls me away from my thoughts.

I attempt whatever swing he did and fail based on how his eyes lighten.

"No. Let me help you." He puts down his ball and stands behind me. The body heat coming off him makes my whole spine warm.

Now this is what I'm talking about.

His hand grazes my arm before circling my wrist like a cuff. He holds on to it with the softest touch that has my heart pounding in my chest and my breathing turning erratic.

Seriously, he's holding your wrist. Come on!

His husky voice is nothing but a whisper in my ear, yet I feel it straight to my core. "Try again."

I move my arm backward. Rowan's fingers remain locked around my wrist, guiding me through the correct follow-through. He repeats the motion a few times.

"Now you try by yourself." He drags his fingers up my arm again before they disappear.

I pout at their loss since he can't see me, and I mess up my swing on purpose because I'm petty.

"No, but you were better this time." He shakes his head and lets out a low laugh.

I'm rewarded with the return of his hand holding on to my wrist as he shows me yet again. This time when he lets go, I try for real. My effort is rewarded with one of his small smiles.

"Perfect. Just like that. Okay, now you try once more." He motions toward the lane.

I take a few steps forward and replicate the motion he taught me. The bowling ball launches out of my hand and rolls straight down the waxed floor, following the path of the tiny arrows.

I suck in a breath as my ball collides with the front pins, making some fly while others roll in opposite directions. Every single pin drops, and a red X lights up above the empty area.

I scream and run straight back to Rowan, who stares at my knocked-over pins. "I did it! I did it!"

He freezes as I wrap my arms around his waist. The fast beat of his heart is hard to miss despite the loud music and crashing pins.

His arms remain plastered to his side like he doesn't know how to give someone a hug back. It only makes me laugh into his chest.

"Come on, you two! We're almost out of time already!" my sister calls out.

I snap out of the moment and jump away from Rowan. His face remains blank, but I know how his body reacts when I touch him.

And it feels pretty good to make someone like him nervous.

CHAPTER TWENTY-ONE

Rowan

"So what do you like to do on the weekends?" Ani steals a piece of cotton candy straight off my cone before retreating to her side of the bench.

This random bench at the corner of Dreamland has become our weekly meet-up spot. While my original intention of joining the mentorship program wasn't altruistic, I've come to enjoy the hour break from my busy schedule because Ani is a decent companion. During the time I've gotten to know her, I've come to realize she shares some of Zahra's best traits. She fills most of the conversation, giving me a chance to sit back and listen. Thanks to her, I can spend an hour not thinking about Dreamland or the demands from the employees.

"I don't do much besides work."

She fake snores. "Boring."

"What do *you* do on weekends?"

She beams. "I hang out with JP. Watch movies. Go to the mall and shop!"

"Sounds like fun," I say with a flat voice.

She giggles. "You don't like those things?"

"No. The idea of going to a mall makes my skin crawl."

"Zahra hates the mall too." Ani grins.

"You don't say." I press my lips together to hold back my smile. Ani always finds a way to bring up Zahra during all our conversations. At first, I thought it was because Ani idolizes her older sister, which she does, but her true intentions became clear after a few meetings. I'm being set up. Ani tries to be slick about it but only a blind man would miss the way Ani's eyes light up whenever I ask a question or two about Zahra in return. She feeds my curiosity while I entertain her little mission.

She perks up. "Actually, you and Zahra have a lot in common."

Unlikely. Zahra's my opposite in every way that counts. I can't compare to a woman who can light up a room with her smile alone. She's like the sun, with everyone orbiting around her to bask in her warmth. Unlike me, who keeps people away from me with nothing but a scowl.

"You always find a way to bring your sister up."

Ani tucks a brown curl behind her ear. "Because you like each other."

"And you know that how?" My voice keeps a neutral tone despite my growing interest.

"She looks at you like she wants to have your babies."

I choke on my sudden intake of air. My fist pounds against my chest as I take a deep inhale. "I definitely don't think that's true."

"You're right. I wanted to see your reaction." She shrugs.

Unbelievable.

"You're a cruel woman." I steal a piece of her pretzel in retribution.

"But my sister does smile at *you*." She says it in the sweetest, most innocent way.

"She smiles at everyone," I grumble under my breath.

"How would you know?"

Shit. Ani's question sounds innocent, but it sheds light on how much I pay attention to Zahra. The smile on Ani's face tells me she probably noticed too.

"It's hard to miss."

"How cute!" she squeals. "I knew it!"

"Knew what?"

"You *do* like my sister."

"I didn't say that."

"No, but you *smiled*."

Well, shit. I didn't notice that. *Get a handle on yourself.* "People smile."

Ani only laughs and shakes her head. "Not you."

"Let's pretend this conversation never happened."

"Sure, Rowan. Sure." She swipes another handful of cotton candy from me as payment for her secrecy.

But something about her smile tells me I'm anything but safe.

I shut off the light in my office and pull out my phone.

> **Me:** Hey. I finished up your drawing. I'll send it over tomorrow.

There's no need for me to message Zahra, but it feels weird to let a whole day go by without talking. Between my busy schedule and her lack of text messages, I've grown restless as the hours have gone by. It's a warning that I'm becoming dependent on her company. Yet I can't find it in me to stop.

My phone vibrates in my hand. Zahra sent me a photo of her cubicle, where she has a hundred Post-its strewn across the wall.

Me: You're still working? It's 10 p.m.

Zahra: Yes, Grandpa. I had a fun idea I wanted to finish before I went home.

Me: What could possibly be better than sleep?

Zahra: Dinner.

I frown as I type out my next message.

Me: You haven't eaten anything?

Zahra: No. I burned through all of my snacks hours ago.

Me: I pity you.

Me: Your work ethic reminds me of Rowan.

I'm a piece of shit for referencing myself, but I'm somewhat interested in her unfiltered opinion of me.

Zahra: Yeah right! I wish.

Zahra: I think the man runs on solar energy because there's no way he's human.

I chuckle low under my breath. That would be convenient and way more time-efficient than sleeping.

Me: Sounds plausible. It would explain his need for taking a walk during his lunch break.
Zahra: How do you know these things?!

Shit. Yeah, Scott, how do you know these things?

Me: Everyone knows to avoid the back lot quad at noon.

Zahra sends a few laughing emojis and another text.

Zahra: Oh. I didn't know this!
Me: That's because you live inside of a warehouse. Go home.
Zahra: I will. I will. Maybe in an hour.

I shake my head and pocket my phone. While I'm pleased that some Creators are taking their jobs seriously, like Zahra, it doesn't make me happy to know she's up this late on an empty stomach.

The walk to the catacombs entrance isn't far from my office. As I walk through the tunnel, I find myself slowing down near the Creators' warehouse entrance.

You could go in and force Zahra to go home and come back tomorrow with a full stomach and a good night's rest.

I walk up the steps and open the door without giving anything a second thought. The path to Zahra's cubicle is one I've memorized, and I find myself stopping at the entrance to watch her work. It's my kind of entertainment, with her working her bottom lip as she grabs a Post-it and folds it into a neat little square. She turns and attempts to throw it in a mason jar. Her shot is too short, and the paper falls to the ground.

"Nice shot."

Zahra jumps in place. "You scared me!" She turns on her heel and looks me up and down. "What are you even doing here?"

I'm struck speechless. *What am I doing here?*

"I wanted to check in and see if anyone was still working." That much is true.

"Why?" She raises a brow.

"I wanted someone's opinion on something." *For fuck's sake. Go home while you still stand a chance.*

"Okay. Hit me." She smiles as she leans against her desk.

What in the world could I ask her opinion on?

"Rowan, what is it?"

"I wasn't sure if our oldest ride is worth keeping."

Her entire face brightens. "Oh no! Don't get rid of it. I love the—" Her grumbling stomach cuts her off, morphing the shade of her face from brown to bright red.

I scowl. "You skipped dinner."

"Umm…how did you know that?" The color of her cheeks somehow intensifies.

Yeah, Rowan. How did you know? Fuck. I keep messing up tonight. Who knew keeping up two personalities would be this difficult?

"You're still here working."

"Right. I'm about to wrap up soon so I'll just—" Her stomach grumbles even louder, and my blood turns into lava, pumping furiously at the pace of my heart.

I pull out my phone. "How do you feel about Chinese food?"

Her mouth gapes apart. "Umm…it's good?"

I dial a local place I have saved after too many late nights working. I'm not sure what Zahra likes, so I order one of everything. It's probably overkill, but I'd rather have her eat something she likes.

I hang up to find Zahra still gawking at me. "What?"

She shakes her head. "I didn't expect you to buy me dinner."

"I'm hungry. You can have the leftovers," I respond as if that solves everything.

"But I'm pretty sure you ordered the entire restaurant."

I remain standing in silence.

Her brows pull together before she wipes away whatever look is on her face. "*All right*. So why are you thinking of getting rid of our oldest ride?" She drops onto the floor where she has an entire array of Post-its, pieces of paper, markers, and more.

Right. The opinion I wanted.

I follow suit and lean against the back partition of the cubicle.

Zahra laughs to herself as I remove my suit jacket and throw it beside my legs.

"What's so funny?"

She waves at my body like it solves my question. "You're sitting on the floor."

I look down at myself. "And?"

"It's weird." She crosses her legs.

I ignore her. "It's an old ride. I'm not sure if it's worth keeping."

She sucks in a breath. "You have to be joking! Is it worth keeping?!"

I nod, knowing this kind of question could stir up an hour-long conversation. And it does just that. While we wait for the delivery, Zahra spends the time explaining the history behind my grandfather's first ride, as if I wasn't aware. She goes into great detail, touching upon all the reasons we shouldn't dare change a single thing. I find myself smiling more than usual because her enthusiasm and passion is contagious.

I'm somewhat disappointed when the food arrives because it cuts her off.

"Did you really need to order the whole menu?"

I shrug. "Wasn't sure what you liked."

She looks at me with a pinched expression. "And why didn't you ask me?" She grabs two cartons from the bag and presses them against her chest with a sigh.

I stay silent and pluck a box of fried rice from the bag. Zahra passes me a plastic-wrapped fork and we both dive in.

She lets out the tiniest moan as she takes a bite of her food. I feel the sound go straight to my cock, and blood starts rushing to a place it doesn't belong.

I take a deep breath. "Why were you here so late? Really?"

She points over her shoulder at the mason jar filled with Post-its. "I was working on a new idea."

"And?"

"And I lost track of time."

"Does this happen often?"

She shrugs. "I don't have much else going on."

"What do you like to do for fun?" The question sounds

natural, as if I care about other activities besides work. Maybe Ani is rubbing off on me with her personal questions.

Zahra smiles. "I like to read."

"For fun?"

She ends up throwing her head back and laughing. My whole chest warms at the idea of making her laugh like that, and a little kernel of pride swells within me.

"Yes. Some people read for something other than work." She speaks breathlessly. "What do *you* like to do when you're not working?"

Text you. "I run."

"Figures." She rolls her eyes.

The hairs on the back of my neck stand to attention. "What does that mean?"

She clears her throat like it can hide the way her cheeks turn the lightest pink color. "Nothing. You have a runner's body." Her eyes look everywhere but at my face.

Hmm. She's been checking me out.

"Not that I check you out or anything," she stammers, and her cheeks only redden more.

I sit up taller, pleased with this new development. "Right."

"Only a masochist runs for fun."

"It clears my head."

"I'll take your word for it."

A laugh bubbles out of me, making my lungs burn from the rush of oxygen.

Zahra grins. "It's a shame you don't laugh more often."

Because I don't have many things to laugh about. I tug at my tie, loosening its hold around my neck. "Don't get used to it."

"I wouldn't dare. I kind of like the fact that it's a rarity because it makes it even more special." Her smile is infectious, making the corners of my lips turn up in return.

No one has called my laugh special. Hell, I don't think I've been labeled special in any other way that wasn't derogatory. It makes me feel...*good*. Appreciated. Valued in a way that has nothing to do with how much money I make or what kind of job I have.

I want to see myself like she sees me. Because in her eyes, I don't feel like I'm a man carrying an entire mountain of expectations on my shoulders. I'm just Rowan, the kind of guy who sits on a floor in a pair of expensive slacks, eating takeout from a carton and loving every second of it.

It hits me, as Zahra grins at me, that I want more of this with her. I need to find a way to make it happen without drawing attention to the fact that I'm two different people in her life.

If only I knew how.

CHAPTER TWENTY-TWO

My sister is up to something. That's the only reason behind her impromptu buddy mentorship event for all four of us. Rowan might be busy but I'm pretty sure my sister has him wrapped around her finger. Ani thinks she's clever but I'm onto her.

But how could I tell her no? The whole point of this project is to help the buddies become more independent, so I would be the biggest hypocrite if I told my sister I don't need her help.

It seemed like a safe bet, but I'm regretting it big time today. Ever since she walked into my apartment with only two pumpkins and a devious smile

"It's no big deal. People forget things all the time." She smiles, revealing the tiniest glint in her eyes that has me tilting my head. I've only seen that look on my sister twice and it led to us being grounded.

"How did you forget two of the four pumpkins?" I wave my hands over the massive pumpkins that make my kitchen look even smaller than it is.

She shrugs. "The pumpkin patch ran out."

"This lie is rapidly devolving." I put my hands on my hips like my mother.

"I'm not lying." Her eyes dart around the entire kitchen to avoid looking into mine.

"They ran out of pumpkins at the beginning of October?" I ask in the driest voice.

"How weird! Must be a shortage."

That little liar. I never thought I'd see the day when my sister attempts to play *my* matchmaker.

I look over at Rowan, wondering what he thinks. He doesn't bother looking at us because he's too immersed in his phone.

Great. What a help he is.

Ani grabs one of the pumpkins off the counter. "JP and I want to do one together."

"You don't say?" I reply dryly. My sister in love is usually adorable and endearing. But right now? It's oddly inconvenient for me.

JP chooses that exact moment to wrap an arm around my sister and give her a kiss on her forehead.

Ugh. Who am I kidding? They're still cute.

"Let's do this!" JP grabs their pumpkin from Ani's arms and takes it to the dining room, where *I* was supposed to work with him.

I sigh and turn around.

I readjust all the supplies in a row. "You don't have to do this if you have something better to do."

He looks up from his phone with knitted brows. "I wouldn't have shown up if I didn't want to do this."

"Why are you here?" I stare at him.

His face remains blank. "Because your sister asked me to be."

My stomach takes a dive, along with my mood. *Stupid girl, thinking he came to spend time with you. Of course he's here for Ani. He's her mentor.*

"Shouldn't you still be working?" I probe. Maybe if I remind him of all his responsibilities, he will run out the door after remembering some kind of email he forgot to send.

"It's a Saturday."

All I can do is stare at him. "I thought you worked every day."

"I do."

"We really need to talk about your work-life balance."

"It's easy when my life is my job. No need for a scale."

I clutch onto the counter while I laugh. "That's the saddest thing I've ever heard you say."

He looks at me with drawn brows. "Why?"

"Because what's the point of having so much money when you'll never have the chance to enjoy it?"

He blinks at me. Has he never considered that before? He might be a sharp guy, but he could use some kind of intervention about his addiction to working.

He shakes his head as if he needed to erase whatever he was thinking from his mind. "If money was no object, what would you do?"

I grin. "The options are endless."

He raises a brow. "That's a terrifying sentiment coming from you."

"Well, for starters, I'd give back to charity."

He frowns. "We support charities."

"Only because it's considered a tax write-off. Have you ever attended a charity event that didn't include champagne and caviar?"

"Don't be ridiculous. Caviar is disgusting." His nose twitches and I find it adorable.

Adorable? I internally groan.

"Well, maybe you should spend a day working at a homeless shelter. Maybe you'd think twice about walking around in shoes worth more than someone's rent."

"I didn't think my question would turn into an inquisition."

I shrug. "You asked. I answered."

"That's all you would do with your endless amount of funds? Donate it?"

I laugh to myself. "Not all of it. I'd save some for myself and buy first edition copies of all my favorite books."

"Books." He looks up at the ceiling like God might intervene. "What about your pins? Wouldn't you want to buy more of those?"

I freeze. "What do you mean?"

His brows pull together. "You wouldn't buy more pins?"

"No."

"Why not?"

"Because that's not how it works."

"Then how does it work?"

I sigh. "It's a long story."

He looks around the empty kitchen. "And? All we have is time."

My muscles tighten. "And that's not something I want to share with you," I snap.

Shit. My eyes widen and my mouth pops open, but I stop myself from apologizing.

His entire forehead scrunches. "I didn't know it was a sensitive subject."

I'm not sure if it's me or my imagination, but the air between us grows heavy until I look away first. "It's…just not something I talk about with many people." Or anyone besides my family and Claire.

"Got it."

No. He really doesn't but I'm not going to unleash that story. There's no way someone like him would understand someone like me. He's put together, and I'm—was…broken.

But not anymore. You're better now. Stronger.

I uncap a permanent marker and move toward the stem of the pumpkin.

"Put the weapon down." Rowan's hand reaches out and halts my movement, sending a wave of electricity up my arm.

His joke breaks the tension between us.

"Out of everything on the counter, this is a weapon?" I point at the knife only a few inches away from him.

"It is when you don't know what you're doing."

"Excuse me? I won our apartment building's pumpkin-carving contest last year."

He raises a brow.

"Okay, well that's a stretch, but I did receive an honorable mention. They gave me a ribbon and everything."

He throws his head back and laughs. It's the best kind of

laugh—rough with a hint of a wheeze. As if he can't take in enough oxygen to support such a rare event. I let the sound wash over me, and all I can think about is how I can get him to do that again.

His eyes open and he startles. "What?"

"Who are you, and what did you do with the real Rowan?"

His brows pull together. "What are you talking about?"

I fumble for my phone. "Could you do that thing again?"

"Laugh?"

"Yes. I need to catch it on camera this time."

He loses the battle with hiding his smile. "What for?"

"Because this is history in the making."

"You're ridiculous." He flips the pumpkin upside down.

"Ridiculously amazing," I finish for him.

His smile evaporates like it never existed.

Was it something I said?

Maybe he's sensitive about people complimenting themselves.

I peer over at his completely symmetrical circle. "What are you doing?"

He grabs the knife and hacks away at the *bottom* of the pumpkin. "Don't ask stupid questions."

"Hey! What happened to 'There's no such thing as stupid questions'?"

"Want to guess who came up with that phrase?" he replies dryly.

I flip him off behind my back.

His smile reappears and I count it as a small victory.

"I'll rephrase my question. Why are you choosing to carve the lid from the bottom?"

He slices away at the last bit of pumpkin before putting the knife down. "Because the experts say so."

"Experts?"

"Yes. The articles I reviewed all stated that cutting a hole at the bottom prevents the pumpkin from caving in on itself."

"Well, wow. I didn't know that." What kind of person researches how to carve pumpkins?

Rowan Don't-Know-What-the-G-Stands-For-Yet Kane, that's who. The man is quite thorough in everything he does.

"Your sister sent me a picture of you with your honorable-mention-worthy pumpkin. I thought I was doing a disservice to everyone if I didn't come prepared."

"How did you know we would be partnered up together?"

His brows pull together. "She told me before."

"And you decided to come anyway?" I hold on to the counter to keep me steady.

He shrugs. How can he play it so cool at a time like this?

"Why did you come?"

"Because I felt like it."

I tilt my head at him. I'm not sure what to make of this kind of revelation. For some weird reason, Rowan wants to hang around me. He is even willing to take time off.

But why? What changed? While we might have this strange chemical reaction to one another, not much has been different between us besides dinner at the warehouse.

Yet he came here to spend time with you.

"Your turn." He shoves the pumpkin at me.

"Gross. Ani does that part." I wrinkle my nose at the pumpkin brains.

He sighs and takes the pumpkin back.

"You're the best!" I grin as I pass him a garbage bag.

He tries to hide his smile by looking down, but I catch it anyway. Another wave of warmth rolls through me.

Together, Rowan and I work on the pumpkin. By the time we are done, I conclude that I genuinely enjoy his company.

CHAPTER TWENTY-THREE

Rowan

I send the message before I can stop myself.

Me: What are you up to?

I fix the pillows behind my head as I get settled into my bed for the night. This is the usual routine now, with me getting home late and texting Zahra once I've eaten and showered. I've only been at Dreamland for a few months, and I've already fallen into a comfortable ritual that can only lead to one thing: dependence.

A photo of some child's homework pops up on the screen.

Me: You're finally learning the alphabet? Nice.

Zahra: No. I'm tutoring kids.

Me: At 10 p.m.? Don't they have a bedtime?

Zahra: Yes, but I can't see my clients at their usual times with my new schedule.

Clients? I didn't even know she tutored on top of everything else she does. When does she find the time to take care of herself if she's so damn busy helping everyone else?

Something resembling a rock drops into my stomach. *Guilt?*

Nope. Maybe indigestion.

Me: Don't they pay you enough as a Creator?
Zahra: I do this as a favor for a single mom I used to work with at the salon. It's only once a week so no big deal.
Me: Why?
Zahra: Because she works a second job and can't afford a tutor herself, so I offered to help.
Me: For free?

The concept makes no sense to me. Who works late nights on top of a full-time job to help someone else?

Zahra: Sure. She needs her money more than I do and I like helping.
Me: But why does she need to work two jobs? They give us free lunch and offer us cheap housing.

I thought those kinds of measures were put in place to help lessen the cost of living.

Zahra: Not everyone can survive off Dreamland's dismal wages.

There's that drastic heartburn again, trickling its way through my chest.

Is that me starting to care? I swallow back my unease.

Zahra: But we make do.

I type out a response before I lose my nerve.

Me: Wouldn't people quit if they were unhappy with the pay?

Zahra: They might. I wouldn't blame them.

Huh. Really? Our annual surveys always report such high employee satisfaction rates.

Zahra: But many people love their job. Some are even multigenerational.

Me: Like you.

Zahra: Exactly!

She tacks on a heart to the message, which is new for her. It makes me smile.

You seem ridiculous obsessing over something as small as that.

Me: It's hard to forget about the ukulele-playing, Elvis-loving family that happens to work here.

Zahra: It's kind of nice that you pay attention to the little things.
Me: Don't set your standards so low.
Zahra: Trust me. My standards were obliterated a while ago.

The burning in my chest cranks up the intensity. I want to do something, but I don't know what, so I settle for the only thing that might make her better.

Me: Who hurt you? Do we need to find their HP address?
Zahra: Haha so funny. Are you expanding your talents to the computer hacking business?
Me: For you, I'd consider it.

And I mean every word.

I've always prided myself on the ability to remove my emotions from any kind of business decision. It took an effort to develop the skill, but I've perfected it over the years. I was the first one to suggest laying off 10 percent of the Kane Company employees when our company lost millions after two bad movies in a row. I've been known to be demanding and clinical, from forcing employees to work Christmas Eve to swapping health insurance policies to trim our bottom line. No amount of crying, moaning, or yelling from our employees could convince me otherwise.

Despite this training, Zahra somehow got under my skin. Her calm and collected conversation about the employee's finances actually got to me. The thought lingers in my head during every encounter I have with Dreamland employees.

Martha is the final straw.

I frown at her. "Why do you need to work at the bar? Don't we pay you enough?"

Her smile wobbles at the same time as her shoddy ankle that desperately needs surgical attention. "Of course."

"Don't lie to me, Martha. I thought we had a connection." I even let her go home early last week, for fuck's sake.

"Sir, our connection is weaker than the dial-up internet at the local library."

Jesus. Dial-up internet still exists? That's almost as sad as the beat-up sneakers she swaps with her work flats.

I'm disgusted by her big toe peeking out from the hole at the front of her tennis shoe. "Why do you have a second job?"

She bites down on her frail lip.

"Don't make me repeat my question."

"Because my husband has a heart condition and his medications cost more than a monthly mortgage." Martha's lips clamp together again.

"Why doesn't your health insurance cover it?"

The glare she sends my way chills me to the bone. She's never been anything but respectful and meek in my presence, but the fire in her eyes could flay the skin off a weaker man. "With the company health insurance policy, the copayments are severely out of budget."

"And you find that your paycheck isn't sufficient."

She nods. "Some months are tougher than others. With the holidays coming up and all..." Her voice trails off.

I picture Zahra's little ice pick smacking into my cold heart with the strength of a jackhammer. With my hand, I rub at the burning spot in my chest. "Follow me."

I walk back to my office with Martha dragging her feet behind me because of her usual limp. "Have a seat." I stroll around my desk and drop into my chair.

She takes a seat across from me. Her eyes move back and forth from me to the grandfather clock at the corner of the room. "I don't mean to be rude, but I can't be late to my job. Every hour counts for someone like me because I don't make as much as the other young ones."

I'm pretty sure that comment aged her another ten years.

The loud breath I release has Martha wincing. "Give me a moment of your time. How long has your husband had this heart condition?"

"He was diagnosed at forty-five, after our grandchild passed away suddenly."

Jesus fucking Christ. A grandchild?

She prattles on. "The stress did him in. Instead of attending our grandbaby's funeral, he was recovering in the hospital. He's never gotten over that still to this day." Her eyes water but no tears fall.

I pinch the bridge of my nose. Something about Martha working late into the night on a shitty ankle because I don't pay her enough doesn't sit right with me. It's my fault she can't afford these things.

Doesn't feel too good to trim the bottom line now, huh?

My skin flushes beneath my suit, with my body temperature spiking. At the moment, I can only think of a temporary solution.

I type out an email to the head of Dreamland finances requesting a bonus.

"What are you doing?" Her voice comes out in a whisper.

I flip the monitor so she can read the email. "Consider this your Christmas bonus."

"But it's October." She puts on her reading glasses and gasps. Her eyes roll into the back of her head as she passes out.

Fuck. This is why I don't do nice things.

Something about my encounters with Zahra and Martha have me itching to learn more about the hidden issues of the park. Something is haunting me, stealing away my sleep as I consider the daily struggle employees have. Medical insurance. Retirement funds. Savings accounts. All of it batters against me like rough waves, and I feel like I'm struggling to stay afloat amidst my growing guilt.

This seems like something my grandfather would find important and worth exploring. He cared about his employees like they were family, and although I can't relate to that, I can pretend for the vote.

So this morning I decided to follow my gut and speak to Zahra. It's time I talk about her concerns as Rowan, the man who can get shit done, rather than Scott, the lonely asshole who has no pull or stakes in Dreamland. If there is someone who will be honest with me about employee affairs, it's her.

I find Zahra's cubicle empty, and a heavy breath escapes my throat. It takes me only a few steps to stop by Jenny's office.

"Where's Zahra?"

Jenny looks up from her computer. "She's doing some recon work. You know, that whole 'boots on the ground' mentality."

"Did we sign up for a war that I didn't know about?"

She cracks a rare smile. "She asked me for a special kind of workday, and I'm intrigued to see what she comes up with after it."

"What do you mean?"

"She wants to explore the park as a guest and take notes."

"A guest," I repeat.

Her cheeks flush as her eyes roam over my face like she wants to gauge my reaction. "I think the idea is genius, and I plan on doing the same for the entire team. Some are hesitant about giving up one of their unpaid vacation days though."

Interesting… Why didn't I think of that? Maybe the fresh take on Dreamland boosts creativity.

I clear my throat. "Consider it a paid vacation day on the house."

Her eyes widen. "Really? We haven't had one of those in years."

You really are a heartless piece of shit. Another thing that's your fault.

I exit Jenny's office and text Zahra through my personal messages this time. I tell myself it's only business. That I'm only trying to meet up with her because I want to discuss semantics and wages and health insurance benefits and employee issues that I've done nothing but exacerbate over the years.

Except the small voice in my head calls me out on my bullshit, whispering how all I do is lie.

CHAPTER TWENTY-FOUR

Zahra

I take a step forward as the line shuffles a few feet ahead. My phone vibrates in my backpack, and I pull it out.

Unknown Number: Where are you?

I scan the thread to check for any past messages but come up empty. The phone vibrates again before I have a chance to tuck it away in my backpack.

Unknown Number: It's Rowan.

Really? What does he want?

I've been keeping my distance from him for the last few weeks, ever since Ani's little stunt to get us together. I'm afraid I'll end up doing something I'll regret. Between the dinner he didn't need to buy me and the pumpkin carving, I'm losing the battle of staying away from him. Plus, I feel guilty about stringing Scott along while becoming more interested in Rowan.

You'll have to pick one eventually.

The thought makes my stomach sour. I grind my teeth together as I type out my response.

Me: What do you need?

I update his contact information while I wait for his response.

Lucifer: Where are you?

I roll my eyes at him ignoring my question.

Me: Touring the park.

Lucifer: Try to be a little more specific.

Someone coughs behind me and points to the massive gap of space I left open. I apologize and speed walk through the queue.

Lucifer: I'm losing my patience.

Me: Then go buy some more.

Lucifer: Funny.

I laugh to myself. Him admitting I'm funny makes my heart slam into my rib cage at an uneven pace.

Lucifer: Please tell me where you are?

Me: Look at you using the word please. And people say old dogs can't learn new tricks.

Good, Zahra. Remind him of your age difference. That should steer him away, given the fact that he's seven years older than you.

Lucifer: This old dog has plenty of tricks he could teach you.

Did he make a sexual joke? My whole body burns from his reply, and I can't come to grips with his shift in personality.

Rowan replies again before I have a chance to move past my shock.

Lucifer: That was highly inappropriate.

Me: I think your phone has been hacked.

Lucifer: I can assure you it hasn't, but I can't say the same about my brain. I tend to do stupid things around you.

I laugh up to the ceiling, feeling way too giddy from his admission. Given his openness, I throw him a bone.

Me: I'm waiting in line for the Spooky Castle ride.

Lucifer: A line?

Me: Allow me to educate you. A line is a thing that patient people wait in when they can't afford to purchase the quick skip passes your company sells for the price of a liver.

One look in the direction of the empty quick-skip line tells me that other park guests agree with me.

Lucifer: If someone offers you a liver for two hundred dollars, run.

I laugh as I throw my phone in my backpack. A couple standing ahead strikes up a conversation with me. They're a sweet couple from Kansas who traveled all this way to celebrate their honeymoon. I ask them a few questions, including their favorite and least favorite parts of the park. They share their thoughts, and I write them down on my mini notepad.

"Hey. You can't skip the line!" a guest calls out behind me.

I turn to find Rowan moving through the line without paying the yelling guests any attention.

How did he get here so fast?

He stops beside me, not even the least bit winded.

"Umm. What are you doing here?" I stare up at him, taking in how ridiculous his suit and Gucci loafers look compared to all of us casually dressed humans.

"You weren't at the warehouse."

"Yeah, I took the day off."

"So Jenny said."

"Why were you looking for me?" I try to keep my voice neutral but fail.

Rowan smirks at me.

The man behind us taps on his shoulder. "Excuse me. You can't skip the line. We've been waiting here for forty minutes already."

He sends a withering glance over his shoulder. "I own the place."

"Yeah right. And I'm Santa Claus." The man tugs on his white beard.

"Google the name Rowan Kane. I'll wait." Rowan taps his shoe against the floor.

There's something about Rowan's voice that makes everyone follow his bidding. It's oddly fascinating to watch as the man pulls out his cell phone and taps away at the screen.

The man's scowl drops as the color drains from his face. "I'm sorry, Mr. Kane. I didn't mean to yell at you. We just feel strongly about line skippers here."

"I'm sure that's the case with anyone who can't afford a quick-skip pass," he responds in the driest voice.

My jaw drops open. "You shouldn't talk to people like that." I turn around, giving Rowan my back. No wonder everyone avoids him. He has the emotional maturity of a robot and the appeal of rush hour traffic.

The couple from Kansas starts up our conversation again, and I focus on them. Rowan's loafer taps against the floor as he faces my back. I don't care if he throws a tantrum. He can wait in the line in silence for all I care.

Rowan sighs so loud, it rattles my bones. Whatever look he shoots toward the couple has them shutting up. They turn around and start chatting with one another, completely ignoring me.

I look over my shoulder to find him staring at me. "Yes?"

"Are you going to finally explain why we're waiting in a line when we can go ahead and skip everyone?"

"I'm experiencing the park from the perspective of a guest

so I can come up with ideas for the very people you're trying to appeal to."

"How noble of you." His nose scrunches. I swear he tried his hardest not to say something insulting this time.

"If you hate the idea so much, then go back to your fancy office. No one asked you to come here. Actually, wait. Why *are* you here?"

"I—" He pauses. "I don't know." His brows draw together.

Whatever is happening in his brain shuts him up. Both of us remain silent while waiting in line, with both of us lost in our thoughts.

Why is he really here, and why does it make me giddy to know he decided to wait in line with me despite hating the idea?

We finally make it to the front of the line after ten minutes. The Spooky Castle ride is one of the classic attractions at Dreamland, based on a haunted castle somewhere in England from one of the Kane Company's movies. Each cart is shaped like a half-moon, with a black seat large enough to fit three people.

A man dressed in an old-school three-piece suit calls out to us. "How many in your party?"

"One," I reply at the same time Rowan says, "Two."

The attendant shifts his weight from foot to foot. "Umm, please hurry. The cart is leaving."

I rush and enter the small black seat. My temple throbs as Rowan slides in and pulls down the lever, trapping us in the cart together.

"Why can't you leave me alone?" I croak.

"I wish I knew." He says the words so low, I wonder if I made them up.

Regardless, I smile at the idea of Rowan wanting to spend more time with me, even if he doesn't know why.

Rowan spreads his legs to get comfortable. One muscular thigh brushes against mine, and I suck in a breath. I'm not sure what's scarier: our cart moving through the creepy darkness or the burst of heat in my belly at Rowan's closeness.

Definitely Rowan. I shift, moving closer to the end of the seat.

"If you scoot any closer to the edge, you'll fall out of the cart and get hurt." He speaks over the haunted sounds.

"I thought you didn't care?"

"Hmm. Maybe I found some fucks to give after all."

My chest tightens as I fight my smile.

The cart carries us into a hallway with evil cackling and the moans of ghosts echoing off the walls. Doorknobs rattle while other doors creak open as we move forward at a crawl.

Rowan's eyes bounce around everywhere as we're taken through the various rooms of the castle. His eyes widen as he assesses the attic space, where a Gothic bride chants over a coffin. "That's creepier than I remember."

I raise a brow. "Aw, are you scared? Want me to hold your hand?"

He rolls his eyes. I find the move so oddly human of him that I end up laughing to myself. The side of his mouth twitches again as he fights a smile, and I mentally dance in celebration.

"When is the last time you rode on this one?" I probe.

His hands tighten on the handlebar in front of us. "When I was ten."

"Ten?! That's forever ago."

"Way to make me feel old."

My entire body shakes from laughter. "Sorry."

"I still remember how Cal used to cry every single time. His reaction always made my mom laugh, so we would bully him into doing it with us over and over again."

I suck in a breath. I've never heard him talk about his mom before like this. "That's sweet that you did that for your mom."

He coughs. "I doubt Cal would agree."

"What was her favorite ride?"

"All of them." He smiles, but it doesn't reach his eyes. I reach out and grab his tight fist. I'm not sure what I thought to accomplish. Soothe him? Provide comfort? What a ridiculous idea. He doesn't need that. I remove my hand, but Rowan latches onto it and holds it trapped against the bar. The graze of his thumb across my knuckles sends a spark up my arm.

I gasp. He rears back and releases my hand.

Our cart continues its slow descent into the morbid graveyard. Talking statues and ghouls fly around. One ghost pops up from a gravestone, and Rowan jumps in his seat, smacking his chest against the safety bar in front of us. It groans from his weight but stays in place.

A rush of laughter explodes out of me. Tears form in my eyes, and I can't blink them away fast enough. "Oh my God. That reaction was totally worth riding with you."

He turns in his seat. His eyes are lit up by the projector ghosts floating above us. "You're evil."

A massive spider drops in front of our cart and Rowan recoils. "Fuck!"

Another laugh erupts from my throat. I've never heard him swear before, probably because it would reveal too much about his mood.

His lips form a tight line, but his eyes remain bright.

"You should've seen your face. Priceless."

He shakes his head.

"I think I might have peed a little from laughing so hard."

"Charming as ever, Zahra."

Something about the way he says the phrase has me grinning like an idiot.

"I've never seen a grown adult react like that on a kid's ride." I discreetly dab at the corners of my eyes again.

"You're not as sweet as everyone thinks you are. Only a wicked woman would call a man out for being afraid like this."

"Do you think they have it on camera? I'll buy that insanely overpriced photo in a heartbeat." My face feels like it might crack in half from how big I'm smiling.

He stares at me for a few seconds before facing forward.

The ride ends too soon. Our cart drags toward the exit and the handlebar lifts, releasing us. Rowan steps out before offering his hand to me.

I stare at it, blinking to check if my eyes are deceiving me. He rolls his eyes once more and grabs my arm, pulling me out before the cart disappears back into the queue. I expect him to let go but he holds on tight as the ride spits us out into a store selling merchandise from the Spooky Castle movie.

"Wait!" I call out as Rowan heads toward the front doors.

He drops my hand, and I walk up to the photo counter. The attendant helps me find the picture I'm looking for.

When he pulls up the image and blows it up, I lose it. My voice becomes hoarse from how hard I laugh.

"Delete it." Rowan speaks behind me. The warmth of his chest heats my back.

I throw my hand up to stop the employee. "No! Please let me buy it first." I stare at the photo with longing. I'm an image of grace while Rowan looks about two shades paler with his eyes threatening to burst out of their sockets. And strangest of all, his arm is plastered against my stomach as if he was protecting me. The notion is sweet, and I want a photo to never forget the memory.

I rush to grab my wallet from my purse. Before I have a chance to count my money, Rowan hands the employee a crisp bill over my shoulder. The Dreamland worker prints and wraps the photo up for me.

I turn around and stare at Rowan's expressionless face. "Why did you pay for it?"

"Because I felt like it."

His response is meant to throw me off, but I'm onto him. I think Rowan likes me more than he's willing to let on, even to himself.

CHAPTER TWENTY-FIVE

Zahra

We exit the store with my new present in tow. I smile up at the sky and breathe in the fresh scent of cookies in the air.

Rowan pulls out a package of Tums from his pocket. He pops one in his mouth and rubs his chest.

"Heartburn?" I prop my sunglasses back on my nose.

"Yup."

"Interesting. I always wondered if you had your heart surgically removed to save you the trouble."

"I tried. Turns out the doctor didn't feel comfortable with the low survival rate."

"Those cowards."

He releases one of his laughs. The kind that's so low, it's hard to hear over the screaming and laughing children around us. The sound sends a warmth through my body I find impossible to ignore.

I really need to get the hell away from Rowan before I do something stupid like kiss him again. "Well, nice seeing you. I better get going—you know, places to go, rides to see and all." I turn toward the next ride on my list.

His shadow follows me. He grabs onto my elbow and turns me with a softness someone like him shouldn't possess. Why is it that whenever this man touches me, it feels like the world stops to take notice?

He releases my elbow with the speed of a snail, his fingers tracing my skin as he drops his hand. "Why are you really doing this?"

I stare down at my sneakers. "I have a creative block."

"And this is your solution?" He looks around the park with a sneer.

"Why did you agree to become the director if you hate this place so much?"

"I don't hate it." His nose twitches.

"Then explain that look on your face."

"I don't answer to you."

"If you act like a child, then you'll get treated like one. Goodbye!" I wave over my shoulder as I power walk out of his vicinity.

He follows, eating up the distance without taking a breath. "I'm coming along."

"Why?" I groan.

"Because I find you interesting."

Rowan is the only person who could call me interesting and make my heart flutter in response. I give in to his request because I'm hopeless when it comes to him.

We continue our journey toward the Kanaloa ride based on one of the Hawaiian gods. I head toward the main entrance, but he leads me toward the quick-skip one.

"We don't have quick-skip passes for that." I try to stop, but his hand finds the small of my back, pushing me forward. Heat spreads from the area his palm covers.

He points at his face. "You're looking right at it."

I snort. "God, that was so corny. I can't even believe it came out of your mouth."

He remains quiet, but I'm pretty sure the hand pressed against my back trembles from silent laughter.

"You know, this defeats the point of me experiencing Dreamland like a regular person. I like talking to people and hearing their opinions while waiting."

He ignores my chatter as we walk through the long, empty halls.

"Why do you want to spend time with me anyway?" I ask.

His pocket rattles again as he grabs the Tums bottle and pops another into his mouth.

"You're not supposed to ride this roller coaster if you have heart issues," I tease.

He shoots me a glare that could refreeze the Arctic. "I do *not* have heart issues. It's indigestion."

"Or a chronic side effect for being an ass all the time." I wink.

He grunts something indiscernible under his breath.

We're shuffled into the waiting area for the coaster. Per Rowan's request, an attendant leads us to the front of the line where the first seats of the coaster are.

I shake my head and point at the back. "That's where we want to sit."

Rowan raises a brow but follows my lead. We take our seats at the back of the cart. Our arms brush against each other as the safety harness is brought down, trapping us.

I look straight ahead as the cart cranks up the lift. The scenic facade of a Hawaiian volcano surrounds us, and warm steam trickles through the air, making it purposefully hard to see.

This is my favorite part. The clicking sound grows louder and my heart pounds faster in my chest as we climb up the side of the volcano. With one last push, the cart goes over the edge, falling straight into fake lava.

I scream, my stomach shooting straight into my throat as the ride twists and turns. Rowan's rough exterior cracks as he laughs, his eyes focused more on me than the ride. I'm not sure what to make of it. Based on the way my chest feels, maybe I need to pop a Tums too.

The next drop steals my attention away, and I yell as we are thrown upside down and through a corkscrew motion. This is one of the best rides in all of Dreamland.

My heart doesn't stop racing until the coaster cart comes to a halt right outside the unloading station.

I turn to face Rowan, wondering what he thought of the ride. "What did you think?"

"I think you popped my eardrums." His eyes are stuck on me, darkening as he licks his bottom lip. His hand reaches out and brushes my crazy waves down.

My once steady heart picks up its pace again, pounding

harder in my chest than a minute earlier. "I could ride this over and over again and never get sick of it."

He lifts a brow. "Over and over again?"

"Yes! Doesn't it make you feel alive?"

Our cart pulls into the station. Rowan makes some fancy hand-twirling motion, and our safety harnesses remain locked in place.

"Umm. What's happening?" The passengers all step off the cart, but we remain seated. Rowan does another hand signal, and the cart takes off again, empty except for us.

"Why are we doing this again?" I speak louder over the cranking gears.

He looks over at me, his face flat. "You said you wanted to do it again."

"Yeah, but I didn't exactly expect us to."

"Well, here we are."

The cart moves forward, cranking up the volcano again.

"Why are you really spending so much time with me? Don't you have other things to do and people to torment?"

He offers a noncommittal shrug. "Maybe I enjoy hearing your screams."

"Freak."

I'm surprised Rowan doesn't send me straight into cardiac arrest when he *winks.* My heart thuds in my chest, and my skin tingles in response.

CHAPTER TWENTY-SIX

Rowan

I'm not sure what the hell I was planning on doing once I found Zahra in the park but joining her on this bizarre day was the last idea on my mind. Yet here I am, a helpless bystander, desperate to be a part of her orbit in any way I can.

Today, I was more than willing to wait in a few long lines with Zahra because she said I needed to experience how the rest of the world lives. I've thrown off my entire diet by eating through half of Dreamland with her. I even agreed to walk through the House of Presidents, also known as Dreamland's most boring fucking attraction, all because Zahra wanted to.

Everything I do today is for Zahra's sweet smiles and soft laughs. She has the magnetism of the Bermuda Triangle, and I'm a lost plane desperate to land.

With the sun fading away, our day is slowly coming to an end. The idea of going back to my office fills me with dread.

"Hurry up!" Zahra yells at me. She takes off toward the German-inspired Christmas village set up in a corner of the park for the holiday season. Dreamland takes advantage of Christmas enthusiasts as soon as Halloween ends. It might only be the first day of November, but the park doesn't miss an opportunity to profit off the holiday spirit.

With massive Christmas trees surrounding the plaza, it's as if guests are transported to a different country.

"Come on!" She checks the time on her phone. "We're going to miss it if we don't pick up the pace." She leads us toward the town square. I swipe two cups of hot chocolate from one of the stations and pass one to Zahra.

She smiles down at the tiny marshmallows swimming at the top of the cup. "How'd you know I like hot chocolate?"

"Because everyone likes hot chocolate."

"I shouldn't. We've basically eaten everything they sell at Dreamland."

"If you complain about your weight, I'll gouge my eyes out with this spoon." My eyes trail down her body, taking in the way her clothes cling to her in the best kind of way. She's got curves I'd love to memorize with the tip of my tongue and the brush of my lips. Blood relocates itself to my dick at the mental image of Zahra in my bed, covered by nothing but a silk sheet.

Her cheeks flush as she catches me staring. "My ex used to call me fat."

My jaw clenches to the point of pain. This is the first time Zahra's mentioned anything about her ex to me, and I wish I hadn't heard anything about him. "I take it that's why he's an ex."

"No. Sadly not. Although I should've taken it as a sign."

"That he was losing his vision?"

She lets out a sad excuse for a laugh, and I realize I never want to hear that version of her laugh again. A weird feeling claws up my chest to make her feel better.

"Seriously, what kind of idiot complains about a woman having curves? Off the record, your body is hot as fuck."

Her cheeks turn into two red splotches. "Please pretend I didn't say anything."

"Why?"

"Because we shouldn't be having this conversation. You're my boss," she whispers the words as if someone can hear us.

My molars press together. "I'm not technically *your* boss."

"My contract begs to differ."

"You report to Jenny, who then reports to me."

"Well, you're my boss's boss, which means I should *definitely* not bring up my ex to you. So be a gentleman and shut up. Kay, thanks!"

I chuckle under my breath as I lean over and talk into her ear. "Gentle is the last thing I want to be around you."

Her skin breaks out in goose bumps. "What are you doing?"

"Having fun."

"Did I miss the start of the apocalypse or something?"

I unleash a small smile. Her eyes expand as she checks out my face.

She clears her throat, grabs my half-finished hot chocolate, and throws the cups away. By the time she comes back, her cheeks have lost their flush. I miss it.

"You're cute when you get all flustered. If it was—" My

response gets cut off by a chanting crowd counting down from ten. "What are they counting for?"

She beams as she looks up at me. "You'll see!"

The crowd yells *one* and chaos erupts. Kids scream around us as foam snowflakes rain down around us. The hidden canisters across the quad spray us all and coat everyone's hair and clothes in fake snow. Christmas music blasts from the speakers, basking the whole area in holiday cheer.

Zahra laughs as I swipe at my shoulder and bring the foam up to my eyes.

"What the hell is this? I don't remember this being here when I was a kid." My parents took us to this same village every year, yet I don't recall snow being a part of the program.

"They added it last year!"

"This better not stain." A pitiful excuse for a snowflake lands on my nose.

Her grin widens as she steps on her toes and brushes it away. "Don't be such a stick in the mud."

Foam rains around us, dropping onto her dark hair and clothes. Kids squeal and run around as they make foam angels on the grass.

"These people act like they've never seen snow before."

"That's because some of us haven't!" She laughs up to the sky.

"Really?"

"Yes. Maybe one day." She holds out her hand to collect more foam.

A child runs right into Zahra, throwing off her equilibrium. I reach out and grasp onto her arms before she topples to the ground. Another little speed demon runs right at her, but I tug her into me before he mows her down. Her hands smack against my chest and her eyes hold mine hostage. She feels perfect in my arms, and I'm tempted to keep her tucked beside me where I can protect her from all the darkness in the world, including myself.

I'm not sure what's happening to me, but all I know is that I'm captivated by Zahra.

A piece of her hair flutters in the wind, dragging across her face. Without thinking, I grab onto the strand and tuck it behind her ear. My skin buzzes at the contact, and I cup her cheek to hold on to the moment. Her brown eyes sparkle despite the setting sun.

Everything around us slows as I lower my head. She meets me halfway, and our lips crash together. I've been craving this since our first kiss. Our bodies mold together like they're two missing parts of a puzzle.

Energy crackles where our lips touch, and I feed off it like a desperate addict. Zahra sucks in a breath. I take the opportunity to trace her bottom lip with my tongue. Her body shudders as her fingers claw into the fabric of my suit.

My head grows cloudy and the noise around us fades as Zahra deepens the kiss. Her tongue teases mine as she wraps her arms around my neck. She tastes like mint chocolate, and I'm desperate for more. It's as if all my senses have been kicked into hyperdrive, with my spine tingling and my lips buzzing for more. More of this. More of her. More of us.

Kissing Zahra is like reaching heaven after an eternity spent in purgatory. Like I've spent most of my life hopelessly ambling around, waiting for her to show me the way back to the light. She's divine with enough wickedness to make a sinner like me want to pray in devotion.

I groan as she presses into me. My growing erection is poorly restrained by my slacks, and Zahra gasps.

Another child screams as they barrel into us and shove us apart. Zahra wobbles, but she regains her balance by herself this time.

She steps out of my reach as she looks up at me with gaping, swollen lips. "So…"

"Go on a date with me." I take a step toward her.

"What?!" She presses a hand against her mouth as if the gesture can stop me from kissing her again.

Am I the only one affected by our connection? *There's no way.* "Should I repeat myself?"

"No! To both questions."

"Why?" I step closer to her, taking in her fresh scent of citrus mixed with the soapy smell of the foam snowflakes.

"Do you need a bigger reason besides the fact that you're my *boss*?"

"That's never stopped you from doing what you wanted before."

Her eyes drop to the floor. "It doesn't matter. You're the last person I should want."

Her words throw me back into the past—of the boy who was rejected until he learned to stop caring.

The vein in my forehead throbs. "Yeah, well, I'm not supposed to be attracted to an insufferable female who drives me to the brink of insanity yet here we are. You represent everything I dislike in someone."

She winces. "That's the way you really feel about me?"

Fuck. That came out all wrong. Somehow, I watched Mr.

Darcy fuck up seventeen times yet still managed to fall into the same trap.

Her eyes shine, instantly making myself feel shittier.

"Shit. I didn't mean it like that." I cup her elbow, but she rips her arm away.

"You know what? Forget this. All I've done is make excuses for your behavior because I was hoping there was a decent guy underneath all that anger. But in reality, you're nothing but a jerk who gets off on making everyone as miserable as you." Her bottom lip wobbles.

No. That can't be true. That's something my father does, not me. I'm practical and blunt. There's a difference between that and being a miserable fuck like my father.

But the way she looks at me makes me consider it for a second.

My chest tightens. "Zahra, I'm sorry. Hear me out—"

"I don't want your apology. It means nothing coming from someone who wouldn't know the first thing about feeling remorseful."

I feel as foolish as motherfucking Mr. Darcy.

You're comparing yourself to the fictional characters she loves now?

You're fucked. Absolutely fucked.

My stomach rolls. I'm tempted to say something snappy, but I hold back. I don't want to be *that* guy anymore. The one who loses the girl before he even had a chance. The same one who hides behind a pseudonym and waits up for her messages because I hate the crippling loneliness that hits me every time I walk into my empty house.

No. From here on out, I'm choosing to be better with her. Even if I made this mistake, I can still keep trying anyway.

"Forget this kiss happened. God knows I will." She turns and walks away without a second glance.

Something about her departure has my chest tightening to the point of difficulty breathing. I go to grab my Tums bottle from my blazer's inner pocket, only to find the damn thing empty. It's a perfect representation of how I feel now that Zahra's gone.

Nothing but empty.

Asking Zahra out on a date like that was careless. I got caught up in the moment and it was the first thing I thought of. It was stupid, especially when she sees me one way while I see her in another light.

I thought I could go back to pretending to be Scott, but after kissing Zahra, I can't do it. It feels…wrong. Like I don't fit into that persona anymore because my interest in Zahra has evolved. I don't want to pretend I'm some loser who has no contact with people. I don't want to pretend anymore. Period.

So I start a new conversation as Rowan. From now on, that's all she'll get from me.

Me: I need you to meet me at my office tomorrow at 8 p.m.

I release a pent-up breath when she finally responds an hour later.

Zahra: Okay.

Her simple answer makes me edgy for the rest of the night. She's not the kind of person to do simple anything, and I don't like receiving a one-word message from her. She would never do that to Scott, yet with me, she doesn't even try.

You sound jealous of your own damn self.

I consider canceling the meeting twice before shoving my phone in a drawer and ignoring any messages Scott received from Zahra. It needs to be done. She'll accept my reasoning behind pretending. It's not like I could admit who I was to her when it's hard to trust anyone besides myself and my brothers.

What if she doesn't forgive you?

She will. There's nothing wrong with what I did. I have no doubt if she was raised the same way I was, she would do the same thing without blinking.

Right.

CHAPTER TWENTY-SEVEN

Zahra

I push my shoulders back and knock on the door to Rowan's office. I'm ready for whatever he might throw at me after our little spat, although my heart feels like it's been permanently lodged in my throat after his text message yesterday.

"Come in."

I open the door and find Rowan seated on the opposite side of his desk. His button-down shirt is wrinkled, and the sleeves are rolled up, revealing his strong forearms. The best kind of vein porn makes my mouth water, and I'm tempted to trace them with my lips.

I stop moving once I look up at his face.

Rowan wears glasses. Thick, black-rimmed glasses that belong on some superhero moonlighting as a reporter. I'm caught off guard by the look. *It's…God…wow.* They make his face look harsher, bringing out every sharp angle. I want to reach out and touch the dark shadow covering his jawline.

It adds to his more rugged, after-hours look. While a clean-cut Rowan is enticing, this disheveled version has my blood pumping to the beat of my erratic heart.

"Have a seat." He gestures to the empty chair across from his desk.

I follow his order, dropping into the chair. It's hard to remain graceful when I'm prone to drooling.

Rowan pulls out some file and drops it on his desk in front of him. His eyes remain focused on his clenched fists on either side of the file, and I'm pretty sure my heart might explode from the irritating silence.

"What's this?" I gesture at the file. "Please tell me that's not an NDA or something nefarious."

He rips his glasses off. I mourn the loss as they slide across the desk. "No. Nothing like that."

"Okay then..."

He won't even look me in the eyes. "I brought you here under false pretenses."

"I'm sorry. What?"

"Hear me out before you do anything." He looks up at me with guarded eyes.

"Umm...okay?"

He clutches onto the file, making it bend. "I made a decision a few months ago that had a longer-lasting impact than I intended. While it wasn't made with the most favorable intention at the time, it quickly became something I enjoyed."

"I'm not following."

He pinches the bridge of his nose. "I don't know how to say this without making you upset."

A cold feeling trickles through my veins. If Rowan is afraid of upsetting me, it can't be good.

"Well, try." My teeth grind together. The blood whooshing through my ears makes concentrating a nearly impossible task.

He releases the folder and slides it in my direction. "Open it."

I open the file with a shaky finger. The very first page is a mock-up of my mandap from the Hindu wedding. I'm stuck in a trance as I flip through pages of sketches I asked Scott to draw for me. There are even a few drawings that never made it into my presentations because Scott and I decided against it.

"Did Scott send you these?" My voice trembles. How else would Rowan have access to all these images?

He shakes his head.

"Am I in trouble? I thought it was okay for me to work with him."

"No. You're not in trouble."

"But how do you have these?"

He releases a heavy breath. "Because there is no Scott."

My chest squeezes to the point of pain. "What do you mean?"

His jaw locks. "I'm the one who's been talking to you this whole time."

After all the hours I've spent feeling guilty over my growing feelings for Rowan and Scott, they were the same person?

"Are you kidding me?" I shake my head as if that can erase the truth.

"No."

Acid inches up my throat. I swallow, trying to ease the lump, but nothing helps.

How could Rowan lie to me like this? I thought he was

safe in a weird kind of way. That his sharp wit and purposeful words meant he was a straight shooter with little time for bullshit.

Oh God. Rowan's impeccable timing makes perfect sense now. Like when he showed up at my cubicle, offering to buy me takeout food after I told Scott I skipped dinner. It would take me hours to sift through all my memories to connect the dots, but I don't need to bother. There's only one conclusion.

I was wrong about Rowan. He's the worst kind of liar and the type of man who made me believe in a lie for months because of whatever sick game he wanted to play with me.

Wetness clings to my eyes but I blink it away. I don't have a right to be upset with anyone but myself. It's my fault I texted a stranger, thinking I could get out of this unscathed. I trusted Scott despite the warning signs I was stupid enough to ignore.

Have fun, Claire said to me time and time again.

Be brave, Ani chanted like a war cry.

And for what? This feeling in my chest at the idea of losing something I never had? Screw that.

I shut my eyes as if it can block out everything unfolding before me. "Why?"

Why would you do this?

Why lie to me for months?

Why pretend you cared about me?

So many questions batter my brain, yet I can't find the words to attack him.

His eyes drop to his fists. "At first, I wasn't sure about your motives. Texting you was supposed to be a way to make sure you weren't secretly conspiring against me after our first kiss."

Is he serious?! "You wanted to spy on me?"

"No. Not spy. I was checking to make sure you were genuine."

I'm floored by the conversation. I can't believe he would only talk to me because he wasn't sure if I would make a scandal out of us. The thought hurts.

He continues. "But I realized I was foolish because you really are this kindhearted person who wanted to entertain some lonely guy you'd never even met."

"A person who doesn't even exist," I snap.

"I'm him. I swear I never lied to you as Scott besides the obvious. And once I realized the mistake I made, I couldn't stop. I started looking forward to our conversations, and I knew you would be upset—"

I hold my hand up and shut my eyes. "Stop."

He doesn't bother listening. "I never meant for everything to get so…out of control. There were plenty of times I considered admitting the truth because I wanted you to look at me the same way you looked at your damn phone."

I don't know what that even means, but I'm not about to ask. "Consider the feeling long gone."

His brows pull together. "You can't mean that."

"Really? What exactly do you feel toward me?"

He rubs his bottom lip with his thumb. "I want to spend more time around you."

I shove the file toward him. "Your feelings are irrelevant. I don't care what you want because I'm not open to any of it. This was all a mistake."

His entire body locks up under his shirt, making the veins in his arms stand out. "I had every intention to stop messaging you, but I couldn't find the courage to stop." His declaration rips at my resolve against him.

I take a few deep breaths and consider his level of betrayal.

No. He's good at lying and saying anything to keep me hooked. No more.

"I can't trust you when all you do is lie." My voice cracks.

His eyes soften around the edges. "I promise that every conversation we had was real. The person I am with you…that's who I am. You probably know me better than anyone." He trips over his words.

"I don't care." I shake my head. How can he expect me to believe a single word out of his mouth?

"I swear I wanted to tell you."

"But let me guess—there was never a right time."

He nods.

I let out a shrill laugh. "You liars are all the same. It's amazing how no matter the circumstance, people like you find a way to justify your actions with the same cliché reason." Lance gave me a similar speech after I caught him in the act with Tammy, and now Rowan's doing the same. The truth is that there never will be a right time to break someone's heart.

He blinks at me. "I understand you're upset—"

A strange noise escapes my throat. "Upset doesn't begin to cover how I feel."

I thought I had a chance with Rowan. It might look stupid now, but we seemed…connected. And with Scott—I've spent too many hours feeling guilty over kissing Rowan while texting him.

At least you know the truth now. Before you invested your heart in a losing battle.

I stand with shaky legs and grab my backpack from the floor.

"What are you doing?" He rises above me.

"I'm leaving. We're done here."

"That's it? I deserve an opportunity to explain myself and make it up to you."

I shake my head. "Are you for real? You deserve nothing but a courtesy hello whenever we pass each other in a hallway."

"You're going to throw months of friendship away because of this? I'm coming clean now when I didn't need to. Doesn't that count for something?"

Does he seriously believe him being honest is some kind of achievement? I stare at him, unsure how the hell he could expect anything close to appreciation.

He's a man who gets everything he wants. You're probably the first person who dares to tell him no.

"We were never friends to begin with. You made sure of that when you decided to lie to me as Scott while manipulating my attraction for Rowan." I release a bitter laugh. "Maybe the reason you don't have friends has nothing to do with being awkward or wanting to protect yourself from other people. It's because you are so damn cynical about everyone and everything. Who would want to open themselves up to someone like that? I sure as hell don't."

He recoils, and I instantly feel shitty. This isn't me. I'm not the kind of person who hurts others on purpose.

I sigh, trying to gain control over my temper. "Maybe one day you'll be open to the idea of showing the world the real you, rather than hiding behind your mask of indifference. Life's too short to hide who you are because you're afraid of getting hurt.

Just like life's too short for me to give someone like you another chance."

I've never seen Rowan wince before, and it makes me sick to my stomach to upset him like this. I don't want to hurt him despite everything he did, but I won't be silenced anymore. I spent too much time holding back because I was afraid of standing up for myself. I did it when Lance stole my idea, and I allowed it when Regina treated me poorly because she felt like it.

Not anymore.

I leave without giving him a second glance.

I slam the door to my bedroom and drop onto my bed in a huff.

Claire pops her head in. One side of her head is still curly while the other side is straight as a pin. "What happened?"

I sit up. "Remember Scott?"

"How can anyone forget *Scott*?" She says his name in a sing-song kind of way.

"Well, I plan on it. I want to pretend he never existed, seeing as he never did." My voice cracks.

"What are you even talking about? Was he a grandpa after all? I had a feeling after he quoted *Casablanca* that one time."

"No. I wish that were my issue. That would be way easier than the alternative."

She hops on my bed and crosses her legs. "What happened?"

My bottom lip wobbles. "Turns out *Scott* is actually Rowan."

Her mouth opens before closing again. "Oh. Wow. I didn't expect that."

I drop my head in my hands. "You and me both."

"How did you find out?"

I spill all the details I know up until this point. Claire listens to every word, only interrupting to ask for clarifications when she's confused.

She clasps her hands together. "Well, this isn't the worst news."

"How could you even say that? He lied!" I grab a pillow and hold it to my chest.

"Sure. I'm not excusing that. But at least now you don't have to feel guilty about being interested in both of them."

"That's because I'm not interested in either of them anymore."

"Well, shit. Of course not. He really screwed up."

"I thought… He seemed—I mean…" I can't find the words to describe how I feel. The other day, I wondered if Rowan could be someone I could see myself falling in love with. But after this, I don't know how he expects me to forgive him. Because if he could lie to my face for months, what's to say he won't lie to me whenever it conveniences him? I was dumb enough to not question him to begin with.

A liar is a liar, no matter what excuse they have. And honestly, I can't imagine anything is worth deceiving me for as long as he did.

CHAPTER TWENTY-EIGHT

Rowan

Am I cynical? Yes.

But afraid? Absolutely not.

I'll prove it to Zahra. I'm willing to put myself out there and be rejected if it shows her I don't need to hide behind a mask. The person I was around her is the same guy I am today, and I'll make sure she doesn't have a reason to doubt me. She's the first person I let down some of my walls for. Not even my brothers know me like she does, so I'm not about to walk away because she challenged me.

I sigh. Tonight didn't go close to plan at all. The way Zahra reacted to my hidden identity was anything but ideal. I might have been too optimistic about the potential outcome, expecting her to forgive me because she understood where I was coming from. But I didn't have a real chance to explain my past and why I would be hesitant to begin with. And honestly, there's a part of me that wonders if it's even worth exposing myself considering the risk of Zahra not forgiving me.

I need to regroup and plan what to do next. Instead of working until late, I wrap up for the night and go home to work out, take a shower, and eat a quick dinner. By the time I drop onto my bed, it's a quarter past midnight.

I pull out my phone and check my emails. The typical pattern I've fallen back into tonight feels emptier than usual. I've gotten used to Zahra's incessant texting and our bedtime conversations about everything under the sun.

I place my phone on my nightstand and turn on the news, hoping to bore myself to sleep.

My phone vibrates, making my heart pound faster in my chest in response. Did Zahra regret what she said in my office?

I swipe my phone off my nightstand. A heavy weight presses against my chest at the message from the group chat I share with my brothers.

Declan: Father received his own letter. It's official.

Cal follows up with a bunch of curse words.

Shit. I had a feeling he received something, so the news doesn't surprise me as much as it should. I'm more curious about what the letter said because my father's relationship with Grandpa had been strained since Mom died. The only reason Father took over as CEO after Grandpa's accident was because Declan was still too young according to Grandpa's will.

Me: Did you find out what it said?

Declan: Nothing to report yet. We should keep tabs on anything he does that we consider out of character for him.

Cal: Do you want the short or long list?

Declan: You spoke?

Cal: He called me last week out of the blue.

Me: What did he say?

Cal: He asked if I needed help. ME.

Cal: Wonder who I should thank for that awkward conversation? Jim, Jack, or Johnnie?

Declan: I warned you what would happen if you got out of control again.

Not this again. Declan already forced Cal into rehab during college. It's the tipping point that pushed their already weakening relationship to its breaking point. Declan might have done it out of love for our brother, but Cal has never gotten over it.

Me: Did he ask you anything about your letter?

Maybe he was trying to prey on Cal because he thought he could get the best answers out of him. They've always had the better relationship out of us three.

Cal: No. I don't think he knows about ours.

Declan: Let's keep it that way.

Good. One less obstacle in my way. The thought of going back to Chicago usually eases my discomfort, but it only adds to my already upset stomach. For the first time, it doesn't feel like an easy choice anymore, and I'm not sure what to make of that.

My first idea to get Zahra's attention is through her love of food. It's worked in the past, so I might as well put my theory to good use.

I find her right where I want her—in her cubicle without any Creators around us.

She stares at her computer before typing away in a blank document.

I drop the paper bag on her desk. "I come bearing an apology dinner."

She slides the bag to the corner of the desk without bothering to look away from her screen. "I'm not interested."

She continues clicking away at her computer. I grind my teeth together, unsure how to get her attention if she won't even look at me. Food should have had some effect on her, especially if she's hungry. Yet it seems to only work if she actually wants my company.

"How about some apology cupcakes I made myself? Ani gave me her recipe." I grab the plastic container out of the bag and place it closer to her.

Okay, fine. Ani baked them under my supervision but whatever.

She looks over at me. Her eyes remain glued to my face. "Are you here for work-related reasons?"

I frown at the coldness of her tone. "No."

"Then get out. I don't want to talk to you."

Shit. This version of Zahra is new. I think it's worse than

how she reacted after I made my stupid comments about her mentorship program.

"At least give me a chance to explain. I didn't go about things the right way the first time, but I have a reason."

"There's no reason in the world that is good enough." She stands, grabs the bag of food, and shoves it into my arms. She tucks the container of cupcakes on top of the Chinese food, watching to make sure she doesn't ruin the icing. I don't deserve that niceness, but she gives it to me anyway because she's just that damn good.

I'm nothing but screwed up—both in my actions and in my way of thinking.

I hate the glare she sends my way. I'm more interested in making her smile, and I feel extra shitty that I'm the reason behind her anger.

If only you had confessed sooner...

"Zahra, I shouldn't have lied about Scott. I used him as a way to—"

My voice is cut off by her packing up her backpack and shutting off her computer. "Where are you going?"

She doesn't bother to look at me. "I'm going home. Maybe you should do the same."

I want to tell her that home is just another empty place that makes me miserable. But I don't have a chance to say a single word as she exits the cubicle, leaving me standing there with a bag filled with untouched takeout food and this void feeling in my chest.

"So let's say someone hypothetically hurt your sister."

"Oh no." Ani presses a hand against her head.

I readjust my position on the bench so I can get a good look at her. "What?"

"*You're* the one who hurt my sister?"

"No." *Yes*. But how does she know that?

"I knew she was upset!" Ani jumps up from the bench and starts pacing.

I bristle. "What do you mean?"

"Because she canceled on us for dinner. She only misses family time when she's sad or sick."

Fuck. That's the last thing I want. "I messed up."

Ani rolls her eyes. "I see."

"How can I fix it?"

"Depends on what you did."

Am I really going to confess my issues to Ani to understand her sister better?

Yeah, I guess I am. "Well, it started with a bad idea." I go off, explaining every decision I made up until this point about Zahra. The more I rehash, the worse I feel about it. Ani's facial expressions don't help.

"What? Say something."

She shrugs. "She really liked Scott. I heard her talk about him to Claire."

I wince. "Help me come up with an idea on how to get her back and I'll owe you anything."

"Anything?"

I nod.

Ani tucks her hair behind her ear. "I don't know. If she thinks you're like Lance, she might never give you another chance."

I'm not going to even entertain that option. "Okay. That's fair. But if you were me, what would you do?"

"Easy. Give her a reason to trust you. A really good reason." Ani answers me like it's the simplest idea in the world.

Except I have no idea how to get someone to trust me. I've never had a reason to do so.

"How do I do that? She doesn't believe anything I say."

"You're a smart guy. Figure it out."

I peer inside Zahra's cubicle. If she feels my gaze on her, she ignores it. The only way I can tell my presence bothers her is based on her tiny frown.

I step into the forbidden zone and take a seat on the corner of her desk. Her eyes narrow at her paper. Today's pin looks like the seventies threw up, with the groovy *flower power* text surrounded by flowers. It matches her vintage T-shirt and bell-bottom jeans. I haven't seen Zahra match her outfit to her pin before but it's cute.

"We need to talk."

Her only response is the crinkling of the pages beneath her tense fingers. The silence grows between us to an uncomfortable level.

"It's considered rude to ignore your boss."

Her jaw ticks.

I peek over at the paper she has in her hands and read the title. *No way.*

I rip the application out of her hands.

She spins in her chair and stares at me head-on. "Give it back."

"No."

Her nostrils flare. "You're acting like a child."

Am I? I'm too far gone to care as I shred the paper into four parts. She blinks at me like I've gone crazy. And honestly, maybe I have, but she can't seriously be considering this alternative. I won't allow it.

"You're not quitting." I dump the job resignation in the trash bin underneath her desk. Because I'm a bastard, I make sure my fingers skim her body. Despite her skin being blocked by a pair of jeans, her soft inhale of breath tells me everything.

No matter the time, place, or circumstance, Zahra is attracted to me. Nothing she says or does will tell me otherwise. While I might have messed up, I'm done giving her time to think things over.

She crosses her arms. "You can't force me to stay here."

"I could."

She gapes at me. "No. Things are getting too complicated."

"Then *un*complicate them."

"I can't simply shut off my feelings and carry on with life like none of this happened." She gestures between us with a slight frown.

"I didn't mean to hurt you." The thought makes my heart squeeze uncomfortably in my chest.

"You lied about who you were for *months*. I felt guilty for being interested in two different guys while you knew the entire time who I was. That's cruel." Her voice cracks.

My entire body responds to the way her eyes shine from unshed tears. Her reaction is nothing close to something I'm equipped to deal with. I don't know the first thing about working through someone else's emotions, least of all when I'm the cause of all the hurt.

I reach out for her hand, wanting to break through her cold exterior. She takes a deep inhale as she rolls her chair as far away as it can go.

Her rejection stings more than I care to admit. I hate the distance between us. We didn't spend months getting to know each other for her to pull away like this.

"Give me one chance to explain myself. If you're not convinced that I'm sorry"—my voice drops out of habit—"then I won't bother you about this again. I'll let you quit."

"Really?" Her entire face lights up.

Her excitement only emboldens me to prove her wrong. "*Really.*"

She nods. "Okay. One try. I mean it."

Her enthusiasm is bordering on insulting. When I told her I had a competitive streak, I meant it. She's not getting away. I only need to find out how to keep her.

"Perfect." I hold my hand out to shake on it.

Zahra grabs my extended hand. My skin sparks with the same feeling whenever she touches me. I trace her delicate fingers with my thumb before letting go. She tries to hide her shudder and fails.

"I'll see you tonight." I can't let her build her walls any higher. Giving her more time will only add to her skepticism about my intentions. I might like a challenge but I'm no fool.

"Tonight?!" she squeaks.

I tuck my hands in my pockets to avoid doing something crazy like touching her. "First rule of business—always discuss the terms before agreeing."

CHAPTER TWENTY-NINE

Zahra

The house is exactly something I'd expect Brady Kane to build for himself. The cute wraparound porch looks empty but well-loved, with a bench swing and a series of rocking chairs moving softly from the wind. It's a house built for a family, and I can imagine he spent many years here with his.

I walk up the steps. My hand hovers over the doorbell, but I'm hesitant to press the button.

Might as well hurry up and get tonight over with. I press the doorbell and wait. The wood door creaks open less than a minute later, and I'm hit with a version of Rowan I've yet to see. I blink twice to confirm he's wearing sweatpants and a T-shirt. He has a new pair of glasses, this time with a tortoise-shell pattern.

My eyes drag across the contours of his body before landing on his naked feet. His entire outfit seems like a completely unfair war tactic against my racing heart. *It's... He's... Ugh!*

I frown. "Hi."

He makes a show of checking me out. Somehow, he makes my bell-bottom jeans and vintage T-shirt feel inappropriate.

He opens the door wider, giving me space to enter. But not enough, because his body remains in the middle of the doorframe, forcing our skin to brush against each other.

He leads me toward a dimly lit living room fit for a family of fifty. The massive couch reminds me of a cloud I want to dive into while the carpet is plush enough to take a nap on.

He points me toward a cushion on the floor.

"This seems an awful lot like a date," I mutter under my breath.

"Don't be difficult. I know you're hungry."

I glare at him, hating that he's right. I drop onto the cushion and cross my legs. He grabs the bag, removes the cartons, and serves me a plate of my favorite pad thai. My stupid heart betrays me, clenching at the smallest hint of Rowan's attention to detail.

Get a grip. It's just dinner.

I straighten my spine. "Well. Let's hear your apology."

"Eat first."

I roll my eyes at his command and keep my hands settled on my lap.

He sighs. "Please eat? I don't want it to get cold."

A ghost of a smile crosses my lips at his request. I only comply because I'm starving. Rowan takes a bite of his food with every bit of elegance I expect from American royalty. If only I looked half that good while eating.

We both eat in silence. I hate it enough to speak up because I can't take it anymore.

"So you like to draw?"

His fork clatters against the plate.

Well, aren't I the queen of casual conversations? I grin at my plate because making Rowan uncomfortable has become my new favorite game tonight.

He picks up his fork and twirls some noodles. "I used to love drawing."

"Why did you stop?"

Rowan's shoulders tense before he releases a shaky breath. "Why do most people stop doing things they love?"

I relate to that question. After everything Lance did, I stopped wanting to create anything. I paused my dreams because it seemed easier than facing the pain of his betrayal. The path of least resistance included shutting down things I loved because I was too afraid of the backlash.

At least until Rowan threw me out of my comfort zone. And for that, I'm indebted to him. It doesn't make his choices correct, but it makes me a bit more forgiving. Because without him taking a chance on my drunken proposal, I wouldn't have finally let go of the last bit of hurt holding me back.

The only person who has power over me is myself. Not Lance. Not my past mistakes. And definitely not fear.

I pluck at a loose thread on my jeans. "I'm not asking about people. I'm asking about you."

"You're not going to make this easy for me, are you?"

"If apologizing were easy, everyone would do it."

He readjusts his glasses in a way that has my thighs pressing together to stop the dull throb. I swear he only wore them to wear me down.

"My grandpa got me into drawing at a very young age."

I stay silent and waiting, not wanting to spook him.

"He always had a special something with my brothers and me, and drawing happened to be our thing. I was the only artistic one of my family besides him so I think he enjoyed having that kind of connection."

"That's sweet."

His lips press together in a thin line. "The bond I had with my grandfather was different from the one I shared with my father. And I think that frustrated my father. He was never artsy and that was all I wanted to do as a kid. It was like he didn't know how to connect with me in a way that didn't involve throwing a ball around." His eyes seem distant, like he's picturing his life at another time. "I don't remember my parents arguing much, but when they did, it was usually about me." He winces. "Dad would get angry because he didn't know how to bond with me, so Mom would cry. It got particularly worse once my mom got sick. I think she was worried my father and I would never be close, and she wouldn't be there to help us."

My entire chest aches at the look on Rowan's face. "Cancer, right?"

His throat bobs as he nods.

"I'm sorry." I grab his hand and give it a reassuring squeeze.

He clears his throat and looks down at his plate. "That was the start of my rocky relationship with my father. Eventually, I gave up on drawing and moved on to more appropriate activities that were expected of me."

I want to beg him to tell me all the stories because I'm desperate to learn more about the man sitting across from me.

Rowan's probably spent years with pent-up emotions. The way he speaks of his mother, laced with pain breaking through his emotionless facade, has my heart cracking.

"What made you want to stop?"

"It's…complex."

I think he might hold back, but he continues. "He might have not intentionally told me to stop, but he made sure to take the joy out of it. Whenever I had an exhibition, he wouldn't show up, so I had to watch all the other kids' parents celebrate while I stood there by myself. It got to the point that I refused to participate anymore, despite my grandfather trying. Then there was a time that he found all the old cards I drew for my mom while she was in the hospital—" His voice shakes. "He ruined them because he felt like it. They were some of the last memories I had of her, and they were gone after a drunken rampage."

"Drunken rampage?"

A vein in his jaw ticks. "Forget I said anything about that."

But I can't. I want to go back in time and protect Rowan.

"It's okay if you can't talk about it." I reach out and place my palm on his clenched fist.

"I owe you after everything." He releases it, giving me room to interlace our fingers.

I give his hand another squeeze before pulling away. "I'm not going to use an apology as a way to pull information out of you. It's your choice to share your past."

He looks at me. As if his eyes are gauging my soul, assessing me for deception. "You mean that?"

"Of course. But will you tell me what made you want to start drawing again? If that's okay."

He nods. "Because your drawings were terrible, and I had this burning desire to help you."

"You started drawing again because of *me*?"

"Yes," he mumbles under his breath.

I smile and nod. "Oh, wow. Why?"

"You almost cried during your first presentation."

"*And*?" This is the same man who told me he had no fucks to give. His wanting to help me without even really knowing me… it makes no sense.

"In the beginning, I only wanted to help you because I thought it was beneficial for me. You have the kind of talent I was looking for to renovate the park and make sure—" He blinks twice, catching himself midsentence.

"Make sure what?"

"Make sure I make my grandfather happy." He frowns again. Does he hate the idea of needing to lean on someone?

"I understand. You have a lot of pressure riding on this project."

"You have no idea," he grumbles under his breath.

"Why didn't you hire someone else to help me?"

"I thought of it but didn't want to."

"Why?"

"Because my common sense escaped me."

"Or you liked me." I try my hardest not to smile but fail miserably.

"Definitely not. I found you oddly annoying and way too nice at the time."

I lean over the coffee table and give his shoulder a shove. "Hey! There's no such thing as being too nice."

"There is where I come from."

"And that is?"

His eyes reflect enough disgust to nauseate me. "A place where people smile too brightly or talk too sweetly because they have every intention of using it against me. It's the whole damn reason I'm cynical in the first place."

"That sounds awful."

"I'm sure you would be horrified to know what kind of people are lurking beyond the park's pearly gates. Dreamland really is some fantasy. It's like this whole damn place is untouched by the real world."

"Tell me about what you had to deal with then. Help me understand why you are the way you are."

His fists clench against the coffee table. "You really want to know?"

I nod.

"Fine. But it's not pretty."

"The truth usually isn't."

He blinks at me. His eyes drag from my face to his clenched fists, where he opens and closes them repeatedly.

He sighs after what feels like a minute of silence. "My first real taste of the scum of the earth started in college when a random girl invited me back to her dorm after a party."

My appetite shifts to nausea at the mention of him being with someone else.

"Before, I had only dealt with the typical stupid teen stuff—like people using me for a private jet or a trip to Cabo."

"Oh yeah, the *typical* stuff."

He cracks the saddest smile before it falls flat. "Well, where

I came from, people have used me throughout my life, but it had never taken a turn toward anything illegal until I became an adult. College was eye-opening. I lost my virginity while unknowingly being filmed with a hidden camera. It cost my father a lot of money to sweep that issue under the rug before she went to the media with the tape."

The food I ate doesn't sit well with his admission. "Are you serious? That's disgusting! Why would you pay her off? She's the one in the wrong."

"Because I wasn't going to risk it. A tape like that could be devastating if it got out, so we paid her to stay quiet and turn it over."

I can't do anything but stare at him.

He lets out a bitter laugh. I've never heard it before, and I hope I don't hear it again because it makes my entire body chilled to the bone. "That was only my first experience. College was full of shit but even that was tame compared to adulthood."

"Oh God. There are things worse than blackmail?" Seriously, I thought money meant security, but realistically, it only further complicates life.

He nods. "I've dealt with it all. Women stabbing sealed condoms with safety pins when they thought I wasn't looking. Someone trying to drug my drink at a bar. There was this one ti—"

I wave my hand. "How can you talk about this like it doesn't bother you?"

He frowns. "Because I got to a point where I learned to expect it from other people. You can't be bothered by something you already anticipate happening."

"I thought these kinds of things only happened in movies." I don't know what makes me more ill—the idea of Rowan with another woman or a woman trying to purposefully trap him with a baby.

"I'm only scraping the surface. Each situation was a lesson for me—a way to prove that my brothers were right about how shitty people are."

My lips part. "How did you survive growing up in a place like that?"

"Because you either bend to the will of monsters or you easily become the prey."

I blink twice, waiting for the end of the joke, yet Rowan's jaw remains clamped shut.

"Is that why you lied? Because you're so used to people doing the same thing to you?"

There it is. The truth laid out right in front of us, waiting for his confirmation.

"I did it because I thought I was justified. I had no reason to trust you at all, and I never imagined I would feel all this."

"Feel what?"

He lifts his glasses and rubs his eyes. "I'm bound to fuck all this up."

I release a shaky breath. "Okay, well, try your best not to."

He pushes his plate away from him. "My initial reason for speaking to you was selfish and cruel. I was interested in uncovering the kind of person you were. I honestly thought you were a fraud, and I wanted to prove myself right."

His words *hurt*. I thought his intentions might have been misplaced but sweet, but this alternative is the worst-case scenario.

"I feel sorry for someone like you who grew up surrounded by so many vicious people. I really do."

His upper lip curls. "There's a reason we live by the motto *money over morals*."

"There are two ways to be rich in life, and one of them has nothing to do with a bank account."

"I see that now. I see that in *you*."

My heartbeat picks up, pounding harder against my sternum as if it wants to tell Rowan it's listening too.

His eyes remain locked on mine. "I thought you would extort me for money after that kiss. Part of me anticipated it, if only to prove you were just as selfish as the rest of us. Because how could you not want to milk me for money if I harassed you like I did? There were times I even wondered if you would attempt something else to only exacerbate the issue."

"That's sad, Rowan. I told you I wouldn't do that."

"I don't have a good track history with trust."

"Yeah, I see." And it makes me so damn sad.

I walked in here expecting to not fall for anything Rowan said because in my head, I thought nothing would be good enough. But this reality…it's tragic. The kind of life he has lived up until this point is anxiety provoking. I'd rather be poor and happy than rich and miserable any day of the year.

"You proved me wrong every time you spoke to me. You didn't even know who I was and you were willing to make me feel like I mattered to someone."

My whole resolve crumbles in front of me like a house of cards.

"I was proud to make your drawings. It made me feel happy

to make you happy." His voice cracks and I feel the sound straight through my heart.

His eyes find mine. "As I spent time getting to know you, I confirmed my deepest suspicion in a completely different way. You are so much more than you let on—but in a way that makes you priceless."

Priceless? Don't you dare cry, Zahra.

"You're selfless, caring, and willing to go above and beyond to help those around you. You tutor kids for free, and you bring a grumpy old man bread and cookies. And the selfish part of me wanted to steal a piece of you for myself. You reminded me of what it was like to not feel so damn lonely all the time, and I didn't want to lose that."

How in the world can I respond to that? I don't have a chance because Rowan keeps talking.

"I took your kindness for granted, and I abused your trust. So for that, I'm sorry."

I blink away my tears. "What made you want to confess?"

"I couldn't keep pretending after our day at Dreamland. I became addicted to the way you made me feel, to the point that I couldn't find a way to tell you who I really was. I was afraid and I didn't want it to end. So, instead of giving myself up, I found ways to spend time with you as Rowan while purposefully stealing the rest of your attention as Scott. It was a stupid idea. It was unfair of me, but I don't regret a single thing except hurting you."

Wetness emerges, making my tear ducts full. I've never heard Rowan talk this much, and I realize it's such a shame. The way he speaks…it's beautiful. He makes me feel beautiful. Not the superficial kind either, but in a way that makes me proud of who

I am. In a way that makes me think he cares about my soul first and foremost.

He might have lied, but his intentions behind continuing the fantasy are so damn sad that I want to cry for him. What kind of person is so lonely, they would willingly text someone with a pseudonym?

The one desperate to be loved back.

My throat tightens. "What about the buddies program?"

He groans. "God. I'm going to sound crazy."

The corners of my lips tug up. "Maybe I like your kind of crazy."

And I truly mean it. Anything is better than the icy exterior Rowan portrays to the world.

"I'm the one who stole all the papers except for one because I didn't want anyone to have your number."

My jaw drops open. "You what?" Holy shit. How far does all this go?

He removes his glasses and drags a hand down his face. "When you caught me, I was angry at myself for feeling so stupid, and I took it out on you. But then once I showed up at the meeting, I realized what you were trying to do for people like your sister. I attended the first one for purely selfish reasons, but I stayed because I like Ani. She makes me laugh and she's sweet, just like you."

My lashes become damp from the unshed tears. No normal man would steal all the papers with my number unless he cared. And the way he talks about Ani… It's so simple, yet it means the world to me. It's everything I wanted with Lance but was denied.

My pounding heart feels like it might escape through my throat.

Rowan likes me.

And he hates it.

My small smile becomes a grin.

"Why are you smiling? Did you not hear a thing I said?"

"You like me," I blurt out.

"No. I tolerate you more than most people. That's why I want to date you."

The laugh that explodes out of me has Rowan rearing back.

"You find this funny?"

"A little. But it's cute."

He sighs.

It clicks for me. "You don't like the idea of liking me."

"I can't promise you that I won't mess up again. I'm learning as I go, but there's something about you that makes me happy in a way I haven't felt before. So if you want to quit, I understand, but go knowing that I never wanted to harm you or make you feel like a fool." He stares at me, making me feel exposed in a whole new kind of way.

He cares about you. Really, truly cares.

"I think part of me wants to dislike you for being mistrusting, but part of me can't help but relate."

He doesn't move or breathe. "What do you mean? You're the most trusting person of all."

I release a sad laugh. After all he has confessed, it's only fair to share my story. "My last boyfriend broke my heart and my trust the day I found him with another woman. She— God. It's something I can never unsee." I've tried to wipe the memory of them from my brain, but some parts still leak through. "And because one blow to my life wasn't enough, Lance—my ex—demolished a part of my heart I'll never get back."

"What did he do?" His voice is low, carrying the same kind of lethality as his gaze.

I look away, unable to hold his stare. "He stole my Nebula Land submission, impressed the Creators, and used the bonus to buy his lover an engagement ring." The words leave my mouth in a rush, sounding clunky and unrehearsed.

He leans over the table, gently cups my chin, turns my head to face him. "While I'm sorry he hurt you, I'm not sorry he let you go."

I shoot him a wobbly smile. "Are you always so selfish?"

His eyes glint. "With you, yes."

I shake my head.

He tucks my hair behind my ear before tracing my earrings with his finger. I shiver, and goose bumps explode across my skin.

"I might be many things but I'm no cheater. And while I lied to you about everything before, I won't do it anymore. That I can assure you."

I swallow, fighting the tightness in my throat. "So that's it? I'm supposed to take your word for it and hope for the best?"

"No, I know firsthand how words mean nothing."

"Then what?"

He leans in and presses a featherlight kiss against my lips. "I'll prove it to you."

"How so?"

His eyes brighten in a way I've never seen before. "Would you rather me show or tell you?" His husky tone makes my cheeks heat.

And the smile on his face? Absolutely, positively devious.

But the way he crawls over to me on his knees?

I'd agree to anything from that one action alone.

CHAPTER THIRTY

Rowan

Zahra's perfume wraps around me like an aphrodisiac. I take a seat in front of her before pulling her onto my lap. The side of her body remains tucked against my chest, giving her space to leave if she wants.

"What's it going to be?" I tuck her hair behind her ear before leaning in to whisper. "Show or tell?"

I'm having an out-of-body experience where I want to do something for myself that defies my usual logic. That doesn't require a list, risk analysis, or excessive thinking. I want to be free, if only for a few months while I'm still here.

My tongue darts out, tasting her skin before pulling back.

She sucks in a breath and leans into me. "Show. Always show."

I chuckle low under my breath. I return my lips back to her neck to hide the way my cheeks burn. "There's no going back after this."

"I say there's no time like the present." She turns toward me and presses a soft kiss against my lips. Her tongue darts out, tracing the seam of my lips. Something inside me snaps. Months of buildup unleash, and I let it all out. Our lips fuse together as we kiss like never before.

My head wages war with my entire body, warning me away from the rush of feelings firing off inside of me. Kissing Zahra is like tasting the sweetest poison.

Zahra twists and wraps her legs around me, pushing her jean-covered center against my growing cock. The friction of her body against my sweatpants has me panting into her mouth.

The entire world fades away as we tease, nip, kiss. Two tongues dueling against one another for dominance. Zahra tugs on my hair at the nape of my neck, adding a touch of pain. I take it as permission to wrap my hands around the globes of her ass and squeeze, making her gasp against my mouth. She forces my neck to the side, giving her the perfect angle to kiss the column of my neck.

My touch becomes exploratory as she gains the courage to do what she wants with my body. Her tongue darts out and tastes my sensitive skin. My head drops back and I groan, which only encourages her boldness. Zahra grinds herself against my stiff cock. I can't stop my eyes from rolling into the back of my head.

Zahra kisses with a wildness I want to match. Like she senses the kind of man I've kept trapped for years and wants to unleash it. Instead of giving in to the fear and pulling back, I bring her lips back to mine and unlock the part of myself I've hidden away from the world.

Heat explodes down my spine as she rubs against my dick in

the best kind of rhythm. I moan into her mouth, and she sucks up the sound like it never existed.

I pull away with a ragged breath. "If you want to stop, now's the time."

She blinks in confusion. "What?"

"If you don't want to keep going—"

Her lips slam against mine, removing any other doubts. With her legs wrapped around me, I rise on shaky legs. She laughs and holds on tighter, making my dick throb as I take the steps up to my room. Each step to my bedroom is a struggle as her lips do all kinds of things to my neck.

I drop Zahra on my bed. She releases an audible breath that turns into a moan as I drop to my knees and make quick work of her jeans.

Her gaze burns as she props herself up on her elbows.

I place a soft kiss on the inside of her thigh before sliding her underwear down her legs. "Enjoying the show?"

"I like how you look begging on your hands and knees."

"I don't beg."

"Practice makes perfect."

I take her challenge for exactly what it is. I shove her legs apart and trail kisses up her thighs before devouring her like a man starved. Her arousal coats my tongue, and my eyes roll into the back of my head. Her groan matches mine. I run the tip of my tongue in a straight line from her pussy to her clit. I'm rewarded with a scream and her back bowing off the bed.

I leave no part of Zahra untouched or unfucked. My tongue brands her pussy, showing her exactly who owns her. Her legs tremble against my shoulders. I drive her to the edge only to rip her orgasm away before she has a chance to explode. She groans and clutches onto my hair in a death grip. I only smile before dragging my tongue from her entrance to her clit, giving it a good suck.

I thought Zahra's laughs were addictive, but the breathless moans she releases are fucking intoxicating. It's something I could hear for the rest of my life and never grow bored or tired. I insert a finger and groan, finding her soaked for me. Her back arches off the bed, and I stop and stare. She grows more restless under my gaze, and I reward her mumbled curse word with a second finger.

It fills me with deep satisfaction knowing this version of Zahra is all mine. No amount of money, fame, or power could steal her away from me. I'm the one she's desperate to have between her legs. It's my name that she screams up to the ceiling as I insert a third finger into her.

She's all mine.

For now.

I shake the feeling away and change my tempo, pumping my fingers into her faster as my lips wrap around her clit and suck.

Heat rushes down my spine as Zahra falls apart in front of me. I don't stop my torment until her moans turn into heavy pants. I press a soft kiss against her thigh before rising on shaky legs.

"Did I meet your expectations?"

"I couldn't spell the word *expectations*, let alone define them right now."

I laugh as I lean over her and prop myself on my elbows.

"You have the best laugh." She runs a hand against my spine, sending another shiver down my body. Her lips press against mine. I shudder as she runs her tongue across my lips, tasting her arousal.

I grab the hem of her shirt and remove it. Her bra doesn't last long after getting in the way of my tongue and her breasts. My lips kiss a path from one to the other, sucking enough to leave a mark after. She turns me into a fucking animal.

All I want to do is bring her pleasure. To have her clawing at the sheets because she can't get enough.

Her fingers reach out and trace the outline of my cock. I grab onto both her wrists and lock them in place by her head. "This isn't about me tonight."

I mean it. I didn't invite her over for sex, but her in my bed happens to be a bonus.

She pouts. "You don't want me to help you with that problem?"

"Take a man out to dinner first."

"Does my pussy count?"

"*Fuck*."

Her legs wrap around me again, and she pulls my hips forward so my shielded erection presses against her heat. She takes advantage of my shock and rips her hands away from my grasp.

"Stop being noble. It doesn't suit you." Her palm traces the band of my sweatpants. She drags them down, along with my boxer briefs. My shirt finds a similar new home on the floor.

"I can't offer anything more than something casual."

She pauses, tilting her head at me. "That's fine."

Really? I expected her to hesitate at the very least. "I mean it."

She rolls her eyes. "I'm sure you do. Now stop being a cliché and get on with the show."

My expression turns predatory.

Zahra's hands drag across my chest, tracing the ridges of muscle. "This is unfair."

"You won't be complaining in a couple of minutes." I reach over to my nightstand and grab a condom from an emergency pack I snagged from the family's private jet last week. She plucks the golden foil packet from my hands before tracing the vein on the underside of my cock with her index finger. My nails dig into my palms.

She teases me some more before rolling the condom down my shaft. Somehow everything she does is sensual, and I'm desperate to experience more.

"Just to be clear, should I scream your name or Scott's when you fuck me?"

I shove her down against the bed, and she laughs as the air gets knocked out of her. "I dare you."

Her toes curl in front of me. *Little hellion.*

"Spoiler warning—if you do, you might not be able to walk home tomorrow." I trace her pussy with the pad of my thumb. I sink two fingers inside of her and withdraw them to find her still soaked.

"Walking is overrated anyway." Her eyes lock on my glistening fingers as I bring them up to my mouth and lick the shine right off them.

Her breath hitches and her eyes widen. I want to recreate that look when I'm fucking the oxygen straight out of her lungs.

Zahra's eyes remain enraptured as I line up my cock and slowly push inside of her. Her legs wrap around my hips, keeping me locked in place.

As if I would ever leave paradise now that I've found it.

She shudders as I slowly withdraw to press into her a bit more. Her back arches as I repeat the move, only this time gaining another inch. Her pussy clutches onto my cock. Each thrust gets me one inch closer to being seated inside her. The heels of her feet press into my ass cheeks, pulling me flush against her.

"Fuck me like you mean it already," she rasps.

A shiver shoots down my spine at her command and I thrust forward one last time to the hilt. Her back arches, revealing her full breasts to me. I bend over and swipe my tongue over her nipple.

Zahra moaning is a sweet harmony to my ears.

I smile against her skin. "I have one last question."

She growls at me, and I find it hot as fuck.

I rise, tracing the curve of her body before giving her ass a squeeze. I withdraw my shaft a couple of inches before slamming back into her. The whoosh of air that leaves her makes me grin. "Do you still want that measuring tape? I can go find one now and settle the debate."

"All good. I'm pretty sure I can feel you in my throat."

Fire spreads across my skin as I pick up my pace. Sweat clings to our bodies as we find a steady rhythm. We're two people, lost to the harmony of our deep breaths, slaves to each other's erotic touches.

I ram into her over and over again. She shakes with every thrust, and I take pleasure in watching her breasts bounce every damn time. I've never seen anything as beautiful as her in the throes of passion. The tight sensation that only seems to happen whenever she's around increases to the point of pain. I push in and out of her like I've lost my goddamn mind, which isn't far from the truth. I immerse myself in the feel of her and hang onto every single sound she makes.

No area of my skin goes untouched. Her nails embed themselves into my back and she bites at the most sensitive place on my entire neck. She's wilder than I could have ever imagined, and I want to test her limits.

It turns out I was right. Little Miss Bubbly does have a hidden side to her. I just never expected it to be this… The woman she is in the bedroom is everything I could have wanted and more.

If this is what it feels like to be around someone who's pure sunshine, I'll willingly accept the burn. Every. Damn. Time.

Her second orgasm shoves me over the edge, and the next thing I know, I'm free-falling along with her straight into darkness.

CHAPTER THIRTY-ONE

Zahra

I've officially passed the point of no return.

Okay, well I passed it the moment Rowan made me orgasm the first time tonight. But it really hits me once Rowan withdraws his softening cock from me and gets rid of the condom.

I'm absolutely useless after Rowan fucked me into near unconsciousness. Whatever I thought Rowan kept trapped under his cool exterior doesn't hold a candle to tonight.

No. Rowan might as well have set my body on fire with kerosene. It was…*wow*. I think I lost some valuable brain cells from the lack of oxygen.

Do I stay? Do I go? I'm completely at a crossroads about what to do next.

Go. Keep it casual like you promised.

I rise off the bed with a groan and grab my shirt off the floor. *Now where's my bra?*

"What are you doing?" his voice snaps.

"Getting dressed?" I squeak, shielding my body from him like he hasn't seen everything already.

My cheeks heat as his eyes slide from my face to the tips of my pink toenails.

With the dim light of the bathroom, I'm able to assess the curves and contours of God's finest work. I think I release a small groan, but I can't be too sure. Rowan clears his throat, clearly covering up a low laugh.

"So…"

Don't be clingy. Act cool.

How does one act cool when they have no idea what's happening? I return to my mission of searching for my missing clothes. My bra hangs haphazardly off the lampshade, and I swoop in to grab it.

"You're leaving?" His brows pull together. Somehow he got ahold of my underwear. I'm willing to part ways with them if he's into that kind of thing. Honestly, I'm open to anything that saves me from this embarrassment.

"Umm. Isn't that what you want?"

"What gave you that idea?"

"Well—umm. You see…" My bright idea takes a dive as his jaw clenches.

"You want to go." A statement rather than a question.

Is that…hurt in his voice?

No. That can't be true.

Or is it?

Ugh. I think Rowan fucked my common sense right out of me tonight.

"Do you want me to stay?" I blurt out.

It takes him an entire twenty seconds to answer. *Yes. I counted.* It was either that or melt into a puddle under Rowan's guarded gaze.

"I wouldn't *not* like it if you stayed."

I laugh. "Oh God. You use double negatives. This was doomed from the start."

The smile he unleashes is my favorite Rowan smile—the kind that's so small, I don't want to blink and miss it. "I did that on purpose."

"Sure you did." I roll my eyes.

He rips my shirt from my hands and throws my bra over his shoulder.

Well then. I guess that debate is settled.

He throws me back onto the bed before pulling the comforter over our naked bodies. I've cuddled before, but with Rowan, it feels more intimate. Especially when he wraps an arm around me because it turns out he's a total clinger.

The shocks keep coming tonight. I'm not sure my heart can hold up against the strain.

Rowan grabs a remote and chooses the streaming app. "Which version of *Pride and Prejudice* are you up for tonight?"

"Maybe I'm in the mood for some horror film."

"Isn't romance considered a subgenre?"

I pinch his side, making him laugh. "Now you're just trying to be funny."

"Trying? I seem to recall you thinking I'm quite funny." He perks up like a total show-off, flaunting his pearly whites that threaten to blind me.

"I found the secret to making you smile!"

"What?"

"Orgasms! Why didn't I think of it sooner?!"

The laugh he lets out is unlike anything I've heard before. His head drops back against the pillow and his entire chest shakes from the sound.

I really, *really* like it.

And I know that's really, *really* bad.

But I end up thinking through every way I can make it happen again.

He dangles the remote in front of me. "Pick or I'll pick for you."

I decide now's a good test to see if *Scott* really meant some of the things he said. After all, maybe he lied about watching all seventeen versions of *Pride and Prejudice* for scientific purposes. "I'm in a Matthew MacFadyen kind of mood tonight."

In typical Rowan fashion, he chooses the right one, proving he really was crazy enough to watch all the movies. The only thing I'm not too sure about is his reasoning for doing so.

There's a small, irrational voice in my head that wants to read into the situation more, but it loses to the stronger voice that says to enjoy the moment and drop all expectations.

My walk of shame is prolonged due to the Kane house being a ten-minute walk away from my apartment. Rowan offered to drive me, but I only rolled my eyes and bid him goodbye with a deep kiss.

I could have let him. There was an honest to God part of me

that was craving that kind of attention. But I needed some distance and a walk to clear my head after a night of mind-blowing sex and worse, good conversation. I hate to admit it, but I'm still hesitant about Rowan's intentions. Dating seems like a dangerous game with someone like him.

After all, we watched the entire movie before getting into a heated debate about classicism and the divide between the haves and have-nots. Rowan tried to lecture me on upper-class problems and I tried to introduce his face to my fist.

Okay, I'm only kidding. Violence is never the answer. Although I did threaten bodily harm in the form of withholding sex, which only landed me a withheld orgasm until I apologized.

Rowan plays dirty. It's the one thing I learned, along with his dick size.

So basically, I have no idea what I'm doing with Rowan, but maybe that's a good thing. I've always been the *labels* kind of girl and it hasn't exactly worked out in my favor.

During my ten-minute walk home, I solidify my positive mindset. I'm all for keeping things casual for now. After being in a long-term relationship that went from zero to a hundred, I'm willing to take things slow and let the relationship grow on its own. While it's risky, I know Rowan cares, so there's no need to worry.

I use my key and unlock the front door. "Claire?"

The apartment is silent except for some noises coming from Claire's room. I'm smart enough to not open her door whenever I hear John Legend crooning from the doors. I value my eyesight far too much to bleach my eyes.

I walk into my bedroom, take a shower, and drop onto my

bed with a smile. John Legend's sweet voice fades into the background as I drift off.

I wake up to the smell of sizzling bacon and Claire belting out off-key to Journey. My stomach grumbles, demanding to be fed after my long night.

I find Claire in the kitchen, cooking and singing into her spatula. "Who's got you in such a good mood?"

Claire jumps in place. She turns down the volume on the small speaker. "Zahra! You're home! I didn't hear you come in."

"That's because you were a bit busy."

Claire blushes. "I've got something to share."

"Me too." I grin.

"You first," we both say at the same time before laughing.

Her smile is infectious. "I met someone!"

"Tell me more."

"Well, remember that sous chef from the Royal Chateau?"

"How could one forget Her Royal Crankiness?"

She snorts as she dishes up two plates of breakfast for lunch. "Well, she apologized."

"What?! How?"

"We ran into each other at the grocery store. It was like a movie."

"How?"

"Well, I saw her and panicked. I accidentally ran my cart into a stand full of oranges, and they toppled over in my rush. It was hands down the most embarrassing thing to ever happen to me in public."

"That can't possibly be true. Remember that time we were at the football game—"

Claire winces. "Even worse. She ended up slipping on an orange and falling."

"And then what?"

"She laughed up to the ceiling after I did a terrible 'orange you glad to see me' joke."

I throw my head back and laugh. Claire goes off, telling the rest of her story that involved an angry store manager, an unnecessary paramedic van, and a date.

Honestly, I have no idea how she's still standing after the last twenty-four hours.

I offer to clean the dishes while Claire takes a seat at the counter.

"Tell me everything!"

I take off with my story, explaining everything Rowan divulged last night and how we ended up in bed together.

"So please tell me that Rowan's looks aren't just for show."

"He's more of an action kind of guy." I grin to myself at the inside joke.

Claire cackles. "Great. I'm glad we now know he can use his tongue for good rather than evil. It's a step in the right direction."

I only laugh to myself.

"So you're what? Fuck buddies?"

I wince at her choice of words.

"Okay. No." She pauses. "How about friends with benefits?"

I shake my head. "We didn't discuss labels."

"Silly me. How could you with his dick lodged in your throat."

My sponge splashes in the soapy water after I lose my grip. "Claire!"

She raises her hands. "What?! You walked into that one."

"We didn't define what we are because there is no us. At least not in that sense of the word. We're just Zahra and Rowan. Two people having fun."

Her brows pull together, and her face takes on a serious note I rarely see. "I don't want you getting hurt. Casual relationships aren't your thing."

"Maybe that's my problem. With Lance, we dove headfirst into a relationship. I'm looking to take things slow."

"Well, hate to break it to you, but you drove past a red light at two hundred miles an hour."

A laugh bubbles out of me. "It's just sex."

"Yeah, and he's *just* the guy you've been texting every night before you go to bed."

I sigh. "Is it wrong to go with the flow and not put us into a box so soon?"

She shakes her head. "Of course not. I only want you to be careful and I don't want you to invest your heart in someone who doesn't plan on reciprocating."

"We're going to keep it casual for now."

The plan sounds solid and foolproof—the perfect way to protect my heart while having some fun.

Or so I hope.

CHAPTER THIRTY-TWO

Zahra

I walk into work Monday half expecting someone to call me out on having sex with Rowan. It's laughable how I'm acting as if I have a yellow sticker on my forehead proclaiming I did the dirty deed with my boss. It wouldn't even matter if they did know. Dreamland doesn't even have a no-fraternization policy. Although it's discouraged for individuals who work within the same workspace, it's not prohibited.

Not to mention, Rowan would never let something like sleeping together get in the way of his decisions. And the idea of him showing me preferential treatment has me wanting to work harder to show him what I'm capable of. To show myself and others that it doesn't matter who I am when my ideas speak for themselves. At least I hope so.

Yet even after creating a game plan, Monday is a complete bomb due to my fraying nerves. Rowan hasn't even graced the warehouse with his presence yet and I'm already falling apart.

This morning, I broke our communal coffeepot after someone asked me how my weekend went. And then, when someone mentioned Rowan's name in the bathroom, I ended up dropping my phone in the toilet.

That one isn't exactly my fault. Two Alpha team members were talking about Rowan in a very inappropriate way while washing their hands. My phone slipped straight out of my grasp and met its watery grave.

It's safe to say by the time Rowan strolls into my cubicle looking fresh as a daisy later this afternoon, I'm fried. Absolutely positively done with the day.

"You haven't been answering my texts."

"Hello to you too." I look up from my computer screen.

"You haven't responded to my messages." His voice is extra edgy, and I'm tempted to dance around at the idea of him worrying over me not answering him.

"Did you miss me?" I bat my lashes.

"No." He answers too fast.

I grin. "It's okay to admit your feelings. I'll wait." I turn my chair and face him.

"Just like you made me wait all day for a confirmation?"

Huh? "A confirmation?"

"Yes. I'm taking you out tomorrow night for a date."

I laugh under my breath. "Don't you think you should ask me first?"

"I don't ask questions I know the answers to."

"We need to work on your manners. They're severely lacking."

He steps into my space and bends down to whisper in my ear. "You weren't complaining about politeness the other night."

"Of course not. Every woman wants a gentleman in the streets and a beast in the sheets," I whisper low enough so my cubicle mates don't hear me.

His eyes glint as he takes a little bow. "Pardon my mistake then. Will you do me the honor of gracing me with your presence tomorrow evening for dinner and cocktails?"

"Emphasis on the cock?" I raise a brow.

Rowan drops his head back and laughs until I join him. It warms me from my head to my toes to see his eyes light up and his lips remain permanently upturned.

Which makes my next comment that much harder.

"I can't go out with you tomorrow. We're having a late team meeting to discuss a few loose ends on previous proposals tomorrow."

"Good thing you have an in with your boss."

"No way! That's an abuse of power."

"What's the point of having all this power if I don't use it?"

I blink at him. "I'm going to pretend you did not just say that."

"Pretend all you want. It doesn't change the outcome."

"But—"

He raises a brow. "Either you message Jenny or I will."

I glare at him. "Your bossiness is losing its charm."

He leans over, placing the softest kiss on my cheek. "We'll have to test the theory out in a few circumstances then. Just to be sure."

"You're always so thorough with everything you do."

He *grins*. "I'll see you tomorrow night." He moves away, taking his cologne and addictive pheromones with him. "And answer my messages from now on."

"I can once I get a replacement phone." I point at a bowl filled with rice.

"Do I even want to know?"

I grin. "Probably not."

Even after Rowan leaves, I can't stop smiling to myself.

Because I'm going on a date tomorrow with Rowan Don't-Know-What-the-G-Stands-For-Yet Kane.

Power wears many faces. Tonight, mine is drawn from the look on Rowan's face when I exit my apartment.

"You look like…a princess." He rubs his jaw.

I beam as I run a hand down the bottom half of my yellow dress, pressing down the puffy tulle. My mom made it for me after I raved about a similar dress on a celebrity. Against my brown skin, the material reminds me of early morning sunrays.

Rowan's gaze becomes lethal. His eyes flick from my corset top to my fluffy skirt.

While he's looking at me, I stare at him. Out of all his suits, this one is by far my favorite. I'm not sure if he knows that. The way the royal blue material plasters against his skin has me wanting to invite him into my apartment and forget all about our dinner plans.

Our eyes connect. He curses at whatever look I have written all over my face. Before I have a chance to say anything, he grabs my hand and hauls me away, muttering under his breath the entire time.

"Garfield."

Rowan's hand on my thigh flexes. "God, no." He hasn't stopped touching me since I entered his Rolls Royce. Apparently, people like the Kanes reach a level of wealth where they don't even have to drive their own cars anymore. At first, I thought it was ridiculous. But then, the freedom gives Rowan the ability to run his hands up and down my thigh. Despite the obscene amount of layers to the tulle skirt, his fingers send flames of heat up my thigh with every enticing swipe.

I peek down at the list of names I saved after wondering what the heck Rowan's middle name was. After searching all over the internet, and some sketchy websites that requested lots of money for a background check, I settled on a list of baby names from a website.

Except I'm twenty names in and have struck out with each one.

"Gary."

His chest shakes from silent laughter. "No."

"Gertrude."

"That's a woman's name."

I shrug. "Your mom could have been progressive."

Shoot. I didn't mean to bring her up. The Kanes are like a vault when it comes to anything related to Rowan's mother. The only thing the general public knows is she died after a long, terrible battle with cancer.

He squeezes my thigh as if he wants to reassure me. "My mother was many great things, but even she wasn't *that* progressive. Thank God."

"Hmm. Okay! What about Glen?"

"You'll never guess, so you might as well give up now."

I make eye contact with him and jut out my bottom lip. "I'm no quitter."

He rubs my lip with his thumb, making heat trickle down my spine in response. "That's why I'll reward you with the story of how I got my middle name. But I must swear you to secrecy."

I hold out my pinky for him.

He bats it away before leaning forward, cupping my cheek with a calloused hand. "A kiss for a secret."

"I've never heard of this game." I smirk.

"That's because it's exclusively ours."

Warmth shoots through my chest at the idea of us having something to ourselves. "I like this game already."

His hand wraps around the back of my neck and tugs me forward. His lips press against mine, soft at first before giving way to a burning hunger. Heat spreads across my skin as Rowan brands my lips with his tongue, tracing a pattern I feel down to my very heart.

He kisses me until I'm breathless and panting. His eyes lose their brightness as they slide from my face to the window behind me.

I hate seeing him this way. "I can stop guessing. You don't need to tell me."

He shakes his head. "We made a deal." The resigned sigh he releases does little to ease the tension from his body. "I don't talk much about my mother."

I reach out and clutch his hand in mine. He holds on to it like a lifeline, barely concealing the tremble in his hand as he squeezes the blood from my fingers. "Some of my memories are confusing since I was so young, but the one thing I remember most about my mom was that she loved King Arthur."

"No way! She was a history buff?"

He looks at me knowingly. I sigh and give him a soft peck for his next secret. I move away but he tugs me back into his chest and deepens the kiss. Like he needs the extra courage to talk about anything related to his mother.

He might not be searching for love but maybe he's looking to heal.

I can help with that. I've been there.

He releases me before taking a few deep breaths. "My mother was obsessed with history and stories that bordered on fantasy. That's actually how she and my father met."

He pauses as if he's not sure if he should keep going.

"Tell me more. Please?" I kiss his cheek.

"She worked at the tutoring center at the university they both attended. My father walked into the building to pick up his friend whose car was at the shop. My mother was working the counter and asked if he needed help."

"And?"

"My father was a straight-A student who attended an entire semester's worth of tutoring sessions for a class he wasn't even taking."

"*No!*" I laugh until I'm hoarse. His parents' story might be better than mine—not that I would admit that to them.

"It's true. Mom even revised his fake essays and homework about King Arthur and his knights."

"I see lying is a Kane family trait here."

He smirks. "We do anything to get what we want."

"Ruthless. All of you," I tease.

He chuckles low under his breath.

"What did your dad say about it all? And how did he get her to agree to a date after pretending for so long?" I need to hear more if only to feed the hopeless romantic in me.

"I don't remember." Rowan's lips press into a thin line, and his hand holding on to mine tenses.

The temperature in the car drops, matching the energy coming off Rowan. My entire chest aches for Rowan's dad. Despite hearing all about his questionable business decisions, I can empathize with anyone who lost their wife. Especially a man who was willing to attend tutoring sessions for no reason but to spend time with the woman he liked.

And I can feel even more empathy for the children who suffered from similar grief.

I give his hand a squeeze. "So what's the connection between that story and your middle name?"

"My mother named my brothers and me after King Arthur's Knights of the Round Table."

"Those are some big shoes to fill. Didn't they find the holy grail or something?"

"Or something." The corner of his mouth lifts again and the tension leaves him like a gust of air. "I have it easy. Declan's the one who has to introduce himself as Declan Lancelot Kane for the rest of his life."

An ungodly giggle escapes me at the idea of Rowan's oldest brother having to bear that kind of cross for the rest of his life. *Lancelot? Really?*

"And you? Mr. R. G. Kane?"

"Galahad," he grumbles under his breath, bringing my attention to the lightest shade of pink in his cheeks.

"Aw. That's cute."

"There's only room for one liar here, and it's not you."

I shove his shoulder. "I mean it! The story behind it makes it that much more special."

His body tightens. "If you tell anyone, I'll have to—"

"Yeah, yeah. Fire me. I got it already."

"I'll have to *fuck you*. But if you're interested in role-playing the other scenario, I'm more than happy to oblige."

"Did you make a sex joke?! I am absolutely scandalized." I speak in a Southern accent while fanning my face.

He shakes his head like I'm the most amazingly crazy person he's ever met. Okay, I'm only assuming, but it seems like a plausible guess.

I hold out my hand. "You have a deal."

CHAPTER THIRTY-THREE

Rowan

"It's not too late to go home." Zahra uses her menu as a shield to block the entire left side of her face.

When I booked a reservation at the finest restaurant in Orlando, I didn't expect her to protest the moment we sat down. Ever since the hostess showed us to our table at the back of the restaurant ten minutes ago, Zahra's been flushed and unable to sit still. I thought wine would help with first-date nerves, but she's already guzzled one full glass.

Is she afraid to be out in public with me? I highly doubt any paparazzi worth their salt would be prowling the streets of central Florida waiting for a celebrity.

I frown, pulling down her menu. "Is it too fancy?"

"No—I mean yes! I mean, look at this menu." She pulls it back up, flaunting it to me while shielding both our faces now. "Any place without prices and lots of French words is a red flag for my bank account."

"You're not paying." I speak in a dry tone.

"Yeah, well, it would be presumptuous for me to assume we wouldn't go halfsies."

"Halfsies." I choke. "What has gotten into you?"

"Nothing." She bites her lip. Her skin goes from pink to red, giving away her inability to lie about anything.

"Are you always this nervous on a first date?"

She frowns. "I'm not nervous."

"You drank a two-hundred-dollar glass of wine in ten minutes."

Her entire face pales. "Two. Hundred. Dollars?!" she whisper-shouts. "Why would you spend that much on a bunch of old grapes?"

I can't hold back my laugh. It's barely audible over the people surrounding us.

Her eyes slide from me to another table across from us where a blond male and female sit.

"Do you know those people?"

She jumps in her chair. "Who?"

I blink at her.

Her shoulders slump as she slides a few inches farther down her chair. "Yes."

"Who are they?"

"The blond guy with tiny hands and a massive forehead is Lance."

You've got to be fucking kidding me. Of all the places? Here? This would never happen in Chicago. There are too many damn people to run into someone I hate.

I blame the lack of restaurants available around the area.

Maybe I can build one on Dreamland property to avoid this from happening again.

Again? You're not staying here past the vote.

I grab my wineglass and take a long sip to quench the sick feeling in my stomach.

Her eyes flit from me back to that damn table at the center of the room.

I frown. "Do you want him back?"

Where the fuck did that come from?

"What?!" Her voice draws the attention of some neighbors. "God no."

"Then forget about him."

"Easier said than done. He's right there with *her*. I hate seeing them because it reminds me—" Her voice trails off.

Of how he broke her heart, I finish in my head.

I hate seeing Zahra this upset. She usually has more positivity in one finger than a damn squad of Super Bowl cheerleaders. Her distress makes me feel unsettled. Like I want to fix it, but I have no clue how especially when I don't know the first thing about dealing with an ex.

"Let's play a game."

What the fuck are you doing?

She perks up, finally dropping the menu and giving me her attention. "You're all about games tonight."

"Would you rather go skinny-dipping in the middle of the ocean or run naked through Dreamland in the middle of the night?"

"I hate running but I hate sharks more so definitely running naked through Dreamland."

I smile. "Naughty girl. You could get caught."

"Good thing I know the boss," she taunts.

The way she smiles at me makes my heart take pause. It's strange—like my entire body can't help but go haywire whenever I'm around her. Whether it's itchy skin, a tightening chest, or a bizarre urge to kiss her, I'm battling a ton of sensations. Sometimes all at once.

"Your turn." I grab her hand, tracing her knuckles with my thumb. Her breath always hitches when I do it, so it's easily becoming my favorite way to keep touching her while in public.

"Would you rather never read a book again or never be able to check the stock market?"

"Hitting me where it hurts." I rub my heart with my free hand.

She smiles. "The fact that you have to think this one over breaks my heart."

I offer her a knowing smile. "I'd have to give up reading books. Sorry."

"Well, this was fun while it lasted." She pulls her hand away teasingly before I latch on to it again.

"You said I never could *read* a book again. Audiobooks don't count."

Her mouth drops open. "You—that's. You can't cheat like that!"

"Life's all about semantics."

"Dating a businessman sucks."

I want to kiss the pout off her face. "I gather it's a bit of a change from the wonderful company you picked up on the dating apps. What about the electrician with the mother?"

She points a finger at me. "I'll have you know that Chip was a very nice man."

"Who brought his mother along on the date."

"I thought it was sweet."

"She asked you if you had a fertility tracker." I take a sip of my wine.

Zahra drops her head back and laughs up to the ceiling. Making her laugh fills me with the deepest sense of pride, knowing I could make her day brighter in some small way.

A new realization hits me hard. For the first time on a date, I'm having fun. There's no predestined agenda or cold conversations about work and business. I'm genuinely interested in hearing anything that comes out of Zahra's mouth, and everything is only amplified when I make her laugh.

Part of me wishes I could be like her where I could live without abandon and move on from past issues that seem to make an appearance at the worst time. It's not possible for someone like me. I've become jaded from life, so being around Zahra is refreshing.

I'm aware that I'm playing a dangerous game with Zahra by toeing the line between dating and more. I can't pursue much more with my deadline and my end goals. At least not with my future in Chicago and hers cemented into the very foundation of Dreamland.

But we can enjoy the present and live for today. That much I can promise.

Zahra waves her hand in front of my face. "Your turn."

I shake my head and return to the conversation. Zahra and I switch back and forth, with her choosing the most outrageous questions for me to pick from. I'm not sure where she comes up with ideas like skiing in a pair of boxers or riding a Jet Ski across the entire ocean but her imagination is endless.

That's why you hired her.

We spend the entire dinner in our little game, branching off into different conversations depending on what kind of answer we give.

Zahra considers her next set of crazy options when Lance steps into our proximity. He gapes at us, his eyes switching between Zahra and me. She hasn't even noticed him yet, too immersed in her head.

I keep my eyes glued to his as I pull Zahra's hand up to my lips and give her knuckles a kiss. She sucks in a breath and her cheeks turn the prettiest shade of pink for me. Lance's jaw clamps down, making him resemble a squashed tomato with a mop of blond hair. He's absolutely average in every sense of the word—from his Brooks Brothers button-down to his poorly pressed khaki pants. I'm sure I could find a dozen like him at the local outlet mall.

I place Zahra's hand back on the table and stand to my full height. Lance has to tilt his head back to stare up at me.

I button my jacket before saying, "Lance Baker. I've heard about you."

He stands taller like a peacock. "Mr. Kane. I wanted to stop by and say hello. Zahra and I go way back."

My blood turns red-hot, pulsing with each breath. Lance extends his hand and I merely stare at it with every ounce of disgust I feel toward him.

"She told me about your Nebula Land submission."

He drops his hand by his side like a rejected stray. "Oh yes. I was shocked my proposal was accepted."

My fist itches to familiarize itself with his face. This piece of shit thinks he can get away with stealing Zahra's idea? It dawns on me that he believes Zahra kept quiet about the whole thing.

What a piece of shit. He probably thinks she's too nice to rat him out, and since he never got caught, there was no reason for him to worry.

Fuck him. I'll seek out revenge in Zahra's name.

"Oh, Lance. Hi. Weird seeing you here." Zahra's voice is wooden.

"I'm celebrating my anniversary."

I keep my face blank despite the urge to tell him to fuck off.

Zahra's entire body tenses. "Isn't it considered bad taste to celebrate the time you started an affair?"

Lance's eyes bulge. His already red cheeks take on a purplish hue.

Warmth seeps into my chest at Zahra's straightened spine and steel gaze. It makes me…proud of her. Of the way she can stand up to others like she has to me.

I pull her into my side. I'm tempted to hide her for the rest of her life, protecting her from idiots like Lance who abused the kind of gift she is.

The wave of possessiveness hits me out of nowhere. I should be surprised, but I'm not shocked. I've always been territorial over everything. Toys. Money. Business ventures. And now…a woman. Although the idea is new, the feeling is not.

Lance turns his attention on me.

"Mr. Kane. I'm sorry to interrupt. I didn't realize you and Zahra were in the middle of a business meeting tonight."

"We're not," I offer in a dry voice.

Zahra shivers as I trace her arm with my finger. Lance's eyes track the movement before ending at my hand pressed against her waist in an intimate gesture.

"Well, I'm sorry to intrude on this…outing."

"Why did you then?" I counter, keeping my voice flat.

His mouth opens and closes again. I don't bother waiting for his limited brain cells to make up some pathetic excuse.

I wave over the hostess. She comes over and places herself between Lance and me.

"Mr. Kane. Can I help you with something?" She keeps her tone light and professional.

"I'd like to send this man's table a bottle of Dom Perignon on my tab."

She beams. "Of course. What occasion are we celebrating?"

"His job promotion."

The hostess disappears with a massive grin on her face.

Zahra's body goes rigid beside me. I caress her hip, toying with the strap of lace through the fabric of her dress. Her body melts into mine despite Lance staring at us openly.

"Job promotion?" he squawks.

"It's come to my attention that you have been a dedicated Dreamland employee for years."

He nods with a grin. His eyes move from me to Zahra, and I'm tempted to shield her from his gaze. The way he looks at her makes me think he believes she talked him up to me.

He's such a waste of good oxygen.

I'm absolutely disgusted by him. "You're officially being transferred to Dreamland Shanghai to work with the Creators there. Effective immediately."

All the blood drains from his face. "Shanghai? *China*?"

"It appears you have two reasons to celebrate tonight. Congratulations."

He sputters some more. His discomfort makes me want to smile, but I hold back. There's only one person who deserves my limited supply and it's definitely not this degenerate.

I look down at Zahra, only to find her already staring up at me. The smallest smile graces her lips, but her eyes tell me everything. She rises on the tips of her toes and places a soft kiss on my cheek.

Her lips make their way toward my ear. "You're so getting laid tonight." Her hot breath makes the back of my neck heat, and suddenly I'm very interested in getting the hell out of here.

Screw dates at restaurants. They're grossly overrated and highly restricting. I'm not sure what I was thinking bringing Zahra to one when she's the kind of person who likes to sit on floors and binge takeout food together.

I give Zahra's hip a squeeze in acknowledgment.

"Congratulations on Shanghai. You should be so proud of your accomplishments, Lance." She gives Lance one last wave over her shoulder before she returns to her chair.

A small part of me rejoices in the fact that she doesn't offer him a smile. Those are all mine, fuck him very much.

Lance stares at her with his mouth agape. The way he ogles her makes me want to deck him right in his crooked nose.

I clap a hand on Lance's tense shoulder and lean in, the gesture seeming friendly to anyone else. "There's a reason men like you hurt women like Zahra. It has nothing to do with her and everything to do with what you're severely lacking." I take a moment to look down at him, not bothering to hide the disgust in my eyes.

All the blood drains from his face, and his body shrinks into itself. It brings me a completely different sense of satisfaction to affect him like this. I'm sure it's only a fraction of the discomfort Zahra probably feels in his presence, but I'm glad to deliver it.

I give him one last pat on the shoulder before turning away.

Zahra's already seated in her chair. Her wide eyes bounce between Lance's retreating form and me. "Are you really sending him to Shanghai?"

"That's up to him." I pull out my chair and sit.

"How so?"

"He can either go to Shanghai or hand in his resignation. It doesn't matter to me as long as he gets the hell off my property."

She grasps my hand. "Why would you do that?"

I shrug.

"You really do like me." She bats her long lashes.

"I already told you this earlier." I shoot her a soft smile, which only makes her beam like the goddamn sun in return.

She grabs the dessert menu from the center of the table. "Actions speak louder than words."

"And what do my actions say?" I lean in and grab the end of her hair, pulling her toward me, so our mouths are only a few inches apart.

"That you care more than you're letting on."

I close the gap between us and kiss her. "Don't go wishing for things that can't happen."

The corners of her eyes soften, reflecting an emotion I haven't seen from her yet. "That's okay. I'll dream big enough for the two of us."

The strange warmth surging through my veins is quickly doused by a chill. That's my biggest worry in one single sentence.

CHAPTER THIRTY-FOUR

Zahra

Lance is moving to China. All because Rowan wanted to make me happy and help me move on. While he might not have said so in as many words, his actions make it extremely obvious.

If Rowan's trying to keep things casual, he's doing a terrible job of it. Seriously, is the man *trying* to make me fall in love with him? Because if he keeps up with these kinds of displays of affection, I won't survive him. I'm already slipping into dangerous territory.

The moment the driver closes the back door to the car, I'm all over Rowan. With the partition up, I feel bold. Reckless. A little bit power-drunk on the idea of Rowan standing up to Lance.

It's hot. He's hot. The whole damn situation is hot.

I lift my dress and slide onto Rowan's lap. His hands find my hips, grinding my lower half against his zipper. He steals my gasp with his lips.

Kissing him feels like a high I don't want to come down from. Like the world seems brighter with him in it, and I want to chase this feeling until the end of time. Our tongues collide, stroking, testing, pushing.

"This isn't safe," he mumbles between kisses.

I grab his seat belt and buckle him in, which earns me a laugh. "There you go."

He pulls me tighter against him. "I wasn't complaining about me."

"You're overthinking things." I trace the line of his zipper, feeling him stiffen under my touch. His grip on my hips tightens.

He undoes the seat belt with a grumble before making quick work of his belt and trousers. I thought Rowan in the bedroom was sexy, but him sitting with his pants halfway down his thighs, rigid cock on display in the back seat of a car is devastating. Because beneath those expensive suits is a man who looks like *this*. For *me*.

My knees hit the floor. Rowan's gaze follows me as I trace the thick vein down his shaft. His breathing grows heavier as I replace my hand with my tongue. I'm tentative at first, tasting the slightest hint of his arousal mixed with some kind of addictive soap.

I cup his balls with my free hand and give them a squeeze. His hips surge forward. Arousal coats my tongue and I lave at it, switching between deep sucks and long strokes of my tongue.

Rowan's hands dig into my hair, his desperation growing as my tempo changes. I'm addicted to the man Rowan becomes with me in private, so unlike his usual quiet, withdrawn self. Because when the walls come down, he's voracious. Greedy. As selfish during sex as he is in a boardroom.

It shouldn't turn me on this much, but I'm a lost cause to our desire when it comes to him.

Rowan is quickly becoming my drug of choice. His heavy breathing. Our battle for control. The way he groans my name like it's a blessing and a curse.

His entire body shudders as I give him one last pull with my mouth. He lets out a hiss of air when I release him and crawl back onto his lap.

He blinks up at the ceiling with a hazy gaze. "This is highly inappropriate for a car."

"We haven't even gotten to the best part."

The smallest smile graces his lips. "Are you going to show me or tell me?"

"Show. Always show." I trail some kisses from his lips to his neck.

His hands slide up my dress, disappearing beneath the layers of fabric.

"You're so stunning that it hurts to stare at you for long periods of time." He leans in and kisses the spot on my neck that steals my breath away.

My entire body warms from his confession. Maybe because I know Rowan's not the kind of man who offers meaningless compliments or flowery words. Everything he says has meaning, and he called me *stunning*.

My eyes get itchy from the emotions swirling in my chest. Rowan makes the thoughts vanish as he tugs my underwear down my thighs. Everything with him feels heightened, from the drag of his calloused fingers across my skin to his warm breath eliciting goose bumps.

I rise onto my knees, giving him room to pull my underwear down my legs. He throws them on the seat while pulling down the cup of my corset, releasing my breast. His lips latch on, and I throw my head back at the sensation. The way his tongue teases me drives me wild.

He groans as I slide my exposed center across his hard, naked shaft. My entire body pulses with need, and warmth fills my belly at the velvet feel of him against me. I slide back and forth once more, eliciting another moan from Rowan. He calls out my name, but it's nothing more than a hoarse whisper under his strained breath.

I turned a rich god into a beggar. A surge of power spirals through me, pushing me to the brink of insanity. I tease his tip and earn a sucked breath. His fingers clench onto my hips with enough strength to bruise.

Our eyes connect. The darkness blazing in his gaze feeds the warmth spreading across my lower half, turning a spark into a fire.

"Your pretty little cunt hasn't earned my cock yet." He lifts me enough to slide his hand between us.

My entire face flames. His hand dips inside of me, removing all my control from the situation. My body clenches around his single digit, and I jump when he adds another. His free hand wraps around my hair and tugs, leaving my neck exposed to his lips and my body arched for the taking.

"I was right all along." His deep chuckle sends another zing of energy down my spine. "You, Zahra Gulian, really are nothing but a fraud. A temptress who hides behind sweet smiles and kind words while hiding this monster within you." His rough voice does something devious to my lower half. He drags his tongue from my neck to my nipple before grazing his teeth across the sensitive skin.

A shiver spreads across my body, leaving goose bumps in his wake.

"But I see you." His touch is punishing. Like he dances across the fine line between anger and lust. It's addictive to know I drive him wild enough to lose all semblance of control over himself. No one knows what kind of animal prowls beneath his skin but me, and I find the secret rather intoxicating.

My body trembles as I become consumed by lust.

He sucks on my neck, leaving behind bruised skin in his wake. His tongue traces the curve, and I cry out.

"And I want you." Two fingers turn into three, diving deep while his lips possess every inch of exposed skin. The pressure in my body grows until it becomes unbearable. I scratch at his shirt, unable to impale his skin with my marks.

"You drive me crazy," he mumbles against the goose bumps on my neck. He withdraws his fingers before slamming them inside me again. "Wild." I gasp. "Out of control." Another punishing assault of his fingers. "Reckless enough to fuck you in the back seat with my driver only three feet away, separated by a plastic divider that isn't made to block out your cries."

The desperate need to come floods me. I swivel my hips and ride his fingers, chasing the wildfire building at the base of my spine.

"I think you like the idea of other people hearing me fuck you until your voice is hoarse." He withdraws his hand.

I mourn the loss, and the buzz in my body turns into nothing but a dull hum. "Maybe I like them hearing *me* fuck *you*."

He grins in a way that makes him look ten years younger. I touch his smile to confirm I'm not imagining things.

He grabs his wallet and pulls out a condom. I'd call him out on being a cliché, but I imagine it's important for him to feel in control of the little things after everything he's been through. The crinkle of a foil wrapper balances out our heavy breathing. His jerky movements rattle my limp body, making me putty in his hands.

He lifts me up, revealing his sheathed cock. One hand holds on to me while he uses the other to trace my slit. The move is gentle and reverent before he slams me down onto his cock. I gasp at the sudden sense of fullness. My entire body freezes from the burn, and I drop my head back. He softly kisses my neck in an unspoken apology. His thumb finds my clit, making my tense body relaxed.

"Show me how badly you want it." He smacks my ass once before pulling back. He rubs his bottom lip, tracing that hint of a smile.

That bastard. He's going to make me work for it.

I use his shoulders as a support while I rise up, taking my skirt along with me. He looks down at our joined bodies where his dick is still halfway inside of me. His eyes don't stray as he licks his lips and stares.

I push back down, making him shudder as my body clamps around his cock. "I might be a fraud, but you're nothing but a beautiful liar. A man willing to do anything to get what he wants. Selfish." I rise to slam down again, building a rhythm that matches our heavy breaths. "Controlling." I swivel my hips which makes his eyes roll back into his head. "An angry man with secret smiles and soft laughs and a golden heart he keeps hidden from the world." My lips find his neck and nip at the skin.

He's my dark storm cloud in the middle of a drought—an

underappreciated beauty that makes me feel equally alive as the sun or the stars.

His fingers tremble against my hips as he releases another groan.

"I think you hate how much you want me. Because to care about me means you have to admit to having a heart." I place a soft kiss against his lips. "So keep telling yourself those pretty little lies. Your secret is safe with me."

I ride him, earning every single moan from his lips. I'm obsessed with teasing him. Each time I rise, I withdraw right to his tip, making him suck in a breath before I slam back down.

Rowan's eyes go completely dark as his hands holding on to my hips squeeze harder. Something inside of him snaps. He takes control, his arms straining beneath the fabric of his shirt as he lifts me before pulling me back down again.

The breath gets knocked out of me with each punishing stroke. Pleasure crawls up my spine. My skin burns with each graze of Rowan's skin against mine. Like someone holds a flame to my skin with each caress.

Rowan's movements become sloppier as control slips from his grasp. Black spots fill my vision before stars burst, sparking to life behind my shut eyes. My body shakes as pleasure rushes through me.

Rowan's entire body trembles as he comes. I don't stop moving my hips until we're both breathless and boneless. My head drops against his shoulder, and exhaustion eats away at the remaining adrenaline in my system.

Rowan runs his hand up and down my spine. My eyes shut

as I try to regulate my breathing and heart rate. The soothing motion of his hand has me drifting into unconsciousness despite his softening cock still inside of me.

I must be half-delusional from my orgasm because Rowan whispers something to himself that I must've dreamed up in my head. "If I had a heart to give, it would be all yours. Free of cost."

My spine tingles, and it has nothing to do with his hand running down my back. I want to tell him he has a heart, but the words get stuck in my throat. So instead, I soak in whatever kind of affection Rowan is willing to share.

CHAPTER THIRTY-FIVE

Zahra

Rowan shows up after our weekly Friday meeting wearing the most annoyingly smug smile on his face.

"Can you go back to not smiling? This isn't fair." I shut off my desktop computer.

His grin widens. "But I like the way you squirm."

I shove my laptop in my backpack. "Asshole."

He leans against the cubicle wall and tucks his hands in his pockets. "If you're trying to turn me off, you're going about it the wrong way."

I think of our first kiss and how much he liked me calling him an asshole back then.

"What are you doing here?" I rasp.

"I wanted to let you know we're going on a date tomorrow."

"Okay…" I play it cool, but inside I'm swooning. Rowan is definitely making his intentions obvious, and I'm so here for it. It's refreshing to not chase him down for a date.

"After we have dinner with your family," he speaks with finality.

"Come again?!"

"Maybe later." He winks.

I clutch onto the side of my desk to stop myself from falling out of my chair. "Don't wink."

"Why?"

"Because my ovaries might implode and that would be quite unfortunate."

He chuckles to himself. "Ani invited me after our last meeting."

"That little conniving—" I'm so not ready to introduce Rowan to my family.

"It's cute how much she talks you up."

Ugh. How can I get annoyed at Ani for that?

I sigh. "I'm not sure you're ready for my family."

"Please. I need to hear all about your parents getting married in Vegas. Their love for Elvis runs deep."

"Don't encourage them. They'll whip out an old album and shower you with stories."

"Ani mentioned they have a video of you performing with your ukulele in the living room. You can consider me quite interested in viewing that family film."

I groan as I lay my head on my desk and raise my middle finger high in the air.

"Aren't you the sweetest thing?" my mom gushes over Rowan the moment he walks through the door with a fancy-looking bottle of wine.

His whole body remains frozen in the doorway.

"Welcome." My dad offers his hand.

Rowan shakes it and greets everyone else, including Claire, who stares him up and down before shrugging like she's unimpressed.

"You came!" Ani all but tackles Rowan, giving him a big hug.

Everyone stares at them. My mom's eyes shine as she clasps her hands to her chest.

My dad turns his head in my direction and gives me an approving nod. "I like him better than Lance already."

"Dad!" I groan.

If Rowan heard him, he pretends he didn't.

"Let's eat!" Mom chants. Claire offers to help serve everyone my dad's favorite food.

Rowan takes the seat next to me, and instantly my parents' dining table feels like it's meant for a dollhouse.

"Have you tried Armenian food before?"

He shakes his head.

"Are you a picky eater?"

He rolls his eyes. "I'll eat anything but caviar."

I laugh to myself. "Great! Then prepare to be amazed. My mom might be from Europe, but she learned all my dad's favorite Armenian recipes."

I grab a utensil and dig into my mom's cooking. Claire makes the recipe every now and then, but nothing compares to my mom's cooking.

"So, Mr. Kane, how are you liking Dreamland so far?" My dad takes a sip of the wine Rowan brought.

He looks down at me. "It's growing on me."

My entire face turns molten under Rowan's gaze.

He gives my thigh a squeeze before looking at my dad. "And please call me Rowan."

Mom grins. "Zahra told us all about the project you're working on. It's so nice that you want to celebrate the park's anniversary."

Rowan's hand fists against his lap. "It's what my grandfather wanted."

"He was a great man," my dad says.

Rowan nods. "I'm glad the people here appreciated him." There's a slight hesitation in his voice.

I grab onto his fist and spread his fingers out before locking ours together. "You don't have to be nervous," I whisper under my breath.

"I'm bad at small talk," he whispers back.

I can only laugh and enjoy the show. Rowan being shy is such a welcome change compared to how he is around everyone in the office.

"How do you like Florida compared to Chicago?" Mom asks.

"It's…hot."

Everyone at the table laughs, and the tension dissipates from Rowan's body.

"It must be a change compared to Chicago. We've always wanted to visit." Dad nods.

"But we haven't had a vacation in years," Ani pipes up finally.

"Why not?" Rowan looks over at my sister with furrowed brows.

"Oh." Her smile drops.

Well, shit. No one wants to be the one to break it to him.

The temperature in the room drops significantly. Rowan's hand grips onto mine harder, like he's afraid to let go.

"Because we can't afford to take vacations even if we wanted to," Claire offers in a neutral tone.

"Right." Rowan's voice sounds strained to my ears.

Mom, bless her soul, changes the topic and somehow salvages the dinner. Rowan seems more withdrawn than usual, which says something. I don't think my parents notice since they have only heard stories about Rowan, but I do. I'm plagued with nausea for the rest of the dinner, which makes eating my food difficult.

Rowan scowls at me shoving my food around my plate like a child. Unlike me, he devours it all and asks for seconds, which only makes my mom happier.

After dinner, my dad claps Rowan on the shoulder before giving him a hug. I'd laugh if I wasn't already on edge, seeing as Rowan remains stiff as a board during the entire exchange.

Together, we walk hand in hand toward the parking lot. Rowan unlocks his car and opens my door for me. I freeze, unable to get inside before I clear the air.

"I'm sorry about earlier," I blurt out.

His hand holding on to the door tightens. "Why would you be sorry?"

"Because you were already nervous about talking and then that conversation happened."

His jaw clenches. "It's not your fault I'm an asshole, Zahra."

I wince. "Don't talk about yourself that way."

"I thought you valued the truth."

I gape at him.

"It's the reality of the situation. I make business decisions that affect people's lives for better or for worse. It is what it is." He looks up at the dark, starless sky.

"But you could change. No one is forcing you to choose one side over the other."

He lets out a bitter laugh. "Running a business is hard."

"So is being human."

He sighs and grabs my hand again, interlocking our fingers once more. "I don't know the first thing about being human."

"That's okay. I'll teach you everything I know." I grin as I drop into the passenger seat.

"That's exactly what I'm afraid of," he mumbles under his breath.

Challenge accepted.

CHAPTER THIRTY-SIX

Zahra

The knocker on our apartment door thumps three times.

"He's here!" Ani doesn't bother to pause our TV show as she grabs my purse and throws it into my arms.

"Who?"

"Rowan!"

My heart picks up its pace, going from a steady rhythm to erratic. "Oh, I'm sorry. You know this *how*?"

"He wanted to surprise you for your date." Ani steps into my bedroom.

Date?! I'm dressed in a pair of old paint-splattered Levi's and a sweatshirt of the Chicago Bulls from the nineties. My fashion choice is barely suited for the local grocery store, let alone a *date*.

"What do you mean by date?" I call out.

"The kind where Rowan whisks you away to show you his surprise." Ani's yell is muffled by the distance.

Well... wow, okay. I'm all for surprises now.

"Hurry up. You're so slow." Ani steps out of my room with the largest suitcase I own.

"Am I moving somewhere?"

She giggles. "No, silly. Rowan asked me to pack you a couple of outfits."

"Outfits? For what?"

She beams. "I'm under contract to not say anything else."

"How did you even get into my apartment and pack a suitcase?"

"Claire." Her grin is infectious.

"How far does this surprise go?" I blow a lock of hair out of my face as I grab onto the handle of my suitcase.

Ani laughs. "It's worth it."

My palms get slippery as I try to hold on to the luggage. I'm not sure what Rowan planned but a suitcase of this size seems like overkill.

"Don't worry about anything. I even packed your sexy clothes." Ani winks.

My cheeks flush. "Oh my God. You didn't! How did you even find them?"

"A sister never reveals her secrets. Have fun!" Ani runs to my bathroom and locks herself inside.

"Claire will be home soon to make you dinner."

"Bye, Mom! Stop worrying about me!"

I tug the door open and find Rowan leaning against the frame with his hands tucked in his pockets. "Fancy seeing you here."

"Hello." He shoots me a small smile.

I nearly melt into the welcome mat when he leans over and

places the softest kiss on my forehead. A buzz starts at my head and travels all the way down to my toes.

He pulls away, taking his addictive smell with him. His hand latches onto the handle of my luggage. "We better get going. We've got a flight to catch."

"Flight?" *Oh shit.*

My life went full-blown Dreamland princess in less than an hour. But instead of a prince on a horse, I ended up with Rowan—the perfect kind of morally gray hero I love reading about.

"Here we are." He squeezes my thigh with his massive hand.

"Are we stopping somewhere before our flight?" I look out the window, checking out the area that is definitely not the Orlando airport.

A hint of a smile crosses Rowan's lips as if I said something cute. Someone opens a gate, and the driver steers the Rolls-Royce Ghost *onto* the runway.

I blink at the sleek black jet parked on the pavement like this is a casual Friday outing. "Are you kidding me?"

"I don't joke."

"Liar."

I'm rewarded with another small smile.

I wave at the plane. "When you said we had a flight to catch, I thought you meant commercial."

"God no."

"Oh yes. Because mini pretzels and babies crying are so aversive."

He nods and gives my thigh another reassuring squeeze. "Good. You get it."

The more time I spend around Rowan, the more I realize he's not just out of my league—he's out of my atmosphere. "We're seriously going on a private plane?"

"Yes."

I mutter a thank-you under my breath as his driver opens the door. I'm stuck staring at the red carpet below me.

Rowan slides out of his seat and walks around the car. "Scared you might get addicted to this kind of lifestyle?"

"That's the last thought on my mind." I take a hesitant step toward the red carpet. I don't think I've seen one anywhere but on the TV. My sneakers seem out of place as they press into the plush fabric and my paint-splattered jeans seem absolutely ridiculous.

He buttons his jacket as he looks over his shoulder. His brows pull down as he assesses me. "What's wrong?"

I point back and forth between us. "You look like you stepped out of a Tom Ford catalog while I resemble someone who sifted through the BOGO bin at Goodwill." I point to my washed-out sweatshirt. "This isn't even a Michael Jordan sweatshirt because that wasn't an option at the thrift store."

The corner of his lip hitches. "I like your style." His eyes drag down my body. His hands latch onto the back pockets of my jeans and tug me toward him.

"I like my style too, but it's not exactly private-jet material."

"Says who?"

"Me!"

"How would you know if you've never been on a private jet before?"

I curse up to the sky. *Dammit. Why does he always have a good point?* "You can be so infuriating sometimes!"

Rowan kisses my forehead like I should be rewarded for being adorable while angry.

"We should get going because we don't want to be late." He removes his hands from my pockets before placing one on the small of my back. With a softness I've grown to appreciate, he directs us up the stairs and into the jet's private cabin.

Whatever I thought private jets looked like inside, this was not it. The toe of my sneaker catches on the black carpet, and I scream as I lose my footing. Rowan's arm shoots out and clutches onto my flailing arm, righting me before I fall face-first.

"Graceful as ever, Zahra." He laughs under his breath.

He deposits my body in a massive seat that is three times the size of those on a typical flight. I stroke the beige leather to confirm this is not a dream.

He drops into the seat across from me. "What's that face for?"

"Nothing."

"You're uncomfortable."

My cheeks burn. I should be thankful to be going on a trip instead of freaking out over the minor things. "No. I'm fine."

He traces his bottom lip with his thumb. "I think you might be the only person I've met who is intimidated by my money and wants nothing to do with it."

"Must be quite the contrast compared to the majority who are mainly intimidated by your personality." My snappy comment is rewarded with a low laugh from Rowan. The sound warms my entire chest.

His eyes lighten as I shoot him a smile. "I like the way you make me feel."

"And that is?"

"Like I'm a real person."

I roll my eyes. "If these are your standards, there's nowhere to go but up."

He laughs again, and this time, I join him.

Okay, I won't admit this to Rowan, but dating a billionaire has its perks.

Perk One: Taking a random flight to *New York City* because he feels like it would be a good date spot.

Perk Two: Visiting New York freaking City!

I'm bursting with excitement as the jet lands on the runway. The moment Rowan told me about our destination, I pestered him with many questions about the city and how often he comes here.

"I've never seen someone look this excited to be in New York before."

"Are you kidding me? This is a dream come true!"

"Hold off on that statement until you get off the plane. I'm pretty sure the smell alone will convince you otherwise."

"What kind of person hates New York?"

"The same kind who loves Chicago."

"Take that back!" I lean over and smack his shoulder.

He grins. "Nope. Not until you come with me to Chicago and confirm what I already know."

I'm pretty sure my heart might burst at Rowan's idea. Planning ahead seems to add another layer to our *casual but doesn't feel casual* relationship.

"People can't take off and fly away whenever the feeling strikes."

His head tilts. "Why not?"

"Because we have jobs and responsibilities."

"Leave dealing with your boss to me."

I shake my head, pretending to be disgusted, yet my heart accelerates in my chest.

Our conversation is cut off too soon by the pilot announcing it's safe to take off our seat belts.

The flight attendant opens the cabin door and all I see is white.

"Snow! Real snow!" I take the steps two at a time and pick up a handful of glittering snow.

Rowan stops beside me. "We got lucky."

"Lucky? How?"

His eyes stay glued to my smile. "There usually isn't snow this early in the season but they just had a storm the other day."

"If that's not fate, I don't know what is." I throw the snow in the air and watch it all fall around me like powder.

I close my eyes and laugh, only to open them to find Rowan staring at me.

The staff makes quick work of our luggage, and before I can blink, Rowan has us settled into the back of a town car. He clutches onto my hand and draws idle circles with his thumb. Each rotation sends a jolt of energy shooting up my arm.

I stare out the window the entire time, taking in the bright lights and endless amounts of people. It reminds me of the Dreamland crowds, but more aggressive. Like people have places to go and people to see, so everyone needs to get the hell out of their way.

I absolutely love it.

We pull up to the valet of some high-rise building covered in glass and steel.

"You live *here*?" I crane my neck back, taking in how the skyscraper touches a cloud. A real freaking cloud!

He shrugs. "Sometimes. It's one of my homes."

"One?!"

He shrugs.

"What's it like to have more money than God?"

"Lonely." His word carries enough heaviness to taint the air around us.

I'm tempted to wrap my arms around him to give him a squeeze. I can't begin to imagine how isolating it is to be surrounded by so much wealth to the point that people stop treating him like a real person. After Rowan's confession, I make a promise to myself to stop gawking at everything like it might disappear any second.

"Okay. I'm going to act cool from now on and pretend none of this fazes me."

"Don't do that. I… It's fun to see things from your perspective."

Fun?! Who knew the man could experience such joy. I'm so caught up in that admission that it takes me a second to realize the rest of his statement.

He likes to see things from my perspective. My chest tightens, betraying me. Dammit. I should have listened to Claire. There's no way things can stay casual between us without developing more intense feelings beyond liking one another. But why would he pursue me as Scott and Rowan if he wasn't interested in taking things further?

I don't think he's using me for sex. There would be no reason behind carting me off to New York if that were the case.

Rowan's hand finds the small of my back again as he leads us through an outrageous lobby with thousands of dangling gems suspended from the ceiling. He doesn't need to press a single button on the elevators. Like he willed them himself, the doors slide open, revealing a shiny car of mirrors.

We step inside and the doors shut behind us.

His hand remains placed against my back. I'm tempted to step away and catch my breath, but he smells too damn good. The air thickens around us as he stares down at me.

"This is one hell of a date."

"Please. We haven't even gotten to that portion of the evening yet."

"Just want to let you know you're setting an unattainable bar for future men. I'll never accept movie theater dates after this."

Good, Zahra. Mention future men to throw him off.

"That's because you're more of a drive-in type of girl anyway." He grabs my hand and tugs me closer. His head tips down and his eyes shut as he leans in. My eyes flutter closed as his lips press against mine. I hold on to him as his tongue traces my bottom lip, asking me nicely to open up. My head grows heavy as my body trembles under his attention.

The *ping* and the swooshing of the doors opening pulls us from our kiss. Rowan's hand latches onto mine. He doesn't let go as he walks us into a penthouse that could make an architect salivate all over the hardwood floors.

"I hope you know I might never leave this place." I walk right up to the massive two-story window that shows off a panoramic view of the entire city.

One of his arms wraps around me, teasing the hem of my

sweatshirt while the other tilts my head to look over my shoulder. "You would give up Dreamland for the city?"

I let out a soft laugh. "No. I love Dreamland. I could spend the rest of my life there and never get bored."

He looks at me with a weird expression I can't place. "Really? Why?"

"My whole family lives there. I'd be crazy to give that up for some random city."

"Hmm." His hand strokes the sliver of exposed skin on my stomach.

"Are you happy giving up the city for Dreamland?" I shouldn't probe but I'm too curious.

"I never thought I could feel happy at Dreamland again, but now I'm not too sure."

I smile. "Really?"

"I might have met the one person who makes the place bearable." His gaze remains solely focused on my face.

His answer makes my breath all shaky and my legs all wobbly. Hopeful little butterflies take flight in my stomach, proving just how far I'm falling.

CHAPTER THIRTY-SEVEN

Zahra

I should have known it was game over the moment Rowan told me to unpack my suitcase.

I kneel on the hardwood floor, unzip my luggage, and throw it open. "Well, this explains the massive suitcase."

Half of it is filled with my regular clothes while the other part is packed with all my regency romances written by Juliana De La Rosa. *The Duke Who Seduced Me* is tucked safely at the top with the protective straps keeping all the books from sliding around.

I rush out of the room to find Rowan, only to run headfirst into his chest.

He laughs as he readjusts me.

"Why is my bag filled with all my De La Rosa books?" I press a hand against my beating heart.

"Because the famous bodice-ripper author is signing books

in New York tonight, and we happen to have tickets to her event." He pulls two tickets out of his back pocket and dangles them in front of me.

My jaw pops open. I jump and grab them from him. "No way!" I throw my arms around his neck. The sudden move knocks him off balance, and he reaches out for a wall before we both topple over.

"You like it." He chuckles in my ear. His hot breath makes my skin break out into goose bumps.

I untangle myself from his neck and return my limbs to my personal bubble. "Like it? I *love* it! How did you get tickets like this at the last minute?"

He clears his throat. "I have connections."

"Okay, *now* I'm impressed by your wealth."

Juliana freaking De La Rosa is standing only thirty feet away from me. The golden bookstore lights shine down on her like a halo, and I'm tempted to run straight into her arms. Instead, I play it cool, only because Rowan holds on to my hand like he's afraid I might disappear or get arrested for stalking.

Surprisingly, Rowan doesn't complain as we jump into line with all the other book lovers. It's a complete one-eighty from us standing in the Dreamland lines. This time, he smiles as I take in my surroundings. He holds on to my books like they're a national treasure, and I'm pretty sure I could kiss him stupid if it weren't for the people surrounding us.

I comment on the woman's bag in front of me and we end up becoming friends instantly. Katie and I compare our list of book boyfriends and discuss what we expect will happen in *The Duke Who Seduced Me*'s season finale. Rowan even offers his analysis of the show which makes Katie about two breaths away from passing out.

When Rowan uses the bathroom, she asks me if he has any single brothers she can meet. My hackles go up, but Katie laughs and seems unaware of who Rowan actually is.

The line moves at a snail's pace. By the time we get to the front, Katie and I befriended her neighbor and mine, turning our duo into a quadruplet. Rowan is a good sport about it all, and I feel kind of guilty I spend our date fangirling with other book nerds.

"Your turn." He nudges me with the palm of his hand straight into Juliana's breathing space.

"Hi! I'm a huge fan." I hold out my shaky hand.

The wrinkles around Juliana's brown eyes tighten as she looks up at me from her table. She has the most ridiculous outfit on that looks like something straight out of a pinup catalog, and I instantly fall in love with her. Her graying hair is secured in a perfect ponytail, and her side bangs swoop across her aging forehead.

"My, my. Aren't you a looker!" Juliana stands and crushes my cheeks between her hands in the most grandmotherly gesture.

Oh my God, Juliana is touching me!

Would it be weird if I ask Rowan to snap a picture?

Yeah, probably. I withhold the urge and take a few deep breaths of Juliana's heavy perfume.

Juliana's grin stands out against her red lips. "Rowan, you didn't tell me your girlfriend is as cute as a button."

Rowan? She knows Rowan?! Why didn't he say anything?

And wait… GIRLFRIEND?!

He clears his throat. "Zahra isn't my girlfriend."

My stomach takes a dive off a very long cliff.

Her eyes slide back to mine. "Well, my dear, you need to lock this man down immediately."

I ignore her because hello, she *knows* Rowan. "I had no idea you knew Rowan!"

Am I dreaming?

Rowan must read my face or something because he pinches my arm for me.

"Hey!"

He shrugs. I grin like an idiot because it reminds me of our first meeting. *He really does remember everything.*

Juliana pats Rowan's cheek like a mother would. "He scheduled this entire event for you because he said you're my biggest fan."

I think the room shifts. "Are you serious?!" I turn and look up at him. "How?"

"Ah, you didn't tell her," Juliana says.

"You planned this whole thing?" I gape at the man who planned an entire book event for me.

"No. I had help."

Juliana cackles. "Dear, without him, my ass would be glued to a lawn chair somewhere in Hawaii right now celebrating the release of my new book."

"But you're here? *For me*?"

"It pays to have friends in high places, doesn't it?" She winks. "His company made my books into the show you love."

"His *company*?!" I'm not sure how I'm remaining upright with the amount of rug she's pulling out from under me.

How could I be so stupid? Rowan's mentioned his streaming company in the past but I didn't connect it until now. "Scott never needed my password to watch TV. Did he?"

He has the audacity to shrug. "No."

"Then why use it?"

"Why else, dearie? Love makes us do silly things," Juliana intervenes.

"Oh, no. We're just…"

"Seizing the day," he finishes for me.

I snap. "Right! One day at a time." I nod at Juliana like that explains every complicated second of my relationship with Rowan.

Juliana wags her finger at us. "You let me know who stops believing the lie first."

I roll my eyes. She is a romance author after all. Of course she's going to believe every couple is destined for a happy ever after. I'm not against one, but I'm also not all for getting my hopes up too soon. Although this book signing has me wondering what next step we might take together.

Rowan deposits my books on the table.

"Why did you use my account then if you literally created the entire platform?"

"I wanted to see what you were interested in."

I'm tempted to cry from how sweet that is. For months I thought he barely liked me, and here he was watching TV on my account to feel more connected.

I wrap my arms around him and give him the best hug. He kisses the top of my head.

"Well, come on now. I have about a hundred more people

to see after you two." Juliana waves me over. She signs each of my books with her name and a short message. People behind us grumble about how long she takes with me, but she is so full of life and hasn't stopped talking to me. I can't help wanting to soak it all in.

Rowan all but drags me toward the bookstore entrance like a child once Juliana needs to move on.

We walk through the front doors and are met with real snowflakes.

"It's snowing!"

"We should be getting another few inches tonight. Talk about freaky weather." He frowns.

I laugh as I run out onto the snow-covered sidewalk and twirl in a circle, trying to catch the pieces with my tongue like a kid.

"Slow down there before you kiss the sidewalk."

The words leave his lips a second too late. My sneakers catch on a slick patch, and I throw my arms out, but there's nothing to hold on to.

Rowan runs and catches me with some kind of superhuman speed, but his boots meet the same fate of the icy sidewalk. We both go down in a tangle of limbs and a plastic bag filled with all my signed books. Rowan turns to protect me and ends up landing on his back. I follow, smacking right into his chest. He lets out an audible breath. His other hand still clutches the bag, protecting all the books from falling out and landing on the wet sidewalk.

"Ouch." I rub my forehead that didn't survive the fight with his muscles. "Are you okay?"

"Ask me tomorrow when my lungs start working again."

I drop my forehead against his chest and laugh until the cold air burns my lungs. He wraps his arms around me, and together, we lose it on a dirty sidewalk covered in snow.

Best date ever.

CHAPTER THIRTY-EIGHT

Rowan

I guess I didn't do too bad. Zahra's had a permanent grin plastered across her face since she found out about the book signing. My only mistake was not swearing Juliana to secrecy about the reason behind the event.

I don't want Zahra to look too much into things. But part of me wonders if it's too late for that based on the way she smiles at me like I make her genuinely happy.

My driver drops us off back at the penthouse.

This elevator ride is different from the last, with Zahra cracking open her books like she wants to double-check for any water damage after our tumble. She's done it twice already, but I don't fault her for being protective over her new prized possessions.

We stroll into the apartment, and Zahra scurries away to put her books back in her luggage and take a shower. I do the same, changing into a pair of jeans and a T-shirt with a faded Dreamland logo.

"So, what's the plan?" She walks down the stairs in a matching jogger set. The fabric outlines every curve on her body, and I find it difficult to be a decent man and look away. Except I'm not anything close to proper when it comes to Zahra, so I take the time to check her out.

She rounds the counter and looks up at me. "You're going to burn a hole through my clothes if you keep staring at me like that."

"Remove your clothes then. Problem solved." I grab onto her hips and tug her closer.

She places a hand against my chest, right above my heart. It races faster in my chest at the registration of her touch.

Her stomach lets out the loudest protest ever. She slaps a hand over it. "How embarrassing."

I cringe at my lack of thinking. We haven't eaten anything since the quick lunch on the plane.

I release her and walk to the drawer filled with takeout menus. "Take your pick."

She flips through the brochures and mini menus before plucking out one for pizza. "When in New York?" She lifts a shoulder.

"You pick that when you could have Ruth's Chris takeout?"

"Who's Ruth Chris?"

I groan. "Pizza it is."

Dinner arrives an hour later, and I set it up on the coffee table. We both settle onto the accent rug in front of the massive fireplace in the middle of the living room. I've never enjoyed eating at a dining table. It reminds me of the time when my mother was alive, back when my father would make it home sober enough for us to eat as a family.

"So you said this was one of your properties. How many do you have exactly?" She takes a big bite of her pizza.

I do the mental math. "Twenty-eight."

"Are you serious?"

"Yes."

Her cheeks lose some of their color. "Okay. Wow. Which one is your favorite?"

I take a bite of my pizza to give me enough time to consider her question. "Honestly, I don't have one."

Her mouth gapes apart. "None of them feel like home?"

"Home is wherever I'm needed for work."

She gapes at me.

"There's some climates I prefer more than others. Like Chicago is great in the summer but my dick is subject to frostbite during the winter."

"And Dreamland?"

I toe around her question carefully. "Dreamland is different."

"How so?"

"There were a lot of bad memories there for me."

Her brows pull together. "Oh. It's surprising you wanted to become the director then."

"I was interested in taking the park to the next level. It was in my best interest to move past the issues holding me back."

It's not technically a lie. Yet her smile still feels like a punch to the gut.

You have no choice but to keep the whole truth from her. You're too close to finishing to jeopardize everything now.

She smiles. "Do you feel better about being there now?"

"I met someone who makes my time there tolerable."

The flush spreading across her cheeks makes my stomach roll. It's hard to eat anything. "Tolerable? I've got to step it up."

She's done more than enough. I clear my throat. "Enough questions about me. I'm curious about something."

"What?"

"Tell me about your pins."

Her entire body language changes from the one question. "It's not a cute story." She looks out at the view behind me.

"I didn't ask for one." I grab her hand like she's done for me every time I need to talk about something difficult.

Her body loosens, and she releases a deep breath. "The first day I attended therapy was the same day I got my very first pin."

I could never imagine someone like Zahra going to therapy. My father told me it was for weak people who were so pathetic, they needed someone else to solve their problems.

"You went to therapy? Why?"

"Because I realized that I couldn't fix myself without putting in the hard work."

"But you're—" I get stuck on finding the right words.

Her laugh sounds sad. "What? I'm nice? Happy? Smiling?"

"Well, yes." Isn't that how it works? Why would anyone who's happy go to therapy?

Her eyes drop to her lap. "Everyone has bad times. And for me, I—there—" She lets out a heavy breath.

Zahra feeling distraught? That's new.

"About two years ago, I fell into a deep depression." She stares down at her hands.

I blink. "What?"

Her cheeks flush. "It's true. I didn't know it at the time, but

Claire was the one who officially told me I needed to get help. She even helped me search for a therapist and told me to try to talk to someone about how I felt."

"I—I don't know what to say."

She sniffles. "I don't even know why I'm crying right now." She furiously wipes her damp cheeks.

I swipe away a tear she missed.

"I know I'm in a better place. But…God. When Lance broke my heart, I could hardly get out of bed. I used up all my vacation days for the year because I wasn't sleeping much and it felt like a chore to even get up. It was like I was going through the motions of life but not really living. Barely even eating. And the thoughts—" Her voice cracks, and I swear I feel it like a punch to the heart. "I hated myself so much. For months, I blamed myself. Because what kind of stupid woman wouldn't realize a man was cheating on her? I felt pathetic and used."

"You're many amazing things, and pathetic isn't one of them." My blood heats at the idea of her thinking anything bad about herself.

She sniffs again. "I know that now. But at the time, I felt so weak because nothing I did could stop this feeling of hopelessness that took over. I tried. God, I really did because I never knew what it was like to be anything but happy. But the harder I tried to put on a face, the worse things got. I eventually hit a scary point where I wondered if life was worth it." She looks down at her trembling hands. "I–I never thought I would be the kind of person who thought I might be better off gone. I'm ashamed I ever even considered it."

I'm tempted to find Lance and pummel his face to match

a fraction of the hurt Zahra went through because someone as sweet as her wouldn't need a semicolon pin if it wasn't for him.

"This is me now. But who I was before, when everything happened—I was a broken shell. I forgot to believe in myself when it mattered most."

The hurt in her voice chokes me, making every breath difficult. Her eyes, always expressive, show every ounce of pain she's felt because of that asshole.

I crawl over to her side of the table and pull her into my lap. She buries her face into my shirt, fisting the material of it as if she needs to hold on.

I've felt many different things in my life, but Zahra seeking comfort from me brings out something in me I can't pin down. It makes me feel needed. Protective. Vindictive toward anyone who hurts her.

I really like her. Our relationship is slowly evolving from something casual into something more, and I'm not entirely against it.

I tug her tight against my chest.

"Claire was the one who started my pin collection after my very first therapy session. She bought me an Iggy the Alien one she found on Etsy, but instead of him holding up his three fingers in peace, he was flipping everyone off. It was a symbolic *fuck you* to Lance."

I shake my head with a smile. "That's illegal trademark infringement."

"Sue me." She grins.

I smile back. "How did you go from one pin to a whole backpack covered in them?"

"Claire made it her mission to find me the most outrageous pins each week. Every time I came back from my weekly session, she would unveil it. Now she gets me two a year, one for my birthday and one for Christmas."

"She's a good friend."

"The best kind. I'm lucky to have her in my life. As a roommate and a best friend."

I squeeze her closer as if it could alleviate some of the pain. "But now you're better?" I try to hide the concern in my voice, but some of it shines through.

She nods. "Definitely."

"For what it's worth, he never deserved you."

And you do?

"Thanks." Her voice is a whisper, sounding so small and unsure.

"If you don't mind me asking, why do you wear the pins then every day?"

"As a reminder and a promise to myself that no matter how hard life gets, I'll keep pushing." Her watery smile makes my whole chest tighten to the point of it being difficult to breathe.

I grab a lock of her hair and tuck it behind her ear. "You're ridiculously amazing."

"Because I wear awesome pins?"

"Because you're you."

I press my lips against hers. It's a soft kiss, not meant to tease or provoke. I'm not sure what it's for but I know it feels right.

She sighs and it makes something weird happen in my chest. Like I can make her content.

I press my forehead against hers. "One day I hope I can be

strong like you. To maybe talk some things out that have been weighing on me."

She sucks in a sharp breath. "Strong like me?"

I nod. My throat grows tighter as if it wants to stop me from spilling secrets.

Don't do it. You open up this kind of wound and you're asking for her to pick at your weaknesses.

But what if she's not like *him*. Zahra is kind, loving, and everything good in the world. She's nothing like my father. She wouldn't judge me. No. Because she actually likes *me*—the complete opposite of him.

An asshole who doesn't care about making others cry, beg, or poor. Someone who's chosen himself time and time again because if I didn't protect myself, no one would.

"I–I was very affected by my mother's death."

Zahra's entire face changes. Her smile drops and her eyes soften around the edges. I'm tempted to stop. To erase that look and never bring up the subject again.

But she surprises me. "A kiss for a secret?"

I nod, unable to get any words out. She presses her lips to mine. The feel of her body against mine urges me forward. To take. To own. To make her remember who I am, regardless of my hidden weaknesses disguised as secrets.

I dominate her lips, branding her with my tongue. Showing her I'm still the man she likes no matter what I might say that makes me seem less than.

Don't be stupid. She wouldn't think that.

She pulls away and cups my cheek. "My secret."

I sigh. Am I really going to tell her about this? *Can I* even do it? That part of my past is under lock and key, submerged somewhere deep within the crevices of my darkest memories.

She wraps her legs and arms around me. Her warmth trickles into my skin, bringing back some kind of heat to my chilled veins.

I release a tense breath. "My dad was a latchkey kid who had access to anything money could buy. Private jets. Boats. A full-time waitstaff. But none of it mattered once my mom came into his life. They are—were the closest thing to true love. At least that's what I was told because I was too young to remember much about them together. But Declan always said that whatever my mom wanted, my dad granted."

Zahra pulls back. "That's so sad."

Shit. "Don't feel sorry for my dad. He's an asshole."

"I feel sorry for *all* of you."

I clear my scratchy throat. "My parents loved Dreamland as much as my grandfather…until everything changed."

"When your mom got sick?"

I nod.

"I'm sorry. No child should lose their mother at such a young age like you did." Her hand reaches out and grabs mine. I open my fist, letting our fingers lock together. The simple gesture shouldn't mean much but holding on to Zahra feels like clutching onto a lifeline. Like I could hold on to her or get swooped up into the darkest corners of my mind.

"One of the last memories I have with her was at Dreamland."

Zahra nods, her eyes reflecting some sort of understanding.

"My mom was everything to us. And the few good memories I have of my parents together include my dad waiting on her hand and foot. If my mom smiled at something, my dad found a way to own more of it. If she cried about something, my dad was hell-bent on demolishing it."

Zahra shoots me a wobbly smile. "He sounds like a man in love."

"Love. Such a simple word for something so devastating."

"Even the best things in life have consequences." Her hand squeezes mine even tighter, cutting off any chance for blood flow. I'm not sure who she does it for but I'm grateful for the grounding caress of her thumb brushing across my knuckles.

"My dad was never the same after she passed, and neither were we." My eyes focus on the fireplace beside us rather than Zahra's face because I can't take her sympathy. Not when I don't deserve it. The selfish monster I've become over the past two decades is a far cry from the boy she pities.

I stare at the dancing flames. "My father treated us like shit because I think he was *scared*. Because taking care of us on his own meant accepting that my mother was truly gone, and he wasn't ready for that. He abandoned us when we needed him most and replaced himself with someone none of us recognized. And instead of losing one parent, we lost both. One to cancer, and the other to his vices." My voice cracks.

"We protected him because we thought he would get better. Looking back, we were too young to know any better. We should've told someone about his issues. But he kept his alcoholism so well hidden. Our grandfather was suspicious, sure, but we protected our father. Not out of loyalty for him, but maybe for our mother? I don't know."

"You were *children*."

"But maybe if we had gotten him the help he needed early, we could've stopped the years of pain we felt after." I shut my eyes, afraid Zahra might catch the wetness building in them.

Men don't cry.

You've always been weak.

Pathetic.

All the memories flood my head at once.

"Pain tests us all in different ways."

I nod. "I think for him, he ruined what everyone else loved because he couldn't stand to lose the one person he cared for most in the world."

"And what do you think he ruined for you?"

"The one thing I was good at. My brothers had sports, or comic books, or special clubs. But me? I was the odd one out. The disappointing artistic one who talked too much and dreamed too big."

Zahra's lips remain pressed together, although I can read a hundred questions in her eyes.

I exhale. "I got to the point that I started resenting myself. All I wanted to do was make my dad happy, but instead, I proved to him time and time again why I failed. Why I was the weakest of his sons. Why my mother was better off never seeing me become such a pathetic child."

A tear trickles down Zahra's face. "You can't believe that."

Look at you making her cry. Always the same disappointment.

I shake the thought away. "I–I don't know. But I changed. There was a shift in my mindset after—" I stop myself from revealing too much. "I withdrew. Learned everything I could from my brothers and stopped caring about anything but proving my father wrong. I spent every day proving why I wasn't a disappointment."

"At the expense of what you loved?"

"It was a price to pay for peace. I didn't think I would draw again—"

"Until you saw my atrocious drawings."

I nod with a small smile. "Because I didn't know it at the time, but I wanted you to see *me*."

CHAPTER THIRTY-NINE

Zahra

I want to kiss Rowan until his lips are swollen and the sad look in his eyes is replaced by lust. Part of me wants to go back in time and protect that little boy who wanted nothing more than to dream and draw and be who he was without being attacked for it. I'd do anything to shield him from his father's ugly words—a result of him hurting just as much as his sons.

I tighten my arms around his body. His ocean-breeze scent washes over me as his head drops to the curve of my neck. He releases a shaky breath.

I'm not sure what this is but it feels *right*.

His heart pounds against his chest at an unsteady pace. "I didn't tell you this for you to pity me."

"Then why?"

"Because…" His voice trails off.

I give him the time he clearly needs. We do nothing but sit here together, basking in the comfort of each other's company.

"You—because—" The fire conceals most of the redness in his face, but I catch the look of terror in his eyes.

I brush my lips across his, leaving behind the faintest kiss. "Because what?"

His heart pounds faster against my chest, the beat becoming alarmingly fast. "Because I like you. It's scary as hell because you make me feel *everything*. And I know I'll disappoint you. That I can't promise much, but sometimes I think maybe I could. If I tried hard enough. If I found a way to make things right."

My entire heart threatens to disintegrate in my chest from the heat spreading through my body. It's the closest thing to a confession of love that I might get from him. And it's a sign of hope.

That he might be in this for more than a casual fuck and a friendship with someone who treats him like a normal guy. That he really could be willing to make things right if he tries hard enough.

I rise up on my knees and press a kiss against Rowan's lips. It's meant to be one of comfort, but he doesn't let me go. One of his hands wraps around my ponytail and tugs while the other grips onto my hips as he deepens the kiss. I moan, giving him better access to my mouth. Our tongues clash together, and blood pounds from my erratic heart to my ears.

Rowan's lips don't break away from mine as he gently maneuvers me so my back presses into the lush rug. He kisses me like he wants to brand me with his tongue. Like he needs to make sure I don't forget him. I wouldn't. Not in a hundred years or a million kisses later. There's something about our connection that has me stumbling for more.

My head grows dizzy as he traces the shape of my body with the tip of his fingers. I move on from his lips and claim the area at his neck, sucking on the skin until I brand him.

He groans as he pulls away. With hungry eyes, he lifts the hem of my hoodie.

"Hmm. That's unexpected." His hoarse voice breaks through my heavy breathing.

Every ounce of blood rushes to my cheeks. "Ani packed it."

"Damn. Way to wound my ego. I thought you picked this just for me." He runs a finger across the obnoxious donuts design. I'm pretty sure this bra hasn't seen the light of day since I was in high school. Pro: It makes my boobs look stellar. Con: It makes me look ridiculous. I can only hope he's desperate enough to skip past reading the "Donut You Want Me" quote plastered across my ass cheeks. I'm not sure I could live that down.

"Do you plan on staring at me all night or are you going to get on with the show?"

His gaze remains focused on my chest. "I like the view."

"I'd like mine better if your face was between my legs."

His lips crash into mine. He rolls us over before I can catch a breath. One of his hands unhooks my bra while the other makes quick work of removing my hoodie. It takes him less than a moment to leave me topless and waiting for him.

He rises up, taking me with him. The area begging for him presses into his erection, and together we moan. His hands are greedy, running across my skin, creating goose bumps wherever they linger.

My head spins as my back hits the rug again. I can't help it. Our lips break apart as I let out a laugh.

"If you're laughing, there's a problem here."

"I can't help it! Where did you learn to move like that?" Another giggle escapes me. I shut up as his body slides down mine.

I don't get a warning. Nothing more than a sharp jolt of my nerves when his mouth latches onto my breast. His tongue swirls, teasing me until I'm moaning and thrashing beneath him. All I can do to ground myself is hold on to his hair and tug.

Rowan is a man with impeccable attention to detail. His mouth might be occupied but it doesn't stop his hands from tracing my other nipple with the gentlest touch. It's nothing but a whisper of a caress, making my skin burn for him. My entire body feels like he drenched me in lighter fluid and set me on fire.

I groan in frustration, and Rowan's mouth detaches with a pop. Flames from the fireplace dance across his face, casting him in a golden glow. "Patience is a virtue."

"Yeah, so is chastity, but you don't see me practicing it."

The corner of his mouth lifts. "I'm trying to be a gentleman. Foreplay is important."

"You fucked me in a car only a couple of weeks ago. The gentleman card has been revoked."

He laughs. It's rich and deep, with enough of a rumble to make my toes curl.

"Stay here." He rises, showing off his impressive bulge pressing against the zipper of his jeans. He undoes the button and zipper partially as he walks toward the kitchen. Drawers bang open and shut before he returns and drops a few condoms on the rug.

He tugs his T-shirt over his head, and I find my mouth

dropping open. I want to trace my tongue across his rippling muscles, memorizing the curves and solid edges. His jeans find the same fate as his shirt on the floor, leaving him in nothing but a pair of skin-tight boxer briefs. My mouth waters at the outline of his cock.

I crawl over to him and trace his bulge with my palm. His head drops back while his fingers find the roots of my hair as I uncover his erection and trace his length with the tip of my tongue. That earns me a groan and a tug of pain at my scalp.

"Prove how much you want me."

Something about his words clangs inside my chest. After everything he shared, his words feel important. Like he half expects me to think of him as lesser-than because he went through life being unappreciated.

I make a mental promise to adore him. To show him that nothing he says could drive me away. I care about the man no one else knows. I even think I *love* him.

My cheeks burn as I take him in my mouth, one inch at a time. He pushes his dick farther into my mouth, and my clit throbs in response. He controls my body like he does a boardroom—with absolute confidence and a deadly restraint that I find intoxicating.

And I fucking *love* it.

He pushes more, and the edges of his nails scrape at my scalp. My moan comes out muffled, but it pulls his attention back toward me.

The tips of his fingers caress my cheek. "I'm not sure what I love more. The way you smile at me with abandon or the way you look with your swollen lips wrapped around my cock."

He *loves* the way I *smile.*

My entire body flares to life, and I take back control. I use my hands to pump him farther down my throat, and the moan he lets out has me wanting to devour him until he releases his control.

I graze my teeth across the smooth skin, and his hips buck forward. Whatever dominance Rowan had over the situation snaps and his demon is unleashed. He fucks me like he hates me. Like I bring out all those feelings he can't stand.

I absolutely love it. In fact, I want more. More of him and more of whatever this is.

The tiny pinpricks of pain barely register as his fingers tug at my hair. He uses me, marking my tongue with his arousal with every shove.

Our eyes connect, and the fierceness in his gaze sends another current of energy down my spine. I cup his balls in response and every muscle in his body *trembles*.

"Don't you dare swallow." He pumps in and out of my mouth over and over again. His shaft shines, and my eyes nearly roll into the back of my head.

He groans at the same time as his streams of hot cum hit the back of my throat. There's so much, I'm convinced I'll choke, but I take deep breaths and follow through with his request.

He withdraws his cock. "Open." His thumb traces my bottom lip, smothering it with the mix of my saliva and his cum.

I stare him straight in the eyes as I show him what he wants.

"Fuck." His gaze *burns*. "Swallow every last drop."

My throat bobs as I follow his command.

He drops onto the rug and pushes me down onto my back.

His lips return to mine, devouring them. He latches onto the band of my sweatpants and underwear at once, pulling away from my lips only to pull them down. The fire casts me in a golden glow.

"You're perfect." He traces the sensitive flesh on the inside of my thigh, making me feel revered. Special. *Loved.* I've never felt as beautiful in my life as I do right now.

He crawls over me. One of his hands slides down my body while his lips find mine again. He kisses me until I'm breathless. Until blood returns to his cock and pre-cum trickles down my stomach, leaving a path of his arousal.

I cup his growing erection, and he shudders above me. Rowan leaves no area of skin untouched or unkissed. It's as if he wants to memorize the shape of me with his lips. His head rolls to the side when I trace my thumb across the bead of pre-cum and use it to help my hand slide easier across his shaft.

Rowan slides down some more until his mouth lines up with the area desperate for him. I jolt when he runs his tongue across me. Sparks scatter like fireworks across my skin, and my hands grab onto his thick locks. He chuckles against me, making the best vibration against my clit. I have an out-of-body experience as Rowan brings me to the brink of pleasure. I claw at him, trying to find something to secure me to Earth.

His lips find my clit and he sucks at the same time as one of his fingers slides into me. I'm granted no reprieve as Rowan propels another into me. My entire world turns Technicolor. Colors burst behind my eyes as I explode around him. He chases my orgasm with a kiss, muffling my moans like he wants to own them.

I'm trembling by the time I come down from the high. He slides his thumb across my arousal before tracing my bottom lip. "Taste how much you want me."

My tongue darts out, licking my lip before teasing the tip of his thumb.

His eyes turn predatory as he flips me over and lifts me up on my knees, changing our direction so I face the city skyline. I'm not sure where to look: at him kneeling behind me or the bright lights shining in front of me.

The telltale rip of foil fills the silence. Heat pools within my lower stomach. My palms press into the thick rug, and I take a few deep breaths.

Rowan's body presses into my back, enveloping me in his warmth. The heat of his breath sends my nerves into overdrive as he presses the tip of his cock into me.

He kisses the base of my spine. "You weren't supposed to make me smile or laugh." He nips at the edge of my ear before tracing my earrings with his finger. "You weren't supposed to work your way under my skin like venom with no kind of antidote." He slides only the tip into me. I push back, but he moves too, holding me hostage.

"And you were never supposed to make me want more."

Heat blooms in my chest. I gasp as he thrusts his cock into me with one push. My body burns from the intrusion, and tears prick my eyes.

"But now it's too late." He smooths out my hair before wrapping it around his hand like a rope.

He tugs. "You're mine."

My arms tremble, barely holding me up. His words batter

against my heart. Rowan usually might not say much, but tonight he won't stop. Each word works its way down to my soul, fusing together the broken bits Lance left behind in his wake.

His hand clutching my hair tightens. "Say it." He slams into me so hard, I slide forward on the rug, burning my knees.

I can only respond with a moan as he slides out of me to do the same thing all over again.

"Say you're mine." He slides out to the very tip, leaving me feeling empty.

"I'm yours," I cry out. I'm rewarded with another rough thrust of his hips, but this time he brushes against my sensitive spot.

Pressure builds within me. The tingling starts at the top of my spine and reaches all the way to my toes. One of Rowan's hands grips onto my hip while the other tugs on my hair, forcing me to look over my shoulder at him. The view in front of us is nothing compared to the one of Rowan coming undone as he thrusts into me over and over. I'm entranced, clawing at the rug when all I want to do is sink my fingers into his skin and never let go.

Forget sparks. Together, we're a raging inferno so blistering, I'm scared that I'll burst into flames if I touch him. It's fitting, seeing how falling for Rowan is like playing with fire. One wrong move can consume me. Ruin me. Turn me into nothing but ashes in his wake.

But I want to risk falling in love anyway in the hopes that we create something beautiful together. Like a diamond built under pressure, with flaws that make us stunning. I want that kind of love with Rowan. The one that is as passionate as a wildfire and as long-lasting as a gem.

One of the hands gripping my hips moves onto my clit. His thumb presses against the sensitive flesh, shoving me into sweet oblivion. Rowan holds on to me as he plunges into the dark after me.

He's perfect. We're perfect. Everything is so perfect, I'm afraid of saying anything aloud. This is more than lust, but I refuse to be the first to admit it. No matter how tempted I am.

CHAPTER FORTY

Rowan

Zahra's hand shivers against mine. "Are you going to tell me where we are going?"

"If I told you, then it wouldn't be a surprise anymore."

She rearranges a scarf over her face. Her entire body trembles despite me lending her my only coat because Ani packed her a jean jacket.

The two pom-poms at the top of her hat bob as she follows me down the busy street. "Does this surprise include something warm to drink? I can barely feel my toes anymore."

"That's because your sneakers aren't meant for this weather."

"I don't think my sister had a clue how cold it gets here." She rubs her gloved hands together.

I should've bought her better winter clothes while we were here. She's trembling like a leaf and I'm afraid she'll fly away with the next gust of wind.

"You're not ready for a Chicago winter if you think this is cold."

"I didn't know I was expecting a Chicago winter anything."

I smack one of her pom-poms. "You're my date for the New Year's Eve gala."

"What kind of selfish people host a gala on New Year's? Don't people like to spend it with their families?"

"Sure, if they're ninety and in a retirement home." I grab her hand and cross the road with her. Despite her neon jacket, I don't trust her not to get stuck in oncoming traffic because she's amazed by all the lights and people.

"Do you ever ask instead of order? First, it was going to New York. Now it's a gala for New Year's. Do I have a choice when it comes to you?"

"Sure. Tonight you can decide how you want to have sex first." I grin. The muscles in my face feel looser this time, like I'm finally adjusting to this kind of gesture.

She smacks my arm with the edge of her scarf. "How generous of you."

"Come on. We're almost there. Just one more street over."

We make it to Rockefeller Center. A crowd of people surrounds the massive tree dazzling with multicolored lights.

Zahra cranes her neck back to get a look at the seventy-five-foot-tall tree. "Wow. This puts the Dreamland tree to shame!"

I'm tempted to make the next tree at Dreamland as gigantic as this one to make her this happy.

I wrap my arm around her and tuck her into my side. "What do you think?"

"That this is the closest thing we have to magic. Seriously, how do they even find a tree that large? The North Pole?"

I choke on a laugh. "More like somewhere in Connecticut."

"Way to ruin the dream." Zahra stares up at the lights while I look at her. I've never cared for silly traditions like visiting the Rockefeller tree but watching Zahra smile as she experiences new things revives a damaged part of me. It makes me want to find other things that would amaze her if only to recreate the same kind of look of wonder on her face.

I'm screwed. Absolutely losing my goddamn mind.

Her eyes light up like the damn tree as she turns and checks out the ice-skating rink behind us. "So, how hard would it be to convince you to go ice skating right now?"

I can't ice skate to save my life. Where Declan and Cal crushed it on their minor league hockey teams, I preferred more creative pastimes. I have a higher chance of chipping a tooth tonight than getting laid, yet I don't care.

"Give me your terms."

She rolls her eyes. "Everything is a deal for you."

I tap her red nose. "You're a fast learner."

Her smile rivals the star at the top of the tree.

Yup. I'm royally screwed.

"There's one last thing I want to do." Zahra clutches onto my hand.

Snowflakes fall around us, covering our coats and hats.

"Ice skating wasn't enough for you?"

She shakes her head. "Can we take a walk through Central Park? *Please*?"

"I lost all feeling below my knees about thirty minutes ago."

I blow a breath just to prove my point. The smoky air disappears into the night.

"That's because you spent more time on your hands and knees than actually skating."

My lungs burn from laughing. The warmth spreading through my chest combats the chilly air.

She drags my hand in the wrong direction. "Come on. It's only a quick walk. I googled it."

"No."

"Don't be such a drag." Her pout, while cute, does absolutely nothing to me.

"Consider myself unmoved by your display."

"Please? There's one last little thing I want to do." Her bottom lip wobbles. Her lashes flutter, collecting snowflakes in their wake.

My resolve melts. I cup her windburned cheek. Her smile grows as I drag my thumb back and forth across her frozen skin.

Damn. My balls have officially become a prisoner of war.

"Fine. But only for fifteen minutes. Your nose is about to detach from your body." I flick the red tip.

Zahra beams. For her smile, I'd do just about anything.

I was a fool for thinking fifteen minutes was enough time. There was no way in hell I was dragging Zahra out of the park without her kicking and screaming. The one little thing she wanted to do turned into two things, and then three. Then, before I know it, I'm making a snowman in the middle of Central Park after doing a ridiculous sleigh ride through the entire place.

"Did you find the buttons?" Zahra lets out a ragged breath. She drops three branches by my boots.

I place the three small pebbles I sifted through inches of snow to find.

"Yes! Perfect." Zahra looks at the rocks like they're diamonds.

Never in my life would I have considered building a snowman to be this much fun. Watching Zahra experience snow for the first time is like being around a little kid on Christmas morning. I've never felt such joy like this before. At least not since I was a little kid myself.

I want to steal more of Zahra's firsts. Anything to recreate *that* smile she has while looking at a pile of rocks and a lopsided snowman. I want to own her smile just as much as I want to own every other part of her.

She laughs as she rolls the head of the snowman around and around, making the ball larger with each pass.

"Are you sure you're twenty-three years old?" I tease.

"Oh, come on. The closest thing I had to a snowman was one made of sand. Let me live a little."

"Remember this moment when you end up stuck in bed with a bowl of chicken soup in a couple of days."

"Who cares? We're living for today."

"That's great and all until I lose nine out of ten fingers from frostbite."

"Aw, poor baby." She grabs my gloved hand and kisses each finger.

"I know something a little lower that could use a warm kiss too."

A laugh explodes out of her. I lean over and peck a soft kiss on the curve of her neck, too tempted by her exposed flesh.

Her eyes heat as she gathers herself. “Let’s go, Jack Frost. We’re almost done.” She runs a mittened hand across my zipper, bringing my dick to life.

Zahra has that kind of power over me. A few touches from her, and my dick is all systems go.

“Where the fuck have you been? You’ve been ignoring me,” Declan snaps the moment I answer his call.

“I’ve been busy.” I lock the door to my office just in case Zahra gets out of the shower faster than anticipated.

“Busy doing what exactly? Scheduling book signings in New York for no other reason except that you’re losing your goddamn mind?”

My grip on the phone tightens. “How did you find out about that?”

“I know about everything that happens within the company, including the fact that you took a vacation for the first time in years. What the hell is going on with you?”

“It’s a long story.”

“Give me the abridged version.”

I drop into my leather chair. “Is this the real reason behind your call?”

“No, but I want to know why you’re acting like a dumbass only a few weeks before the vote.”

“I decided to spend a weekend doing something I liked.”

“Save me the bullshit excuse about New York.”

“I don’t need to give you an excuse. You’re not my keeper.”

“No, but I’m the one who’s going to knock some sense

into you when you've clearly lost your goddamn mind over a woman."

What the fuck? He knows about Zahra? "Who told you anything?"

"I have eyes and ears everywhere, Rowan."

"Stop poking around in my affairs. If I wanted to tell you what I was up to, I would."

"No, you wouldn't. You never do."

I chuckle low under my breath.

He sighs like he's carrying the weight of the world on his shoulders. "I'm worried about you."

I roll my eyes. "Don't be." It feels pointless to even say it. Declan might act like a hard-ass, but I know it comes from a good place. His protective instinct has been ingrained in him from a young age.

"I don't like the idea of some woman manipulating you into taking time off so close before the vote. It's suspicious."

My jaw clamps down. "I don't see how that's possible when it was my idea."

"You actually like her?" He laughs mockingly.

"Is that so hard to believe?"

"And to think I considered you my more intelligent brother. What a disappointment."

My molars grind together. "Declan, I'm in the middle of something so either get to the point of your phone call or I'm going to hang up."

"The letters have been sent to Grandpa's chosen voting committee."

Fuck. This is the last kind of stressor I need. "Any word on who he picked?"

"No, but you need to get your shit together because we're all depending on your presentation."

"I've been prepping for months. There's no way I don't have this vote locked down."

"Good. Once you get the approving votes, you'll spend a month transitioning the next director into the role and they'll take on the project from there."

"I thought while you were settling everything with your letter, I could stay here and oversee the project myself." The idea slips out of me. If I stay at Dreamland, it will give me time to work through my feelings for Zahra without sacrificing anything in the process.

If we fizzle out, I go back to Chicago like planned.

And if you don't?

The silence coming from Declan's end of the phone makes the back of my neck prickle.

"I thought you were joking." He speaks after a whole minute.

"No. What's the point in me moving back if you still haven't gotten married yet?"

"You're going to shadow me and take over a portion of my CFO role so I can concentrate on finding my future wife."

My teeth grind together. "Give me six more months as the director. It'll be less confusing for the employees to have a director for a whole year."

"Since when do you care about confusing employees?"

"It's my job to care."

Declan's low laugh carries through the small speaker. "No. It's your job to finish up and move back to Chicago after the vote."

"Grandpa said I have to be director for *at least* six months. But he never stated when I had to leave."

"I'm well aware of what Grandpa said. It doesn't change the outcome for you. I've already chosen the next director and he will be contacting your secretary after the vote."

"You're not the CEO yet. You can't force me to move back whenever you snap your fingers."

"Let's be real. The only reason you're interested in staying there is because of a woman. You don't even like Dreamland, so cut the shit."

My nails dig into my palm. "No. That's not true. I actually enjoy this job."

He sighs in a way that reminds me of when we were kids and I begged him for dessert before dinner. "Rowan, if you really want to be the director, you can go back to Dreamland once I secure my CEO position. Until then, let's get everything sorted out with each of our letters before you go changing the plans."

Fuck. I put him on speaker and run my hands through my hair.

How am I supposed to choose between my brother and Zahra? My distress over the decision is laughable after everything Declan has done for me throughout my life.

I hate that my brother has a point. I hate that I know I owe him this much, despite my feelings toward Zahra. Declan was always there for me when my father was drunk or absent. He was the one who taught me how to ride a bike just like he was the one who stayed up late helping me with my homework despite having his own. Hell, he sacrificed an Ivy League education so he could stay in Chicago to take care of Cal and me. In some ways, he became a parent figure when I didn't have one.

All I feel is abdominal distress at the idea of choosing him over Zahra. Nothing about moving back to Chicago seems easy, especially now.

You were the one who wanted something casual with Zahra. Get over it.

I release a heavy sigh. “Okay.”

I expect some type of relief at agreeing to his plan, but instead, I feel a heavy weight pressing against my chest. Because to please my brother, I’m bound to hurt the one person I’ve grown to care about.

CHAPTER FORTY-ONE

Zahra

"You can't go to work like this." Claire uses a pair of tongs to throw my empty tissue box in the trash.

After I came home from the airport, my condition slowly deteriorated. It started with feeling bone-tired and it devolved into me cradling a box of tissues all through the night while I slept. I went to work yesterday but I ended up having to spend half the day working from home because everyone kept staring at me every time I blew my nose.

Rowan was right after all. I did catch a cold because I was too stubborn to go inside.

I cover my mouth with my elbow as I let out another wet cough. "I have to go. We don't have much time left before the project deadline."

"One day off isn't going to make much of a difference."

"But I need to—"

She shakes her head. "But nothing. I already made you some chicken soup last night after I heard you hacking up your lung."

I press a hand against my pounding head. "Thank you."

"It's the least I could do. You look like death."

"I feel like it too." My laugh turns into a series of coughs. Each breath makes my lungs burn in protest.

Claire brings me a fresh glass of water before leaving for work.

I grab my phone and send Jenny an apology email. She replies back within a few minutes telling me to get well soon and not to worry too much about them.

I pull up my chat with Rowan. He's been a bit off since our last night in New York. I'm not sure if it's the stress of the job getting to him or maybe the fact that he needs some distance after spending so much time together. I really hope it's not the second option.

Me: I think I'm coming down with something.

Rowan: I told you Central Park wasn't the best idea.

I cringe. It probably wasn't the smartest move to stay outside in the cold but the memories were totally worth it.

Me: But it was so much fun.

Rowan: So are drugs. That doesn't mean people should use them.

Me: How would you know?

Rowan: ...

Me: I have a feeling you're the funny type when high.

Rowan: I will neither confirm nor deny.

Me: Creative type?

Rowan: Zahra. Enough.

Ugh. He's no fun today.

Rowan: Do you need any medicine?

Me: I think I know the cure.

Rowan: Enough cough medicine to knock out an elephant?

Me: Close but no. Watching the next episode of that true crime documentary we started over the weekend.

Rowan: My house. Tonight. 6 p.m.

Me: You're leaving work early?

Rowan: I felt like taking some time off anyway. Jet lag and all.

Jet lag? Yeah right! We stayed in the same time zone and he knows it.

Me: Feel free to admit that you're starting to like me at any time.

Rowan: These are the ramblings of a person hopped up on too much cough medicine.

I grin. That's the man I know and love.

Love? Oh shit. Can I really love Rowan?

How could I not? He's thoughtful, reserved, and so damn sweet to me that I completely forget how he hates the general population. He drives me wild in the best kind of way and he makes my heart race whenever he's in the same room as me.

Oh, yeah. I'm in love with Rowan Kane.

The real question is does he love me back?

"Come on, Zahra. You've got to eat something." Rowan's voice sounds far away, like he's on a different kind of radio frequency.

I shove his arm away from my shoulder and sink further into his silky sheets. I'm drawing a blank on how long I've been using his house as an infirmary tent. All I know is his bed is a hundred times better than mine and I never want to leave.

I'm pretty sure my sinuses make up three-fourths of my brain by now, and my left nostril hasn't felt fresh oxygen since yesterday when Rowan picked me up from my apartment.

"*Zahra.*" He turns me toward the edge.

"Go away," I mumble.

He flicks me on the forehead. My head pounds in response, and I wince. I open my eyes to find a distressed version of Rowan. I've never seen him look like this before. His hair is unkempt and he has purple bags under his eyes.

I trace his unusual stubble. "You need to shave." My voice croaks before I let out a wet cough.

Ugh. Disgusting.

"You slept through breakfast, lunch, and—" He checks the time on his watch. "Dinner. It's time to get some food in you before you pass out." The rare high pitch of his voice makes my head throb harder.

"*Shh.* Talk lower." I place a finger against his lips. "Wake me up in another—" My sentence is cut off by my body attempting to expel one of my lungs through my throat.

"Here. Take a sip of water. *Please.*" His voice cracks. He all but shoves the metal straw in my mouth.

I take a sip. "Happy now?"

He frowns. "No."

"I feel like I'm dying."

His grip on my chin tightens. "Don't be dramatic. You have a cold."

Is that *worry* I hear in his voice?

"Okay." I turn over and give him my back. "I'll be up in an hour. I promise."

"I'm going to call a doctor to come check on you."

"Doctors still do house calls?"

"For the right price."

I cough again, but this one doesn't stop. My chest rattles from the sheer intensity of it. There's a sharp stabbing pain poking me in the lungs, and it takes every ounce of energy to breathe.

His hand stroking my hair freezes. "Shit. I'll be right back."

Rowan places a kiss on my forehead before tugging his phone out of his pocket and exiting the room. His murmurs carry through the door, but it takes too much effort to listen in on his conversation.

I shut my eyes and give in to the darkness pulling me under.

I wake up to someone opening my eyelids and shining a flashlight on my face. I try to put some room between us, but I only end up falling back on my shaky elbows.

"She's been sick for three days straight already."

"Three days?!" I regret the loud shriek as soon as it leaves my mouth. My head and lungs work, revolting against me one cough at a time. The pulsing intensifies the more I hack.

"In my professional opinion, she needs to be taken to a hospital."

"Hospital?" Rowan and I both speak at the same time. He practically spits the word out.

I look over at him. He looks almost as bad as I feel, with days' worth of stubble covering his face. The bags under his eyes stand out even more now because of how red his eyes are. He looks like he might keel over any second.

My chest aches for an entirely different reason than my illness.

The doctor stands and packs up his medical bag. "She's severely dehydrated and needs proper medical care."

"Anything else you suggest?"

"Based on the symptoms you described and what I see and hear, it's probably some kind of viral pneumonia. Her tissues are covered with green mucus and she has a fever. If you don't take her to the hospital tonight, she's going to end up in the back of an ambulance soon enough."

Pneumonia? Shit. No. That sounds scary. The only person I know who got pneumonia was one of my parent's friends and he didn't make it.

I want to cry, but I don't think I have enough water in my body to produce tears. I sweat it all out on day two.

While Rowan sees the doctor out, I sit up and fumble for my phone. I should call my parents and let them know about how sick I am. Except I can't find my phone anywhere within the sheets or on the nightstand.

Did I leave it in the bathroom? I slide out of bed and stand on weak legs. My walk to the bathroom steals all my energy, and the room spins.

I grab the handle for stability and push the door open. My legs give out at the same time, and all I see is black.

CHAPTER FORTY-TWO

Rowan

I dismiss the doctor and shut the front door.

Pneumonia? How the hell did Zahra go from making snow angels in Central Park less than a week ago to a nasty case of pneumonia? She went from the sniffles to bedridden faster than I've seen anyone decline.

Something thumping against the floor makes the ceiling vibrate.

"Zahra?" I bolt up the stairs and throw open the bedroom door at the end of the hall. The pulse point at my neck throbs to a wickedly fast beat as I walk into the empty bedroom. The sheets are nothing but a haphazard mess, empty of the severely ill woman who should be sleeping.

My eyes snap to the bathroom door.

"Shit!" I don't think. I don't breathe. I do nothing but run toward a set of tan legs peeking out from the doorframe. My knees slam into the marble beside a small puddle of blood.

"Zahra? Zahra! Are you okay?" My voice croaks.

I drag her useless body into my arms. With a shaky hand, I swipe her hair away from her face. She's pale. *Too* pale. Like the life was drained out of her somehow within the five minutes I went to show the doctor out. I'm pretty sure a piece of my frozen heart shatters right off.

She doesn't respond, and her eyes remain shut. Her chest rises and falls from her shallow breaths, and I exhale slowly, relieved she's breathing. A trail of blood seeps from a nasty gash at the top of her forehead.

I'm careful not to jostle her as I fumble for my cell phone in my pocket and dial 911. They ask too many damn questions, and I'm at a loss for answers except to tell them to get here fast.

"Zahra." I reach for a hand towel within arm's distance and press it against her head wound.

She doesn't wince. Doesn't blink. Doesn't do anything but lay there in my arms, absent of everything that makes her so very her.

Her smile. Her laugh. Her constant flushed cheeks whenever I'm around.

My chest squeezes. "Zahra!" I squeeze her body against mine, hoping something snaps her awake, but I'm met with silence. Her soft exhales are the only thing keeping me from losing my shit.

"Zahra. Wake up!" A drop lands on her forehead. I look at the ceiling but don't find anything leaking. Another drop splatters against her face, trickling down into the blood trail.

It takes me a second to realize the water is coming from me. My tears.

Always crying like a little girl. My father's slur of a voice slithers into my ear.

"Come on, Zahra. Wake up." I shake her body.

She moans as she reaches for her head, but I push it out of the way.

"Thank fucking Christ." I can't understand whatever gibberish comes out of her mouth. There's a mix of incoherent words which only adds to my concern that she fucked up her head from the fall. Nothing makes sense, and I'm worried I might have further aggravated her head injury when I shook her.

"Fuck!" I drop the towel and grip her harder to my chest.

Did I harm her? In my desperation, I didn't think. Didn't consider the pros and cons of moving her body. I reacted and lost control, yet again.

Her blood seeps into my shirt, sticky and clinging. My entire body trembles as I hold on to her.

What the fuck was I thinking shaking her body like that? She already has a head injury.

Fuck. That's the thing. I'm not thinking. I allowed my already useless emotions to get to me.

She wheezes, turning one cough into a whole coughing fit.

The sound of the sirens grows closer. Only then do the tears stop falling.

I've never ridden in an ambulance, and my skin remains permanently clammy during the entire trip while the paramedics work on stabilizing Zahra's condition. Zahra is somewhat coherent, responding to a few questions with her eyes closed.

Zahra winces as they bandage up her forehead. The monitor's beeps become more erratic, a staccato matching the beat of my heart.

Her pain makes me want to rage. To throw shit around and scream because I feel like it's all my fault. I shouldn't have left her alone while she was half-lucid. Hell, if I had said no to half the shit we did in New York, we might not even be in this position.

Is this how my dad felt when my mother was rushed to the hospital time and time again? This burning desperation to do something yet the inability to fix anything?

The thought hits too close to home. How could I have been this much of an idiot? I willingly became like my father, giving in to a woman's every whim until they took over all my thoughts and influenced my actions. I've rearranged my schedule, took nights off to attend mentorship events, and went on vacation when I should have been working. Fuck. I was even willing to give up my future as the CFO to stay with her at Dreamland.

What the hell is wrong with me?

The truth is I became soft and easily swayed by her. And for what? To willingly subject myself to this feeling of powerlessness?

Fuck that. I absolutely despise whatever is wreaking havoc on my head and heart. If I never feel it again, I'd consider myself forever grateful.

This is why I should've listened to my gut instinct when I first met Zahra. There was something about her that warned me away, but I didn't pay enough attention.

A tremor runs through my body, but the adrenaline still coursing through me doesn't let me give in to exhaustion.

The doors open and I'm pushed out of the way as they roll Zahra out and through the emergency room bay. I feel like I'm having an out-of-body experience as I walk through the sliding doors. I'm hit with the offensive smell of antiseptic cleaner.

I'm running on autopilot, completely missing the nurse calling for my attention.

"Are you family?" She taps on my shoulder again, pulling me from wherever the hell my mind keeps drifting to.

"What?"

"Family or friend?" Her lips purse.

"Fiancé." I've seen enough TV shows to know how it works around here.

She gives me a quick scan as if she can detect my lie, but she shockingly nods.

"Fine. Follow me." She leads me into a waiting room. The peeling linoleum tile and the flickering fluorescent light in one corner add to the tightness in my chest. There are a few people seated at different corners of the room.

My hands shake. I haven't been to a hospital since my grandpa's accident. And before then, my mom's death. Hospitals and I have a bad history and a low success rate. And now, it's a place where my present and my past have collided.

The nurse moves to leave, but I call for her.

"I want my fiancée placed in a private room," I blurt out.

She looks down at her clipboard. "Once she's stabilized, that's up to her insurance policy. Is she on your plan?"

My jaw clenches down. I have no idea what kind of insurance Zahra has, let alone if they allow for private rooms.

Knowing the insurance plans your employees have, do you really expect anything more?

My selfishness has a way of coming back to bite me in the ass. And the worst part is it's only just begun.

CHAPTER FORTY-THREE

Zahra

"Ani, can you shut off the alarm?"

Beep. Beep. Beep.

"*Ani.*"

The same incessant beeping continues. I open my eyes and come face-to-face with a heart monitor. I bolt upright in the bed, and my chest aches in protest.

I stare at the IV embedded under the skin of my left hand as I try to comb through my memories. The last thing I remember is going to Rowan's house to watch TV in bed.

So how did I end up here? My fingers trace the clear tubing that leads right into my nose. I follow the line with my eyes, landing on an oxygen tank.

"She's awake." Rowan's raspy voice has me turning my head toward the sound.

He hangs up the phone and tucks it into his pocket. The

look on his face has a chill spreading across my skin. It reminds me of how he used to stare at me before everything changed between us, and I hate it.

"Don't move." He stands and steps toward the bed.

"What's going on?" my voice croaks. Every word takes a ton of effort I struggle to produce.

He fills a small plastic cup and passes it to me. "You're in the hospital."

I take a sip of the water before speaking. "I gathered that much. But how did I end up here?"

His lips remain in a flat line. He looks ragged and tired in a way I've never seen him, with days' worth of stubble and bags under his eyes. I blink at his wrinkled hospital gift shop T-shirt.

Everything about him is all wrong.

I smooth out the blanket covering me. "Are you okay?"

"I will be." He says the statement with such absolute resolve. I want to believe him, but he can't even look me in the eyes.

Goose bumps explode on my arms. "Do you want to tell me why I'm here?"

It feels like a whole minute goes by before he finally looks at me. "You were dehydrated, bleeding from your head, and tempting fate. You're lucky to be in this bed rather than the morgue."

"Morgue? That's drastic for a couple of stitches and a cold." My brows pull together, and I'm hit with a sharp pain at the top of my head. I touch the spot. My fingers hover over a giant bandage.

His jaw ticks. "Don't touch. With your good fortune, you'll pull a stitch and bleed all over your new gown." He brushes my hand away with a gentleness that fails to match his tone.

"How did I end up getting stitches?"

He caresses my cheek with his thumb. "I found you passed out in my bathroom after you knocked your head against the floor."

"Oh my God." My lungs ache, making it hard to breathe normally. I wince at the burning sensation.

"What hurts?"

"The real question is what doesn't." I shake my head and regret it.

"Don't do that."

I rub my eyes. "I can't believe I ended up here."

He stands taller. "The doctor says you'll go home by the end of the week."

"What day is it?"

"Friday."

"Friday?!" I end up coughing after my outburst.

How is it Friday already? The last day I remember fully is Monday, when I had to call in sick.

"You've been in and out of it from your fever and then your head injury."

"How many days have I been here?"

"Two. They want to keep you here for observation before letting you go home."

I rub my eyes. "This all sounds so expensive."

His nostrils flare. "The only thing you need to worry about is getting better."

"That's easy for you to say. I can't afford my deductible or whatever it costs to have oxygen therapy and overnight hospital stays." I shift in the bed, but Rowan places a hand on my shoulder, stopping me.

Darkness crosses over his face. "It's already paid for."

My pride shrivels up at the idea of being so financially insecure that he needs to cover my medical bills. "I don't know how to repay you."

His entire jaw clenches. "I don't need your money."

"Is everything okay?" My voice is a hoarse whisper.

He releases a deep exhale. "It's good you're more coherent."

That wasn't an answer to my question but I'm afraid to ask more. He tenses when I reach for his hand.

"I'm sorry you had to go through all this. I can't imagine how scary it was for you."

The vein in his forehead pulses. "I was *terrified*, Zahra. I found you barely breathing, with too much blood coming out of your head. And when I got you to wake up, you were talking gibberish. I thought you had permanent *brain damage*." His voice cracks. "The few minutes before the ambulance got to my house were the scariest of my damn life and I couldn't do anything to fix it." The way his voice cracks has my heart splintering with him.

"I'm really sorry. I don't even remember going to the bathroom."

"Stop apologizing. You sound ridiculous." He drops my hand and gives me his back. His back shakes as he lets out a deep breath.

"Minus the amazing?"

His heavy exhale is the only response I get.

I take a deep breath to calm myself down, but I end up wheezing. "Are you sure that you're okay?"

"Stop worrying about me and save your energy for what matters."

But you matter, I want to say. But the words get trapped in my throat, held down by this worry that something isn't right between us.

The heart rate monitoring machine betrays my nerves.

Rowan turns around and glares at the machine. His jaw locks and the vein in his temple makes a reappearance. "I mean it, Zahra. Relax."

"Will you stay while I sleep?" I feel pathetic for asking.

He remains silent.

Acid churns in my stomach and inches up my throat. What happened while I was resting? It's like the man I spent the whole weekend with in New York is gone, replaced by this cold version. It reminds me of how Rowan was when I first met him, which pains me more than I care to admit.

He squeezes my hand once before taking a seat across from me. "I'll stay."

I offer him a small smile which he returns with a forced one.

The beeping machine fills the silence. Each breath is taxing on my energy, and I lose the battle with consciousness. Darkness swallows me whole, worries and all.

CHAPTER FORTY-FOUR

Zahra

"Uno!" Ani throws her arms in the air, flaunting a wild card. Rowan throws his stack of cards down.

As much as I love Rowan spending time with my sister, his intention is clear. He's using her as a buffer to avoid talking to me. Anytime my family comes to visit, he immerses himself in small talk. It's highly suspicious, but I'm too tired to talk to him whenever we're alone again.

The silence ends today. I'm never going to truly get better if I'm worried about our relationship.

Despite the way my chest contracts at him ignoring me, I can't help but smile at how he treats my sister. I never thought he would bond with her during his time as her mentor. Their bond really is something special, and it makes my eyes water while watching them.

Rowan is perfect. I never thought I would meet a man like

him. It was supposed to be casual, but it's developed into so much more. From him taking off work to stay by my side at the hospital to him planning a whole book signing just to make me happy, his actions scream *more*.

If only I could figure out what is bothering him because his evasiveness is only adding to my stress.

The nurse strolls into the room and checks my vitals. She asks some questions and writes information on the whiteboard across from my bed.

"The doctor should be stopping by soon to check on you. You're responding nicely to the antibiotics, which means you might be able to get out of here tonight." The nurse smiles and exits the room.

The warmth seeping through my chest is quickly replaced by a chill. Rowan's jaw ticks as he stares at the closed door.

Ani's phone beeps. She looks down at the screen before smiling at me. "I need to go. JP is waiting in the parking lot with his mom." She grins at Rowan before giving me a kiss on top of my head.

"Have fun!" I call out before coughing.

Ani shakes her head. "Gross."

I stick out my tongue.

Ani grins at Rowan as she says goodbye, and he returns it with one of his own. I shouldn't feel jealous at how sweet he is with her, but I've been deprived of his kindness ever since I was admitted to the hospital.

I tuck my shaky hands under the blanket to hide how he makes me feel. "Is everything okay? Really?"

His tight smile doesn't reach his eyes. "It will be."

What does that mean? I want to hold him hostage until he gives me an honest answer.

"Are you still upset about what happened in your house?"

He makes a noise in the back of his throat. "No."

"Then what's going on? Tell me something more than a few words strung together. Something happened, and unless you're open with me about it, I can't fix it." My voice cracks, revealing how exerted I truly am.

His eyes soften. "There's nothing to fix. You need to concentrate on getting better rather than on us."

"Is there still an us?" I voice the one question I've been avoiding since I woke up in this place.

His Adam's apple bobs and his eyes slide toward the window. "I—you—" He stumbles over his words.

Oh God. He's hesitating? He never *hesitates.*

"I need you to tell me what's bothering you. Now." I'm putting my foot down. I've had enough of the cryptic answers and half-truths. Whatever Rowan has to say, I'm a big girl. I can handle him and way worse.

"We can talk about this once you're hom—"

"Cut the bullshit, Rowan. What's your problem?"

His eyebrows rise at my tone. "You want to know what's my problem?"

I nod.

"*You.* This whole damn situation." He throws his arms out in my general direction.

My muscles lock up. "What do you mean?"

"We were supposed to be something casual. Something *fun.* This isn't even close to what I want or need in my life. I have a company to run, a park to oversee, and a lot of shit to work through. People are depending on me, and I'm stuck making sure you're okay because I feel responsible."

I wince.

He continues on like he's not taking a sledgehammer to my heart. "I never asked to play your dutiful boyfriend. That's not the man I am."

My lungs protest from my sharp inhale. "You…you can't mean that."

We have a connection, no matter how hard he tries to deny it. Sure, while we might not have an official label, we have something special.

He clears his throat. "Us hooking up and going on a couple of dates was supposed to be a way for me to pass some time at Dreamland."

"*Pass some time.*" How dare he minimize what we have like that.

He shuts his eyes. "I've lost track of what's important."

And you're not it. He doesn't need to say it because it's written all over his face. Tiny fissures in my heart spread, cracking with each hurtful word he wields like an invisible knife.

"I never take off time for work—not even on Christmas. But I felt obligated because you got hurt in my house. I've even postponed important meetings and blown off a shit ton of paperwork because…"

"Because what?" *Say you care. Say you want me anyway. Say you might be scared, but some things in life are worth the risk.*

Say anything but nothing.

He stands, staring at me with an expression similar to the

ones he has during boring presentations. I've never felt so insignificant—not even when Lance left me. I truly thought Rowan and I had something special. The forever kind of connection I have been hoping for all my life.

I was so wrong.

I let out a bitter laugh. "I don't know what's more pathetic—the fact that you deny how much you care about me or the way I'm actually surprised by all of this."

Nothing but beeping machines fill the silence between us, matching the rapid beat of my heart.

I shake my head. "The problem isn't work. And it's definitely not us changing from casual to more, which is your own damn fault when you kept doing things that showed you cared. You made me believe in some fantasy. You made me want *more*."

His blank stare sends another chill down my spine. "I always meant to keep things casual. That's what we agreed on."

"Well, you did a really shitty job at that. You didn't have to *play* the role of a dutiful boyfriend because you were already acting like one!"

He takes a step back at my outburst.

Breathing hurts, but I don't care. "Every decision you've made up until this point has all been because you *care*. Because deep down, I think you love me even though you're too damn scared to admit it." My voice cracks and I let out a wheeze because my lungs struggle to cooperate.

"Love was never an option. If I made you believe otherwise, I apologize. I would never subject you to that kind of misbelief when I'm moving back to Chicago soon."

He might as well have slapped me.

"What?"

He stares out the stupid window again. "A new director will be taking over Dreamland at the end of January."

If I wasn't attached to an oxygen machine, I'm not sure I would be able to breathe on my own. "Did you—" I rasp. "Did you know this the entire time we were together?"

No. He couldn't have. I'm sure he would have said something about it. What about his anniversary renovation plan? I don't understand why he would spend months of his time on a project of that scale for nothing.

"Yes."

"Did you consider staying longer…" *for us?*

Rowan breaks my heart all over again when he shakes his head. "I was always meant to go back."

You're a fool, Zahra. He's been hiding this all from you since day one. I sniffle, trying to hold back the tears threatening to burst.

"That's not what I asked, and you know it. Stop playing your mind games and tell me the truth."

His jaw ticks. "My personal feelings on the matter are irrelevant."

I stare down at my trembling hands. "Why are you moving back?" *Why are you giving up on us because you're scared?*

"My future is in Chicago."

My heart feels like Rowan clutched it in his cold fist and ripped it out of my chest. "So you say." My voice cracks.

God. How could I have let myself fall for Rowan despite knowing deep down the kind of man he was?

The muscles in his jaw become more pronounced. "I regret hurting you. This was all a mistake."

A mistake. I think a knife to the heart would be less cruel than this conversation. I'm the one who made a mistake. I thought a lot of hopeful things, but most of all, I thought Rowan loved me enough to face the demons holding him back. But this isn't some fairy tale. Change doesn't magically happen because someone threw pixie dust in the air or made a wish on a shooting star.

No. That's not how real life works. People need to put in the work to fix themselves, and while I've done it, Rowan hasn't. He's too afraid. Too selfish. Too consumed by his drive for *more*, without even realizing what exactly he wants more of. I thought he wanted more of me, but I put stock in something make-believe.

"I'm sorry for hurting you." His voice drops to a whisper.

The lump in my throat becomes a living, breathing thing, blocking my ability to breathe. "And I'm sorry for ever thinking you were better than the selfish, cruel man everyone labels you as."

He flinches. It's the first sign of real, raw emotion I've seen from him today.

He looks away and nods. "I see."

A tear betrays me, sliding down my cheek. I swipe it away. "I'll find a way to repay you for everything because I want nothing to do with you or your money again. Even if it takes me my whole life to pay off this damn room, I'll do it."

His throat bobs. "I don't want—"

I cut him off before he can sink his claws further into my heart. "I'm feeling tired all of a sudden."

He nods. "Of course. I never meant to distress you while you're feeling this way."

I say nothing.

"Do you want me to stay until your parents come back?" He looks at the chair closest to my bed.

"No. I'd rather be alone, but thanks for everything again." My voice is cold and withdrawn—a perfect match for him.

"But—"

It's immature, but I turn my back toward him and the door. I don't want to talk anymore. I'm too afraid I might lose it in front of him. Tears stream down my face, creating a wet spot on my pillow.

Rowan lets out a deep breath. His footsteps match the beat of the heart monitor.

I jolt when his hand brushes across my hair.

He presses his lips against the top of my head. "You deserve the world and more."

The door to my room clicks closed, leaving me behind with nothing but beeping machines and my painful sobs to keep me company.

CHAPTER FORTY-FIVE

Rowan

I exit Zahra's hospital room with a tight throat and a burning sensation in my chest. Hurting her was the last thing I wanted to do, but it's necessary. Loving her isn't an option. I have too much at stake and not enough flexibility to have her and the lifestyle I've spent my entire life pursuing. Earning my shares of the company needs to come first. If not for me, then for my brothers.

Zahra might not see it my way, but this is all for the best. We never had a future past two months, and it would have been cruel for both of us to keep pursuing something that had an end date. I didn't realize how much my feelings were developing until I found her bleeding in my bathroom. Breaking her heart was inevitable. But I found my timing less cruel than leading her on because I wanted more time before I left Dreamland for good.

This was the right choice, no matter how hard it feels right now. If difficult decisions were easy, everyone would make them. These are the kinds of choices that make me good at my job.

That's what I tell myself as I walk out of the hospital despite the heavy feeling pressing against my lungs.

For the fourth time tonight, I turn my body and try to find a comfortable position. It's been three days since the hospital, and I have had maybe ten hours of sleep total.

I swipe my phone off the nightstand and check the time.

Three in the fucking morning.

If I can't get a full night's rest, I'll be running on fumes by the end of the week. And with the vote fast approaching, I don't have time for this shit.

I grab a pillow and tug it against my chest. It still smells like Zahra's perfume, and I feel stupid pressing it against my face and taking another sniff.

The tightness in my chest returns with greater force.

You're the one who wanted this. Think about your end goal.

But what good is an end goal if I don't feel happy when everything is decided?

My blood heats in my veins, and I launch the pillow across the room. It lands with a soft thump near the door. Instead of feeling relieved, it feels as if someone is squeezing my throat.

Nothing makes the uncomfortable feeling go away. All my rationalization tactics fail, and I'm stuck staring at the ceiling, wondering if I made the right choice. It sure as hell doesn't feel like it.

Not even a little bit.

I thought I could get information out of Ani about Zahra's recovery, but she is ignoring me. Every text I've sent Ani has gone unanswered. I'm going a bit crazy since Zahra took a whole week off after she was discharged from the hospital.

All I want to know is if Zahra is feeling better. But Ani didn't show up to our usual meetup spot last night, and I was stuck eating my pretzel and hers. The ripple effect of my actions is starting to hit me like a tsunami.

I've resorted to stalking my buddy at her workplace because I hate the fact that she's mad at me. If she were anyone else, I wouldn't care. But Ani's grown on me during my time at Dreamland.

"Hey." I tap on Ani's shoulder.

She tenses before turning around. "Hi. Can I help you with picking out some candy, sir?"

"Come on, Ani." I pretend her words don't bother me.

Her frown adds to the growing tension in my shoulders.

"I don't want to talk to you."

"Too bad. I'm your boss."

She makes a disgusted noise as I grip her elbow lightly and take her to the empty back room of the candy store.

"Spit it out." She stomps her foot.

The fist around my heart tightens as she shoots me a hard look I've never seen on her before.

"I thought we were friends." Ani and I built a bond over the last few months, and I don't want her pushing me away. I've grown to like her as a friend. The idea of her not talking to me anymore makes me sadder than I care to admit.

She shakes her head. "That was before you hurt my sister."

"So what? We're not friends anymore?"

"Nope."

"You don't mean that."

She scowls. "Zahra's my best friend and you made her *cry*."

The inhale I take burns my eyes. "Your sister and I are—"

"Done. She told me." Ani's bottom lip wobbles.

"I didn't mean to hurt you too."

"I helped you hurt her. With the pumpkins, and New York." Her eyes shine from unshed tears.

Fuck. Ani feels responsible for my actions? I never meant for her to carry the burden of my decisions.

"None of this is your fault." I place my hand on her shoulder and give it a squeeze.

"No. It's yours because you're a big baby who can't admit you like her."

I can't hold back my sad laugh. "If only life were that simple."

"You told me excuses are for losers."

Damn. I never thought she would use my own mentor advice against me. I had told her the same words in the context of trying to move out of her parents' apartment and become independent.

It might seem like an excuse to her but I have my reasons.

She sighs. "Thanks for helping me and making me feel better about moving."

Is she seriously trying to give me the brush off right now? "Ani—"

"You're not my friend or buddy anymore. I quit." She lets out a heavy breath.

Her rejection stings. I've genuinely enjoyed spending time

with her. We bonded over many things from being the youngest sibling to our love for pistachio ice cream.

The fact that she can't even look me in the eyes anymore sours my already darkening mood.

"Ani!" Someone opens the door.

"I've got to get going. Merry early Christmas, Rowan." She offers me a half-assed wave before she escapes the room.

I'm left with an empty feeling I can't seem to shake, no matter how hard I try.

Silence greets me when I walk into my house. After meeting with Ani, my day went from bad to complete shit. Nothing could keep my mind from drifting to thoughts about Zahra. I even caved and texted her, only to be ignored. It was supposed to be a simple conversation to lessen the building pressure inside of me, but Zahra didn't even bother answering my message asking how she was feeling.

I change into workout gear and go for a punishing run around the property. My feet slamming against the pavement helps relieve some of the tension from my muscles, but it's not enough to calm my mind.

By the time I run toward the gravel driveway of my house, my breathing is ragged, bordering on painful.

My eyes land on the forsaken swing. The one I never found the time to take down because I was too busy.

Or too much of a coward.

My molars smash together. I stomp through the house and toward the garage where my grandpa kept some tools and his old drill. I'm on a mission to remove that damn swing.

The same swing my mother read fairy tales to us on. Where she and my father would cuddle together while my brothers and I ran around the front yard. And the place where she took her last breath, with my father clinging to her cancer-riddled body while we all cried together.

I hate that fucking swing more than anything in the world. There's nothing I want more than to remove the bolts and turn the whole damn thing into a bonfire.

I plug the cord into the wall with an unsteady hand. One test proves that the drill still works, and I grab a chair from inside to give me the height to reach the top bolts.

My hand shakes when I press the drill into the first screw. Every muscle in my arm groans in protest as I press the button. The screw rotates over and over before it drops straight onto the swing bench.

One down, three more to go.

I get off the chair and move it toward the other side. Resuming my position, I align the drill with the next screw. I freeze at the etched letters engraved right into the wood above my head.

My vision clouds as I trace the annotation. It's jagged like it was done with a sharp knife, but the handwriting is unmistakably my mother's.

My little knights,

Love with all your heart and show kindness in all your actions.

Mommy

I trace the words with a trembling finger. It's been years since I heard the phrase, and it hits me like a punch to the gut. My mother lived by her words in every single one of her actions. She spoke them to us every morning before we went off to school and would whisper them to us every evening before bed. The words sink their claws into me, tearing apart whatever justification I had for the decision I've made.

Would my mother be proud of the man I am now? Part of me would surely hope so but another part of me knows I've done a lot of messed-up things in my life because that's all I know. I wasn't raised with the kind of values my mom preached—at least not once she was gone.

I understand I'm not in the business of making everyone happy, but there's a difference between being business savvy and being unnecessarily cruel. I chose the latter over and over again without feeling a damn thing because it was the easy choice. Cutting back on better health insurance was a shitty ploy to get my father to allow me to sit in during board meetings. He wanted me to earn my stripes before I was given a seat at the table, so I decided to go for the big guns. Just like it was simple to vote against increasing the minimum wage and widen our profit margin. I was willing to think about the company first while proving to my father that I had what it took to develop my own streaming company with Kane money.

I chose myself every damn time because it was *easy.*

Show kindness in all your actions.

It's a joke to linger on those words. Everything I did was at the expense of others while everything my mother did was based on her love and compassion. I forgot she was like that. I *made* myself forget because I think deep down, I didn't want to remember the woman she was. Because I knew she would be disappointed in me. My actions over the years have been anything but kind, done from a place of greed and anger. I've shown little mercy, let alone *love*.

Whatever son my mother raised died along with her, and I feel nothing but shame.

A wave of regret hits me all at once. I discard the drill, take a seat on the chair, and allow myself to come to terms with the monster I became at the sacrifice of my mother's most important values.

I stop by Zahra's cubicle, hoping to catch her on her first day back from her sick leave. I enter the space, finding her drawing something on a…tablet? The brand is the same as mine. Whatever she's drawing on the tiny screen is being mirrored on her desktop monitor, and honestly, it doesn't look half-bad.

"Is that a wheelchair?"

She jumps in her chair, dropping the plastic pencil by her feet.

I lean over at the same time as her, and our heads smack into each other. She hisses at the same time as I wince.

Our eyes lock. I brush my hand across hers before releasing my grip on the pencil. She sucks in a breath, and I smile on the inside.

I'm happy to see that some of her color has returned, although she seems to have lost some weight. I frown at the hollowness of her cheeks.

Her brows pull together as she scowls. "What do you want, Mr. Kane?"

Mr. Kane? My jaw clamps down on my tongue to stop me from saying something stupid.

She raises a brow in a silent taunt.

"I needed to speak with you."

She remains silent. *I see she's not going to make this easy for me.*

"I came to…" *To what? Confess how I feel in the middle of a busy workday?*

"Yes?"

"To ask if you would come over tonight."

Her mouth drops open. "You're joking."

Fuck. She thinks I want to make a move on her? This is why I don't talk about feelings.

"No—shit. I'm not saying this right. I want to talk to you. *Just* talk."

"Yeah, well, I don't want to talk to you." She turns toward her little tablet and tinkers away at her design.

I blink at the computer. It hits me that she is creating her own design instead of working with me.

Because she doesn't need you anymore. I'm not sure why the thought makes my throat tight. I feel like I'm being replaced and forgotten by the one person who really saw me. The person who believed in me and supported me when she had every reason to despise me for what I represented.

"Zahra, hear me out. I can't sleep. I can't eat. I'm stuck in a constant state of nausea and heartburn, no matter what I eat."

"Sounds like you can feel after all." She scowls.

"*Yes.* Are you happy? I *feel* like shit, ever since I left you in that damn hospital room, knowing full well you were crying because of me."

"No. I'm not happy that you're upset. On the contrary, I want you to be happy with your choices." She speaks with such a neutral tone as if I didn't break her heart.

"Why?" *Why do you have to be so goddamn selfless all the time?*

"Because I want you to look back on your choices and know they were worth it in the end."

Except a lot of my decisions don't seem worth it, despite how necessary they felt in the moment. I want to tell her that and a lot more if she will only give me a chance.

"Give me a chance to explain myself. I've been…thinking about everything. And I made a mistake. I shouldn't have let you go because I was afraid. You were right. But I want to try again. With you." My speech is stilted and awkward but it's genuine.

She releases a resigned sigh, and my heart drops with it. "No. I'm not falling for this again. I gave you a chance and you blew it."

"But—"

"No buts. What happens if you change your mind again? I won't take that risk. I've been through enough, and honestly, I deserve better than anything you could half-heartedly offer me."

I'm stuck slack-jawed, staring at her.

Her back tenses. "I need to get back to work. I'm on a deadline."

"I could help you with that. No strings attached." I take another look at the drawing.

Say yes and give me a chance.

"I think you've done enough." She turns her chair, giving me her back.

She's dismissing me. I've never felt so…awful. There's an uncomfortable swell in my chest and a tightness in my throat that only intensifies the more I stare at Zahra's back.

She's really done with me, and it's all my fault.

CHAPTER FORTY-SIX

Zahra

I relish the taste of my fresh glass of orange juice. It's taken me a whole week after coming back from the hospital to regain my taste buds. While I might have been going a little stir-crazy from all the bed rest, I was grateful for the break from Rowan and the Creator team. I wasn't sure I would have had enough strength to be in the same room as him without crying or yelling.

Yesterday was a good test of my strength and I passed with flying colors. I was able to stay strong and look Rowan right in his dejected face without giving in to his request.

"This ended up in my stack of mail." Claire drops an envelope in front of my plate.

"This is from two weeks ago!" I point at the date.

She shrugs. "I know, and I'm sorry. I promise to get more organized next week."

I laugh without any pain today. "You always say that!" I yell at her back.

She chuckles under her breath as she walks back to her mess of a bedroom.

My fingers brush across my name written in cursive with an old ink pen. The return address is listed as the Kane Company.

That's weird. I grab a knife from the kitchen and slice across the top.

My fingers shake as I pull out a folded piece of paper. I open it and my mouth drops open.

Brady Kane sent me a letter! It's dated from before his accident, at around the same time we were working through the finishing touches on Nebula Land.

Dear Zahra,

I apologize in advance if my words are scrambled. It's hard to sum up my thanks but I'll try, if only because you deserve to know how much of an impact you had on my life. Even an old man like myself can learn a few new tricks, or at the very least be reminded of the old ones they've long since forgotten.

Gratitude? From Brady freaking Kane?! I'm the one who should be grateful that he took the time to work with me for a whole month.

Before I met with you about your proposal, I was in a dark place. I felt lost and unsure about myself for the first time in many years. But then you came into my office with a huge grin and all this pent-up imagination waiting to be explored. I was immediately impressed with your sharp mind and honest heart. It took me a while to understand why I felt an attachment to you, but I realize it's because you reminded me of my younger self. Of someone yet untouched by money, fame, and the expectations that dull even the strongest creative minds.

My chest aches, and my breathing grows ragged with each sentence. It has nothing to do with the residual effects of my sickness and everything to do with all the feelings boiling inside at Brady's confession.

I know you aspire to become a Creator one day. Whenever you feel like you're finally worthy (whatever the hell that means—I did all right with a community college education and so can you), I want to help you achieve that dream. So wherever you are and whatever you're doing, know that you'll always have a Creator job at Dreamland if you want it. All you need to do is contact my old secretary, Martha, and she'll get you a contract. No interview necessary.

Tears spring to my eyes. Brady was endlessly supportive of my dream, even though I kept telling him no. I think he would be proud of me if he knew the strides I've made over the past few months.

I have one tiny favor to ask in return. As a part of my will, I've asked my grandson to become the director of Dreamland for six months and create a special project meant to improve the park.

He what?! I clutch the letter with a death grip.

I have personally selected you to participate as a voting member on my committee. You will be expected to either approve or reject Rowan's plans.

Me?! Oh my fucking God. Did Rowan know this entire time I was supposed to be on this committee? Acid in my stomach makes me want to retch into the nearest toilet, but I take a few deep breaths before I keep reading.

> *You reminded me why I created Dreamland. Your passion for the park was one I lost along the way and your unique ideas stoked excitement in me that had long since been forgotten. Because of that, I know you're the right person to help me one last time. It might seem like a big request but you're one of the people I want to be a part of the change Dreamland needs. So please join my committee and vote for the future of the park.*

My hands shake as I read the rest of Brady Kane's letter discussing semantics and scheduling. After rereading it twice, it slips from my fingers and flutters to the floor.

Did Rowan know this entire time that his grandfather wanted me to vote on the project he's spent months working on? Why else would he hire me—someone he said wasn't important enough to be missed?

No. That can't be it. Right? There's no way he knew.

But why else would he hire someone like you with limited qualifications who tore apart Dreamland's most expensive ride?

He has an endless stream of Creators he could have hired to ensure Dreamland was in the best hands to win this vote. His reason behind pretending to be Scott seemed reasonable, but now I'm wondering if it was another ploy to poke around and see if I would admit to being a part of the voting committee. What if his whole speech yesterday in my cubicle was a way for him to pacify me so I wouldn't screw him over?

With each question, my doubts grow stronger.

What if everything about us was always a lie?

Claire lifts the pillow from my face and hugs it to her body as she takes a seat. "What's wrong?"

"That fact that Rowan was born."

"I thought we blacklisted his name from the apartment!"

"That was before I received a letter from Brady Kane that exposed his grandson."

Claire's eyes might pop out of their sockets. "WHAT?!"

The words tumble out of me as I share the story about the vote and all the theories I have. I even tell her about how Rowan tried to invite me over to his place after everything, which only adds to my suspicions.

Claire somehow reins in her emotions until I finish. She jumps off the couch and grabs her phone from her bedroom. I track her pacing as she taps away at the screen, with her cheeks all red and her hair going everywhere.

"That no good piece of shit—" She jabs at the screen of her phone with a frown.

"What are you doing?"

"I'm trying to calculate how long someone can survive from blood loss after being castrated."

I drop my head back and laugh. "Physical aggression is never the answer."

Claire pats my hand as she sits back down, tucking her phone into her pocket. "Oh, Zahra. It's cute how innocent you see the world."

"And that is?"

"Like you were never told Santa Claus isn't real."

I drop my mouth open in faux shock. "*What?!* Santa's not real?"

Claire rolls her eyes half-heartedly. "Fool."

"Seriously. Your answer to everything is to cut, maim, and kill. That's not really the kind of solution I'm looking for here."

"Only because you couldn't afford a good lawyer after."

We both end up laughing at that.

I poke her with my foot. "Seriously. Castration?"

"You know how the saying goes. Act like a dick, lose said dick."

A loud laugh escapes me. "No one says that!"

"Then maybe it's time people did. I mean that fucker seriously thinks he can manipulate you like that? Un-freaking-believable! Does he even have a conscience?"

My entire body aches at the thought.

"Debatable." I sigh. There was a time I thought he did, but who knows anymore. Although he seemed genuine when he stopped by my cubicle, I can't be certain who the real Rowan is anymore.

CHAPTER FORTY-SEVEN

Rowan

I enter the last Creator meeting before the holiday break. While the employees might take time off, I'll be working day and night to finish up my presentation for the board.

Jenny stands at the front of the room and everyone nods in my direction as I take my seat. I scan the room, searching for the one woman I can't get out of my head. Zahra's usual seat is occupied by a different Creator.

A pressure pushes against my chest, making my breaths ragged. Jenny doesn't say anything about Zahra's absence.

The first Creator presents on some decent idea that will never make it out of today's meeting. I've already vetoed it in my head.

The door creaks open behind me. I turn to find Zahra entering silently, minus her jangling backpack. It throws me back to our first meeting. A ghost of a smile tugs at my lips before they fall back into a flat line.

Her eyes scan the room before dropping to the only empty chair, located right next to me. If she's annoyed by the seating arrangement, she doesn't show it. She pulls out the seat and slides into the space. All the cells in my body fire off in unison as I inhale her faint perfume.

As presenters go up, Zahra remains stiff while ignoring my presence. It irritates me more than I care to admit.

By the time it's Zahra's turn to present, I'm fidgeting in my seat and struggling to think about anything but her.

She stands and clears her throat.

I go rigid in my seat, checking her over for any signs of sickness. She takes a sip of her water before going up to the podium.

"Today, I'm presenting something a little different. It's not exactly about a ride, so I understand if it isn't accepted as an option for Mr. Kane's project." She doesn't even bother looking in my direction while she speaks about me, which only adds to the tightening pressure in my chest.

"I'm interested in making Dreamland more inclusive for our guests. As a salon worker, I met lots of children who experienced life's hardest challenges. I began to take notice and write down their concerns. After years of working, I came to one conclusion. As a sister of someone with challenges herself, I understood the guests' chief complaints—even though I think my sister would punch my arm if she heard me use that kind of *c-word*."

Some Creators laugh. I'm enthralled by her and the confidence she displays. It's a complete shift from the woman who didn't feel like she was worthy of being a Creator.

"Dreamland isn't only made for the more privileged who can afford quick-skip passes, hundred-dollar entrance tickets, and overpriced food and drinks. It's made for the able-bodied. For those kids who were born with a leg up—no pun intended. So my idea is to change the very foundation of the park and shift the way we view our guests."

All I can do is stare in silence as she goes through various slides covering different ideas. From wheelchair costumes to sensory hours for children with autism, Zahra meets the demands of children and adults alike who are often overlooked at Dreamland. She delivers all the content with the biggest smile on her face. The more she talks, the stronger the longing grows in my chest.

I want to steal her away from everyone and tell her how proud I am of her. And to confess how sorry I am about everything I did and said.

Because I care for her.

Because I want to be with her regardless of any obstacles.

And because I want to be a man my mother would be proud of, and I want to do it by Zahra's side.

I sit taller in my chair, wanting to gain her attention. To have her turn that smile on me so she can see how proud I am of her idea. But she doesn't look at me. Doesn't even bother turning in my general direction at all. It's like I don't exist. I ask questions to try to get her to look at me, but she answers smoothly, staring straight ahead at everyone.

If anyone notices anything amiss, they don't show it.

With each ignored opportunity, the feeling in my chest intensifies. The burn only increases as Jenny stands and gives Zahra a hug.

"Amazing job, Zahra. You're going to do such big things one

day. I just know it. It's a shame we won't have you here after the holiday break."

I blink a couple of times. "Repeat that."

Jenny's spine straightens. "Oh, sorry, Mr. Kane. I didn't think you wanted to be kept up-to-date on things like these."

I ignore her and look at Zahra. For the first time, her eyes find mine, but they're devoid of all emotions.

I detest it with every fiber of my being. "You're quitting?"

"I gave Jenny my two weeks' notice on Tuesday."

I do the math. If she submitted it a few days ago, and next week is a holiday break, then she's not coming back. The realization sits like a rock in my stomach.

She stares at me with a blank expression.

"Today is your last day?" I snap.

Jenny decides to play pacifist. "We'll all miss her very much."

She didn't quit after coming back from her sick leave, so what changed? I stay silent, stewing in the potential reasons for Zahra submitting her two weeks' notice. Jenny claps her hands together and wishes everyone a happy holiday.

Each employee goes up to her, switching between hugs and high fives as they each say their goodbyes.

Fuck. No. This wasn't supposed to happen.

Why would you expect her to stay after everything you did? What have you proved to her besides the fact that you're a selfish fuck who chooses yourself every damn time?

"Everyone is dismissed except for Ms. Gulian." I step toward the podium, hoping to cage Zahra in.

Zahra's body stills. Our gazes clash together as I stand in her direct eye line.

The Creators move along like I'm not glaring a hole into Zahra's face. They each wish me a merry Christmas before exiting the room, buzzing with excitement to be let out early.

I stand between the podium and the door, leaving her no option but to get through me. "You can't quit."

"I can and I did."

My fists ball up my sides. "But we had a deal."

She shrugs. "Today was the last day of our presentations anyway. It's out of our hands now."

"There are going to be other ideas that need Creators' input."

She holds her chin up. "That's no longer my business."

"Zahra—"

She holds up her hand, stopping me. "Why did you hire me?"

I don't blink. "Because you're good at what you do. Today is a perfect example of how talented you are. Imagine what else we could do if you—"

I can practically see her walls dropping one by one. Her entire demeanor changes, from her shoulders slumping to her eyes clouding.

"Why couldn't you leave me alone?" Her voice cracks. "Why did you have to manipulate my feelings for you?"

I take a deep inhale of breath. "What?"

She looks away, hiding the mistiness of her gaze from me. "Did you hire me as a Creator because you wanted me to become emotionally invested in the project before your grandfather's vote?"

Vote? No fucking way.

"Vote?"

Her tiny fists tighten. "I was chosen for Brady's committee, but I'm sure you already knew that. Didn't you?"

Zahra is on the committee? This has to be some kind of sick cosmic joke. Out of all the people my grandfather could have picked, he chose *her*?

All the pieces connect. In my letter, he had mentioned meeting someone at Dreamland who helped him realize his mistakes. I don't know how I didn't think about it being Zahra sooner. Grandpa wasn't the kind of person who met with random employees, yet he discussed Nebula Land with her. He even helped her redesign it. His damn note on her file was the biggest breadcrumb of all, and I completely overlooked it.

Shit. And the way she looks at me—it's like she doesn't recognize me. It pierces through my damn heart.

I fucked up. Big time.

"Was any of it real?" Her voice cracks.

"Of course it was." I reach out to cup her cheek, but she takes a step backward.

It sucks a whole lot.

"I never knew about you being chosen for the vote," I say.

"And what, I'm supposed to believe anything that comes out of your mouth? All you've done is lie or tell half-truths ever since we met." Her laugh sounds so hollow and unlike her that it makes my chest ache.

Instead of asking Zahra to stay at Dreamland and work for me, I now have to convince her that I never knew this was his plan.

Good luck with that. "You have to believe me on this. I knew a vote would happen—that much is true—but I had no idea who my grandfather would pick."

She shakes her head. "It doesn't matter what you say. I can't trust you."

I grab her hand and place it against my chest. The heat of her palm adds to the spreading warmth through my chest. "I swear I'm not lying. I know I might have hidden some truths and lied to you in the past"—she flinches at my words—"but I would never use you for something like a vote. I'm better than that."

She rips her hand out of my grasp. "That's the thing, Rowan. I think you *think* you're better than that, but from everything I've seen, I have no reason to believe you're anything but selfish. You choose to think about one person and one person only—and that's yourself."

Her words slice away at me, making my breathing difficult. She looks at me with a pinched expression, and I've seen that kind of gaze enough times in my father's eyes to label it as disgust. It hurts far more this time, knowing it's from Zahra.

She walks around me to grab her belongings. "I'm quitting because I have no interest in working for you or your company anymore. I want to work for a place that wants to make a real difference in people's lives because they care, and your company isn't it."

She exits the room, leaving me with nothing but the lingering smell of her perfume and the memory of her teary eyes looking at me with nothing but hate.

CHAPTER FORTY-EIGHT

Rowan

I should go home after landing in Chicago, but I tell my driver to take me to my father's place. After everything that happened after Zahra's presentation, I've had something bugging me. It took me an entire flight to realize I have unfinished business to settle before I can finally move on.

The pressure I've placed on my own shoulders to live up to some unattainable goal of proving my father wrong has poisoned enough of my life. I wanted him to recognize my worth for years when he couldn't even see past his own misery. And now I'm done. I'm letting go of that boy who wanted to be seen by the entirely wrong person.

I press the doorbell with one gloved finger. It takes my father a few minutes to open the door to his town house on the edge of the city.

His eyes widen behind his glasses. "Rowan. Come on in." He opens the door.

I take a moment to assess him. His eyes seem clear and sober, and his breath lacks the distinct smell of whiskey that I've grown to pair with his drunken outbursts.

I guess he's sober enough to get through this conversation.

I hold up my hand. "That's not necessary. I have a couple of questions to ask you."

His brows knit together, but he nods anyway. "Okay."

"Do you think Mom would be proud of the man you've become since she died?"

My father's mouth drops open. I don't think I've seen him look surprised like this before. The color leaches out of his already pale face, making him look ghostly.

A heavy gust of wind blows toward us, snapping him out of whatever thoughts he had.

"No. I don't." His head bows.

"Why did you change?"

"Because I was an angry, pathetic man who wanted to drown everyone in my grief so they could feel hurt like I hurt."

I blink at him, caught completely off guard by his candid answer. Out of all the responses I considered, the words he spoke never even made it on the list.

He sighs as if this conversation is draining him of all his energy. "Any other questions?"

"Do you regret falling in love with my mother?"

"Not at all."

I could have sworn he would say yes. How could he not after all the pain he clearly went through? "Why not?"

"You'll learn that the best rewards come with the biggest consequences. Because nothing that great is given for free." He shuts his eyes.

If a man like him would do it all over again, that's all I needed to hear. Because if he would make the same choices only to relive decades of grief, then there's something about love that must be worth the pain.

I made a huge mistake based on a complete lie I told myself year after year. I spent my entire life thinking love makes people powerless, and it does. My father is living proof of that. Love does make people helpless, but only because they willingly accept it. Because to love someone else means to trust them enough to not abuse the power they have over you.

Despite how Zahra might feel about me, I trust her. I trust her with my whole damn heart and my future. There's not a procon list in the world that could keep me away from her anymore.

I know what I have to do. The decision comes easy, relieving some of the tension pressing against my chest like an anvil.

I nod. "That's all I needed to know." I turn, leaving my father gaping at my back as I finally ditch the last of the weight holding me back from moving on with my life.

Now I need to break the news to my brothers.

Declan scoops up another forkful of mashed potatoes like I didn't tell him I'm not coming back to Chicago after the vote. "No."

My fists remain hidden below his dining room table. "I didn't ask for your permission."

Cal's head bounces between us. "Are we seriously going to fight on Christmas?"

I ignore him. "I'm not coming back."

"Okay. I guess we are." Cal grabs his drink and raises it toward me in solidarity. "Finally, it's your turn to be the problem child for once. Welcome to the club." He takes a deep swig.

Declan scowls at Cal before turning his glare at me. "We already discussed this in-depth."

"It doesn't matter what we decided before. Things change, and I'm not giving up my position as the director, so find a new CFO."

The muscle in Declan's jaw ticks. "How could you possibly prefer being the director of a *theme park* over becoming the CFO of one of the top companies in the world?"

"Because I met someone special and I'm not going to give her up for some goddamn desk job thousands of miles away where I would be miserable without her."

Declan looks at a loss for words.

"Holy shit," Cal whispers under his breath. "Are you serious?"

I nod.

Cal blinks twice before speaking again. "What have you been hiding?"

"Nothing I want you poking your limp dick around."

"Now I *definitely* need to visit Dreamland. Our baby brother has been keeping some big secrets from us." Cal elbows Declan with a smile.

Declan shoves Cal away. "It's only considered a secret if I had no idea."

Cal stares at Declan. "You knew this whole time and you didn't tell me?!"

"He took a vacation. That in itself was a cause for alarm. Try to use some of the few brain cells you have left, Callahan."

"Fuck you." He glares at Declan before turning his head in my direction. "I hate feeling left out."

Declan refocuses his irritation on me. "You're doing all of this because of a girl?"

"No. I'm doing this because I like who I strive to be when I'm *with* that girl."

"Damn. Rowan might not speak much but when he does—" Cal does a chef's kiss. "Poetry."

Declan shakes his head, clearly not sharing Cal's sentiment. "You've completely lost your goddamn mind."

I shrug. "Maybe. But at least it's fun."

Cal laughs.

"You'll be begging me for the CFO position in six months." Declan crosses his arms.

I shake my head. "I won't."

Cal claps a hand on Declan's shoulder with a smile. "Cheer up, buttercup. I can lend a hand and help you with your duties until you find a new replacement."

"The job requires more math abilities than adding two plus two."

"I think my little brain can keep up." Cal taps his temple. He might have ADHD, but he has the highest IQ out of all of us. If only he had the drive to apply himself.

I speak up. "You know, Iris could help you with some of the workload. I saw how well you worked together, and she could definitely handle some of your tasks while you search for a wife."

Declan rubs his chin. "Maybe. I'll have to think it over."

"Rowan, we're supposed to protest against Iris working more hours." Cal sighs. "Poor girl probably forgot what the sun looks like with all the hours Declan makes her work."

I don't care about Iris or her schedule so long as I get what I want. While I might be interested in changing some of my old ways, I'll never stop being greedy when it comes to Zahra. She will always be the exception to any rule and the one person I'm willing to screw the world over for. Because if she's not happy, I'll ruin whatever stole her smile, myself included.

I grip onto the plastic bag with a choke hold as I slam the knocker on Zahra's apartment door. After my jet was grounded for an extra hour today due to Christmas Day traffic, I couldn't make it back as early as I would have hoped. But I'm here now and ready to speak to Zahra. Since everything is settled with the director position, I can use it as a bargaining chip to show her my good faith.

I don't want her to leave Dreamland because of me. I want to work with her, side by side, and make this place everything she has dreamed of.

Claire opens the door with a frown. "What do you want?"

"Is Zahra home?"

"It's Christmas."

"But you're here, and she wouldn't leave you alone on a holiday."

Her eyes narrow into two tiny slits, and I know I got her. "She doesn't want to speak to you."

"I'll let her decide that," I reply with a flat tone.

She crosses her arms. "Why are you really here?"

"Because I need to talk to her. It's important."

She raises a brow. "On *Christmas*?"

"Claire? Who is it?" Zahra turns the corner and freezes in the entryway.

I take a good look at her. Her hair is thrown up in a messy bun I want to unleash, and her body is hidden beneath the most hideous Christmas pj's. My hands itch to grab her, yet I remain leaning against the doorframe.

"Zahra." My voice carries a raspy tone to it.

She ignores me. "I got this, Claire."

"You sure?" Her friend's gaze slides from Zahra to me, going from soft to edgy in a second.

Zahra nods and walks toward the door. Claire doesn't bother looking in my direction as she walks down a hall back to her room.

"What do you want, Rowan?" Zahra crosses her arms.

"I want to talk."

"On Christmas?"

What is up with these two and Christmas? It's just a holiday—more of an inconvenience than anything else.

I take a deep breath and dangle the bag in her eyesight. "I brought an activity to convince you to give me an hour to talk."

Her eyes bulge. "Are you serious?"

I frown. "Yes? I researched the best strategies for gingerbread house making and thought we could give it a try while you hear me out. I even bought Popsicle sticks to work as stabilizers."

She says nothing.

Come on. Say something. "I thought we could make homemade icing because the one in the box looks disgusting."

Whatever I said snaps her out of her thoughts. "Oh my God. You actually think a gingerbread house is going to make things better?"

Shit. "Well, no. But I remember you mentioning how much you liked them, and—"

She holds her hand up. Her face is all scrunched up as if she is in pain talking to me. My nauseous stomach sinks into dangerous territory. I'm tired of being sick to my stomach. It makes me feel disgustingly pathetic and in the mood to wallow, and I despise any sort of self-pity.

"Rowan, *you* ended things with *me*. We can't just pick up where we left off and pretend to go back to something casual."

"Good because I don't want anything casual anymore."

Her eyes shine. "You're only doing all this because of the vote."

I release a frustrated breath. "I'm not doing this for a damn vote. If you want to vote against me, then do it. Hell, I encourage you to, as long as you give me a chance to explain myself."

Her mouth pops open before closing again.

I reach out to tuck a strand of her hair behind her ear. "I mean it. Go ahead and do what feels right. The vote is the last thing on my mind right now. You're more important."

Her head drops as she takes a deep breath. She looks back up at me with watery eyes, and it pierces me straight in the chest. "I wish I could believe you. I really do. But I'm tired of giving people all the chances in the world only for them to realize I'm not worth it in the end. Because I am, and no one is going to convince me otherwise anymore. Not even you. I don't want to be used for entertainment while *passing the time*, just like I don't want to be labeled as some *mistake*." Her words are laced with hurt, and it only fucks me up more inside.

I regret ever saying those things to her. When I broke things off with her, I thought I was doing the right thing before it got out of control. Truth is, it already was, and I was too stupid to realize it.

I'd rather feel out of control and still have Zahra than whatever the hell this is without her. I can't go back to the way things were before she entered my life.

"Merry Christmas, Rowan." She doesn't bother waiting for my reply as she shuts the door in my face, leaving me behind with a heavy feeling in my chest.

Zahra ignoring me is nothing but a challenge. I decide the only way to get her attention is to do something ridiculous. And by ridiculous, I mean making the damn gingerbread house myself and sending her a picture. The structure is damaged after falling too many times to count, and the roof keeps sliding off, but I'm committed.

I place the final gumdrop on the roof and grab my phone before the entire thing caves in on itself.

I'm sorry. One of the gumdrops slides off the roof, ruining the letter *m*. I'm quick to fix it and snap a photo.

I attach the photo to my text chain with Zahra and send it, along with a *missing you* message.

I'm not sure why I expect some acknowledgment back. Maybe I was stupid to hope she would take pity on me doing the whole damn thing by myself.

I was wrong. My text goes unanswered, which only adds to the intense feeling in my chest every time I look over at the stupid house.

None of my strategies are working. If Zahra truly thinks I was only with her because of a damn vote, then I'll prove to her that I'm here to stay, with or without her approval. That I've changed because of her and all the kindness she has shown me over the months.

I can only hope she chooses me in the end.

CHAPTER FORTY-NINE

Zahra

Today is the last day I will have to see Rowan's beautiful, manipulative face ever again. That's the only thing that keeps me motivated as I walk into the boardroom located within his office suite on Story Street. Everything was coordinated by some Kane employee sworn to an NDA, including the time and place.

I'm the first one to arrive of the panel, which only adds to my nerves. I pull out my notebook from my backpack and start doodling nonsense to keep my mind occupied.

The door creaks open and Martha strolls in.

"Martha!" I jump up and give her a hug. "Is Mr. Kane asking you to help him set up?"

She shakes her head. "Nope. The late Mr. Kane asked me to be here."

"*Really?*"

She shows off her sweet laugh lines. "Don't sound so surprised. I worked for that man for decades. I know this park better than him, and he knew it."

My laugh is interrupted by the door opening again. Whatever warmth lingered from Martha's hug is quickly sucked out of me as Seth Kane walks into the room.

Oh shit. Brady chose Rowan's father as part of the board? It takes a lot of self-restraint to not explode on Mr. Kane after everything I've learned about him. If looks could kill, he would have been eviscerated by my stare alone.

He ignores Martha and me like we don't exist, probably because to him, we don't. The only people worthy of his attention are those who either share his blood or share his business interest. His sharp suit and emotionless face hide the awful man lingering beneath. I'm tempted to rip apart the vile man who would call his own child pathetic and make them feel lesser than for being *different*.

My fists ball up beside my jeans.

Martha pats my hand. "Now, now. This isn't the time for anger."

I sigh and take a few deep breaths. "I'm not upset."

She leans in and whispers. "It shows you still care about him. Good."

Good? What is going on here?

"I don't know what you're talking about."

"Oh, darling." She pats my cheek. "I put two and two together when Mr. Kane asked me to get him Juliana De La Rosa on the line. And given our conversation about her books, I connected the dots."

Martha is so damn smart. We sit next to one another while

Mr. Kane takes the seat across the table. Two more unknown people enter the room, but I'm pretty sure one of them is the director of the Shanghai park.

"Did Rowan know you were on the board?"

"Rowan? God, no. I can't wait to see his reaction later."

I stare at her.

She presses a hand against her chest. "Wait. Did you think Rowan knew you were on the board?"

I nod, unable to speak because my heart's lodged in my throat. This whole day is going to be an information overload.

She laughs and wraps me in another hug. "No. That's half the fun in today's meeting."

"*Fun?*"

"Of course. Brady had a flare for the dramatic. This whole shindig is his way of making his grandkids work for it."

"Work for what?"

Martha is cut off by Rowan entering the room. He looks extra devastating today, in a sharp black suit and a matching black tie. His eyes collide with mine. It's like all the air is sucked out of my lungs and my head grows woozy.

Snap out of it.

Rowan looks around the rest of the room. Everyone stands and shakes his hand. He says hello to each person by name, and I let out a breath of relief at him at least being aware of his target audience.

Why do you care? He lied to you for this stupid vote.

When he gets to me, he holds out his hand. I grab onto it, and a similar buzz rushes through my body, starting from my fingers before spreading all the way to my toes.

"Ms. Gulian. Thank you for being here today." The timbre of his voice does bad things to the lower half of my body. His eyes linger on my flushed cheeks, and his thumb caresses my hand before he lets go.

I clear my throat. "Mr. Kane." I nod and take my seat.

He steps toward the front of the room and turns on the projector. His presentation is already set up, and I nudge Martha.

"Have you seen it yet?"

She zips her lips and throws the invisible key away.

Rowan steps away from the podium as he holds on to the clicker. He gets through some of the basic openings, including expressing his gratitude for our time and whatnot. His eyes always find mine at the end of his sentence, like he actually wants my approval.

He clicks to the first slide, showing a black-and-white picture of his grandfather in front of a half-complete castle. "My grandfather asked me to determine Dreamland's weaknesses and create something worthy of his legacy. Upon first inspection of the park, I had wondered what I could possibly do that hasn't been thought of before. Dreamland in many ways is perfect."

I turn my attention from Rowan toward his father. It's obvious where Rowan learned his flat affect from because I don't think I see any reaction from Seth Kane beside his eyes blinking.

At least he's not frowning yet.

"I spent the past six months working with the park developers to come up with a renovation plan that would stand out above the rest. Creators spent countless hours developing new ride ideas, land concepts, float additions, and more. I had every intention of showing those designs today—in fact, I created a whole presentation centered around expanding Dreamland."

Mr. Kane's finger taps once against the table before stilling. *Is that his tell? If so, what does it mean?*

"Over the last month, I spent time breaking down my grandfather's words. I came to the realization that finding weaknesses means more than increasing revenue or allocating funds better."

He moves on to the next slide, a picture of Brady with the entire Dreamland staff in front of the castle. If I squint, I can find myself still rocking braces since my parents snuck me in the photo when I was only a teen.

"During my grandfather's time in a coma, the weaknesses slowly became overlooked because of our strengths. The more Dreamland grew, the easier it was to ignore the smaller issues because more money meant more success. My grandfather wrote how there was a special person who helped him realize his mistakes, and I was fortunate enough to have met the same individual." He offers me the smallest Rowan smile to ever exist.

Is he talking about me? Brady Kane referenced me in his letter? My entire chest warms and my heart threatens to burst.

"This person showed me how money becomes meaningless when we ignore the very people who help us make a profit. They were vocal about the issues with Dreamland, and I was intrigued by these so-called weaknesses. I began interviewing employees at random from all departments, and what I found was shocking."

The next slide is an image of *Ralph*. "This is Ralph. He's been a dedicated ride mechanic at Dreamland for the past fifty years, making him our oldest employee besides my grandfather. When I asked him how he felt about all the Dreamland wage changes and insurance benefit cuts, he told me it didn't matter. Of course, I thought that was a bizarre statement. Out of the two hundred employees I interviewed, Ralph was the only person who said *it didn't matter*. So, naturally, I asked him why that was. And he told me that he recently found out he has stage four pancreatic cancer and his health insurance couldn't cover the kind of treatment he needs."

Ralph has cancer? My eyes become misty from tears I try to hold back. I fail and end up sniffling loudly. The way Rowan looks at me has me wondering if he's silently offering his apology.

The next slide is a picture of Brady smiling with an arm wrapped around Ralph's shoulder. It looks like Ralph is fixing a cart from Dreamland's first ride. "Ralph is one of our oldest employees at the Kane Company, and our—my—selfish business practices are limiting him from receiving proper cancer treatment." He clicks and the next slide appears, this time with hundreds of photos. "There are hundreds of similar stories, from people struggling to work two jobs to employees being unable to afford appropriate health care procedures because of limited finances. No person should have to choose between supporting their family or putting their medical needs first."

He lets out a deep breath. "As the director of Dreamland, I want to protect people like Ralph. Because in the end, our employees are our biggest strength. Without them, there would be no Dreamland worthy of the success we have accrued. Therefore, I am suggesting the minimum wage is raised to meet standards consistent with what we expect from our employees."

Seth Kane speaks up. "And what hourly wage do you suggest?"

Is this part of the procedure? Can we all yell out random questions whenever we feel like it?

"A 50 percent raise at the very least."

"That is an extreme increase, given the fact that you voted against the previous wage change."

The two board members I don't know both look at each other. My hands start to tremble, wondering what the heck is going to happen next.

Martha pats my knee and gives me a reassuring smile.

Wait. Does she know about Rowan's presentation? Because if Rowan didn't know Martha was part of the board, maybe he did a mock presentation in front of her.

Rowan doesn't seem the least bit flustered by his father's questions. He changes to the next slide. "Based on research conducted, higher wages are associated with increased profitability. Top corporations have already made this pledge based on data-driven facts. If we increase wages, we boost efficiency, thus enhancing the overall Dreamland experience for our guests."

His father leans forward. "Why would we need to work on employee satisfaction if we are performing beyond expected each quarter?"

Rowan's next slide includes a breakdown of some kind of exit survey from guests. "When I surveyed over one million guests during my time here, over 72 percent of them said Dreamland employees played a key role in their overall experience. On a different question where they were asked what differentiated the Dreamland experience from competing theme parks, 68 percent of guests chose the cast member experience. That means regardless of what rides we have, the employees are the ones who make the difference." The slide changes to an employee satisfaction survey.

I remember filling it out myself but I didn't realize it was for

Rowan's presentation. I'm paralyzed in my chair as I stare at the bar graphs and numbers, trying to make sense of everything I'm seeing.

"On the flip side, over 50 percent of our employees said they would seek a job elsewhere in the next five years if Dreamland wages remained the same. Employees' reasons for quitting included an interest in saving up for retirement, a need for affording childcare, a desire to save for their children's college funds, and an interest in receiving better benefits, including health care."

Rowan's father *tap-tap-taps* again. Either he's a pro at Morse code or he's silently showing his approval. I mean, how can he not? I'm trying my best not to stare at Rowan because I didn't even know he was working on all this. It proves that he *listened* to me, both as Scott and Rowan. That he took everything I had to say about the employees and applied it to his presentation.

My entire body vibrates from excitement.

"By not increasing our wages nor improving our company benefits, we are shamelessly giving up our best asset. Our employees are the hidden reason why we stand apart from our competitors, and it's time we treated them as such. Therefore, I stand by my choice to increase wages and reinstate benefits to preserve the future of Dreamland."

His father blinks.

Martha sits up with a smile. "In the past, you've mentioned only being interested in temporarily serving as the director. What happens if we approve these plans and you change your mind again in a year, given the fact that you were the one to introduce cut wages and benefits?"

Damn, Martha. Sheath those claws. My eyes bounce from her

to Rowan. I expect annoyance, but I'm nearly put into cardiac arrest by Rowan's small smile.

"Another good question. The employees of Dreamland will be my utmost priority, given the fact that I plan on remaining here, serving as the director for as long as they'll have me."

I almost fall out of my chair. *What the fuck is going on here?* Rowan's gaze burns into my skin, drawing my eyes back to his.

The man next to Rowan's father speaks up. "Are you no longer interested in becoming the CFO?"

"No."

The same gentleman turns back to his companion and begins whispering.

Rowan's father crosses his hands together. "Why should I vote yes and approve your plans when I can vote no and take your twenty-five billion dollars?"

"Twenty-five billion dollars?" I croak.

I think I'm going to be sick.

Martha looks over at me with a shy smile. "Here. Have some water."

Seth Kane's eyes snap from his son to me. He stares me down in the same kind of way that makes me feel like I'm being picked apart.

I gulp down half the glass in one go. Water sloshes out of the rim, splashing all over the table.

"The main reason I am interested in receiving my shares is because I want to retain enough power to make the best choices for my employees. Dreamland makes up 20 percent of our entire company's revenue. I can be the kind of director who works to push us to new limits while protecting our employees. I *want* to be the one. As I said earlier, I have created countless plans with the Creators that include expanding Dreamland beyond our one park." He looks around the room at each person. "I have the slides ready to present if you need further evidence to support your decision to approve of my change. While I am interested in renovating the park beyond anything Dreamland has seen before, my first priority is the employees."

WHAT?! Is this how board meetings usually go? I almost regret making fun of them when I first met Rowan because this is *intense*.

Rowan's father raises his hand. "That won't sway my decision." His voice is flat.

My elation dies, replaced by acid crawling up my throat. Rowan's face remains neutral but the tiny vein above his right eye becomes more prominent.

Would his own father really vote no? After all of *that*? I know he's heartless and all but even he has to be somewhat impressed by his son.

If it wasn't uncool, I would stand up and give a standing ovation.

The two men shake their heads.

Martha lifts her wrinkled hand. "I would like some clarification on something."

The corner of Rowan's lip lifts. "Yes?"

"I am interested in hearing about your plans for employees with disabilities."

For the first time during the entire presentation, Rowan's cool exterior cracks. He blinks at Martha, who sports a mischievous smile.

"I thought you were on his side?" I lean in and whisper in her ear.

"I am." She winks. "There's one thing left he hasn't covered."

Rowan clears his throat and clicks through so many slides, I become dizzy from the motion.

He stops on a slide that has my breath catch. Because unlike Ralph's slide, this one has a picture of Ani. My beautiful, larger-than-life sister who has her arm wrapped around JP's shoulder.

"This is Ani. She's one of our youngest employees who happens to come from a family of Dreamland workers. I was partnered with her for a pilot mentorship program. She quickly schooled me in all things Dreamland, including our lack of diversity in the hiring process."

I don't know why my eyes fill with tears, but they do. A single tear slips out, and Martha, like the cunning mastermind she is, slips me a tissue. I'm pretty sure she asked this question on purpose if only to see me cry.

"I was confused because I know our procedures and how we strive for an ethnically diverse cast. But then Ani told me how there aren't people like her—people with disabilities, both visible and invisible. So during my time I was supposed to be mentoring Ani, it turns out she mentored me. She taught me what it meant to live a life like hers, and I started doing my own research. So, to answer your question, Martha, I plan on expanding our hiring process to include more people with disabilities. I would also like to move forward with a full mentorship program to meet their demands. I want Dreamland to be the first of its kind."

More tears run down my face. I'm a complete mess, staring at the photo of my sister with JP. I never thought my pilot program would lead to a change like *this*. Never in a million years.

"This project will be addressed in three major phases, starting with the new mentorship program. Once that is complete, I will move forward with a Creator project that will emphasize Dreamland's promise for inclusivity. We will be expanding our costumes and souvenirs to include wheelchair, crutch, and prosthetics accessories to account for the population of children at Dreamland who are often ignored. Additionally, we will emphasize a new promise to families by creating the first-ever sensory celebration. This opportunity will give children on the spectrum the ability to enjoy Dreamland."

I swipe at my face, trying to erase the tears. I'm shocked Rowan took my last creation and applied it in his presentation. With so much on the line, it means the world to me that he is willing to risk his *twenty-five billion dollars*.

If that's not him showing how he cares, I don't know what is.

"Any other questions?" Rowan looks over at me.

I shake my head, hoping my eyes scream how happy and proud I am.

"Thank you for your time today." He shuts off the projector and exits the room.

Wait, that's it? He doesn't stay for the deliberation or something?

A random man walks in with a briefcase. He passes us each a sheet of paper with our names on it and a pen.

There's a lot of legal jargon I have to read three times before understanding and a simple checkbox asking if I approve of the revisions for Dreamland.

No matter how much Rowan has personally hurt me, there's

no question in my mind anymore that he's the right man for the job. I would be stupid and petty to vote against him.

And because you love him.

No. That has nothing to do with this. He proved he deserves the chance to change Dreamland for the better, and I'm not going to be the one to get in his way.

I wait outside the main conference door. Everyone exits one by one except for the person I've spent ten minutes waiting for.

What on Earth could he be waiting for?

The door opens and Seth Kane strolls out of the place like he owns a personal catwalk at home. For a second, I consider if I should really go through with my plan.

Yeah, fuck it.

"Mr. Kane?" I tap on his shoulder.

"Yes?" He looks down at me with a raised brow. Ugh. The way he stares at me has this strange ability to make me feel two inches tall.

"I wanted to say that although you might be *considered* a good businessman, you've done it at the expense of being a terrible, verbally abusive father. And one day you're going to look back on your life and regret the way you treated your children, and I hope it hurts you as much as you hurt them. So fuck you and fuck off."

I swivel on my heel and catch Martha staring at me with a big grin and a thumbs-up. I'm sure to blow her a kiss on my way out the door while using my other hand to give Seth Kane the middle finger.

There's no other way I would want to spend my last official workday at Dreamland.

CHAPTER FIFTY

Rowan

I thought once I left the board room, the panic would hit me. But as I sit in my office, waiting for Grandpa's lawyer to finish with the vote, I feel a strange sense of calm wash over me.

I've accepted my fate, regardless of what the board decides. If I don't receive my company's shares, I can still stay on as the director. My brothers will be pissed, especially Declan, because of the fallout with my father. I get that, but I did everything possible on my end to gain the upper hand.

Instead of going with my original presentation with the best of the Alpha and Beta team ideas, I went with my gut intuition. It was a stressful change, but Martha helped me power through. And damn, I did not expect my secretary to be one of the votes. I can't believe she hid that from me while helping me with the presentation.

At least I can guarantee myself one vote.

And maybe two.

Zahra seemed moved by the entire thing, but I wouldn't hold it against her if she decided I wasn't worthy of the position or the power associated with the shares. While I'm annoyed my father let out that secret, I think it was his way of letting me know that he is aware of our stakes. Somehow his letter from Grandpa must have said more than I bargained for.

There's a knock on my door. Martha opens it and pops her head in. "Your father would like a word with you."

"Let him in." Might as well get this over with.

My father strolls into my office.

"Have a seat."

He remains standing. "I don't plan on staying long."

I raise a brow. "Here to gloat?"

He shakes his head. "No. I want to tell you that I'm proud of you."

I wait for the other half of the statement, picking apart where I went wrong. The silence grows as I come to the realization that he really only wanted to say that.

"Why?"

He ignores me. "I wish you the best of luck running this place. I'll expect you at the next board meeting, ready to deliver a more concise presentation regarding your budget plan for all of this."

Did I really win the approval of the voters or is this some joke to string me along?

"What are you saying?"

"Your grandfather would have been proud of the man you've become."

Another message.

He exits my office with a nod, leaving me to stare at the spot where he stood, wondering how the hell I pulled that off.

The lawyer enters my office soon after my father and confirms what I already know. The committee approved of my changes and he will be contacting me next week to discuss my finances. It feels surreal to finally put all this behind me. I'm looking forward to actually getting things done rather than discussing it.

I text my brothers and let them know that my part of the plan is complete. Now it's up to them to secure their parts.

I pull up my messages with Zahra and text her, hoping she will finally give me the chance I need to convince her that I'm serious about us.

Me: Will you come over tonight and hear me out?

Me: Please.

I tack on the second message for bonus points.

Her response is instant.

Zahra: Okay. Only because you asked nicely.

Zahra: But don't get your hopes up.

Too late. For the first time in weeks, I finally smile.

I pace the front porch. The wood creaks under my shoes with every step. A twig snaps and I look up to find Zahra walking up the driveway wearing the same white dress as earlier. The colors of the sunset make the perfect backdrop for her, and I find myself getting lost in how beautiful she is.

The only thing missing is her smile. After today, I swear to never make her feel anything but happy around me. While it might seem like an impossible goal, I'm all about achieving the unattainable.

Zahra walks up the steps, keeping her face neutral. She makes a move toward the front door but I steer her toward the swinging bench I've come to appreciate. I'm hoping it brings me some courage to get through everything I'm about to unleash.

Now's a good time to wish me luck, Mom.

"So…" Zahra rocks back and forth, making the swing move.

"When my grandfather sent me here as part of his will, I never thought I would meet someone as special as you. It was supposed to be a simple project. But I should have known things wouldn't go according to plan the moment you fell into my lap—quite literally. It's like life kept throwing you in my way time and time again hoping I would get the memo. I was too stubborn to realize that you were always meant to be mine, Zahra. And because of that, I made mistakes. I lied about who I was. I refused to trust you even though I knew deep down I could. And most of all, I pushed you away when you did nothing but open your heart up to me without any reciprocation. I took your love for granted when I should have cherished it. Because to be loved by you is a gift. One that I threw away because I was too stupid and selfish to give you that kind of power over me in return."

Her eyes soften around the edges, and she pulls my hand onto her lap.

"You were right when you said you deserve better. You always have and you always will. But I refuse to let you go. I *can't* let you go because you're the one person in this entire world who makes me want to smile, and I'm too damn selfish to let the best thing in my life get away from me because I'm afraid."

Her eyes fill with tears, but she blinks them away before they fall.

I give her hand a squeeze. "Truth is, I'm terrified of falling in love. But I'd rather trust you with my heart and risk you breaking it than live another day without you in my life. I want to be the kind of man that deserves a woman as beautiful, selfless, and kind as you. It might take my entire life to achieve that kind of goal, but as long as you're by my side, I'd consider it a life worth living."

Her bottom lip wobbles and I trace it with my thumb.

"And while I know I don't deserve you, I'll spend every single day proving to you how much I love you."

A tear slips out, and I brush it away with the pad of my thumb.

"What about moving back to Chicago?"

"Fuck Chicago. There's nothing I want more than to stay here with you and build a life together."

"A kiss for a secret?" Her voice cracks.

I nod.

Her lips press against mine. I sigh as I wrap my hand around the back of her neck and pull her close. I pour every feeling into that kiss, hoping she understands how much I care about her. How I never want to let her go.

She pulls away with a ragged breath. "I love you too, Rowan. And I would be more than happy to protect your heart from the world because you make me want to be a little bit selfish too." Her smile rivals everything else in the entire world.

Zahra's it for me. I know it with everything in me, and my intuition has never been wrong before. There's nothing in the world I'll find more beautiful than her. Not the sun. Not the moon. Not even the entire galaxy compares to the light she radiates wherever she goes.

CHAPTER FIFTY-ONE

Zahra

Rowan's lips only leave mine to carry me up the stairs without falling. My legs stay wrapped around his hips during the entire journey until he throws me on his bed and rips off all my clothes.

He kisses a trail from my lips to my hip bone, making me feel so pretty my eyes water. His hands drag down my thighs. He's sure to tease me as he moves, caressing my skin with the faintest touch that has me gasping.

"I love the little noises you make because they're all mine." His gaze burns into me as he traces the curve of my breast with his index finger. My skin pebbles in his wake, and my clit throbs.

"But I especially love the moans you make when I do this." He drops to his knees before his tongue drags across my center. My hips buck off the mattress, and Rowan presses his palm flat against my stomach, holding me down.

"I thought I knew what it meant to be selfish, but then I met you. I want to own you in every way that matters. Your time. Your smiles. Your heart." His devious smile sends a shiver down my spine.

There's no other word to describe the way he worships me. I feel like I'm laid on an altar, with Rowan showering me with his devotion. He uses his tongue as a weapon, turning me into nothing but putty beneath his hands. My world shifts to black as I shut my eyes and get lost in the feel of his tongue fucking me into oblivion.

His hands grip my ass and squeeze, making me gasp. "Eyes on me."

My eyes snap open as I stare down at him. He keeps his gaze locked on mine as he sucks on my clit, proving how much he owns my body and heart. My head drops back on its own while my eyes roll into the back of my head.

He pulls away and presses his thumb against my clit. "What did I say?"

I rise on my elbows and stare at him devouring me. It's sensual, the way his mouth moves. Our gazes hold as he pumps another finger into me, bringing forth another wave of pleasure. He thrusts in rhythm with his tongue. I'm gasping and grabbing at sheets, trying to hold on to keep me grounded.

Rowan doesn't like that. His actions scream it, and his movements are frenzied. He wants me wild and begging because every action after says so. His fingers become relentless, teasing my G-spot like he owns it. I buck under him, but his hand remains steady, pressing me into the sheets, forcing me to do nothing but feel.

My orgasm hits me out of nowhere, like a massive wave of pleasure, starting from my head and moving its way to my toes.

I feel completely numb as the jangle of his belt buckle fills the silence. I'm unable to move and do anything.

Rowan kisses his way back up my body. "I love you so damn much, Zahra."

It's amazing how three little words could set off an entire swarm of butterflies in my stomach.

"Would you be willing to try something new with me?"

I thought alpha Rowan was sexy, but there's something about his hesitant voice that has me running a hand down his back in support.

He places a soft kiss against my lips. "Do you trust me?"

I take a deep breath. After everything we've been through, I shouldn't. We might have some work to do, but I know Rowan loves me. He gave up his future in Chicago for me. His actions speak the loudest words, even if it took him some time to get there.

"Yes. I do."

"Good. I don't want to use a condom with you."

"I'm sorry. What?" I blink. While he knows I'm on the shot, I never expected him to ask something like this. Not with his kind of history with women.

He cups my cheek. "I don't want anything else between us anymore."

My eyes become all misty. I shouldn't cry, but it's hard to avoid based on the swell of emotion in my chest.

After being manipulated and abused by too many people, he is willing to give up this last bit of control he has over his life and trust me.

I nod, unsure if I can speak because of how tight my throat feels.

The smile he offers me is one I will never forget for the rest of my life. He stands back up and tugs me toward the edge of the bed with enough power to make me yelp. My legs are thrown over each of his shoulders. I nearly melt into the sheets as he places the softest kiss against the inside of my thigh.

Rowan lines his cock up with my core. "Now that I have you, I'll never let you go." He pushes into me slowly.

I claw at the bed beneath me. "I don't want you to."

"It's cute that you think you have a choice." He pushes more, stealing my breath away. His hands dig into my skin, holding me steady as he slams the rest of the way.

This time, the sex is different. Every touch feels like a promise and every kiss a vow. Rowan's pace is punishing in a completely different way—with his slow thrusts.

He doesn't stop worshipping my body as he whispers in my ear.

"I'm not sure what I did right in my life to deserve your love, but I'll stop at nothing to protect it." His lips find mine and he softly kisses me. "I'll work every damn day to make sure you always have a reason to smile, even if it means sharing them with the rest of the world." He withdraws to slide back into me, this time with a bit more desperation. "And I'll ruin anyone who threatens your happiness."

I lose the battle with my eyes, and tears slide down my cheeks. Rowan kisses away each of my tears in a silent promise.

And with a few more strokes, we fall together like we're meant to.

Rowan holds me tight against his chest. I trace a mindless pattern across it, following the lines of muscle.

"So, I might have said something uncharacteristically mean to your father after your presentation today."

"While my father is the last person I want to speak about while naked in bed with you, I'm too curious to pass this up."

I laugh as I smack his chest. "Well, I might have told him to fuck off."

Rowan explodes. His laugh is heavy and harsh, like he can't get enough oxygen into his lungs.

I absolutely love it and I can't wait to make him do it again.

"You've got to tell me this whole story from beginning to end." He wheezes.

"There's not much to say. Martha bore witness to me telling him off for being a lousy father."

"You said this in *public*?"

"Yes?" *Was I supposed to say it in some secret hallway?*

"And what did he say?"

"Nothing."

Rowan blinks. "You told my father how much he sucked as a parent and to fuck off and he said *nothing*?"

"Umm...was he supposed to?"

"I've heard him fire employees for breathing on him the wrong way."

"That seems a bit extreme."

"You don't know him like I do."

"Thank God. It's those small blessings that get me through the day."

His chest shakes from silent laughter. "I don't even know what to make of this. My father would never stand for that kind of talk from anyone."

He grabs his phone and texts his brothers about this latest update.

I drag a finger across his chest. "Maybe he already knew I quit."

Rowan shakes his head. "I doubt that. I didn't let Jenny file your notice, so you're still considered an employee in every way that counts."

"WHAT?!" I sit up.

Rowan tugs me back down and holds me flush against him. "I couldn't let you go."

"Yeah, well, you can't hold my notice hostage because you felt like it. That's illegal."

He shrugs. "According to your contract, I can do exactly that until you complete an exit interview with me. That's why you always check the fine print."

My lips gape apart. "I thought I wasn't special enough for fine print."

"You're so damn special to me that I don't plan on letting anyone in your vicinity who isn't family or female."

I roll my eyes. "You're too possessive for your own good."

He flips us over so he can hover over my body. His hips roll into mine, pressing his hardening cock into me.

"How does this conversation turn you on?"

His lips drop to the spot on my neck he's already marked

and bruised. "Because why talk about being possessive when I can show you instead?" Rowan proves exactly what it means to be cherished by him, all night long.

His love is something a girl could get addicted to, so it's a good thing I have the rest of forever to love him back.

EPILOGUE

Zahra

My whole family lines up behind the massive red ribbon. Rowan's brothers, who are as unfairly handsome as my husband, stand beside him.

Rowan tucks me into his body and kisses my temple. "Are you ready?"

A camera flashes, catching the moment. There's a lot of press here for the official opening of Nebula Land. It might have taken us three years to complete, but it was so worth it. The moment guests enter the space, they're immediately thrown into a completely different planet where Iggy the alien hails from. The ride Lance submitted got an upgrade and still remains a key attraction of the land, and I've come to accept it. Because without that billion-dollar hunk of metal, I might have never met the love of my life.

I imagine Brady is smiling down on us today.

"I can't believe this is happening. Do you think people will like it?"

"They'd be crazy not to." Rowan passes me the giant silver scissors.

"You trust me with a weapon like this?"

The moment he lets go, both my arms fall from the sheer weight of the metal.

"Okay, maybe not my best idea." He places his hands over mine and holds them up to the ribbon.

"Those are heavier than they look in the movies."

He lets out a soft laugh only I can hear. Another camera flashes in our direction.

"They caught you smiling on camera!" I gasp in mock horror.

"How much do you think I need to pay him to delete the image?"

"I'm not sure. Everything saves to a cloud now—"

"Are you both going to get this moving? I want to go on the rides!" Ani pops her head out from behind my back.

"What she said!" Cal calls from the other side of Rowan.

"We're having a moment," Rowan snaps back at his brother.

"We've all had to live through three years of your *moments* already. I've heard some of them too," Cal calls back.

"Hello! My parents are right there." I glare at Cal.

"They're jealous," Rowan whispers into my ear before placing a kiss on my cheek.

"Not really. You both are gross." Ani makes a retching noise. She's so full of it, especially when JP hangs all over her like an octopus.

Claire runs up to us with her kitchen smock half undone

and her hair everywhere. "I made it!" She throws her sweaty arm around me before taking up a spot next to Ani.

"Finally," Rowan grumbles under his breath.

"You were stalling for Claire to make it?"

Don't cry, Zahra.

"Of course. Without her, you might have never submitted that drunk proposal in the first place." Rowan smiles effortlessly, with every ounce of love in his eyes.

Goddammit, Zahra. Don't cry or else you'll give it all away.

"Thank you for always being so thoughtful."

"I made you a promise, didn't I?" He rotates the ring on my finger once as if to remind me it's still there. As if I could forget. I'm pretty sure my diamond can be seen from outer space because it's that obnoxious.

My eyes water, but I blink away the remaining tears before they can escape. "Ready?"

My husband smiles back at me and lifts the scissors higher. "Take it away, Wife." His voice drops, sending a wave of heat down my spine.

He hasn't stopped calling me that since we got married last winter in the snow. And every single time, it sends a rush of something through my body, making me feel every bit owned by him.

I call out to the crowd. "Thank you for joining us today. Nebula Land holds a special place in all of our hearts because we know how much it would have meant to Brady. While he can't be here today, I'm sure he's looking down at us, just as excited as we are. Iggy was his favorite character, although he might not have admitted it in so many words. Brady cherished his first drawing because it represented him, a young immigrant who felt like he traveled to a completely different world when he came to America. Iggy became a way for Brady to channel his happiness, excitement, and fears. In itself, Iggy is an extension of Brady in many ways—of the values Brady wants to spread with his movies. So we are thrilled to open Nebula Land up for all of Dreamland to visit and love as much as we do."

Rowan and I snip the ribbon together. Everyone cheers around us, clapping and hooting. Some kids run toward the entrance of the land while our family members mingle.

Someone grabs the scissors from Rowan's hands. "You did—"

Ani calls Rowan's name like we had planned before. I knew out of all the people, he couldn't resist answering her. His soft spot for my little sister has only grown over the years, and now I use it to my advantage.

My mom bustles over, swapping my enamel pin for my new one. She gives me a wink before turning back to my father.

Rowan wraps his arm around me from behind. He kisses the crook of my neck before turning me around so we face each other. "I'm proud of you. That was an amazing speech."

"Just amazing? I can do better than that. Let's call the reporters back here and have a redo." I twirl my finger like he does when he wants something done.

"You're crazy, you know that?"

"Hard to forget when you tell me every single day."

He cups my cheek with one hand. "I do love to be consistent."

Finally, on cue, his eyes drag across my face before trailing down my body. He tilts his head and blinks twice. "What is that?"

"What?" I blink innocently.

"Whose pin is that?" He flicks the pin on my chest, making it tremble.

I protect the little piece of metal showing off a bun inside of a tiny oven. After I took a pregnancy test at Claire's apartment three weeks ago, she surprised me with this little gem for my birthday.

I thought today was the perfect time to announce it to Rowan. Because we started with Nebula Land and ended up here, together with our families, years later.

"Mine." I grin.

He blinks again like his brain needs to process all this information. "You're pregnant?" His voice is a whisper.

I nod my head up and down. Rowan forgets about everyone around us as he kisses me until my lips are swollen and my head goes woozy from a lack of oxygen.

I look up at my husband, finding his cheeks streaked with a few tears. Like all the times he's done with me, I swipe them away like they never existed.

He wraps his arms around me and kisses my head. "You're the best damn thing that ever happened to me. Thank you for giving me the chance to be the dad I never had but always wanted."

My entire heart dissolves in my chest. There's nothing I want more in life than to share Rowan's love with our child. Because to be loved by him is to be cherished and protected unconditionally, and in a world like ours, it's a gift. One I never knew I needed but can't imagine living without.

EXTENDED EPILOGUE

Rowan

"This one, Daddy!" Ailey slams the book into my chest before bouncing onto her bed. Her Princess Cara pajama dress puffs around her, and her dark hair flies straight into her brown eyes. She shoves the waves out of her face.

I don't need to look down at the book to know which one she chose. It's the same book she picks every single night before bed.

I tuck her in before taking a seat on the edge. "Are you sure you don't want to pick a different one?" I dangle the book I created in front of her.

"No! I want to hear about you and Mommy!" She has the same grin as Zahra, and it makes my chest all warm and tight to make my daughter smile like that.

I never thought a gift I designed for Zahra's babymoon would have this long-lasting impact. Ailey requests for me to read the picture book every week like clockwork, and it fills me with pride to know she loves my work as much as her mother.

"Okay. But just one story. You're up way past your bedtime today." I don't want to miss the fireworks show with Zahra. It's our nightly tradition to watch from the porch.

"I promise!"

That was easier than I thought. She always asks me to read at least three stories before bed, and I give in every damn time. I'm a sucker for her single dimple and big brown eyes.

I place a soft kiss on her forehead before opening the book to the very first page I drew. "Once upon a time, there was a sad man who received a letter from his grandpa."

"And then what?" Ailey grins like she doesn't know the entire story from start to finish.

I read the next few pages explaining who I was and what I needed to do.

Ailey's entire face lights up as I flip the page to a drawing of Zahra opening the auditorium door. I'm drawn in a dark corner, staring at her like an angry idiot.

"It's Mommy!" She giggles. "You're mad at her."

I laugh to myself. "It made me grumpy when Mommy didn't follow the rules."

"Boo! I don't like rules."

"You're definitely your mother's daughter." I tap her scrunched-up nose with a smile.

I continue reading the story. Ailey's eyes slowly drift shut much sooner than I expected, probably because of our long day at the park for Ani's birthday.

I give Ailey a kiss on the top of her head before shutting off her bedside lamp and leaving her room.

I walk outside and into the refreshing January night.

"She's out already?" My wife shuts off her book light before closing the book.

I grab the book from her lap and place it on another chair. "She fell asleep before I got to her favorite part." I take a seat on the swing and pull her against my side. She moves forward an inch so I can wrap my arm around her and rest my hands on her bump. If I'm lucky, I can feel the little guy kick once the fireworks go off for tonight's show. He's always extra active during them.

"Maybe it's time you made an updated version so she can read about herself and her baby brother." Zahra pats my hand.

I tuck her hair behind her ear before kissing her shoulder. "I'll get working on it tomorrow."

"You spoil her."

I shrug. "There's nothing wrong with that."

She looks up at me. "Really? Just last week, you shut down Princess Cara's Castle while you had a tea party with Ailey. It's getting out of hand."

"It was only for an hour."

"On a Saturday in the middle of busy season!" Zahra laughs, making her belly vibrate against my hands.

"I do not see an issue here when we own the park."

She shakes her head. "Mark my words. She's never going to find a man who holds a candle to you."

I release a low laugh. "It's almost as if that's the point."

Zahra laughs until she wipes the corners of her eyes. "I should have guessed you would be like this."

"Ridiculously amazing?" I tilt her chin so I can kiss her lips.

"No." She smiles against my lips.

"Ridiculously impossible?"

She shakes her head, and I end up kissing her cheek. "Negative. But close."

"Ridiculously in love?"

She grins against my lips. "That's the one."

I kiss Zahra with every ounce of affection I feel toward her. I'm a lucky bastard who married the woman who knows all my faults and loves me despite them. Zahra is my best friend and my one and only love. The woman I look forward to kissing every morning and the last person I want to see before I shut my eyes at night. The mother of my children and the person I look forward to watching the Dreamland fireworks with every night until we are both old and gray.

She gave me a second chance at life, and I plan on making the most of it with her for the rest of my days.

Thank you!

If you enjoyed *The Fine Print*, please consider leaving a review! Any review, however short, helps spread the word about my books to other readers.

Join my Bandini Babes Facebook reader group for all things romance and bookish updates.

Scan the code to join the group

Also by Lauren Asher

Throttled

Dive into my Formula 1 world with Noah and Maya, a brother's rival forbidden romance.

Collided

A story about two friends who complete a naughty bucket list together.

Wrecked

An enemies-to-lovers forced proximity romance featuring a Formula 1 bad boy and his PR agent.

Redeemed

If you like fake relationship romances with a grumpy hero, check out Redeemed.

Terms and Conditions

The second book in the Dreamland Billionaire series, featuring an inheritance clause, a marriage of convenience, and two people determined NOT to fall in love.

Scan the code to read the books

WHAT'S NEXT FOR THE DREAMLAND BILLIONAIRES?

Final Offer, a second-chance romance featuring Callahan Kane and his mysterious ex.

Acknowledgments

Mom—Thanks for always pushing me to chase after my dreams even when they scare me.

Mr. Smith—I appreciate you always. I'm not sure what I would do without you poking holes in my plot points while also teaching me all about corporations and health insurance benefits.

Mary—Thanks for helping bring my books to life. I'm lucky enough to not only call you my kick-ass graphic designer but also my good friend!

Julie—Thank you for always helping me when I need it most. Your friendship and support mean so much to me, and I'm happy to share this journey with you.

Erica—Some people have editors, but I get a two-for-one friend too. Your voice notes always make me laugh as much as your random texts. Your encouragement to pursue something new (not better) helped push past my fear and complete this project, so thank you!

Becca—Without you, I'm not sure this final copy would be close to what it is now. I'm so glad Erica connected us and that you fit me into your schedule. Your support and reassurance were everything I needed, and you really challenged me to take this book to the next level. I can't wait for the next project together!

To my TFP beta readers (Brit, Rose/Kylie, Amy, Brittni, Nura)—Thank you for your honesty, support, and willingness to read my draft on such a time crunch. You're the biggest heroes, and none of this would be possible without your constructive feedback.

Nura—Trust your instincts. Without them, there wouldn't be an extended bowling scene. ;) Also, I appreciate you and your endless excitement about my projects. Every author needs a hype person, and I'm happy you're mine!

To my teams—Thanks so much for always supporting me and promoting my books. It means so much to me to have readers like you wanting to spread the word about my worlds and characters.

To Kimberly and everyone at Brower Literary & Management—I appreciate how much time and effort you put into helping me grow. You have helped make some of my biggest dreams come true, and I'm so thankful to have you as part of my team.

To Anna, the Piatkus/Little, Brown marketing team, and everyone else helping me over in the British Commonwealth—I am so grateful for everything you have done to support me and share the Dreamland Billionaires with the world.

To Christa, the marketing team, and everyone at Bloom Books—I'm so thankful for the time, energy, and love you put into helping me. Thank you for turning something that felt like a dream into a reality.

About the Author

Plagued with an overactive imagination, Lauren spends her free time reading and writing. Her dream is to travel to all the places she writes about. She enjoys writing about flawed yet relatable characters you can't help loving. She likes sharing fast-paced stories with angst, steam, and the emotional spectrum.

Her extra-curricular activities include watching YouTube, binging old episodes of *Parks and Rec*, and searching Yelp for new restaurants before choosing her trusted favorite. She works best after her morning coffee and will never deny a nap.